Rightside/
Wrongside

by

Cathy Hester Seckman

Rightside/Wrongside

Cover Art by *Kim Mendoza*

The Wild Rose Press, Inc.
PO Box 708
Adams Basin, NY 14410-0708
Visit us at www.thewildrosepress.com

Publishing History
First Edition, 2023
Trade Paperback ISBN 978-1-5092-5082-0
Digital ISBN 978-1-5092-5083-7

Published in the United States of America

The old man dozed over his paperback. Even in a busy week his job was boring as hell. What made it worthwhile, besides the status and the pay bag, was the free bed. Old Willie lived right in the Transfer Cabin, backed up against the Border Fence in Cody, and that suited him fine. He took his meals at a bar down the street—had a few good friends there—and spent most of his free time nodding over a book or stoking his small stove.

It was a nice quiet life, a safe life. Nobody bothered the man in the Transfer Cabin. Yeah, it suited him fine.

The bell rang, startling him out of his doze. It wasn't a simple ring, for boxed goods or vehicles through the big Door, but the four-note flourish they used for a baby. It sounded again, signaling two to transfer. "It never rains but it pours," he mumbled, and limped over to answer the bell.

When the ready light flashed on, Old Willie pulled out the heavy metal Drawer set into the back wall of the cabin. He smiled down at the two sleeping babies.

"Welcome to Wrongside," he said softly.

Dedication

For my late parents, Jenny and Andy Hester, who read bits of this book 14 years ago. See, I did finish it.

Chapter 1

Alanna Olaffson, newly installed Rightside president, shed her rank and privilege when she donned the basic Guardswoman's uniform, vest, and helmet. Her staff had tried to talk her out of it, but she believed that joining this raid into Wrongside would solidify her campaign promise to end smuggling once and for all.

"All set, Ma'am?" Sgt. Kirannen Sobriski, second in command of the strike unit, gave the president the once-over. She hadn't voted for the woman.

"Call me Alanna," the president answered, snapping her belt buckle closed. "I'm good to go."

The squad left ahead of schedule and was in-country by ten thirty p.m. easing through a dry wash in the barren Plains of Wrongside.

The trouble, Alanna had to admit, was that in spite of her determination, she did feel like a burden. It had been years, after all, since her compulsory service. She wasn't entirely sure she could still—

"Stop here." The low command came from above and behind. The sergeant, last in line, moved smoothly into position. The squad would wait until the smugglers met on the road above. Half the women were with Kirannen, the other half with the captain on the far side of the road.

"Basic flanking maneuver," Alanna muttered to herself. "Surround and contain, nice and easy."

1

"More exciting than training exercises, eh?" The guard beside her, face streaked with camouflage paint, grinned, her teeth startlingly white in the faint glow of the moons. "It's my first time through the Fence. I can't wait."

A hiss from Kirannen silenced the guard. In the quiet, Alanna heard the low whine of a truck engine coming from the south. The truck bumped over rough gravel and came to a halt a few yards short of Kirannen's guards. At a nod from the sergeant, the women silently leapfrogged right, one by one, until they were directly below the truck.

Within a few minutes, a second truck arrived from the north. This one, if the intel was correct, contained Rightside women with a cargo of guns stolen two days ago from the New Cleveland Armory.

Alanna listened as truck doors opened and closed, as booted feet rasped against the gravel road. There were muffled greetings. A cargo door rattled up. She heard the hoot of a desert owl and turned her head to look at Kirannen. The sergeant's fist was in the air, three fingers raised. Two. One.

"Halt!" The captain's voice rang out. "By Rightside law, I order you to halt, put your hands in the air. Now!" Kirannen's women scrambled up the short rise, gained the road, and formed up in a shallow half circle to surround the trucks, rifles at the ready. The captain's women did the same. In the uncertain illumination of headlights, Alanna made out two groups of smugglers, frozen in shock.

Trouble started when a man lunged into the back of a truck, rolled over one shoulder, and came up spraying bullets from a machine gun.

In an instant, the scene erupted. Strobe-like flashes shot from gun barrels. Shouted orders and the roar of gunfire echoed. Kirannen spun sideways, clutching her arm. The woman beside her dropped, and the coppery smell of blood was in the air. Alanna dove over the downed guard, landing hard in a prone position, rifle out and ready. She sighted on the man in the truck and tried a shot. It pinged wide, but the man flinched and his gun swung up. Bullets spread high and wide above the now-charging guardswomen.

Alanna saw Kirannen dart to the man in the truck, one arm cradled to her chest. With her other arm, she slammed her rifle into the man's legs, knocking him sideways. The machine gun clattered out onto the gravel.

The battle was over in minutes. Disorganized smugglers were no match for trained troops. A dozen smugglers lay facedown, hands cuffed behind them. Two men were dead, and many of the rest were wounded. Four guardswomen had taken hits.

Alanna stood to one side, breathing hard, fighting back the adrenaline rush.

The smugglers were quickly sorted. Women were bundled into a truck for transport back to Rightside. A sergeant disarmed the men, recorded their names, took photographs, and sent them back south.

The squad returned to Rightside just after midnight.

"You did okay, Alanna." The captain slapped her on the shoulder as they climbed down from a truck. "Your shot went wide, but it gave Kirannen time to rush the man, and that was key. Glad to have you along."

Alanna nodded sharply, not trusting herself to speak. Her legs were still shaking.

The guard who'd spoken to Alanna in the ditch came hesitantly to the captain, looking from her to the president and back again.

"Yes, Guard?" the captain barked.

"I just had a question about the op," she managed. "Why did you take photographs of those men?"

The photos, Alanna already knew, ensured a harsh punishment.

"Insurance," the captain said, unbuckling her bulletproof vest. "In case they've given us false names. We'll distribute the names and photos to every Red Cabin. It's our best deterrent since we have no interest in maintaining a men's prison."

The guard paled. "You mean they can't—they'll never—?"

The captain nodded grimly. "They'll never be allowed into a Red Cabin again. From now on, for as long as they live, they'll never have sex. They'll never get sons."

Chapter 2

In one of Rightside's hospitals, a group of women gathered in close. They hadn't heard the morning news of the successful raid into Wrongside. They wouldn't have cared if they had heard.

"It's time to push now, honey," Jessie murmured. Tenosha did as her nurse said, panting harder. The pain was building again. She wasn't scared of the pain, but of the outcome. Why had she ever let her mother talk her into this?

"Bear down, Tenosha," the doctor said sharply. "Bear down *now!*"

Tenosha bore down and groaned.

Above the girl's sweat-beaded forehead, her mother, Carole, hunkered down for the final minutes. She curled her fingers tighter around Tenosha's wrists and pulled in a deep breath. Tenosha wasn't the only one who was hurting. Carole had struggled and cried and sweated this out right at her daughter's side, where she belonged. It had taken eleven grueling hours, but now they were almost home. Her daughter was about to give birth. Would it be female or male?

Tenosha turned her head fretfully. "Mama? Don't go away, Mama."

"I'm right here, sweetie," Carole said. She touched the deep dimple on Tenosha's chin, an old trick that always reassured her daughter.

"Again, Tenosha! Push again! I can see the baby's head!"

The doctor was excited, Carole could tell. She was young and enthusiastic and probably hadn't delivered many babies. Fleetingly, Carole wondered about the woman's statistics. She had heard all the obstetricians kept tabs on their female/male ratio of births. It was like a badge of honor or of shame for them.

Tenosha was screaming now, and Carole could hear the exhaustion behind the sounds. She cupped her daughter's face in one trembling hand. They would all be glad when this was over, for better or worse.

"Almost there, hon," the doctor crooned. "A little more, a little more, a lit—"

In the abrupt silence, Carole knew. She knew, and so did everyone in the room. So did Tenosha.

"Oh, no," Tenosha sobbed, whipping her head back and forth on the sweat-stained pillow. "Oh, no, Mama, nooooo."

"It's male," the doctor said flatly. She cut the umbilical cord, placed the squalling newborn on a nearby cart, and draped a blanket indifferently over the tiny red body. She pulled off her gloves with an angry snap and jerked her head toward the door.

"Arrange for transfer," she told Jessie, "and get it out of here."

"Do you want to see him, honey?" Carole asked her sobbing daughter. She sneaked a hesitant glance at her grandson and almost gagged.

"No!" Tenosha was horrified. She squirmed on the gurney, trying to get closer to her mother and farther from the baby. "Let's just get out of here, Mama. Okay, can we go?"

Carole looked pleadingly at an older nurse.

"Of course," the woman said soothingly. She busied herself with the afterbirth and cleanup while the doctor strode angrily from the room.

Now she patted Tenosha's hand and backed the gurney out of the delivery room. She began a familiar litany, one she delivered almost daily to similarly horrified mothers.

"This happens all the time, Tenosha. It has to happen, you know that. We can't live without men, after all. You wait and see, next time, you'll have a girl, and everything will be fine. Just put this behind you, Tenosha. We all do. Yes, everything will be fine."

In the sudden quiet of the delivery room, Jessie was alone with the baby. She shot a glance at the door to make sure no one was lingering, watching, then reached out a finger and stroked the baby's dusky cheek. *So what if it's male*, she thought defiantly. *It's still a baby.*

She was admiring his dimple when she realized what was wrong. Her head came up. She could see Dr. Angelloni through the glass window, stripping off scrubs.

"Doctor!" she shouted. "Doctor, I need you!"

Instinct propelled the woman back through the swinging door, then she slowed down as she remembered the baby's sex.

Jessie already had two fingers on the baby's sternum. "He isn't breathing."

"What do we care?"

"You don't mean that. Four. Five." Abruptly, Jessie bent forward to blow into the baby's mouth and nose.

Angelloni hesitated, swaying on the balls of her feet. Natural antipathy warred with professional responsibility.

"Doctor, now! Please!" Jessie pulled in a breath and restarted her count. "One. Two."

Angelloni's face blanched, but the order did get her moving. She stepped forward, called for backup, and took over smoothly. In less than five minutes, the baby was breathing normally on his own.

The doctor peeled off yet another pair of gloves, more slowly this time. She dragged the surgical cap off her hair and twisted it uncertainly in her hands.

"Thank you," she finally blurted out. "I'm still not comfortable with male babies. He deserves a chance to live, like anyone else."

Jessie smiled her relief. "I'm just glad it was this simple. He's fine now, ready for his transfer. Thanks to you."

****

Jessie crooned a lullaby as she wheeled the baby quickly to the Transfer Room at the far end of the obstetrical ward. Another male, born earlier that morning, slept quietly in a carrier.

"These two to go," she told Sashi. "That'll probably be it for the day."

"On a bad roll, aren't you?" the clerk commented. "That's five this week."

"Yeah, well," Jessie said automatically. "Next week'll be better."

Sashi's new assistant, a young girl just out of school, looked askance at the second male. "Two at once," she marveled. "My friends can't believe where I'm working. It's too bizarre. I don't know how anyone has the nerve to get pregnant when they might have a male."

****

The technology existed, of course, for determining a baby's sex in utero. Rightside scientists hadn't lost all of their pre-Settlement knowledge from Earth. But by common consent, no obstetrician made use of it. If a pregnant woman knew she was carrying a male, she would choose not to carry it to term. Enough of that, and then where would they all be?

Working quickly, Jessie readied the new baby for his journey. She flipped him back and forth, measuring, weighing, footprinting, and recording his stats. Jessie wasn't aware of it, but she was still singing softly.

"How can you be so casual?" the assistant asked, shuddering.

Jessie smiled. "It's just a baby, Birdie. Here, touch his skin."

"No!" Her reaction was just as violent as Tenosha's had been, and Jessie pursed her lips.

"I was nervous at first, too. But after a few weeks you won't even think twice. It sounds almost sacrilegious, I know, but a baby is a baby, male or not. There are thousands of them just on the other side of that Fence." She gestured to the back of the room, where a Transfer Drawer was set into the wall. "If they weren't over there, we wouldn't be over here."

Sashi chimed in with her opinion. "Give her a break, Jessie. You know how the new ones are always shocked. I think it's just the idea that they're seeing babies, not adults, and this is a hospital, not a Red Cabin." She turned to the young girl.

"After all, we never think about men outside the

Red Cabins. For any reason except sex, I mean. It's hard to remember they start out as babies, just like we do. Imagine this one as a toddler or a nine-year-old."

"Oh, man, that's too disgusting!" Birdie cried. "Oh, I don't want that picture in my head!"

"Welcome to our world," Sashi said. "The rest of Rightside has no idea what we do here. Have you seen a male baby pee yet?"

The thought of finicky Birdie being squirted by a tiny penis was too much. Jessie collapsed into a chair, feeling the last of the day's tension bleed off in her laughter.

"I can't stand it," she gasped. She flapped a hand at the two women. "Stop, before I have the hiccups."

Birdie wiped her streaming eyes and subsided into horrified giggles. Sashi composed her face with an effort.

"Okay, you're right," she said. "But what would we do if we couldn't laugh about it?" She glanced at the babies and grimaced. "It really is disgusting. The Earth pioneers knew what they were doing when they put the men behind the Border Fence. With all their fighting, we'd have been extinct before the end of the first year. Women saved this colony, and we keep it strong."

"Yeah, but we still need men," Jessie said. Laughter forgotten, all three women stared down at the sleeping babies, at the reality they lived with every day.

"We can't get cloning perfected fast enough," Sashi said. She gathered up paperwork. "Come on, Birdie, I'll show you how to copy these for transfer and file the originals."

The girl trailed out after her. "This job is so weird," she complained. "I don't know how to feel. Part of me is sort of titillated. Part of me thinks it's hilarious, and the rest of me is just appalled. Is it always like this around here?"

****

The old man dozed over his paperback. Even in a busy week, his job was boring as hell. What made it worthwhile, besides the status and the pay bag, was the free bed. Old Willie lived right in the Transfer Cabin, backed up against the Border Fence in Cody, and that suited him fine. The women across the Fence never seemed to mind how often he hit the off-duty button. They probably knew the men could only afford one Transfer man per cabin. He took his meals at a bar down the street—had a few good friends there—and spent most of his free time nodding over a book or stoking his small stove.

It was a nice quiet life, a safe life. Nobody bothered the man in the Transfer Cabin. Yeah, it suited him fine.

The bell rang, startling him out of his doze. It wasn't a simple ring for boxed goods or vehicles through the big Door, but the four-note flourish they used for a baby. It sounded again, signaling two to transfer. "It never rains, but it pours," he mumbled and limped over to answer the bell.

When the ready light flashed on, Old Willie pulled out the heavy metal Drawer set into the back wall of the cabin. He smiled down at the two sleeping babies.

"Welcome to Wrongside," he said softly.

****

The babies didn't even wake up as Willie started his paperwork. That was good—it would give him time to heat some bottles after he finished.

11

He puzzled over the babies' names, rolling possibilities slowly across his tongue. "Trader, Travis, Trevor? Brandon, Bert, Brock, Buford?"

Willie liked naming babies. It was his favorite part of the job. The last few transfer agents had been lackadaisical about it. Most folks around here were named Bob or Mike or Tom but Old Willie tried to be creative. He had an antique pre-Settlement book on baby names, and it was brittle and dog-eared with age and use.

"Henry, Hollis, Hoss, Hud?"

The dark-haired baby let out a wail.

"Okay, Hud, you little asshole, couldn't wait till I was finished, could you?" Willie scolded. He picked up the crying infant and slung him over one shoulder, cradling the head carefully.

"You'll just damn well have to ride over here with me till I get you a bottle warmed up," he said, heading for the kitchen.

The baby, lulled by the warmth of Old Willie's body and the rumble of his voice, drifted back to sleep.

Willie peeked down at the closed eyes. "Little asshole," he commented absently.

Chapter 3

"I don't care if all of Rightside disagrees with me," the president argued. She propped her hands on her hips and frowned at her two least favorite Cabinet secretaries.

"If we don't impose this new tax, we can't rebuild the dam on the North River. If we can't rebuild the dam, it'll break in the spring floods. If it breaks, we'll—"

"We'll all suffer," the Secretary of the Interior finished. "We know that, Madam President, and we agree with you. The tax has to be collected. But this isn't the way to do it."

Secretary Maud Adams frowned down the length of her sharp, twitchy nose. It was a private joke among the top-ranking legislators that the secretary's nose, which jutted straight out from her unfortunately narrow face, had gotten that way from inserting it too often into other people's business. Maud's nose sniffed busily most of the time, making it impossible to ignore. The president put up with her because she needed Maud's additional influence with southern voters.

Maud didn't care for the president, either, but was careful to keep her dislike concealed. She suspected the feeling was mutual. Regardless, Alanna Olaffson was her boss. And for once, she was absolutely right about the tax. It was just—

Giulia Saracco, the Treasury secretary, worked up the nerve to clear her throat. "Let us develop a new proposal, ma'am," she suggested. "Give us a few days, and we'll submit some alternative ideas. If you'll just be patient with us—"

Alanna threw up her hands. "All right, all right. Do it. Just get out of my office.

"Now!" she added when the Treasury secretary failed to move fast enough. The secretaries scurried, and Alanna flopped down in her desk chair.

"Man!" she swore. "Will this day ever be over?" She looked at her watch, then abruptly sat up and buzzed her secretary.

"Tawny, isn't Laran here yet?"

"Just coming up the elevator now," Tawny's voice reassured her over the intercom. "She's probably soaking wet, though. It's been raining all day."

Alanna smiled and looked out of the window. She hadn't noticed, but it was indeed raining. A gray drizzle splashed disconsolately against the tall windows of the Government Building's executive suite. Skeletal, winter-bare trees bent before a cold wind. She was glad her daughter was home.

"Doesn't matter if she's wet," she said airily as she passed Tawny's desk on her way to the elevator. "The kid's never been sick a day in her life."

Alanna swooped Laran into a big bear hug. "How you doin', short stuff?" she greeted her daughter happily. "Did you have a good day at school?"

"Uh-huh," a very damp Laran nodded, squirming out of her mother's arms. "How 'bout you?"

"Mommy had an awful day." Alanna sighed, taking Laran by the hand. "Come on into my office, sweetie. I want to hear about yours."

Alanna's office was furnished traditionally, with a child's table and chairs in one corner and a wall-mounted box for toys.

Laran rushed to her table and began pulling papers out of a small red bookbag. "We did maps in history today, Mommy. Wait till you see!"

Alanna pulled up a pint-sized chair and sat down with her daughter. The country could run itself for five minutes.

Anyone watching them would have thought, as Tawny often did, how similar they were despite the thirty-year difference in their ages.

Eight-year-old Laran sported a belligerent shock of short, spiky white-blonde hair that stuck straight out from her head in all directions. Beneath the stylish hairdo were brown eyes with short, no-nonsense lashes, a straight nose, and a full mouth given to impulsive grins. Epicanthic folds at the inner corners of her eyes betrayed the input of her father's genes. Her small body was sturdy and muscular from non-stop activity.

Alanna had the same spiked hair, though hers was darker with age. Her eyes were blue rather than brown, but she shared Laran's body type. Thank goodness, she often thought, that Laran mostly had her looks. Some girls didn't resemble their mothers at all.

"See my map, Mommy?" Laran said proudly, spreading it out on the table.

Alanna admired her daughter's handiwork. "You made a gold star for New Washington," she commented.

"That's where we are," Laran said smugly. "And look, here's where Grandma lives." She pointed a pudgy finger at the large northern city where Alanna had been born.

Alanna noted the fat blue line of the North River where it intersected with New Cleveland. If that decrepit old dam ever did break her mother would be one of the first to suffer. Congress *had* to impose that new tax! If they didn't—

"—to me, Mommy!"

"What, sweetie? I'm sorry, I was woolgathering. What did you say?"

Laran giggled at the thought of her mother, the president of the whole country, gathering wool. "I said, you aren't listening to me. And before that, I said, did you know why all the cities have 'New' in front of their names?"

"No," Alanna lied. "Why do they?"

Laran took a deep breath to give some drama to her statement. "Because they aren't the original cities, that's why! They're all named after cities on Earth!"

"Earth!" Alanna pretended surprise. "What's that?"

"It's a whole other *planet!*" Laran whispered dramatically. "It's where we *came* from!"

"Sweetie, didn't you already know that?"

Laran squirmed. "Yeah, I guess I did, but Mommy, our teacher *explained* it all to us. She told us how people came in a spaceship and about the Territory War and everything."

Hoping to skip over the images of rape and destruction, Alanna asked, "Did she tell you about the Final Confrontation?"

"Uh-huh." Laran wiggled away from her mother, stood up, and prepared to act out the most significant moment in the history of the Colony.

"The women had a meeting with the men to tell them what to do."

"And do you remember what Milina said? The first president?"

"Oh, yeah, she was the one who was—I forget the word."

"Married," Alanna supplied. "That meant one woman lived with one man all the time. His name was Yong Zhang. It'll probably be on your test."

Laran wrinkled her face in disgust. "Yeah, married."

"And what did Milina say?" Alanna prompted.

Laran straightened up and pushed her damp hair off her forehead. "She said all the men had to stay behind the Border Fence all the time. They could only see the women when the women said it was okay. Then Yong, he got real mad, and *he* said, 'Whose side are you on, anyway?'"

"And what was Milina's answer?"

Laran took a deep breath, drew herself up proudly, and recited the most famous words in the history of the planet.

"Milina said, 'I'm on the right side, and you're on the wrong side.'"

"Very good!" Alanna laughed and clapped her hands enthusiastically. "You got every single thing right! You'll be the best history student in the whole school!"

"Mommy, you hardly even looked at my map yet. See my Border Fence?" Laran ran a pudgy finger over the gentle S-curves of the hundred-mile barrier that separated Rightside from Wrongside.

"That's a beautiful fence," Alanna said admiringly.

"Are these dots the cabins?"

"Yep. Our teacher says we're going on a field trip to a Transfer Cabin sometime to see how we trade stuff with the men."

"Stuff…" Alanna echoed. Fleetingly, she thought of her own male babies that had gone though a Transfer Drawer years before she struck it lucky with Laran. Where were they now? Did they live? Were they happy? She couldn't imagine their lives.

Alanna sighed and brushed a hand over her daughter's still-damp hair. It did no good to wonder about fathers and brothers and sons. The old truism offered scant comfort, but it was all the comfort there was for a woman of Rightside.

"The red dots are the Red Cabins. How come they're called that, Mommy?"

"No one knows, sweetie. They've always been called Red Cabins, ever since women and men started to meet in them."

"I'm *never* gonna do that!" Laran was adamant.

Alanna laughed again, this time knowingly. "That's what every little girl says," she told her daughter. "But just wait until you grow up. You might change your mind. I'd like to be a grandma someday, you know."

The intercom buzzed, and Tawny's voice filled the room apologetically.

"Sorry to disturb you, boss, but the vice president is on the line from the Senate building. She wants to know if you've reached a decision yet on the new tax."

Alanna blew out an exasperated breath and called across the room to her intercom. "No, we haven't. But tell her our two favorite secretaries are working on some alternatives."

"That should make her day," Tawny said dryly.

"Made mine," Alanna answered. "Sweetie," she said to her daughter, "why don't you go up to the kitchen and get Martha to make you some hot chocolate? Mommy still has work to do."

At the mention of hot chocolate, Laran scrambled to her feet, maps and history lessons forgotten. "See you later, Mom," she called on her way out the door.

"Later," Alanna echoed, her mind already back on the tax problem. Absently, she looked at her daughter's map, tracing the North River down the length of the country as it paralleled the Border Fence. Eighty percent of the population of Rightside lived within twenty miles of the Fence, if she remembered her demographics. And that meant eighty percent of them also lived within twenty miles of a potentially life-threatening flood should the river dam ever break.

She went back to her desk to look at the engineer's report again, and it still said the same thing. The dam was in imminent danger of failing. And the spring rains were only three months away.

Alanna shook her head angrily. How had this ever been allowed to happen? When the jubilant Fidelity Party had swept her into office last fall after a sixteen-year domination by the Constancy Party, they had expected to have to clean house. Little did they know how dirty the house would be.

"Dams crumbling, tax bases eroding, schools falling down, people out of work— Man!" Alanna swore again. "Where do we start?"

First things first, she decided. After Congress imposed the new tax—and they *would* impose it—she

19

and the Interior Secretary could structure a quick repair and rebuilding plan that would put at least some of the idle construction crews back to work. Their paychecks would provide some tax money, and then…

Alanna whistled as she worked. She was not aware that in another part of the building, her daughter, complete with chocolate mustache, was regaling Martha with more details of the Final Confrontation.

Nor was she aware that, in yet another part of the sprawling government building, a nervous Treasury Secretary and a vindictive Interior Secretary were wishing out loud that Alanna Olaffson had not won the last election.

Chapter 4

"What the hell is that?" Eighteen-year-old Davy dropped two limp rabbits on the floor of his father's cabin and unshouldered his shotgun. The object of his scrutiny slept peacefully, unaware of his half-brother's rude curiosity.

"A baby." Tom Redwolf, Davy's father, was a man of few words. "Name's Hud."

"Hud," Davy repeated stupidly. "A baby."

His father made no answer. He sat in the kitchen, elbows propped on the table, chin propped in his hands. He was staring at the unlikely sight of an infant asleep in its carrier in the middle of his kitchen table. As the two watched, the baby stretched and sighed, then snuggled back into a deeper sleep.

Davy shook his head slowly, unable to take it all in. "Is this baby—*yours!?*"

His father grunted, then made what was for him an uncharacteristically philosophical comment. "Surprised the shit out of me, too."

Davy sank into a kitchen chair. It was mind-boggling. He didn't even know his father still went to the Red Cabins. He had been itching to go himself, but hadn't quite gotten up the nerve. Other boys had told him some stories... To think that his own father had gone to see a woman was just mind-boggling.

"How did he get here?" Davy was all curiosity.

"Transfer man brought him. I still had some bottles and stuff around, from you."

Davy nodded thoughtfully. He had seen his friends take care of their baby brothers. "Can I touch him?"

"Suit yourself."

Davy rubbed the back of one finger cautiously across the baby's cheek. It was the softest thing Davy had ever felt. "He'll have to go to the Corral sometimes, right?"

"Only when neither of us will be here," Tom grunted. "I'll show you what to do when I'm at work."

The Corral was the local daycare center, where babies and toddlers spent their days or nights while fathers worked. Since Davy didn't have a regular job, Tom wouldn't need the Corral too often. Davy didn't know whether to be excited or nervous about taking care of his baby brother.

****

Down at Bally's Cafe, the news was all over. Tom Redwolf had finally got himself another boy, after years of trying. They had begun to think there was something wrong with his pecker.

"Ain't me," Tom always said, embarrassed as hell. "It's them damn barren women I get."

What Tom didn't know, and what no self-respecting Rightsider would have told him, was that the woman who favored him, and whom he had been seeing regularly for six and a half years, already had four daughters and was using birth control. It was only when the woman dropped him and he lucked into another that his seed finally found fertile ground.

"You should of seen his face," Old Willie said now, drinking the first of his free celebratory beers.

Bally was always good that way. The transfer man got a free setup for every baby he delivered. It made it nice.

"Tommy almost pissed his pants when I showed up on his doorstep with that baby. After he got over the shock all he could do was stare at that baby like it could hang the moons."

"He should be real proud," Mike Dannon put in. "He worked hard enough for it."

That brought another round of raucous laughter, and Old Willie nearly choked on his final swallow. "Well, boys, I got one more to deliver tonight. I'll see y'all later."

"Where's this one going?" Bally asked. He had the second baby out of its carrier and was patting its rump, joggling it up and down. If the baby had been older, it might have laughed to be tickled by Bally's crinkly salt-and-pepper beard.

Old Willie sighed. "Little Tyler here's going to Frank Gibson's place."

The laughter died out. Bud Hopper, who was the local lawman, spoke up. "Willie, one of these days you and me will have to do something about Frank and that brood of his."

Everyone in the bar knew what he was talking about. Frank already had five boys, and every one of them was worse than his father. They seemed to come by it naturally. Frank kept the boys in line with an iron fist, and maybe that was part of the problem. No one wanted to see Frank get another kid to ruin.

Old Willie shifted uneasily on his feet. One thing he didn't need was trouble with the likes of Frank Gibson. "Nothing I can do, Bud," he whined. "Frank's the father. I got the papers right here. Boys got to go to their fathers."

Bud heaved to his feet. "I know, Willie, I know. But I think I'll walk along to Frank's with you, just for the hell of it."

"That'd be real nice, Bud, real nice." Willie limped to the bar to collect baby and carrier, then the two men stepped into the gloom of the late afternoon.

Willie pulled up the collar of his coat against the late winter wind and shivered. "Wish I had me a truck," he complained. "I'm too old to lug babies and supplies around town."

"Stop back at Bally's and see Mike Dannon," Bud suggested absently. "I heard he wants rid of that blue truck."

"I might," Willie answered, though he knew there was no way in hell he could afford it. He was lucky to have a job and a bed at his age.

It was near a mile out to Frank's place, so the men put their heads into the wind and trudged off down the muddy main street of Cody. Bud carried the baby. Willie was grateful, but he wished the lawman wasn't such a wet blanket. Still glowing slightly from the beer and the camaraderie of the bar, Willie talked a mile a minute, but Bud mostly answered in grunts.

Walking easily beside the old man and swinging the carrier in one hand, Bud was doing some hard thinking.

Frank was a problem, and that was a fact. He walked on the wrong side of the law too often for good sense. Sure, everybody did it now and then. Bud Hopper himself, before his lawman days, had been known to run a little crazy sometimes. He once shot a man when a bar fight turned bad and got away with it because the man pulled a knife.

But Frank was a hard case. He was in tight with some boys up in Bozeman. They had a nice black-market operation going, and they sold everything from smuggled penicillin to pornography right under the mother-loving table. Bud and his Bozeman counterparts cracked a piece of the operation now and then, but they never caught the big boys. One of these days, he swore, he'd collar Frank Gibson red-handed and send him to the slammer for good. Hell, the kids'd probably thank him.

In the meantime, though, there was this problem of the new baby. Aside from the fact that everyone hated to see another Gibson grow up bad, it was a damn shame to sentence an innocent baby to the life he'd most likely lead in Frank's incompetent hands. Everyone knew Frank drank up most of his illegal profits. He didn't feed the kids right, and until last winter, when Bally got up a fund and bought out the general store, none of the Gibson boys had a decent winter coat, nor socks neither.

Why should Gibson get another baby, Bud thought resentfully, when there were men in town who'd give their right arms for a son? Look at Tom Redwolf—he'd waited damn near twenty years for his second kid. And Bud himself—

But he pushed that thought away. The old-timers said the more you thought about it the more you jinxed yourself. It'd happen. Someday when he least expected it, Old Willie would come knocking on his door, and boy, then wouldn't he celebrate! Why, when he got a son, he'd—

"Here we are, finally." Willie's gusty sigh broke

into Bud's reverie. The old man eased up on his bad leg and propped it on the front stoop of the ramshackle Gibson cabin. "Damn, I got to get me a truck."

Their knock was answered by snot-nosed Tonio, age four.

"What do you want?" the boy said around a mouthful of something.

"Your father home?" Bud grunted.

"Yeah."

"Then let's see him!" Bud growled, pushing the boy aside.

"You got a reason to be here, lawman?" Frank Gibson loomed out of the darkness of the room, unshaven and unsteady, a bottle in his hand. Bud had never understood why women liked Frank, with his dangerous blue eyes and his long blond hair, but they obviously did. How else could he have gotten six kids?

"I'm just taking a walk with my friend, Old Willie, here," Bud said pleasantly. "He's got some business with you."

Frank's cloudy eyes shifted to the carrier in Bud's hand, and he let out a cackle of glee.

"Hoo-eeee, boys, look here! Is your old man a stud, or what? We got us another rug rat!"

Bud grimaced and stepped farther into the room. "You don't look like you're in any shape to take care of a new baby, Frank," he said easily.

"What's it to you?" Frank lowered his blond head and stared suspiciously at the lawman.

Bud swept some clutter off a kitchen chair and made himself at home. Willie hovered nervously. With the carrier on the table in front of him, Bud was the center of attention for the five boys, who ranged from

Chad, age sixteen, to Jase, age three.

"Brian!" Frank barked to a medium-sized towhead. "Round up them baby bottles. And some diapers."

"I ain't changing no more crappy diapers," Brian muttered rebelliously. "We just got Jase out of them, and we sure as hell don't need another baby filling them up."

Frank aimed a backhand at Brian, who ducked it with the ease of long practice. "I said, go get some!" Frank roared. "Now!"

Brian disappeared. The kid's rebellious statement had started Bud thinking. He had an idea, and he pounced on it.

"That's a smart boy you got there," he commented casually.

"Brian?" Frank snorted. "He couldn't find his ass in the dark with both hands." He shot Bud a look. "And like I said, what's it to you? I still ain't heard a good reason for you being here."

Bud decided to be as honest as possible. "I was at the bar when Old Willie here came in with the baby, and it started me thinking. I wondered what you'd do with another rug rat around here. It ain't like you got any shortage of boys. I mean, I can't see a man like you wanting to be tied down with babies all the time. You've got better things to do."

Willie was decidedly nervous now. What was Bud leading up to? Bud knew as well as anybody that Frank had no thoughts of taking care of a new baby. He'd make the older boys do it, like he always did. It was a joke downtown that Chad was lucky he ever grew up, without an older brother to look out for him.

Frank was frowning, obviously trying to clear his

booze-fuddled brain. "Tied down?"

"That's what I said." Bud shook his head sorrowfully. "I can't see it myself. What do you need with another baby?"

Frank giggled and reached out to rub the baby's head. "Can't do nothing about it now. He's here. Cute little sucker, ain't he? What's his name, Willie?"

"Tyler," Willie muttered. Suddenly he was no longer proud of his fancy naming. With an old man's instinct, he could feel tension starting to build. Whatever Bud was up to, he wanted no part of it. A transfer man was usually safe in these parts, but only if he kept his nose where it belonged.

"You remember what to do, don't you, Frank? Ain't been that long since Jase. Keep his head covered, and feed him every four hours. Take him over to see the doc in a couple weeks. Bud, I got to get back. You coming?"

Bud waved his hand vaguely. "In a minute, Willie. I got a proposition for Frank, here."

"A proposition?" Baby forgotten, Frank took a swig from his almost empty bottle. He didn't pass it around. "And just what kind of proposition could you have for me, lawman?"

Bud took a deep breath and said it straight out, like it was the most natural thing in the world. "Why, I could take that baby off your hands," he said. "Way I see it, I ain't got no boys, and you got too many. I could raise him for mine, and you'd be footloose and fancy-free, for a while."

Frank spewed the mouthful of liquor across the table, choking and spitting. A few drops hit Tyler on the back of the head, but the baby slept on, unconcerned.

Willie stopped his cautious backward shuffle to the door. The kids were staring at Bud, open-mouthed with shock.

"Give you my boy?" Frank gasped through the liquor burn. "Give you—my boy?"

"It's just a baby," Bud said off-handedly. "Plenty more where that one came from, for a stud like you."

But Frank, even half-drunk, was having none of it. He stood up beside the table, swaying and pulling in deep breaths. He looked down at the baby, then up at Bud. Down at the baby. Up at Bud.

Chad slapped Jase and Tonio across the backs of their heads to get their attention, then pulled them silently from the room. Misha, the second-oldest, dropped to the floor and scooted behind a chair. He wanted to watch.

Bud lowered one hand casually below the level of the kitchen table and loosened his holster strap. He'd seen Frank in action before.

It happened in an instant. Frank swung the liquor bottle back in a short, vicious arc to connect with the kitchen wall, where it shattered in a thousand glittery pieces. A few landed in the carrier with Tyler, but no one noticed.

By the time Frank pulled back the neck of the bottle and pointed its jagged end at Bud, the lawman had reacted. He was standing. The business end of his revolver was pointed unswervingly at Frank.

"Take it easy, Frank," he said softly, almost whispering. "I was just thinking out loud, that's all."

Old Willie cleared his throat nervously. He didn't want to get into this, no, he didn't, but that baby was still his responsibility. And in Wrongside, babies were

29

very important commodities.

"That's right, Frank, nothing to get hot about. That's your baby. I got the papers right here. Babies got to go to their fathers. Everybody knows that, yessir. Bud didn't mean it."

"Shut up, old man," Frank spat, swinging the bottle neck in his direction. Willie instantly shrank back, trying to make himself as small as possible. He held up a protesting hand and shook his head silently.

Frank turned back to Bud. "You get it straight, lawman," he growled. "Willie says this baby's mine, then it damn well stays here. Ain't nobody messes with me and mine, you understand?"

Bud straightened, nodded, and lowered his gun, but he didn't re-holster it. "No problem, Frank. It was just a thought."

Frank giggled suddenly, a sinister, drunken giggle. "Damn dumb stupid one, you ask me." He threw the jagged hunk of glass toward a trash can and dropped into a kitchen chair. He flapped one hand at them in dismissal. "Go on, get out of my house."

Tyler started to cry as Bud and Willie left the cabin. It was a weak, fretful newborn's cry, and it made Bud's heart turn over. Feelings he usually shut down welled up inside him. A baby. A son! What he wouldn't give—

Chapter 5

Jessie Sandova, the newest obstetrical nurse at New Washington Hospital, hummed softly in her pink and white bathroom as she applied eyeliner with a deft touch. Everything was right tonight. She was sure of it. There were even full moons. She picked up a tube of lipstick and went over everything in her mind one more time.

She was halfway between her periods. The slight cramping she'd felt this morning reassured her that she was ovulating.

She looked perfect tonight. Unlike some women, Jessie always took pains with her appearance. She stepped back from the mirror and ran her hands over the red silk that clung to her slim hips. She was proud of her high, firm breasts, her shiny brown hair, and the perfect heart shape of her face that framed smoky violet eyes. She nodded her head approvingly. Any man would thank his lucky stars to be chosen by her.

Jessie returned to the mirror to finish her makeup. Her sister, Diana, chief administrator of the Pennsylvania Avenue Red Cabin, was on duty and on the lookout. Jessie had specified someone young this time, young and full of testosterone.

She giggled at the sacrilegious thought and smeared her lipstick. She felt good. Tonight was the night.

Half an hour later, Jessie almost danced into the Red Cabin, actually a nondescript brick building at the east end of the hospital, paired with the hospital's Transfer Cabin. The place was packed. Full moons, it never failed.

"Hi, Kareen." She breezed past the front desk. "Where's Diana?"

"In the back," Kareen answered. "She's got one for you."

"Great!" Jessie hurried past the waiting area and interview rooms on the left. Meeting rooms stretched down the right side of the building. Muted music and laughter drifted out to the hall. Jessie felt a flurry of anticipation in the pit of her stomach.

The viewing room was all the way at the end. Two older women and a gaggle of young girls were there, walking up and down in front of the one-way glass like buyers at a cattle auction.

"Look at the shoulders on that one, Annie," one older woman said admiringly.

Her friend crinkled her nose. "I like the studious type. All those muscles sort of scare me."

The first woman snorted in disgust.

The younger girls couldn't stop giggling. "Look at the one standing beside the desk!" one of them whispered. "He's new, and look how young. He's got to be our age!"

"Tell me you're not gonna pick him!" the girl next to her whispered back.

"Why not?"

Jessie, walking past them, thought she could hear both bravado and fear in the girl's voice. When girls first started to have sex, they typically went for older, safer men. It was only the more confident older women who craved muscular and younger male bodies.

"I could handle him," the girl was insisting. "I'm tired of saggy old men. Besides, I'd ask for cameras."

"Hey, Sis!" Jessie's older sister Diana looked up from a pile of printouts at her corner desk. Diana was plump where Jessie was thin, but they shared the same violet eyes and black hair.

She stood and swept the papers aside. "Have I got a hot one for you!"

Jessie giggled. "Lead me to him, Di!"

Diana shook her head. "Not yet. It's his first time, and they just yanked him up for more paperwork. I only caught a glimpse of him. Where did I put those stats?" She rummaged through the drift of papers.

Jessie, tantalized, lifted one perfectly groomed eyebrow. Like the girl who was currently horrifying her friends, Jessie was ready for a young guy. "First timer, huh? Sounds interesting. I've never had one before."

"I have." Diana looked up from her papers and gave her sister a wicked grin. "It's a gas. They can go forever, once they get the hang of it. And think of all those millions of virgin sperm, just looking for a—"

"Diana!" Jessie was scandalized. Even if they were in a Red Cabin, the place where it all happened, it was still outrageous. Jessie was so excited she could hardly stand it. "Spare me the lurid details, okay? Just tell me when I can have him."

Diana frowned. "Not for a while. I told Hank over the intercom that I had a match for the kid, but he just grunted at me. You know men."

Jessie nodded, licking her lips. And she was about to know one better.

"I already have his blood work," Diana continued, "and it checks out okay. You're absolutely not related."

Kareen burst into the room just then, waving a sheaf of papers. "Diana, you'll never believe it. Susan just called off work. Her baby fell down the stairs and had to get four stitches."

Diana flopped into her seat in a flurry of printouts and consternation. "Oh, the poor kid. But what are we going to do without Susan? On a Saturday night? With full moons?" She groaned. "Where's Sydney?"

"Doing interviews. I can't break her loose, there's a line a mile long."

"Amber?"

"Off tonight, remember?"

"Then no one's on the Balewa girl?"

"No, she's still waiting for her tour. Which was supposed to be Susan's job tonight, if you remember."

Diana stuck out her lower lip and blew her bangs up off her forehead in frustration. "Well, I can't do any tours. Who'd give the room assignments?"

Jessie, who had been watching this exchange sympathetically, broke in. "I'll give the tour. I spent two summers working here, remember? Let me help out while I'm waiting."

Diana jumped up, scattering papers everywhere. "Oh, Sis, that'd be great! Her name's Cara, and she's in the first waiting room." She hesitated. "You remember how to give the pitch, don't you?"

Jessie nodded confidently. "How could I forget?"

Kareen patted Jessie's arm in appreciation and rushed from the room. Diana dug out an information sheet on Cara, along with some first-timer notes. She pushed them toward Jessie, then turned to the women at the mirror, who were ready to make selections.

Jessie walked back up the long hallway, studying Cara's stats. She was eighteen, healthy, using birth control. She wanted an older man, one with a record for gentleness. No surprises there.

As Jessie passed the door to Room 4, Kareen was just sitting down in front of a video screen in the hallway. The monitor showed the interior of the meeting room, where a young girl waited nervously beside the bed. Kareen pressed an intercom button.

"I'm going to let him in now, honey. Are you ready?"

The girl nodded.

"Now remember," Kareen continued, "I can see everything and hear everything. If you need help, just call out. I'm right outside."

The girl nodded again, then pulled in a deep breath and held it as a door in the opposite wall opened slowly.

Jessie smiled, thinking of her own first time. She left Kareen to it and entered the waiting room.

"Cara Balewa?" she asked. A dark, thin girl with a cloud of frothy black hair stood up.

"That's me. I guess."

Jessie nodded sympathetically. "You're nervous, I can tell, but don't worry about it. Everyone is, their first time. My name's Jessie."

They sat on either side of a small table and Jessie spread out her notes. She tried to put the girl at ease as they waded through the preliminaries.

"You've seen the introductory film, right, Cara? You know how the Red Cabins operate?"

The girl nodded hesitantly. "Yeah. I guess so."

"Let's review a couple of points anyway, okay?

We want the gene pool to be as diversified as possible. That means you should visit Red Cabins in other cities as often as possible." She waved a hand in the direction of Wrongside. "We've determined that there are fewer than 250 men who use this one.

"More importantly, the Red Cabins are the only places on the planet where women and men meet face to face. We meet for sex, and that's all. No other reason." She looked sternly at the girl. This was the most important point they had to drum into the first-timers.

"Whether you want to get pregnant or you just want to enjoy sex, that's the only reason you see a man. You don't have heartfelt talks. You don't confide in him. You don't make him your friend. Most importantly, you don't tell him anything about life in Rightside. It's dangerous."

She lowered her head to look into Cara's downcast eyes. "Do you know why it's dangerous, honey?"

Cara frowned in confusion. "Because we're in control?"

"We're in control," Jessie repeated patiently. "We've had control of the planet for seventy-one years. We grow most of the crops, we supply all of the technology, and we provide good lives for our women. We control sex."

Jessie curled her lip and waved a contemptuous hand. "The men just sit over there in Wrongside and play their war games and shoot their guns. They live in hovels and eat squirrels for supper and take our charity. They're animals. The only way we stay in control is by keeping them ignorant. If they knew how we live and how good our lives are compared to theirs they'd try to take over again."

Jessie sat back in her chair and folded her arms. "That's why it's so important for you to keep the details to yourself, Cara. They can't know anything about us."

Jessie wound up for the final pitch. She'd always been a little uncomfortable with this part. She didn't see the necessity, herself. But if Cara didn't give the right answer, the poor kid would never be allowed to see a man as long as she lived.

"We women have a pact, Cara. A secrecy pact. And as a woman of Rightside, it's up to you to honor it. Never make a man your friend. Never tell him a single detail about yourself or about life in Rightside. I need you to swear to that, Cara. Will you?"

Cara, wide-eyed, nodded her head slowly. "I will," she said breathlessly. "I swear. When you put it that way—I never realized—"

"Well, now you do," Jessie finished briskly. She pushed a sheet of paper toward Cara. "Sign your pledge. I'll witness it, and we'll be ready for the tour."

****

Jessie flung open the door of an unoccupied meeting room. "Here we are," she began. "Every room is the same, with a bed, a table and chairs, and a small bathroom through here." She pointed. "The men come through this door." She pointed again. "It leads to the other side of the Border Fence."

She opened a drawer in the nightstand and pulled out a sheaf of perforated cards. "These are the appointment cards you saw in the film. If you want to meet the same man again, just write the date and time on both ends, and give one half to him. He'll show the card to the Wrongside clerk, and you'll show yours to our clerk, so she can put it in the computer. If a man ever misses an appointment with you, we'll bar him for five years. We can't let them think they can make any decisions about sex.

"And this is the alarm." Jessie pointed to a wall-mounted box within reach of the bed. "You remember the emergency evacuation procedures you saw in the film, don't you?"

Cara nodded vigorously. That was the most important thing, as far as she was concerned. "It's just like a fire alarm. You punch this button. The alarm goes off, and someone will rescue me. If someone else pulls the alarm and I hear it, I leave immediately."

Jessie nodded, pleased with her student. "It doesn't matter what you're doing. If you're in the middle of sex, if you're in the shower, whether you're dressed or not. Don't say anything to the man, just leave as fast as you can. You'll only have thirty seconds."

There was one more thing to show the newcomer. Jessie pointed to a small video camera recessed into a corner of the ceiling. "This camera will be on for your first time, and any other time you request it. We'll be watching everything to make sure he never hurts you."

Cara stepped back, alarmed. "You mean he might hurt me?"

Jessie shook her head reassuringly. "All the men know that if they ever hurt a woman, they'll be barred from the Red Cabins for life. This camera is just for insurance."

Cara relaxed a little. She looked around the small room, licking her lips nervously.

"How do I pick the man I want?" she asked timidly. "My mom said they won't know I'm looking at them."

Jessie nodded and led the way out of the room. "That's right. Come down the hall with me to the viewing room. I'll show you."

In the viewing room, now crowded with more women making selections, Jessie led Cara up close to the glass. On the other side, a row of men sat on a bench, staring vacantly at the women.

Cara gasped and jumped back. "They're looking right at me!" she exclaimed.

Jessie smiled. "No, they're not. It's one-way glass. We can see them, but they can't see us. They think they're looking at a mirror."

Cara sidled closer. She had seen pictures of men, of course, and videotapes, but this was the real thing. In just a few minutes, if she didn't chicken out, she would actually be touching the real thing. Kissing. Holding. She moaned and shrank away from the glass. Red spots of color burned on her pale cheeks.

"I can't do it. I just *can't*."

Jessie put a sympathetic arm around the girl's trembling shoulders. She had recognized a face at the far end of the bench.

"Come on down here, hon, let me tell you about this one."

The two walked to the far end of the glass, where Jessie pointed out a middle-aged man with dark hair and a sparse but well-kept beard. The man wasn't tall, but he had broad shoulders and a quiet air of confidence. His beard was shot through with gray, and he had friendly, slanted eyes.

"His name's Bud," Jessie said with a soft, reminiscent smile. "I picked him for my first time. He made it really easy for me, and I've enjoyed sex ever since."

Cara pulled in a ragged breath and looked timidly at the man on the bench. "I'm not sure."

Jessie withdrew her arm. "It's your call, Cara. Only you know if you're ready for this."

On the other side, a door at the end of the bench opened, and a young boy walked through. He sat next to the older man, grinned at him nervously, and said something.

****

Bud laughed. "You ain't kidding, Davy. They put you right through the damn wringer with all those questions."

Davy shifted on the hard bench. He couldn't be still. "What're we sitting here looking at this mirror for, anyway? What are we waiting for?"

Bud shook his head. Kid was so naive it wasn't funny. "Don't Tom tell you nothing, boy?"

Davy shrugged. "He don't talk much."

Bud understood that, he guessed. "These are one-way mirrors," he said, gesturing at the long line of glass.

****

From the viewing room, Cara watched his broad gesture and smiled.

****

"The women are on the other side, looking us over like prize cattle. They can see us, but we can't see them. They make their choice, Hank calls your name, and off you go. Sometimes you wait for hours."

Davy was aghast. "What if none of them ever pick you?"

Bud gave a loud guffaw. "Happens to Bally sometimes, him being so ugly. But he keeps trying. Sooner or later somebody picks him. Usually later."

Hank ambled down from the far end of the bench, shuffling papers. "You're up, Bud," he said absently. "Another first-timer."

The narrow room erupted with loud hoots and cat-calls.

"Yo, Bud, hubba hubba!"

"Show her the devil, Bud!"

"Hoo-eee!!"

Red-faced, Bud shuffled out. Davy cracked his knuckles and continued to wait.

****

Ninety long minutes later, Davy shifted his numb ass on the hard bench for the thousandth time. He'd whiled away some of the time by studying himself in the two-way mirror, wondering what a woman would think of him. He looked pretty regular, he figured. Bronze skin, black hair, high, sharp cheekbones, and a strong nose. He was plenty muscular, too, but did women care about that? Probably not.

He was more embarrassed than nervous now. Maybe he should just get up and leave. Pretend he had to take a leak or something. A dozen men had been called. Davy had been here longer than anyone.

He stood up and stretched, hoping to look casual. "Got to pee," he mumbled to no one in particular. He was deeply mortified. It would be a very long time before he dared the Red Cabins again.

Hank got up from his desk, still shuffling papers. "Davy Redwolf," he announced. He looked up. "Hey, you're Tom's boy."

Davy nodded, holding his breath. His throat was suddenly as dry as sand, and he couldn't trust his voice. Did this mean—?

"Room 5, kid. You're about to get your balls broke in."

Davy barely heard the catcalls this time.

Chapter 6

"Well, Davy," Jessie said, cocking one red-silk hip and propping a hand on it. "Was I worth the wait?"

Davy's knees unhinged, and he very nearly fell to the floor of Room 5. He opened his mouth, but nothing came out. He forgot to close it. He could only stare.

Her voice! No one had told him her voice would be like that, all sweet and soft and husky. And her eyes! They were a funny shade of blue, like a flower, and the way they looked at him—and her hair!

Jessie uttered a soft laugh. "Come over here, lover boy, before you faint. You're doing terrific things for my ego, but I need you alive and kicking." She extended one hand and gestured toward the bed with the other.

Davy looked down at his own hand, which didn't seem to be attached to him anymore. It was reaching out to take Jessie's. Davy waited for the two hands to touch, sure that when they did, something cataclysmic would happen. Touch a woman! He was going to touch a woman!

The orgasm caught him unawares. He hadn't even realized he had an erection. Her incredibly soft hand touched his, and that was all it took. He ejaculated in one violent spasm that shook his body like a leaf. He closed his eyes and let the aftershocks ripple through him. Deep down in his throat, he groaned.

Alone in his bed at night, taking a guilty, solitary pleasure, it had never been like this.

Jessie watched his closed eyes and struggled to keep from laughing out loud. She knew enough about men to realize that if she laughed now, it would be a very short night. By the time Davy opened his eyes, she'd decided how to handle it.

"Oh, my," she said with an admiring smile. "I made you wait too long, didn't I? Don't worry. There's more where that came from." She reached for his other hand and pulled him down on the bed. "Let Jessie show you."

****

Bud twisted across his narrow bed, tangling his legs in the blankets. In his new position, the rising sun caught him full in the face.

"Damn all." He groaned, opening one eye in a squint. He pulled a corner of the blanket over his face and tried again.

No use. It had been a rough night, and he might as well stop trying to sleep.

He groaned again and sat up, rubbing a hand across sleep-bleared eyes. He stumbled to the bathroom and washed his face, then propped his hands on either side of the sink and stared into the spotty mirror.

"What's all this for?" he asked his reflection. "Why're we doing this?"

He thought back to last night. Another first-timer. He seemed to have a reputation for that. Sometimes he thought the damn women must keep track. Hell, they probably had a file on him. "Treats you nice. Knows how to make you come. Good with first-timers."

What a laugh. Why did men put up with it, he

wondered resentfully. Why didn't they just storm the mother-loving Border Fence and blow a hole in it? It could be done.

He watched a drop of water trickle down his forehead and disappear into an eyebrow. Yeah, it could be done if the men in Wrongside could ever agree on a day to start. A place to meet. Who would be in charge. And what explosives to use.

The women knew that would never happen. It was what made them so smug.

Sunday was Bud's day off. It was traditionally a day of rest, but some men didn't bother. Maybe the women did. Bud didn't know. But he liked his Sundays, so he always took that day off. Today he thought he'd run down to Jackson Hole and visit Ricky.

****

"Hey, bro, long time no see!" Ricky gave him an enthusiastic hug.

Ricky preferred men. It was not uncommon in Wrongside, and it didn't stop Bud from loving his brother or enjoying his company. But he still didn't like it. Ricky was choosing not to have sons, while Bud yearned for them.

He pulled away a little too quickly. Ricky noticed, but he was used to it. He shrugged.

"What brings you south, Buddy?"

Bud shook his head. "I don't know. Cody just seemed too small for me all of a sudden. I ain't due for vacation till summer, so I did the next best thing."

"Well, I'm glad to have you," Ricky said with a smile. "Come on in. Clyde's just making lunch."

Bud disliked Clyde Wether, though he hardly knew him. The feeling was mutual, but they both loved

Ricky, so they adapted.

Clyde, sighing, added water to the soup and took an extra loaf of bread out of the pantry. At the last minute, he sliced some dried meat and cheese onto a platter. He'd seen Bud eat before.

The three men sat late over lunch while Bud regaled them with stories of the first-timer. Cara, her name had been.

Neither Clyde nor Ricky had ever been in a Red Cabin, and neither had any intention of going, but they were fascinated all the same.

"*How* long was her hair?" Ricky asked for the third time.

"Did she really cry?" Clyde mused. "A woman crying. What an image." Clyde was an artist and looked the part, stick-thin with a wispy beard and shoulder-length blond hair.

"Just a little," Bud said uncomfortably. "She was scared, that's all. If she'd cried any harder they'd have booted me out of there for sure."

Later, Bud accompanied Ricky to his office for an appointment with a student. Ricky was a history teacher at Wrongside's only university. Bud himself hadn't gone beyond the mandatory tenth grade, but he was proud of his brother.

After a supper of grilled venison and dried vegetables, the three men sat around the fireplace with a jug of Ricky's homemade wine. Bud had two glasses before he broached the subject that had been on his mind all day.

"Why is it like this, Ricky? Why do the women control everything, and why do we accept it? You're a history teacher—explain it to me."

Ricky took his arm off the back of the couch and sat forward, cradling his glass. Firelight etched his bearded face, so much like Bud's that it was like looking in a mirror. Their father had always believed they must have had the same mother, but of course he hadn't known for sure. No woman would have dreamed of telling him that Milina, founder of Rightside, had been the brothers' grandmother. Bud and Ricky were the sons of Milina and Yong's only daughter.

****

"That's a tough question, Buddy. When my students ask it, I always tell them to go back to the beginning. What do you know about the Territory Wars?"

Bud shrugged. "Same thing everybody knows, I guess. The women and men fought over the best lands, and the women won."

Ricky shook his head. "That's the simple version, the one they tell boys in their cradles. The truth is the men were doing all the fighting. Against each other. The women were hiding in the woods, scared to death. We fought ourselves into exhaustion, then the women stole the guns and drove us behind the Border Fence because they were afraid we'd kill them all."

Bud waved the details away with one hand. "But how do they stay in control? That's what I can't figure out. Why didn't we ever take Rightside back? We're stronger than they are, aren't we?"

"Physically, maybe."

"So why didn't we ever fight again—men against women?"

Ricky sighed. "Because the women won't, that's why. They don't want anything from us but our seed.

47

We give it to them on their terms because they provide us with almost everything else. We don't know much about Rightside, but we all know what's wrong with Wrongside. Look at us. We're fragmented. It's been seventy-one years, and although things are better now than they've ever been, we still don't have a representative government. Education is low priority. We don't even have social services."

Bud had never heard of those. "What the hell are social services?"

Ricky gestured impatiently. "On old Earth. Before the colonization. Women and men lived together back then in the same towns. Same houses, sometimes."

Bud recoiled at the thought, but Ricky nodded. "It's true. It's in the history books. Men and women lived together and governed together. They had what they called social services. Old people got a stipend to live on when they couldn't work anymore. Health care was free and universal. The government took care of the roads, built bridges, ran the schools. There were hundreds of universities. There were museums everywhere. Hell, there was free trade back then—and *communication*."

"Communication?"

"Yes. Look at Wrongside. We only have a few radio stations, and outside of Jackson Hole, hardly anyone is interested enough to listen to the news. We have one mother-loving newspaper in the entire country, and no one but the history teachers remembers what a magazine was. The only reason we have art in our lives"—he gestured at Clyde—"is because we have so little else in Wrongside.

"The only things we manufacture are munitions,

leather, and liquor, and we only do that because the women won't supply us with them. We keep some farmers and bakers in business because we'd starve without them. The women can't or won't provide us with all our food. We only get meat when we hunt for it because most of our domesticated stock has to go to the women to pay for the things we don't manufacture. Trucks. Kitchen sinks. Paper. Wristwatches. Even electricity.

"And look at our technology. Seventy-one years ago, *men* helped move us to other planets when Earth's climate went to hell. Men even piloted the spaceships, but we couldn't build one today if our lives depended on it. The women have kept their old knowledge, but we men have degenerated almost to a pre-technology level. The few computers we have at the university came from Rightside. No one here knows how to build them or repair them, for that matter."

Ricky was getting wound up now. The faults of Wrongside were always a hot topic. "But government—that's where we really come up short. I've been told that Rightside has a constitutional government, with elections every year. It's representation of the people, by the people, for the people, the way it was meant to be. What we have here—"

Ricky stopped and shook his head suddenly. He flopped back against the couch and stared at the fire, disgust written across his bearded face.

Bud knew exactly why Ricky was so disgusted. Commander Sherman, the chief of state in Wrongside, had been entrenched in office for years. Bud couldn't recall the date of the last election, but it had been a while.

Each commander governed indifferently, keeping loose track of a cadre of lieutenants who oversaw the nine districts of Wrongside. The lawmen, Bud among them, enforced what law there was in the individual towns.

It was a system ripe for abuse, and there was plenty of that. The most recent scandal involved a lieutenant caught taking bribes to lose shipments of free Rightside drugs that had been destined for Wrongside's five hospitals. The desperately needed drugs had ended up on the black market, where their under-the-table sale to the same hospitals lined the pockets of various crooks and politicians. Everyone knew the story, and no one really cared.

Ricky shook his head again. "Sometimes I don't think anything can change Wrongside. We've been entrenched in this way of life for so long that nothing can pull us out. We might just as well accept it."

Bud shook his head impatiently. "Still, aren't things better now? Remember when we were kids? There were still outhouses, at least up in Cody. Hardly anyone had a truck; lots of folks still rode horses. Pop and his brothers never even finished grade school, let alone high school. Seems like we're better off now."

"We are," Ricky admitted. "The picture isn't quite as bad as I've painted it. Because Sherman has been in power so long, things are definitely more stable, and it allows us a little leisure for art and music. Look at Clyde. He's known throughout Wrongside, after all. Culture—yeah, I guess we have some culture now. The university orchestra is even talking about doing a tour this summer. You might see them up in Cody, even Bozeman. But it still doesn't mean we'll ever get along with the women."

"But if we could just talk to them, ask them—"

Bud never finished the sentence, because Clyde chose that moment to jump in and change the subject. "Talk to the women? What a silly idea. I've been doing something better than that, Bud."

"Better than what?" Bud was startled into asking Clyde a direct question, something he rarely did.

"Better than talking to women. I've been trading with them."

"You?" Bud didn't bother to hide his contempt.

Stung by the scorn in Bud's voice, Clyde jumped up from the couch and left the room. Bud was trying to force himself to apologize when Clyde returned, carrying a small soapstone sculpture carefully in two hands. He set it on the hearth with a flourish and sat back to enjoy Bud's reaction.

The sculpture, exquisitely done, was of a woman with a baby. Bud had never seen anything like it, and he knew without asking that no man had carved it.

"It's called *Mother and Child*," Clyde said softly.

"Mother," Bud repeated. For once, it wasn't a cuss word.

He studied the sculpture more closely. The baby seemed to be female. That was the amazing thing. It had long, delicate eyelashes, beautifully rendered in stone, and a fineness of features that Bud had never seen on a male baby. The mother—even in his mind, he stumbled over the word—had a tender and loving expression that seemed out of place on a woman. It was such a *fatherly* look. To see it on a woman's face was almost obscene.

Bud, along with all the men of Wrongside,

accepted that where there were male babies, there must be female babies, but he had never given the idea much thought. He assumed, correctly, that the women kept all the female babies, but he had never applied that assumption to his own life.

Studying the sculpture, a question dawned in his conscious mind for the first time. "Ricky, do you think I ever made a female baby like this? Do I have a-a—" He groped for a word that was not in the Wrongside vocabulary. His brother, the historian, furnished it for him.

"A daughter? It's entirely possible, Buddy. Entirely possible."

The brothers looked at each other. Ricky knew of Bud's longing to be a father. They also knew that if Bud did have a daughter, neither of them would ever know.

"Best not to worry about it," he said gently. "Concentrate on getting a boy. That's all you want from women."

Bud shook himself. "It's not what Clyde wants from women, looks like. Where'd you get this, anyway?"

Clyde flipped shoulder-length hair back from his face in a distinctly female gesture, though of course neither Ricky nor Clyde himself realized that. Bud, a veteran of the Red Cabins, recognized it at once and curled his upper lip in disdain. Clyde didn't notice.

"Oh, it wasn't hard," Clyde gushed. "A little bribery, a little sneakiness, a little danger. It was a breeze."

Bud growled deep in his throat. "Sounds illegal as hell to me."

Belatedly, Clyde remembered his partner's brother was a lawman. "Oh!" he gasped. "Oh, it wasn't like that at all. No, no, no, no!" He swept the statue from the hearth and cradled it protectively in his arms. Ricky rushed in to salvage the awkward moment.

"He didn't do anything illegal, Bud. Unethical, maybe," he admitted, shooting Clyde an exasperated look. "But not illegal."

Clyde's smug look was back. He liked it when Ricky took his side against Bud. Bud looked from one man to the other, shook his head, and capitulated.

"I give up," he said. "Tell me how you got it."

Clyde placed the sculpture carefully back on the hearth and told his story. It turned out that Simeon Hasad, the art dealer who bought most of Clyde's paintings, was seeing the same woman regularly. Older women liked it that way, though they were careful to keep the relationships superficial.

"Her name is Toller Sheridan," Clyde whispered.

Over the course of several years, the two had become friendly. That was illegal in Rightside, but not in Wrongside. In Wrongside it was just unheard of.

"Hard to believe," Bud said, shaking his head. "They're friends. They shoot the breeze, talk about stuff that isn't sex?"

"Friends," Clyde insisted. "They talk about art."

"Art?"

Painting in particular and the arts in general were one of the few thriving industries in Wrongside. Because the men had little beauty in their everyday lives, they looked for it in art. Clyde was known and respected throughout the country for his work with watercolors. Ricky, though he'd had the good sense never to tell his partner, knew that one of Clyde's best works, *Man at Dawn*, hung in Bud's bedroom.

The dealer, Clyde continued, and the woman who favored him turned out to have mutual interests. Toller was the owner of a gallery in New Atlanta, across the Border Fence from Jackson Hole.

"But the arts are in decline over there," Clyde said. "No one's buying, and more importantly, no one's selling. Toller thought she'd do better over here."

Bud was aghast. "You mean you bought this? From a woman?"

Clyde nodded happily. "Isn't it beautiful? See the detail here on the baby's fingers? And see the way the light catches this plane?"

"Forget about the light!" Bud couldn't believe what he was hearing. Rightside and Wrongside traded for a lot of things. Besides the indispensable commodity of their sperm, men provided women with fresh meat, tanned leather, and lumber in return for electricity, male babies, and such factory-produced goods as the women were willing to let them have.

But Bud had never heard of men and women trading anything personal or cultural. The two groups knew almost nothing about each others' lives. That was the way it had always been.

Until now, apparently.

Now, looking at the statue, Bud felt like a trespasser. He felt as though he was looking straight into the heart of Rightside—into the heart of a woman. He couldn't imagine anything more intimate than this portrait of mother and child. More intimate or more alien.

Bud was speechless. He might be uneducated, but

he was far from stupid. He knew, better than happy-go-lucky Clyde, that the presence of this single piece of art in Wrongside could change the very fabric of their lives.

****

Much later, Bud started the long drive back to Cody. He had a lot to think about. Clyde and Ricky had told him that Toller was smuggling small paintings and pieces of sculpture to the Wrongside dealer through the Red Cabin where they met. Simeon had developed a small, select market for Rightside art and was feeling pretty pleased with himself. Toller was less pleased, but she appreciated the gold coins—legal tender on both sides of the Border Fence—that Simeon paid her.

According to Toller, Clyde had said, what she was doing was seriously illegal in Rightside. Maintaining personal contact with a man, trading secretly with him, and letting Rightside culture into the hands of men were all offenses punishable by long jail terms. There were no laws against such things in Wrongside, simply because the subject had never come up.

Now that it had, Bud, the lawman, faced a decision. Should he report the goings-on to his lieutenant? He wouldn't mind getting Clyde in trouble for buying smuggled art. He knew that although there was no law against it now, there soon would be if the facts were known. The current Wrongside administration was deeply suspicious of women and would want no part of women's culture.

But Bud, like Ricky, didn't personally see anything wrong with what Toller and Simeon were doing. Ricky believed that any new idea could only be good for his stagnant country. For his part, Bud believed the statue could be the first tiny chink in the hundred-mile Border Fence. The Fence, he was beginning to believe, should never have been built in the first place, and the sooner it cracked, the better off they'd all be.

The sooner it cracked, he admitted to himself, the sooner he could answer a question that had very suddenly assumed importance in his mind. Did he have a daughter? And if he did, could this statue be his passport to her? Maybe, if he handled the situation carefully, he could meet Toller. Talk to her. He could find out if the women kept track of which men fathered which female babies. She seemed accessible. If she would talk to Simeon about art, maybe she'd talk to him about babies, especially if she thought the lawman could get her into trouble if she refused to cooperate. It was worth a shot.

Driving home through the cold darkness of the winter night, Bud felt confident. He had a new purpose, the beginnings of a plan, and things were looking good. In his mind he developed a sugar-coated fantasy. Somewhere misty and far away, he met his daughter. She was tiny and feminine, and she had his father's brown eyes. She called him "Pop."

Chapter 7

Davy threw back his head and screamed. It was a jubilant, rising howl that ended on a long, ululating note of triumph. Far back in Davy's ancestry, half a galaxy and a dozen or more branches down the family tree, there had been an Oglala Sioux named Red Wolf. The old hunter's ghost rose up behind Davy now and threw back its own head, joining in the triumphal scream.

Davy had made a clean kill. The deer had dropped dead in its tracks when Davy's single bullet pierced its carotid artery.

The animal was not actually a deer, but that's what Davy called it. The flora and fauna of Rightside/Wrongside were not exactly the same as that of Old Earth but were near enough to make no difference. The first colonists had simply called the plants and animals they found by the names of whichever Earth plants and animals they most resembled.

The same had been true of the cities, in a way. The women, in their orderly fashion, had named their capital New Washington. Cities to the north had been named for cities of the northeastern United States, where most of the colonists had been born. Cities to the south had been named the same way. The men, enamored of the lawlessness and danger of the new colony, had given their settlements brash, brave Western names that spoke of gunslingers and pioneers.

Though it was north and east of everything that mattered, the high plain where Davy stood with his kill evoked the West of the nineteenth-century United States. An empty, windswept prairie filled the long miles between Wrongside's towns and the ocean that covered most of the planet. Men only rarely crossed the Plains to visit the sea, and no one stayed.

Large, slow, stupid bovines that the men called buffalo grazed the wild grasses. Animals that resembled the foxes, coyotes, rabbits, and eagles of Earth filled their ecological niches across the Plains and along the banks of the wild Missouri River that bisected them.

The men hunted continuously, but in seventy-one years, they had not managed to decimate the Plains' wildlife to any appreciable extent. This was mainly due to the scarcity of men. From the bare hundred who had founded Wrongside the population had grown to a few thousand, but they were spread down the hundred-mile length of the country.

Most men hunted in the valleys and copses that dotted middle Wrongside, or in the far southern forests. Only those who hunted for a living came to the Plains regularly; others came once or twice a year for buffalo meat that they salted and stored. Those who didn't hunt at all depended on small domesticated herds of sheep and cattle, though most of the meat from those herds went straight to the women to pay for manufactured goods.

Davy liked the lonely Plains. It was nearly sunset now. He hadn't seen another person all day. Since leaving school the year before, Davy had spent a lot of time up here with his father's battered old pickup. He was a good enough hunter to supply their humble needs and still have meat and skins left over to sell. A buffalo hide was worth four gold coins at the tanning factory where Davy's father, Tom, was a night foreman.

Davy made a swift, expert cut down the length of the deer and breathed through his mouth as the stinking entrails spilled out. He finished the job as quickly as he could, leaving what he didn't want for the buzzards. The rest he loaded in the back of the truck. He walked to a nearby stream and broke a thin skim of ice to wash up. Ahead of him, to the west, the sun was setting in a blaze of crimson glory.

Davy didn't often get a deer. They were more cautious than the buffalo. The venison would be a welcome change, and the bones would make nice toys for Hud.

It was hard to believe how fast the little guy was growing. Davy and his father spent endless hours just watching Hud grow. Tom had begun to unbend a little with this second chance at fatherhood, and Davy was grateful.

He remembered how his father had been years ago, before age and disappointment had crept up on him, rendering him morose and silent. He never talked about his problems, but Davy knew he'd been bitterly disappointed to have sired only one son. The family was happier now. Davy had even told Tom about Jessie.

"Took a shine to you, did she?" Tom had asked.

Davy had nodded happily. "Seems like. She's been asking for me regular ever since the first time, right after Hud came. She says I'm virile, whatever that means."

Tom had shrugged. "Means she takes a shine to you. Enjoy it while it lasts, boy, but don't get too caught up."

Davy was enjoying the hell out of it. His thoughts were never very far away from Jessie. Even now, as he dried his arms on an old rag, he was thinking about her soft white breasts and the way she liked for him to kiss them.

He hadn't told Tom this part, but he and Jessie had been doing more than screwing. They talked, sometimes for hours. Once a buzzer had even sounded in their room, and Jessie jumped like someone had stabbed her, said she'd stayed too long. The talking was almost as good as the sex. He knew all about her job and her family now, and he'd told her about Pop and Hud and hunting on the Plains. She'd said it was illegal for women and men to trade personal information, so he kept it to himself.

But mother, they loved talking. They even liked to sit and stare at each other without even saying a word. The way he felt about Jessie was something he couldn't explain. She said it might be love. Love was something in old Earth storybooks, though, and he figured she must be wrong.

****

Some twenty-eight miles away, in the lab of the New Washington Hospital, Jessie was thinking about the same thing. She was nervous, and to take her mind off of it, she closed her eyes and thought about Davy's mouth on her breast, where it had been last night. With the other men she'd seen, her primary thought had always been her own pleasure. The men themselves didn't matter. They were just faces and bodies.

Davy was more than a face. For some odd reason, he was more important than his sperm. Jessie was young. There was plenty of time to have babies. In the interim, she was enjoying Davy tremendously. She even wondered if she might be in love like it said in the old storybooks.

But their delicious interim was about to be rudely interrupted by the very thing Jessie had just decided could wait. Halfway across the lab, a technician looked up from her work. She raised one thumb in a victory salute. "It's a go, Jess. You're pregnant."

Chapter 8

Motherhood was a blessing, Alanna Olaffson believed, but it could also be an irritating nuisance.

"Laran Lee Olaffson, stop that right this minute." She had a headache, and it was only eight in the morning. Laran was disgustingly cheerful as she skipped around the breakfast table, singing and clapping her hands. She skidded to a guilty halt at Alanna's angry tone.

"Sit down and eat. You'll be late for school," Alanna muttered. "I didn't mean to yell at you, honey. Mommy has a tough day ahead."

And that was the understatement of the year. Today she presented Congress with her restructuring plan. She had held office for five months now. Out of necessity, she'd rammed some pretty unpopular measures down the lawmakers' throats, including the dam repair tax. Now it was time to conciliate, to placate, to smooth over the troubled waters and get the legislators back on her side.

If that was still possible.

A knock on the kitchen door interrupted her musings. Laran skipped to answer it.

"Hi, sweetie. Morning, boss." Vice President Kai Makele maneuvered through the door carrying an armload of papers. She was a large, competent woman in her fifties, a tough legislator, and a valuable friend.

Alanna had known and respected her for years, and when the time had come to choose a vice president, Kai's name had been first on her short list.

Kai would be invaluable in the months ahead, working behind the scenes to smooth the way for Alanna's reforms. She had been busy already this morning.

"No, thanks," she said, refusing Alanna's offer of breakfast. "I've already eaten. Twice, in fact. This job is awfully hard on my girlish figure, you know."

"How come, Aunt Kai?" Laran asked, around a mouthful of muffin.

"Because I have to be nice to all the cranky legislators and invite them to eat. I sweeten them up with homemade chocolate doughnuts and homemade soup and homemade lemon meringue pie—courtesy of my mom, by the way—so they'll like us and listen when your mother talks."

"I don't get it." Laran polished off one muffin and started another. "Why should they listen to my mom just because your mom feeds 'em?"

Kai laughed. "It's called politics, honey. The whole time they're stuffing their faces, I'm stuffing their heads full of facts and figures. By the time the meal's over, they not only know my mom is a fantastic cook, they know your mom's a fantastic president."

"Oh." No longer interested, Laran changed the subject. "Mom, can we get a puppy?"

The women burst into laughter, and immediately Laran looked injured. She was old enough to know when she was being laughed at but not always old enough to know why.

"No, we most certainly cannot get a puppy!"

Alanna was more exasperated than amused. "Laran, we talked about this. After my presidency, when I don't have to travel so much, then we'll see about a dog. Not before." She ruffled her daughter's hair. "Understand?"

"Yeah, I guess so," Laran mumbled. She ducked her head away from her mother's hand and munched disconsolately on her muffin. She paid no more attention to the women as they discussed strategies for the day ahead.

It wasn't fair. She'd be eleven years old by the time her mother's presidency was over—almost grown up! She wouldn't even need a puppy then. She had the meanest mother in the whole world.

"Hey, you! Frowny-face! Hustle up. It's time to go." Alanna was stuffing papers into her briefcase and gulping the last of her coffee. Expertly, she swept Laran's dishes from the table and dumped them in the sink for Martha, the housekeeper.

"I want you to wear your sweater today. It looks cold."

Laran made a face and kicked the table leg. "Man," she swore, careful to keep her voice low.

Sweater and lunch bag in hand, Laran ran out the back door of the Government Building after her long-legged mother. Alanna would walk her to school, two blocks away, then return across the plaza to the Congressional chamber. Kai went straight to the chamber to test the waters.

The block-long Government Building housed not only the vaulted, richly decorated Congressional Chamber, but the somber Judicial Chamber, a set of Cabinet offices, Alanna's and Kai's offices in the second-story executive suite, and presidential living quarters at the back of the third floor.

The building was nearly sixty years old but had been built well and served its purpose. It was sandstone, as were most buildings in New Washington. Each section had its own lavish entrance of marble with pillared porticos—Rightside architecture owed a lot to the classic Greeks of old Earth.

"Are you ready for this, Kai?" The vice president was greeted by Giulia Saracco, secretary of the Treasury. Giulia hesitated under the Congressional portico, lacing and unlacing her plump fingers as if unable to decide where to go.

"You don't look very ready," Kai answered with a wry smile. She would never understand why Alanna had chosen Giulia for her cabinet. The woman might be a financial wizard, but that was her sole asset. Except when it came to figures on a page, Giulia was indecisive and cowardly, incapable of the hard decisions necessary for leadership.

"I'm not," she admitted now. Worry lines were etched across her forehead, and she bit her lip. "I don't know how Alanna can face them after the dam repair tax. If it was me, having to go up there on the podium, I don't know, I just couldn't."

"Then it's a good thing we're not depending on you, isn't it?" Kai didn't bother to hide her disgust.

Giulia, stung by the sharp words, looked away hastily. She caught sight of Alanna and Laran across the plaza as they disappeared around the corner of a building.

"There she goes now," the woman said, eager to change the subject. "That Laran is so cute. She looks just like her mother."

"Yes, she does." Kai smiled at the compliment. Her own daughters were grown and gone, so she was always ready to talk about Laran. "Know what she came up with this morning? She wants a puppy. Can you imagine? Of course, Alanna had to tell her no, but it's a shame. Every girl should have a puppy."

"I have one." Giulia's eyes were dreamy. "Her name is Fluffy. She has the cutest little corkscrew tail. It whirls around when…"

Kai stopped listening, but she nodded politely at all the right intervals. Kai had been in politics for a long time, and she was very good at it. As she lingered at the door with Giulia, pretending interest, she shrewdly scanned each arrival.

Maud Adams, secretary of the Interior, was coming up the steps. Alanna had threatened to fire her two months ago in the wake of the dam repair fight, so she must now be counted an enemy. It had come to Kai's attention that Maud was spreading dissension in the ranks.

Some said that even timid Giulia Saracco was listening to Maud's whispers. But Giulia only nodded absently as Maud passed them, then continued with her happy reminiscences of Fluffy.

Kai smiled encouragingly at Giulia but took one casual step to the left so she could eavesdrop on Maud's greeting to a representative from New Atlanta.

"How's it going?" Maud's long nose sniffed busily, and she wasted no time on pleasantries. "Did you have any luck with the boss?"

"She likes the idea." The reply was equally terse. "But right now, the whole thing hinges on your ace. Have you approached her?"

"I tried once. She's as nervous as a man without a gun. I had to lie through my teeth."

"Keep after her. We might need her."

Maud, noticing Kai's casual glance, took the woman's arm and drew her away into the shadows of the porch.

Kai sighed. If what was going to work? What ace? Who was the boss? She played the conversation over in her mind, locking in every detail, every nuance. She and Alanna would analyze it later.

"… but then, would you believe it, Fluffy went right over and laid her head in Mama's lap!"

Kai laughed obligingly. "Fluffy must be quite a dog."

"Oh, she is!" Giulia gushed. "Another time she found a…"

The next noteworthy lawmaker to ascend the steps was the opposition Constancy Party's chairman, from wet and humid New Tampa. The woman was an astute politician, and Kai had always admired her from a distance. No one was close to the chairman except, just lately, Maud Adams. That was odd, since the women claimed allegiance to opposing political parties.

But Maud had once been a member of the Constancy Party, Kai recalled. She had switched to the Fidelity Party years ago for reasons no one ever clearly understood. Could Maud be thinking of switching back? Could the chairman be the boss Maud had mentioned?

"… but Fluffy had it hidden the whole time." Giulia was smiling fondly. She was obviously at the end of another story.

Kai smiled broadly. "What a smart dog!" she

enthused. "No wonder you love her. But look, here comes Alanna back from school. It's time we went inside."

Giulia nodded happily and drifted away, awash in fond thoughts of Fluffy. Kai waited for Alanna.

"Save me an hour later this afternoon," she said from the corner of her mouth. "We have to talk."

Alanna nodded without speaking, and the two swept into the Congressional Chamber. As far as they could tell, all thirty congresswomen were present. Infrastructure was a hot issue.

The Speaker of the Congress stepped up to the podium as Alanna and Kai took their places behind her. The speaker zipped through the preliminaries and finished with a flourish. "Women of Rightside, I give you President Alanna Olaffson!"

Kai clapped obediently and looked attentive, but her eyes were scanning the chamber. She caught the meaningful glance that passed between Maud and the party chairman, but she missed entirely the nervous apprehension with which Giulia Saracco regarded them.

Chapter 9

Out on the Plains, Davy Redwolf knew nothing of the political machinations of the women. He was still thinking about Jessie and her soft, white breasts. He was totally unprepared for the crack of a rifle shot and the spank of a bullet just inches from his hand as he reached for the door handle of the pickup.

He whipped around and slammed his back painfully against the bed of the truck. Adrenaline spilled into his bloodstream in a frantic rush. His eyes darted left, right. Where had the shot come from?

Another rang out. This time it was closer, whistling past his cheek to shatter the driver's side window. A shard of flying glass sliced into his temple. Davy dropped to the ground and rolled through the dust under the truck. One shoulder thumped painfully against the battery, but he kept going through to the other side.

He crouched against the back tire, breath whistling through his teeth. His shoulder hurt. His face throbbed. Blood dripped onto his trembling knee.

"Think you're *going* somewhere, *boy?*"

Davy started and almost fell over. The drunken shout had come from the right. He eased an eye up over the truck bed and searched the boulders at the base of a low rise on the far side of the truck. He saw nothing.

"What you got in your *truck*, boy?"

This time his eye caught movement. Two men,

maybe more, were standing in the high grass in front of the boulders. As he watched, the men stirred and began to move forward. Davy ducked down against the tire. He wondered if he could reach his rifle back by the tailgate. Even if he could, it wasn't loaded.

"Stand up there, boy, let's—uh—yeah, let's have a *look* at you!"

Davy swallowed, heard the dry click in his throat, and hoped his voice wouldn't crack. "What do you want?" he shouted. "What are you bothering me for?"

"Stand up, boy." A different voice, neither drunk nor disjointed, compelled Davy to stand up slowly. He couldn't cower behind the truck all day, he guessed.

Four men stood on the other side of the truck. All were armed. One, an evil-looking drunk, was reeling slightly, using his rifle to keep his balance. The second wore two handguns strapped low on his thighs. He had bronzed skin and pale, incongruously blue eyes. Davy didn't recognize either of them.

The third man was Frank Gibson, and the fourth was his oldest son, Chad. Frank laughed and stepped forward. He flicked his blond hair back with a quick, practiced movement of his head.

"Well, if it ain't Tom Redwolf's boy," he drawled congenially. "Look here, Chad, it's your old friend, Dave."

Chad shot Davy a black look from under his thick blond eyebrows. "Ain't no friend of mine," he muttered.

"What?" Frank pretended to be amazed. "No friend of yours? Why, I thought you two was best buddies."

Davy shifted nervously. This was looking bad. Chad Gibson had carried a grudge against him ever since grade school when Davy had beaten him to a pulp for stealing his favorite knife.

"Never mind that now, Frank," the blue-eyed man cut in sharply. "What did he see?"

Frank waved a hand impatiently. "I told you he couldn't have seen nothing. Can't hardly spot the truck from here."

Involuntarily Davy glanced toward the boulders again and to the dirt road that ran around the far side of the rise. He could just see the front bumper of a pickup jutting out. What were they doing way up here? Smuggling? The Border Fence was just a few miles away. Suddenly this looked more than bad. This looked awful.

Davy tried a nervous laugh. "What do I care if you're up here hunting? So am I. Got me a deer. Want to see it?" He made a move toward the back of the truck.

The blue-eyed man's guns were in his hands before Davy completed his second step. "Hold it right there, boy," he said softly. "You ain't going nowhere."

Davy obeyed. He stood facing the men over the bed of his father's old gray pickup. Suddenly he wanted Tom. He needed Tom the way only a boy could need his father. *Help me, Pop!* he cried silently. *Help me be strong, help me get out of this, help me now!* But Tom was twenty miles away, smiling idiotically at Hud's attempts to roll over.

Davy licked his lips and tried again. "Hell, maybe you guys didn't have no luck. I could share. I mean, if you want any of this here meat—"

"Shut up, Davy! We ain't out here shooting no deer!"

71

Frank Gibson threw a backhanded slap that caught his son across the face. "Shut up yourself, idiot! You want to drive down to Cody and tell the rest of the town while yer at it?"

Chad retreated sullenly, pressing the grimy back of one hand to his split lip.

Frank returned his attention to Davy. He smiled, and Davy held his breath. Frank's right hand held the barrel of his rifle while his right foot held the stock up out of the dust. He swung it casually, loose, and ready for action. In contrast, Davy felt as tight as a coiled spring.

"We got us a kind of a delicate situation here, Dave," Frank said softly. "You see Chad's right. We ain't deer hunting."

Davy shrugged nervously. His head hurt. He had to concentrate on keeping his knees locked straight. "Makes no difference to me. I don't care why you're up here. Time I get home, I'll probably forget I ever saw you."

The evil-looking one giggled into his rifle barrel and swayed drunkenly. "Hear that, Frank? He's gonna forget he ever saw us. Hoo-eee, that makes me feel lots better!"

Frank shot him a quick, disgusted look. "You shut up, too, Eddie. Let me think a minute."

The blue-eyed man stepped forward. "Think as long as you want, Frank. You'll still come up with the same answer. There's only one." Smoothly, with an almost leisurely attitude, he raised one pistol, took aim, and shot eighteen-year-old Davy Redwolf in the chest.

Davy threw up his hands, and with a comically surprised look on his face, he spun to the right and fell face-down in the dirt.

****

Time passed.

****

Davy blinked his right eye. A gray, flinty piece of rock, flat on one edge and notched on the other, swam into focus for half a second, then swam back out. He decided he must not be dead.

He could feel the left side of his face pressing painfully into the dirt of the road. He could feel the right side of his face exposed to a chill breeze. Somewhere beneath him, a monstrous pain waited to pounce. It hovered just there—and there—on the knife-edge of tolerance. As long as he stayed still, the pain would hover, sucking at his will and his sanity but never quite overcoming either.

If he moved, Davy knew, the pain would crash into him like a sledgehammer and bash him out into nothingness.

The bullet had carved a red tunnel straight through his body, just north of his lungs and east of his trachea. Another few inches either way, and Davy would have been trying to breathe through the small, round, ragged hole in his chest.

The hole in his back was much bigger. The gaping exit wound pumped blood sluggishly, washing out bits of flesh and bone.

When he fell, Davy's right leg had folded under him and broken cleanly in two.

He heard the scrape of a boot on rock. His first instinct was to get up and run, but a stronger instinct—perhaps the ghost of Red Wolf—forced him to lie still. If they thought he was dead, so much the better. He closed his right eye.

Through the waiting haze of pain, he heard the drunk's voice.

"That cat's dead, Frank. Deader than dirt. Gaugh, look at the mess!"

"What'll we do, Pa?" Chad's voice sounded shaky and sick. Davy was glad.

"Why we're gonna drive away, boy." Frank Gibson's voice was hard and flat, like the piece of rock. "Just drive away. We was never even here. We come through way east of here early this morning. Been in Bozeman since lunchtime, visiting with Cousin Eddie here. Ain't that right, Eddie?"

"Sure, Frank, since lunchtime. That's right, I remember particular, on account of—"

"Put a cork in it, Eddie." The blue-eyed voice already sounded bored. "We got cargo to deliver, in case you forgot, and we're late. Let's go." There was a pause. "You know, Frank, I could use me a new set of wheels."

"Forget it, Trask. Everybody in Cody knows this truck and even some in Bozeman. Besides, we never saw it, remember?"

"Yeah, right." There was a peculiar scraping noise, and Davy felt dirt patter over the back of his head. He heard a low, cruel laugh and the sound of boot heels fading.

Davy opened his eye and contemplated that gray, flinty piece of rock. Just beside it was a shiny splinter of glass, perhaps the same splinter that had sliced his temple what felt like a hundred years ago. Davy devoted another hundred years to a study of the splinter. No blood on it, he finally concluded. It couldn't be the same splinter. Damn shame.

He heard the low, fading hum of a truck motor. At least they were gone. That was good news and bad news. Good because they wouldn't shoot him anymore. Bad because now that they were gone, he was going to have to move.

Davy was not particularly brave, but he was tough. No one survived in Wrongside without being tough. Weaned on gunslinger tales, honed in schoolyard fights, tempered by solitary tracking and hunting, Davy was ready for this. Not willing, maybe, but ready. He slid his left arm in toward his body, planted his hand in the dirt, and levered himself up onto his left hip.

The pain was no more and no less than he had bargained for. He sat gasping and retching for a minute. Black dots swam in and out of his vision, and gray mist threatened to swallow the dots. Slowly, he gained control. He knew the bullet must have missed his lungs, and that was good. But he was dizzy and lightheaded from pain and loss of blood, and that was bad.

He knew his leg was broken, and that was also bad, but the bullet had spun him only a few feet from the truck, and that was good. The problem was going to be climbing up into the truck.

The trucks the women of Rightside manufactured for the men of Wrongside looked pretty much like those of old Earth. The cabs could hold three men comfortably, and the beds were big enough for half a dozen boys or one good-sized buffalo carcass. They were battery-powered and could hit a top speed of forty-five miles per hour, downhill with a tailwind. The distance from the ground to the seat of the cab was just about thirty-six inches.

Davy sprawled on the ground, considering his moves. He knew he'd have to do it right the first time. Getting closer to the truck would be easy. Opening the door wouldn't be too hard. Driving the truck wouldn't be impossible. Yeah, it was climbing in that might kill him.

He set about it, hitching his good leg forward and dragging his bad leg behind. His left arm supported his violated torso, and his right arm hung uselessly. It took about five minutes to get in position. After a rest, it took another five to open the passenger door, prop it with his head, and push it wide. Then he rested again, panting and sweating and dribbling blood from the gaping hole in his back.

It was another twenty minutes before Davy fell groaning over the steering wheel of the truck. He swam in and out of consciousness once, twice, maybe a dozen times. When his head finally cleared as much as it was going to, he pressed the starter, let off the brake, and headed the truck down the road.

****

Bud Hopper was sitting in the dark in his living room, thinking and drinking. He'd been doing that a lot lately. He needed to figure out the best way to approach Simeon Hasad, Clyde's art dealer, and through him, the mysterious Toller. Bud hoped that by threatening her with exposure he might force her to help him in the search for his daughter.

That he had a daughter, Bud did not doubt. He knew it as surely as he knew his own name. From the moment he had seen Clyde's sculpture, he had known his daughter lived in Rightside. All he had to do was find her. What he'd do then, he didn't know, but he had to find her first.

Bud's cabin sat at the upper end of the north-south road through Cody. It was an hour after sunset, and the town was quiet. It was so quiet that he heard the truck from a long way off. It was coming down from the Plains, maybe a hunter caught by the dark far from home. He waited for it to pass his cabin and continue into Cody. He listened as the truck slowed and turned toward his house, then jumped as it struck the corner of his front porch with a tired jolt.

Bud buckled on his gunbelt before he stepped outside. The front of the truck was buried in his porch railing, and he could see a figure slumped over the steering wheel. He recognized the truck. With an exasperated shake of his head, he vaulted the twisted railing and wrenched open the driver's side door.

"Tom Redwolf, you drunk old fool! What are you—"

Davy's bloody body slid bonelessly out of the truck and into Bud's arms.

Chapter 10

With a sigh of regret for his clean sheets, Bud lowered Davy carefully onto his bed. The boy wasn't quite dead, but what a mother-lovin' mess. There was blood everywhere, and if that wasn't a bullet hole, Bud would eat his lawman's badge. He threw a blanket over Davy and went out to find the doc.

He stopped by the tanning factory on the way, so Tom was already waiting, washing the blood from his son's face, when Bud got back with Doc Medina.

The physician, a thin, intense young man just out of the university, went about his work in silence. He had been raised in a placid hamlet south of Jackson Hole, and the rough lawlessness of northern Wrongside still dismayed him. This was the fourth bullet wound he'd patched in as many months. He cleaned and bandaged the bullet holes, stitched the head wound, gave him a tetanus shot, and started an antibiotic drip.

Tom held Davy's shoulders while the leg was set. Over the doctor's bent head, he looked at Bud with silent anguish in his eyes.

"I got no idea what happened," Bud said in answer to the unspoken question. "I was just sitting here half asleep when the truck bumped into the porch. Davy was already passed out by the time I got outside. Where was he today?"

"On the Plains," Tom said briefly. "Shot him a

deer. It's in the back of the truck."

"And then somebody shot him, that's certain. Did you find the bullet, Doc?"

"No." Medina straightened up, perspiring slightly from his efforts. "The bullet went straight through the upper right side of his chest, luckily, exiting at the top edge of the shoulder blade. No involvement with the lungs or major arteries. The worst damage is to the muscles of his upper back. He's going to have trouble using that arm after this."

"How about his leg?" Bud asked.

"Nice, simple break. It should heal cleanly." Doc Medina shifted his gaze from Bud to Tom. "You're his father?"

Tom nodded.

"We need to talk about this bullet wound. It's not life-threatening right now, but I'm worried about how it will heal. It could very easily abscess." He hesitated, knowing his next words would not be welcome.

"I want to take him to the university hospital down in Jackson Hole."

Tom pulled back suspiciously. "We got our own hospital here in Cody."

Doc Medina turned away to wash his hands in the bowl of hot water Bud had brought. He stated his case as bluntly as he could.

"Yes. I work there, remember? And no one knows better than I do how limited our facilities are. I can't take care of Davy here. If we don't get him to Jackson Hole, he'll probably die. It's as simple as that."

Tom looked down at his unconscious son. With a calloused hand, he stroked the damp hair and touched the neat stitches that now closed the gaping wound in

Davy's temple. He let his gaze wander down his son's body, past the white chest bandage with its spots of red, to the splints and tape that held the broken leg together. He looked up at the doctor, licked his dry lips, and with them shaped one word:

"When?"

Doc nodded his head. "In the morning. He needs rest right now, and it'll be a rough ride. I can haul him in my truck, but you'll need to come along to hold him steady."

Tom squared his shoulders. "I'll take some time off work."

Bud stirred. "Let me go tomorrow, Tom. No, let me." He put out a hand to stave off Tom's automatic rejection of the idea. "It's official business, anyway, seeing how he was shot. You stay here, go to work, lay in some supplies. You'll need the time off more when Davy comes home."

"Bud's right," the doctor put in. "Davy's going to need round-the-clock care when we get him back."

While Davy drifted in an uneasy, red-hued dream, the three men made plans.

****

In the gray light of the next dawn, they loaded Davy, wrapped in blankets and bolstered with pillows, into the enclosed bed of Medina's truck. Bud climbed in with him.

Outside the truck, Tom stood with a sleepy Hud cradled in his arms. He looked old all of a sudden, with fresh worry lines etched across his face and the suddenly heavy weight of fatherhood bowing down his shoulders. His mouth worked as if he had a hundred things to say.

"We'll take good care of him, Tom," Bud promised.

Tom nodded. "Keep him steady," was all he said.

As the truck pulled out, headed south down Cody's rutted main street, Bud watched Tom. The other man never moved, just stood there in front of the cabin with both arms wrapped around the baby. The rising sun slanted its first beam of light onto Tom's face, highlighting its anguish. His still figure dwindled as the truck picked up speed.

When Tom was finally out of sight, Bud sighed. He looked down at the still-unconscious Davy, and to no one in particular, he said, "I wish I could love a child like that."

****

During the first leg of the two-hour drive to Jackson Hole, Bud did his best to keep Davy comfortable. The boy moaned and tossed but never quite regained consciousness. Once or twice Bud checked the fresh bandages around Davy's chest. They were slowly turning red, and Bud knew without looking that the sheet beneath him would be red, too.

How much blood could a man lose? Halfway to Jackson Hole, Medina stopped, and the two men traded places.

"Do you know how to get to the hospital?" Doc asked.

Bud nodded. "My brother works at the university. Rick Hopper."

Doc started, then smiled. "Of course. You look like him. Mr. Hopper was one of my favorite teachers in college. Brilliant man." He gave Bud an odd look, then climbed into the back of the truck.

As Bud took over the wheel, he smiled ruefully. He knew what the look meant. How did a brilliant man like Ricky Hopper ever get a rum-dum, childless brother like Bud, who lived alone in a shack on the edge of town and never even finished high school?

Yeah, well. Sometimes Bud wondered that himself.

When they got to the hospital, Medina mobilized a small army of nurses and orderlies to put Davy in bed, make him comfortable, and start a blood transfusion.

"I've ordered x-rays," Doc told Bud briskly. "Right now, I've got to find Dr. Brassard and ask his opinion of this chest wound." He hesitated. "We're going to be a couple of hours."

Bud raised both hands in a gesture of dismissal. "I'll leave you to it. What say I meet you here after lunch?"

Doc nodded absently, already turning back to his patient.

A little at a loss, Bud wandered out of the hospital and onto the university grounds.

The women of Rightside had four universities, one in each of their major cities, but in Wrongside there was only the one. Rightside boasted more than a dozen hospitals. Wrongside had five, and the other four were just glorified first aid stations. If you were seriously ill in Wrongside, you either came to Jackson Hole, or you died.

Bud didn't know anything about the assets of Rightside, so he was always properly impressed by the single asset of Wrongside. The university and hospital occupied a cluster of stone buildings up against the Border Fence at the northern edge of the town. The hospital was housed in the largest building. It boasted thirteen physicians and surgeons, some physicians-in-training, a corps of nurses, and some orderlies for grunt work. The hospital was kept supplied with drugs and equipment by charitable donations from Rightside, and its physicians owed much of their knowledge to textbooks sent over by the women.

The university itself provided training for physicians, nurses, and a few veterinarians. There was a good art school and even a small engineering school. Wrongside's aspiring teachers made up the rest of the student body. Perhaps five percent of Wrongside's men were college graduates. Thirty percent were high school graduates.

Bud walked across campus to the history department, intending to invite Ricky to lunch, but his classroom and office were empty.

"Mr. Hopper?" a secretary repeated in answer to Bud's question. "He's gone for the day. Took the boys on their annual field trip to the Fence."

"The Border Fence?"

The man gave a slight shrug of his shoulders over the oddities of teachers. "He does it every year. They go out and visit some of the older parts of the Fence, tour a Transfer Cabin, the works. Mr. Hopper thinks it makes history come alive."

Bud smiled. That sounded like Ricky.

"Any message?"

"Just tell him his brother was here, bringing a kid to the hospital. Say I'm sorry I missed him."

"Will do."

Bud wandered out onto the campus again, enjoying the thin spring sunshine. He looked up at the Border Fence, thinking about Ricky and history. The Fence was forty-five feet high here, clearing the tops of the two-story buildings. At some places in the country it was a lot lower, but it was always too high to see over. The women liked it that way.

The sight of the Fence made him think of his daughter again. She might be right on the other side, just a few feet away, for all he knew. The idea of her was always in his mind now, floating beneath the surface and ready to pop up at any moment. He let her pop up now, with her big brown eyes and her tiny, delicate, oh-so-feminine face. Bud's eyes remained focused on the familiar brick Fence, but across the surface of his mind, his daughter danced. Slowly, he nodded his head. He turned his back to the Fence and walked away.

****

Bud was ready when an unsuspecting Clyde answered his knock. He put up a hand to slam the partially open door back into Clyde's astonished face.

"Want to talk to you, Clyde," he barked in what he thought of as his lawman voice. He shouldered his way inside.

"Wh-what about?" Clyde gave ground immediately. He shrank back against the wall, wondering what he had done to deserve this.

"About art," Bud said, enunciating each word carefully.

Clyde stood up straight and tried to gather some dignity. "In that case, you'd better come back to the studio." He led the way, his back stiff with outrage and dislike.

Bud followed Clyde through the house to his south-facing studio. The large, light-filled room was littered with art supplies and smelled nauseatingly of paint and turpentine. Clyde's current project, Bud could see, was a nature scene. Flowers and tall, windswept grasses filled a large canvas. There was just a suggestion of craggy hills in the background. On one side of the canvas, the field of flowers seemed to stretch into infinity. On the other side, all greenery stopped with barren abruptness at the dun-colored Border Fence. Bud liked it immediately.

"What are you going to call it?" he asked.

"Limits."

Bud nodded approvingly. "Pretty profound for a twerp like you."

Clyde did not try to hide his scorn. "I'm impressed, Bud. You actually know what that word means."

"What word? Twerp? Yeah, it means little, rat-faced son-of-a—"

Clyde slammed a thin wooden palette against a table, breaking it in two. "Did you come here for a reason?"

But Bud refused to be hurried. He prowled around the studio as though that were his sole purpose in coming. "Is this what you call a canvas-stretcher?" he asked idly, digging through a box of equipment.

"Yes, it's a canvas stretcher." Clyde said through clenched teeth, ripping it out of Bud's hands. "And I'll thank you not to touch. This is delicate equipment."

Bud picked up a battle-scarred, paint-smeared block of wood. "Yeah, this looks real delicate."

"Stop it!" Clyde sounded a little desperate, and the idea made Bud smile.

"Stop what?" he asked innocently.

"Beating around the bush!" Clyde drew himself up

to his full height, which put his determined chin at just about chest level with Bud. He injected as much sternness as he could into his thin, high voice.

"Look, I don't know what you're doing here when Ricky isn't even home. If you think you can waltz in and harass me and stick your big, grimy fingers into my business, well, you've got another think coming." Clyde was shaking with indignation now, breathing hard, with a dangerous glint in his eye.

Bud laughed. "Calm down, you little twerp. I just want to ask a couple questions, that's all."

"About what?" Clyde was immediately suspicious.

"About art, like I said. I want to meet this dealer of yours, Simeon Hasad. I might want to buy some stuff from him."

Clyde snorted in contempt. "He'd laugh you out of the gallery. You don't know the first thing about art."

Bud gave Clyde a big, toothy grin. "But I know what I like." He reached up and plucked Clyde's *Mother and Child* figurine from its place of honor on a shelf. "And I like this one."

Clyde snatched the figurine from the desecration of Bud's hands and cradled it protectively. "How dare you!" he cried.

"I dare most anything, Clyde," Bud said softly. "Right now I want Simeon's address, and I dare you to keep it from me." He advanced on the smaller man. Clyde shrank back. The two men only tolerated each other for Ricky's sake, and now Ricky wasn't here. Clyde gave more ground, still clutching his figurine.

Bud, in his lawman's way, had already reconnoitered the room. Now he maneuvered Clyde straight to his desk.

"Write it down," he said shortly. "Then write a nice little note that introduces me as your good friend Bud, who appreciates fine art. Tell Simeon how you hope he'll take good care of me."

The resentful Clyde did as he was told. "Someday," he said furiously, moving his pen in rigid jerks over the paper, "you'll pay for this."

"Sure I will. And thanks," Bud said cheerfully. "I'll shove off now. Sorry, I can't stay for lunch. Oh, and if you ever tell Simeon what you really think of me…" he paused for effect, "…I'll break your fingers."

Bud let himself out.

****

Simeon Hasad lived and worked in a graceful, by Wrongside standards, building in the heart of Jackson Hole. Bud had to ask directions twice before he found it. It rose from the dusty street in slim white elegance with its tall windows and fluted columns. Bud, used to the unpainted clapboards and squat brick rectangles common in most of Wrongside, gaped at it. Whoever this Simeon was, he must be a hell of an artist himself, to live and work in a place like this.

He found Simeon in the main gallery, supervising the setup of some new sculptures. The art dealer was younger than Bud had imagined, maybe in his late twenties, early thirties. He was tall, slim, and ruggedly handsome, with wavy black hair and intense, smoldering black eyes. His chin jutted out aggressively with a blue-shadowed cleft. No wonder Clyde likes him, Bud thought wryly. Ricky had better watch out.

"May I help you, sir?"

"You Hasad?" Bud asked shortly.

"Yes, I'm the owner. Could I show you some

paintings? Maybe something with a Plains theme?"

"Plains theme? No, thanks. I've seen enough pictures of buffalo skulls. I had something a little more sophisticated in mind." Bud walked over and laid a hand on a tabletop granite sculpture, an exquisite rendering of a water lily. "Though I might get me a little statue."

"Oh, you're interested in sculpture. We have some good horse studies in the back. Let me—"

"No, not horses." Bud stopped him. "I was looking for something a little nicer than that. Here," he said, pulling Clyde's letter from his pocket. "Maybe this'll help."

Simeon studied the letter, then looked up to reappraise his customer.

"Money's no object," Bud said carefully. He looked directly into Simeon's eyes. "I want something really special. Something like the piece you just sold to Clyde."

Simeon looked right, then left, then back at Bud. The workers were occupied setting up a base for a life-size nude.

"Come with me," he said quietly.

He led Bud to an office in the back. He took out a keyring and opened a locked cupboard behind the desk.

"I don't usually show these pieces to strangers. It's rather an exclusive collection. But I'll make an exception for a friend of Clyde's."

Bud smiled widely. "That's real nice of you, Si."

The art dealer handed him a tiny sculpture, smaller than his hand. It was of a feminine hand, palm up, fingers slightly curled in a curiously defenseless position. Looking at it, Bud felt an overwhelming need to enfold the hand, to cover it with his two beefy ones and protect it.

"It's beautiful, isn't it?" Simeon's tone was hushed and reverent.

"I'll take it," Bud said shortly. He didn't trust his voice to say more. He set the sculpture down carefully, and stuffed his hands into his pockets while Simeon made out the bill. What now? He wanted to ask about Toller. He wanted to grab Simeon by the throat and make him produce her.

But did he dare make threats? The dealer was no Clyde, limp and pliable and easily frightened. How far would Bud get if he tried to use force?

On the other hand, how far would he get by being friendly? He tried out a few sentences in the privacy of his mind. *"Clyde said you're buying these from a woman named Toller. Could I meet her?"*

Fat chance. Simeon would smell the law all over that one. Even if it wasn't actually a crime to buy Rightside art, Simeon was no fool. He would know it soon would be a crime if too many people found out.

In the end, paralyzed by doubt, Bud did nothing. He paid the bill with every gold coin in his moneybag, then mumbled something about wanting to make another purchase soon. He tried to console himself with plans for the future. He'd buy more art, get Simeon's confidence, then try to meet Toller. He couldn't rush things. The Border Fence wasn't built in a day, after all. He wouldn't crack it in a day, either.

Chapter 11

By the time Bud returned to the hospital, Davy was awake, more or less. Doc had him pumped full of painkillers and antibiotics, but his eyes were open, and he was just able to talk.

"Tell me what happened, Davy," Bud began encouragingly. "Just take your time. We got all day."

Davy's voice came out in a raspy croak that sounded like all the dust of the Plains was caught up in it. "Don't much know what happened," he croaked. "These guys…" He shifted in the bed, grimaced, and stared at the wall.

"What about them, Davy?" Bud prompted. "Where did you see them?"

Davy's eyes wandered from the wall to Bud's face, where he focused them with an effort. "On the road," he whispered. "Couple dozen miles out. Near the Sleeping Woman, where them boulders line up along a rise." He frowned. "Know where?"

"I'll find it," Bud said briefly. "Why did they shoot you? Was it an accident?"

Davy tried to laugh, but it turned into a weak coughing spasm that brought Doc Medina on the run.

"What are you doing?" Doc cried angrily. "He's not in any condition to talk to you!"

Davy flapped his left hand weakly at the physician. "Want to tell Bud," he insisted in a dry rasp. "Let me tell Bud."

"Just talk slow, Davy," Bud said. "Slow and easy."

"No accident." Davy fixed his eyes on the lawman. "Was no accident. They was smuggling something, don't know what. Something they didn't want me to see."

"Who was smuggling, Davy? Who?"

"Frank Gibson. Chad Gibson. Two other guys. From Bozeman. Their cousin Eddie and—" He coughed again, and Bud waited.

"Which one shot you?"

Davy frowned. "Fourth guy. Blue-eyed. Had two guns strapped on. Mean."

Bud couldn't breathe. He'd been wanting to nail Frank Gibson and his gang for years. It didn't look like Davy could testify to any actual smuggling, but he could haul the bunch of them in for attempted murder, at least. Doc had heard the testimony plain as any witness.

He patted the boy's hand. "You rest, Davy. We'll send your Pop down in a couple days to bring you home. Time you get there, the Gibsons and their buddies'll be in jail."

Davy smiled vaguely, and Bud took his leave. He waited for Doc in the truck.

****

"That was some story," Medina said weakly when he joined Bud.

"What do you mean?"

Doc shook his head as he pressed the starter and released the brake. "It's just mindless violence. They could have killed him!"

"They tried to kill him," Bud corrected. "Their bad

luck that they didn't." He gave Doc a wry look. "You just ain't been in Cody long enough. We ain't quite so civilized up near the Plains as you are here in Jackson Hole. Down here, it takes you years to work up enough nerve just to kick the commander out of office. Up home, people get shot regularly for being in the wrong place at the wrong time. Like Davy."

Doc slowed the truck as they left town, seemingly reluctant to leave the safety of Wrongside's capital city. He sighed. "I guess I should have thought twice about moving up there."

Bud guffawed. "You'll get used to it, Doc. We ain't all bad. There's some good people in Cody."

"Good people? Outside of you and Tom and Bally, I haven't met any. And besides, it isn't just that. Cody's so far out of the mainstream that I feel like life is passing me by. At least in Jackson Hole there's the university and the art galleries."

Bud nodded. "My brother calls it culture. And you're right, we ain't got much in Cody. But there's some." He nodded, looking out of the truck window at the sluggish Missouri River that paralleled the road. "Yeah, some."

"Where?" Doc scoffed.

"Believe it or not, Old Willie, the transfer man, has the best library in a hundred miles. And they ain't all shoot 'em, smash 'ems, either. He's got some real strange books, antiques, even, from old Earth. Ask him sometime, he'll show you. And lots of us care about art." He looked sideways at Doc. "I've got a couple paintings by Clyde Wether."

"Clyde Wether! He's the best artist working today! You must have paid a fortune!"

"Nah. My brother gave them to me. Clyde and Ricky live together."

"They do?" Doc was having trouble driving in his excitement. "Then you know him personally?"

"Mmmmm."

"What's he like? Is he as awesome as you'd think? I'd love to—"

"Awesome?" Bud snorted at the thought. "He's a sneaky little twerp. But I do like his work. We get back to the house, I'll show you what I got."

They stopped for lunch at a café, then changed drivers. Bud, trying to stay awake, returned to a comment Doc had made that morning.

"So why did you move to Cody?"

Doc sighed. "It's a long story and not one I think I ought to tell the sheriff."

Bud laughed. "Well, now you got me interested. You kill somebody?"

"Would you care?"

Bud shrugged. "Not if he needed killing."

There was silence.

"Smuggling, then?"

Doc snorted. "Not unless you count me."

A little chime sounded in Bud's head. The guy had tried to smuggle himself? "Must have failed, eh?"

Doc snorted again.

"Now I'm really interested," Bud allowed. "And I got to hear the story. How about this? Anything you say to me in this truck stays right here. I think a lot of Tom Redwolf, and you just saved his boy's life."

Doc hesitated, then shrugged. "The story's been festering in me for a while now. Maybe I'd better just get it out. No consequences, right?"

"My word."

"It started in university. You might not realize it, but Rightside physicians will collaborate with us sometimes. Scientists and scholars, too, I think."

"Ricky's dropped a hint or two. And he seems to know more about Rightside history than he should."

Doc nodded.

"I was working on a research project about inherited diseases. I wanted to know if males could inherit disease from their mothers."

"Inherit?" Bud didn't know the word.

"For instance, if your father or your—um—mother has red hair, you're more likely to have red hair."

"Huh. Imagine that."

"One of my professors thought it was a critical research avenue, and I should pursue it. He suggested I send a query to Rightside. There are channels for that. We use the medical department's computers. The women won't necessarily answer, but if they think it's important enough, they will."

"Someone answered, I'm guessing."

Doc heaved a heavy sigh. "Someone did. It was another medical student, as it happens, and she was intrigued, so she got permission to research it and answer me. Her name was Milina."

"Wasn't that the woman who betrayed the men back in the beginning?"

"It was an appropriate name for this student."

"What'd she do to you?"

"It was nice at first," Doc admitted. "We corresponded through the computer for a couple of months, and things got sort of friendly."

"With a woman?"

"Believe it or not," Doc sighed. "I guess it was careless of both of us, but we were too young and stupid to realize it. We even had a private joke. Once when we'd made a breakthrough, she typed, *Bingo!* I asked her what it meant, and she said it was a game people used to play on old Earth, and it meant you'd won or scored a point, or something. From then on, whenever we made progress, one of us would type *Bingo!"*

As the men neared Cody, Doc talked on. "After I graduated, I stayed at the university, working at the hospital. Milina and I still communicated once in a while. Then one day at a Red Cabin, the woman who picked me didn't give me her name, but when she—you know."

Bud nodded.

"She said 'Bingo!' I said, 'Milina?' and she said, 'Trev?' That's my first name, Trev. Anyway, we had a laugh over it, said it was fate, but she seemed kind of uneasy, seeing me in person. There was a message on the computer the next day. She was going out of town for a while, it was nice knowing me."

"Harsh," Bud said.

"Since when are women nice to us, anyway?" Doc asked bitterly. "I guess I went kind of crazy. Quit my job, did some heavy drinking. Finally, I hatched this grand plan. Milina must have been pressured to give me up, I figured. Someone found out we were too friendly. I'd find a way to get across the Fence, and we'd escape somewhere, live happily ever after."

"A man and a woman? Together?"

"I told you, I was kind of crazy. And I'd read some of those old Earth romance books. Anyway, I spent the next year trying to get across. I was too big for a Transfer Drawer. I couldn't bribe anyone to let me hide in something big, go through a Transfer Door. I drove all the way up to the Plains, thinking I'd find a way across there, but I couldn't. I went to the ocean next."

"All the way to the ocean? Mother, hardly anybody goes that far. Nobody I know, for sure."

"There's a good reason for that, Bud. Nothing out there. Someone must go, because you can buy saltwater fish in Jackson Hole, if you have enough money. But no one lives there. It's desolate. And the North Fence? It goes right out into the mother-loving ocean for miles."

"Well, hell, why?"

"Because of men like me, I guess. I drifted back home but couldn't stay. I didn't seem to belong there anymore, so I came to Cody."

Doc was silent after that, and fell into an uneasy doze. Bud had a lot to think about as he drove. Here was another man unhappy with the way things were with Rightside. It seemed like they could get together, maybe do something to change things.

By the time the two men got home, Bud had made up his mind to cultivate Doc's friendship. He showed Doc the Wether paintings and the new sculpture.

****

"Are you sure you gave him an appointment card?" Diana was getting distinctly irritated, and Jessie knew it was because Diana thought she was too attached to Davy. Diana probably thought it would be best if Davy missed this appointment. That meant Jessie couldn't see him again.

"Just as well," Diana continued.

"What?" Nervously, Jessie paced back and forth in

96

front of her sister's desk in the corner of the viewing room. "What's just as well?"

"That the kid misses his appointment." She gave Jess a motherly pat on the hand. "You're getting too attached to him. You know that's not allowed."

Jessie sighed. "Yeah, I know, but I really like him. And he hasn't missed it yet." She looked up at the wall clock. "He's got another ten minutes before it's official. He'll make it."

"I hope not," Diana said under her breath. But Jessie didn't hear her. She was staring at the door.

"Di, look! Isn't that the president?"

Diana scrambled to her feet and hastily straightened her jacket. She was around the desk with her hand outstretched before Alanna was all the way through the door.

"Madam President! How nice to see you again! It's been quite a while. How can we help you? Are you looking for some excitement tonight? Some entertainment?"

Alanna laughed. "Neither one. How about some good old-fashioned relaxation? I could sure use a break."

"Of course!" Diana bustled back to her desk and picked up a sheaf of papers. "We have a good selection tonight—look, Bally's here. I know he's not much to look at, but if you want relaxation…" She lowered her voice and finished with a laugh.

Watching them, Jessie was amused enough to forget her anxiety for a moment. Diana was so impressed by important people. If Alanna Olaffson said, "Jump," all Diana would say was, "How high?"

Personally, she thought the president looked awful.

Sure, she'd had a rough few months since the election, but that was no excuse, in Jessie's mind, for letting yourself go.

Jessie, who always looked exquisite, had a healthy young girl's contempt for the older, slower, more tired woman. Looking at Alanna now, she missed the determination in the squared shoulders and the steely intelligence of the penetrating eyes. She only saw Alanna's tired face and the way tiny lines of aggravation gathered around the corners of her pale lips.

"Let me just look a while," Alanna was saying. "It has been a long time, but I still remember a few faces. Maybe I'll see someone I want."

"Of course, of course," Diana said hastily. "Take all the time you need, ma'am. We'll be here."

****

Alanna walked slowly down the length of the glass in the viewing room. She was in the mood for something, but didn't quite know what. It had been a long time since she'd seen a man—more than a year, in fact—and it had occurred to her recently that she missed sex.

"Is that normal, Kai?" she had asked the vice president at the end of one particularly difficult meeting. "I mean, I've always felt Laran was enough for me. I don't really want more children, and I definitely don't want to go through another pregnancy at my age, so why should I still want sex?"

"Because you're a woman." Kai, with her inestimable practicality, had gone straight to the point. "I've got fifteen years on you, Alanna, and I'm a grandmother seven times over, but I still want sex. It's just biology. It's natural."

Alanna had frowned and stirred uneasily at that. "Well, it shouldn't be. I hate the thought of being dependent on men for our very happiness. It doesn't seem right."

Right or not, here she was back in the Red Cabins. Her biological itch wanted scratching, to put it crudely, and only a man could do it for her.

She considered a tall, good-looking man with long blond hair. He'd gone to some effort for his Red Cabin night, wearing a sleek, barely-buttoned shirt and low-slung jeans that looked like they'd been painted onto his lean frame. His hair was neatly combed and tied back in a neat club. He carried a bottle of wine. After some thought, she remembered his name. Frank had fathered one of her male babies.

What would happen, she wondered suddenly, if I chose him, took him to a meeting room, and asked him about my son? Would he even know what I meant? Did they give him my baby to raise, or do they give them to just anybody? He'd be almost grown now. Is he a good boy? Does he look like me? What's his name?

Alanna put a hand against the glass to steady herself and pulled in a deep breath. Her heart was thumping painfully in her chest, and she thought she might faint. The room grayed out for a second. She moaned. What was she thinking!? What was she doing? This was crazy!

"Ma'am?"

Alanna felt a soft hand against her back. "Ma'am? Are you all right?" Alanna took another breath and looked up. Blue-violet eyes, sharp with concern, swam into focus. Jessie steadied the older woman with both hands. "I'm a nurse," she said. "Let me help you."

Alanna let the girl lead her to a chair. The supervisor was there instantly, fussing like a mother hen.

"President Olaffson!" Diana cried in dismay. "Are you all right? Let me call someone to take you home. Do you need a doctor? Jess, do we need a doctor?"

****

Jessie ignored her sister. She took the woman's pulse, which was rapid but slowing. She felt her clammy forehead. "I don't think we need a doctor," she said finally. She looked at the president. "You were close to fainting, but I think you'll be all right in a few minutes. Are you pregnant?"

Alanna gave a weak laugh. "No, not that. Maybe I'm more tired than I thought. I tried to go to bed early tonight, but I just couldn't sleep. I thought if I came down here…"

Jessie nodded briskly. "You're probably right. You're just too stressed out. What you really need is a good—"

"Jessie!" Diana gasped. "You can't talk to the president like that!"

Her scandalized tone set all three of them laughing and broke the tension of the moment. Diana, relieved that her VIP was not going to be sick after all, laughed the loudest.

"Although," she giggled, "if we can't talk like that here in a Red Cabin, where can we? Madam President, let me introduce my sister, Jessie Sandova."

"It's nice to meet you, Jessie." Alanna extended her hand and smiled. "And thank you for your help." She tossed her head toward the glass, behind which

Frank Gibson still lounged, unaware of their scrutiny. "It wouldn't do for the president to keel over at the sight of a man, no matter how handsome."

Diana wrinkled her nose. "You don't want that one anyway, ma'am. I've had him, and he's a little too handsome for his own good."

"I know." Alanna stood up, gathered her dignity, and dismissed Chad Gibson's father with a casual wave of her hand. "I think I need someone a little more restful tonight."

"How about this one?" For the second time recently, Jessie steered someone toward Bud Hopper. "He's one of my favorites. See those eyes? Gentle, too. He's just what you need tonight."

"Bud," Alanna said softly. The corners of her mouth curled up in a reminiscent smile. She turned to Jessie. "I saw him for a while several years ago. I'd almost forgotten him." She called to Diana, who was halfway back to her desk. "I think I'll take Bud, Diana."

****

Bud smoothed down his hair as he stood in the buffer, already locked out of the men's side but not yet admitted to the women's side. He hoped it was somebody good. He didn't need a whiny first-timer or an ugly old witch tonight. He'd come to the Main Street Red Cabin half-hoping to find Frank—and he had—but he'd stopped short of an arrest. Tonight, with Frank half-liquored up and feeling his oats, was not good. Tomorrow morning, with Frank asleep in bed and fuzzy with a hangover, was better.

Tomorrow he would finally arrest Frank. He hoped the bastard was enjoying his last night of freedom. Bud was too keyed up to sleep. Since he was here, he needed a good woman and he needed one bad.

The door to Room 5 made its irritating buzz, and Bud pushed it open. "Alanna!" he said with a wide grin. "Ain't you a sight for sore eyes!"

"Hello, Bud." Alanna returned his smile and moved easily into his welcoming embrace. She had forgotten how satisfying it felt to hold him.

He wrapped his long arms around her and breathed in the good woman's smell of her. Of all the women he had seen—and Bud was a popular choice for many in New Washington—Alanna had always been his favorite. He couldn't tell her that, of course. The rules of behavior between Rightside women and Wrongside men were subtle but complex and deeply ingrained. Bud knew them all, though most times, he didn't understand them.

What difference would it make, he wondered as he caressed Alanna's silk-clad breasts, if he told her she was his favorite? Whose business was it if he and Alanna became friends, like Toller and Simeon? And who should care if he asked Alanna whether she had any brown-eyed daughters?

He sighed. He was tired of thinking. He tipped Alanna's chin up and smiled down at her. "So what's new?" he asked lightly. "You still wearing them lacy bras that hook in the front?"

Alanna raised one eyebrow. "Think you're man enough to find out for yourself?"

Bud's happy laughter boomed out, and he swept Alanna up off her feet. "Let's dump you down on this bed, lady, and we'll see if I'm man enough."

****

Alanna remembered how much he loved

undressing her. She shivered in anticipation as he straddled her on the big bed. He took off his own shirt first. She let her eyes roam over the broad muscles of his shoulders, and the thick downy hair, going gray now, that covered his chest. Alanna lived among women twenty-seven hours a day. She was too used to soft bodies and thin voices. Now, she reveled in Bud's masculinity.

She watched his hard, horny fingers fumble with the tiny buttons of her blouse. She closed her eyes, the better to feel the roughness of his hands on her skin. Soon they were caught in the ancient rhythms of love. Impulses that were older than time guided Alanna's hips as they rocked, slowly at first. Slowly.

A little faster now, and she felt the tide surge. Rightside's small moons were dark now, but she felt the pull nonetheless. She groaned and rode with it all the way to shore. She clutched at Bud's back, raking narrow furrows with her fingernails as the waves crashed upon the rocks.

Bud groaned and panted with a harsh male sound that sent an additional quiver through Alanna's already vibrating nerve endings.

"There!" he gasped. "Think I'm man enough now?" He laughed weakly and rolled away from her. "Not as young as we used to be, I guess."

"Speak for yourself, Buddy," Alanna murmured. She felt good—really, really good. For the first time in months, she felt knitted together, all in one piece. Her bones moved easily in their sockets, and her tired muscles rode lightly beneath her skin. Everything was right for a change. Only a man could put you back together like that.

Bud stared up at the ceiling, at the blind eye of the camera. "Funny, you should call me that."

"Call you what?"

"Buddy. Nobody but Ricky has called me that since I was a kid."

At first, Alanna was silent. You weren't supposed to trade personal information. It was one of the basic rules of the Red Cabins. But she was feeling good, and eventually, curiosity won out. What could it hurt, after all?

"Who's Ricky?"

"My brother. He's a historian. Teaches at the university, down in Jackson Hole."

"You're kidding." Alanna propped herself up on one elbow. "Wrongside U has history professors? I never knew that. What do they teach, military tactics?"

"They teach other teachers, mostly. Artists. And some doctors. Few engineers. We have roads in Wrongside, you know. Some of them are even paved in concrete."

"Wow." Alanna was fascinated, in spite of herself. As president, Alanna had been briefed on Wrongside's system of government, and there were monthly teleconferences with Sherman, but Alanna still knew little about the men's personal lives. Artists. He'd actually said artists. And engineers. She looked down at Bud, enjoying their languor and the idle conversation.

"You must be proud of your—brother," she said, stumbling over the unfamiliar word. She knew what it meant, of course, from books. "Do you have any more?"

"Brothers? Nah. Me and Ricky are pretty alone in the world since Pop died. Neither one of us has any

Rightside/Wrongside

boys."

The atmosphere in the room changed subtly, from comfortable to uneasy. They were treading toward dangerous ground, and both of them knew it.

I should stop, Alanna said to herself. The taboos of seventy-one years jangled in her head like warning sirens. She looked right into Bud's eyes and saw the same taboos written there.

"Who's Pop?" she asked him.

Bud's breath caught. "Our—" he stopped to clear his throat.

"Our dad," he said. "Pop was our father."

Alanna's face flattened with shock. The word sounded so obscene, uttered here in the quiet by a man. Bud pressed on.

"How about you? You got any kids?"

Alanna froze. She was no longer amused by the conversation, no longer titillated by their brief foray onto forbidden ground. She sat up and swung off the bed, reaching for her clothes.

"It's late," she said shortly. "I'll be going now." Behind her back, Alanna heard Bud pound at the mattress. She knew he already regretted their illicit conversation more than she did.

"Hey, no offense," he said softly. "I'm sorry, Alanna. I've had a lot on my mind lately, and I just got talking out of line, that's all."

With one hand on the doorknob, Alanna looked back at him. If it had been any other man, Alanna would have shrugged off the question with a laugh and never given it another thought. But this man was different. This man had fathered Laran. His question struck right into her heart like a barbed lance.

It would be dangerous to see him again. She knew that. He had easily disarmed her defenses and slipped around the edges of the strict rules that governed female-male contact. Maybe it was just a slip on his part. She studied him. His hair was tousled from their lovemaking, his face soft and worried. The mat of hair on his chest looked crushed and damp. Satin sheets were puddled around his hips, and one hairy leg dangled to the floor. Involuntarily, she smiled. He might be dangerous, but she did enjoy being with him.

"Maybe I'll see you here again sometime," she said and slipped through the door.

In the hallway, Alanna paused to collect herself. She shook her head. She had always had trouble separating the idea of men from the idea of having children. What, she thought suddenly, would Laran think of Bud? She shook her head. It was ludicrous. They would never meet. Rightside women kept careful track of which men were related to which women. No matter how many times Laran came to the Red Cabins, she would never be allowed to choose Bud or his brother.

Alanna pushed the thoughts out of her mind once and for all. If they didn't stay out, she would find a good therapist.

But the image of his luminous brown eyes, so much like Laran's, followed her up the hallway. They watched as she stopped at the supervisor's desk.

"Thanks, Diana," she said with an easy smile. "That was just what I needed."

"We aim to please," Diana said happily. "Bud's a cutie-pie. Are you going to see him again?"

Alanna barely hesitated. "I didn't make an

appointment, but yes, I think I might. Why don't you call me next time he comes in? If I'm free, I'll come down."

"Of course," Diana said. "Let me just make a note."

Chapter 12

Spring gained ground in Rightside and Wrongside. Up on the Plains, the prairie grass slowly greened. Buffalo herds moved to their summer pastures, and tadpoles outgrew their ponds along the shallow Missouri River. In the pleasant woodlands of Rightside mothers and daughters took long hikes with picnic lunches, and in the dusty streets of Wrongside fathers and sons played ball.

In Rightside, Jessie Sandova reveled in the new and strange feelings of pregnancy and privately wondered how she could get a message to Davy. Not that she would tell him about the baby, or anything. She just wanted to talk to him. That's all.

Over in Wrongside, Davy lay flat on his back in bed and concentrated on remembering Jessie's face. It was the only thing that kept the pain at bay. He knew that missing the appointment with Jessie was serious, but the women would understand once he explained. It wasn't his fault. They wouldn't stop him from seeing her again.

In Rightside, Alanna juggled the heavy demands of the presidency with skill and intelligence, and mountains of fortitude. At odd moments, she thought of Bud and smiled.

Bud, in Wrongside, was tightening his case against the Gibsons. It had been easy to sweep the two of them into custody the morning after he'd seen Alanna and easier still for the Bozeman lawman to pick up their half-wit cousin, Eddie. But he hadn't been able to track down the fourth man, the one who shot Davy. Maybe he'd take a ride up to Bozeman, try to get something out of Eddie.

****

Diana hummed softly to herself as she tapped the keyboard. It was a slow night and she was catching up on some paperwork.

"Hey, girl, what's happening?" Sydney Postern, her second-in-command, breezed into the viewing room. Syd had been on sick leave with a croupy baby and was anxious to get back in the groove.

"Not much, Syd. Dull night, huh?"

"No kidding. Susan said you've had the president in here a few times."

"Herself," Diana said smugly.

Sydney tapped a pencil against her teeth and looked around the large viewing room. Only four women were at the window making selections.

"I haven't seen your sister in here lately," Syd commented. "How is Jessie?"

"Pregnant," Diana said. She was looking forward to being an aunt. "But she's feeling all right. She just hasn't come in because she's mad at me. I wouldn't let her make a new appointment to see Davy Redwolf after he missed their last one."

Sydney made a face. "She should know better than that. You never let a man—"

"—think he can control sex," Diana finished. "I know. Jessie's all right. Her hormones are screwed up, that's all. You know how it is."

Sydney smiled. She did indeed know how it was. She glanced through the one-way mirror into the men's side, and her smile widened. "Speak of the devil," she giggled. "Isn't that him?"

Diana looked up. She had to study the figure on the other side for a minute before she knew it was Davy.

"Man," she swore. "He looks half dead."

Davy had swung into the narrow men's waiting room on a heavy wooden crutch. It was crudely made, Diana noted, not at all like the light aluminum crutches the women used. One of his legs was bandaged and splinted, and one arm lay across his chest in a sling. On his forehead, a wicked, half-healed cut ran jaggedly from temple to eyebrow. Diana could see that it had been stitched.

Davy was talking to Hank, the administrator on the men's side. The two seemed to be arguing. Davy gesticulated wildly with the bandaged arm, then winced.

"What's he doing?" Sydney whispered. Davy now had the attention of every woman in the viewing room. Diana got up and moved closer to the one-way mirror.

"Hank must be telling him he can't make his own appointment to see Jessie," she guessed. "He's just a kid. Maybe he needs to learn the facts of life first-hand."

The man and boy continued to argue. Hank, old and beaten down by a lifetime in Wrongside, had begun by shaking his head, but now he was nodding reluctantly. Finally, he shrugged his shoulders in defeat and lifted his telephone.

"Ma'am," he said softly.

Diana returned to her desk and stabbed impatiently

at her phone speaker. In spite of her righteous indignation at this seeming presumption, she was curious to know what the boy had said.

"Yes, Hank, what is it?"

"Ma'am, I've got a boy over here—"

"Yes, yes, I can see him. What does he think he wants?"

Davy was staring, not at Hank and his intercom, but at the one-way mirror. It was almost as if he could burn a hole through it with his eyes. The six women in the viewing room, mesmerized by the boy's haggard face, watched intently. They saw Hank shrug his shoulders.

"Well, he wants me to give you a message for a Jessie Sandova. He says to tell her he's sorry he missed his appointment, but he got shot last week, up on the Plains." Hank hesitated, then went on.

"I know this ain't the regular way we do things, ma'am, but it warn't his fault, and—"

"That's enough." Diana cut off his explanation sharply. "Hank, tell me, what rule covers this situation?"

The six women heard his gusty sigh over the speaker. "Women communicate with men at their convenience. Men do not communicate with women," he recited flatly.

"Thank you." She disconnected the phone with a vicious slap, watching with satisfaction as, over on the men's side, Hank flinched at the sound.

"Good handle, Di," Sydney said admiringly. "He'll think twice before he ever tries that again."

The two watched with satisfaction as Davy turned, defeated, to the door. Hank, cowed by the reprimand, was sitting obediently at his desk. Diana had returned to her computer screen, and Sydney was halfway to the door when all hell broke loose.

"No!" With a cry of rage that even the women could hear behind their protective glass, Davy Redwolf went crazy.

"You can't keep me away from her!" he howled, whipping back to the mirror. He screamed all the rage and frustration that had bubbled in his broken body for days.

"I *need* her!" he screamed. "You don't understand. *I need Jessie!*" He lurched to the mirror and slammed his left shoulder against it. "Jessie! I know you're there, Jessie. I know, I know." He was sobbing now, lunging against the mirror.

On the other side, inches from Davy's tears of rage, the six women watched in horrified fascination. Diana sat frozen at her desk. She threw one wild glance at Sydney but got no reaction. She couldn't breathe.

Davy backed away from the glass. Chest heaving, he swayed on his one good leg. He tried to stare through the darkness of the mirror to the women he knew were on the other side. He had to get to them. He had to get to Jessie.

Without further thought he lifted the heavy wooden crutch and slammed it into his reflection. Pain flared across his chest.

"*Jessie!*" he screamed again. And again. *Slam!* The long glass shivered as he struck at it.

"Go get her, kid." Laughter erupted behind him. Davy spun around, nearly overbalancing on his one good leg. On the bench, half a dozen bored men had been waiting to be chosen. This was rare entertainment, and they wished Davy all the luck.

"Well, don't stop now, Davy." Mike Dannon's leering face swam into Davy's view. "Go get her!"

Davy looked wildly for Hank, expecting the older man to stop him, but Hank was enjoying the show as much as the others. Still smarting from his reprimand, Hank hoped Davy would just bust on through and lay one upside that bitch Diana's head.

"You're already in trouble, boy," he said happily. "Keep going."

Davy turned back to the mirror. Gritting his teeth against the pain he knew would come, he pulled back the crutch and struck again. The glass sagged and cracked. One more blow, and he'd have it out.

On the other side, Diana's paralysis broke. She lunged across the desk to slap a red button on the wall. With the other hand, she stabbed out at the manual override on her desk-to-desk intercom. An alarm klaxon whooped into life as she screamed, "*Lockdown!*" Her magnified voice blared through every room on the women's side of the building.

"Emergency lockdown in thirty seconds!" she shouted. "Thirty seconds to lockdown! *Lockdown!*"

In Room 3, a woman and a man embraced, seconds from orgasm. At the first hoot of the klaxon the woman braced her hands against the man's chest, hiked her legs farther to get a purchase with her feet, and shoved. The man went sprawling.

In Room 14, a man dropped the bottle of champagne he was about to open. The bottle broke and showered his legs with bubbly. He looked wildly around the room. The scream of the klaxon seemed to come from everywhere.

"Tawny?" he shouted. "Tawny, what—?" The woman burst out of the bathroom, catching him full on the chin with the edge of the door.

In Room 22 a woman and man sat bolt upright in bed, shaken from sleep. "Lockdown?" the man said, confused. "What's a lockdown?" But the woman was no longer beside him. He looked up in time to see the women's door slam shut.

In the viewing room, Diana and Sydney shoved their four customers unceremoniously out of the room. Sydney, last out, took a final look at the bulging mirror. Davy was still pounding on it with his crutch, but the blows were weaker now. Though it was bulged and starred with a dozen cracks, she thought most of the reinforced glass would hold. Behind Davy, she could see the rest of the men, urging him on with hoots and catcalls. One of them took off his shoe and threw it at the mirror. Sydney slammed the door.

Behind her, Diana waited at a computer station. Sydney turned and looked at her. Both women nodded. Diana pushed a button. All over the building, they heard the snicks and bangs and clashes of metal locks, dozens of them sealing every room that connected to Wrongside.

The klaxon died. Diana drew a shaky breath. "I never thought I'd have to do that," she whispered. "I hope all our women got out."

****

Later that same night, Sheriff Bud Hopper was dragged out of bed by a chastened Hank and taken through dark, deserted streets to the Main Street Red Cabin. He stared in disbelief at the shattered mirror of the waiting room. Broken glass had already been pulled

114

out at one spot, and Bud could look past it into something no man had ever seen—the viewing room of the women's side.

Looking into it, Bud felt disoriented and confused, as though a gaping hole had been torn in the very universe, and he saw the unimaginable unknown. Facing him, across the vast gulf of the broken glass, was an angry woman. He had never seen her before. Flanking her were four more women, armed and in uniform. Bud supposed they were the law.

Bud forced himself to concentrate. The woman was speaking.

"—are the local representative of authority?"

"Yes, ma'am. I am. Name's Bud Hopper."

"I know your name." She didn't offer hers. She gestured contemptuously at the broken glass. "What do you propose to do about this?"

"This?" he repeated dumbly. "Well. This. I suppose Hank here could get a handyman to fix it up. You'd have to give us the glass, though. We ain't got none of that reinforced stuff over here."

"There's a lot you don't have, Hopper," she said acidly. "Brains, for one thing. I don't expect you to repair the mirror. We'll see to that. I do expect you to take care of Davy Redwolf."

Davy? Davy did this? Bud pulled his head back in a gesture of negation. "Ah, ma'am, Davy's just a kid. You don't understand. He's had a rough time of it here lately. If he did all this, me and his daddy'll have to give him a talking to, but—"

"A 'talking to,' as you so quaintly put it, Sheriff, is not enough." Diana propped her fists on her hips and enunciated each word carefully. "You will find this boy

115

and arrest him. You will put him in jail. You will throw away the key."

Bud shifted his feet and looked away. Diana took it for weakness, but Bud was trying hard to control his temper. He didn't look back at her until he had it damped down good.

"Begging your pardon, ma'am," he said in a deceptively gentle voice. "But I don't see as Davy has actually broken any laws, here."

Startled, Diana said the first thing that came into her mind. "You don't call destruction of property a crime?"

Bud laughed once and shook his head. "Ain't our property, now is it? It's yours. And him destroying it ain't against any laws we got here in Wrongside."

Diana spoke through clenched teeth. "I'm talking about a more basic law here, Hopper. I'm talking about the rightful, lawful, necessary separation of the sexes. We have maintained this separation for seventy-one years, and we are not about to let a foolish child endanger our natural way of life.

"It goes without saying that Davy Redwolf is barred from the Red Cabins for life. It also goes without saying that you will jail him and punish him. If you do not—If you do not," she repeated stridently, overriding Bud's objections, "we will stop all transfers through the entire length of the Border Fence." She let that sink in.

"Including, of course, the transfer of all male babies."

****

Davy was in jail a half hour later.

"No other way, Davy," Bud said with real regret. He closed the metal door of the cell and let the lock

116

snick quietly into place. Beside him, Tom looked on with stricken eyes. Baby Hud slept unconcernedly against his shoulder.

"How long, Bud?" Tom asked.

Bud sighed. "Till the judge comes through, I guess. Couple weeks." He struck at the metal bars in frustration. "But I'll be damned if I know what the old fart can charge him with. Like I told that woman, he ain't actually done nothing wrong by our laws."

Bud peered curiously in at Davy, who slumped, exhausted, on the bunk. "Why'd you want to get all riled up like that, anyway, boy? She's just a woman."

Davy looked up at Bud from beneath lowered brows. "I love her," he said sullenly. "I need to see her."

"Why?"

Davy thought, opened his mouth, then shut it again. He couldn't tell the lawman and his father the real reason. *Because I almost got killed last week, that's why. Because Jessie's the best thing that ever happened to me in my life, and I can't live without her, that's why.*

Bud shook his head, finally. "You ain't never going to see her again, Davy. They barred you from the Red Cabins. For life."

Beside him, Tom let out a gusty sigh. He hadn't heard that part yet, but he should have guessed. He held Hud a little tighter.

The news brought Davy up out of the bed, and he stood swaying on one foot, grasping the metal bars with his good hand for support. "That can't be right, Bud!" he gasped. "They can't do that!"

"Oh, yes, they can," Bud corrected him. "This is Wrongside, remember? The women over in Rightside,

117

they can do what they want."

"But Jessie don't want that!"

"It might not make any difference what your Jessie wants," Bud said. "She's got to live by their rules, too. What other choice does she have?"

Davy looked away, lost in thought. "I got to see her," he mumbled. "I got to know what she wants. I got to tell her—"

"Look at me, Davy." The boy's eyes cleared, and he looked warily at Bud.

The older man's tone was angry and straight to the point. "Whatever crazy shit you're thinking, you forget it right now. No woman is worth this. All you need to think about from here on out is getting healthy again, so you can help feed your family. Your pop's been through enough with you."

Even as he said the angry words, Bud's heart went out to the boy. Davy would never touch a woman again, never smell her skin, or watch her comb her hair. And unless that Jessie was already pregnant, Davy now had no chance of ever fathering a son.

Davy looked guiltily at his father. "I'm sorry, Pop," he whispered.

Tom looked at his son. "You get yourself some rest," he said quietly. "I'll be back tomorrow."

Bud reached through the bars to touch Davy's shoulder. "Tom's right. Get some rest. I'll send Doc down in the morning, let him take a look at you. Meantime, be quiet in here. No hollering. Frank and Chad Gibson are at the end of the hall, and I don't want them to know you're here."

Davy nodded and slumped back on the bed.

Chapter 13

Bally's Cafe was buzzing by eight o'clock the next morning. The regular breakfast crowd got the bad news served up with their toast and eggs.

"Closed?" Mike Dannon's mouth dropped open. "How could it be closed? It can't be closed."

"Oh, yes, it can." Old Willie was fair bursting with the news. "The Main Street Red Cabin is shut tight and locked up. Hank says they're stirred up like a nest of hornets over in Rightside. He says the women are gonna keep it closed till that there glass mirror is fixed, and they put in all new security and shit."

"Well, hell, that don't matter," Bally put in. "What's to stop us from driving up to Bozeman, or clear down to Jackson Hole? Their Red Cabins ain't closed."

Old Willie shook his head. "The damn women, that's what. Hank says they're *punishing* us." The indignity of that made his voice shake. "Like a bunch of snot-nosed *brats*."

"Punish *us*?" Rollie Leon weighed in, pushing his two-hundred-and-eighty-pound bulk up to the bar. He was heavy on muscle and short on brains, but the men deferred to him because he could pound you into the dirt if you didn't. "What'd *we* do?"

Willie snorted. "We're men, ain't we? That's enough for them."

"So how're they gonna stop us from driving up to Bozeman?"

Willie shook his head again. When you were the transfer man, you got to know a little more about women than you learned in a damn Red Cabin. Him and Hank, between them they knew enough about how women controlled men to scare them both shitless. Patiently, he explained.

"They can't stop us from driving, Rollie. Use what little brains you got. They got our *names* and our *pictures*, all of us in Cody, on a computer list or something. All they have to do is give the list to the other Red Cabins, and we could go sit in their waiting rooms till this time next year. They'd never call us."

"But that ain't *fair*!"

Mike's aggrieved tone was beginning to get on Willie's nerves. The transfer man wasn't comfortable, being the center of attention like this. It was dangerous. But that didn't stop him from getting a guilty sort of enjoyment from it. He shifted his feet, sighed importantly, and spread both hands.

"Let me lay this out for you, nice and simple. The women're scared. They know we could force ourselves on them if we tried. Hell, Davy almost got to them, and he's only eighteen. If Rollie here had been the one pounding on that window them women would still be screaming."

There was nervous laughter at this, and Rollie gave a sideways leer and hitched at his belt. Every Wrongside man, at one time or another, had wondered what would happen if the Border Fence was ever breached. Some had had lustful dreams of rape and pillage, of ripping through seventy-one years of rules and regulations to take what they wanted when they wanted it. Davy's puny attempt had set them all wondering anew, but Willie's next observation brought them back to earth with a heavy thud.

"The one thing we got to have, here in Wrongside, is sex. Now, hold on." He held up his hands to stop the ribald laughter. "Think about it. If we couldn't have sex with the women, we wouldn't get them babies, would we? And if we couldn't get babies, why, in fifty years the tumbleweeds would be down from the Plains, rolling through town, and there wouldn't be none of us left to care."

This sobered the men. They stopped their posturing and backslapping and gave Old Willie their full attention.

"That's why they're punishing us now, to make us think about that. Supposing they decided to close the Red Cabins for good? All the way up and down the line?"

The men thought about this. Not only would they lose the babies, they'd lose women. No more soft, feminine laughter. No more flower-scented hair. No more wrapping your arms around a woman and just holding her.

"Now wait a minute, Willie." Bally slapped a meaty hand down on the bar. "If they did that, they wouldn't have any female babies, either. They need us just as much as we need them."

Willie nodded. "I'll grant you that one. They never would close all the Red Cabins. But they can close ours. They can shut us Cody men out long as they want to, just to make a point. They want us to *know*—really *know* that we can't threaten them like Davy did. Or

Cathy Hester Seckman

they'll shut us off permanent. Simple as that."

"But it just ain't *fair*," Mike whined again. "It's that damn Davy Redwolf's fault, not ours. Why're they after us for something he did all by himself?"

Now it was Bally's turn to snort. "Even I can see that one, Mike. They can't get to Davy direct, except for barring him from the Red Cabins for life. They want *us* to punish him. And they're gonna keep the Cabin closed till we do."

"Enough said," Rollie growled. "Let's go string him up. We ain't had a hanging here since who knows when. We'll stuff Davy's body through Willie's big Transfer Door and send it on over to the women. See if that satisfies them."

"That what you want to do?" Bally asked in disgust. "Knuckle under?"

Bud Hopper walked through the door just in time to hear Rollie's threat. He might have known the first talk of lynching would come from him. He'd been waiting for it.

"I've been thinking about that very thing, Rollie," he said easily.

"Then you're my man," Rollie returned smartly, slapping Bud on the back. "Let's go. Who's with us?"

"What I've been thinking about," Bud continued in the same easy voice, "is better than hanging."

Old Willie shifted uneasily and backed up another step. Talk of hanging was bad enough, and this sounded worse. Willie wanted no part of any of it. He had to keep his nose clean. But before he sidled out the back door, he wanted to hear Bud's plan.

"We'd all get what we want," Bud was saying. "The women would get the satisfaction of knowing we

122

did away with our troublemaker, we'd get back in the Red Cabins, and Davy—who never broke any Wrongside laws, remember—would get off free."

"Now, wait just a damn minute!" Rollie roared. "He's the reason the Cabins are *closed*. Why should he get off free?"

"Because he didn't do nothing wrong," Bud said reasonably. "And he *ain't* the reason the Cabins are closed. The *women* did that to us. All Davy did was put a crink in their fussy little rules. Why would we want to hang him for making the women mad? We should give him a medal."

Bally laughed at that, a hearty belly laugh, and it defused the tension. "A medal?" he laughed. "Hell, I'd even pay for it. Many hours as I've sat waiting till some woman felt like doing me a favor—"

"So what's the deal, Bud?" Mike Dannon put in. "What do we tell the women?"

"Why, that we hung him. Who's gonna tell them any different? Think they'll come over here and check?"

The bar erupted into guffaws at that, and Rollie's lynching idea was forgotten. The men liked the notion of putting one over on the women, and the more they thought of their hero, Davy, languishing in jail, the less they liked it.

"Let's go spring him, Bud," Bally suggested.

"Yeah," Rollie agreed, enthusiastically jumping to the other side of the fence with no trouble at all. "We'll have a parade right down Main Street. Show Davy we like his style."

"Hey, why is he still in jail, anyways, Bud?" Mike asked. "This is your idea. Why haven't you sprung him already?"

Bud had needed to check public opinion first, find out what kind of reception Davy would face if he got out, but he didn't tell the men that. Even now, he thought he'd let his amnesty idea percolate through the community for a few days before letting Davy go.

"Waiting for the judge," he said now. "Thought I'd run the plan past him first." And that wasn't such a bad notion, either. Bud had been telling everyone who would listen that Davy hadn't broken any laws, but maybe he should get that straight from the judge, just for safety's sake.

Mike nodded sagely and wandered out the door. Bud caught Bally's eye, and the other man dipped his head slightly. With Mike on the move, it wouldn't take long for Bud's idea of amnesty for Davy to spread.

****

Old Willie thought on that conversation, back in his cozy Transfer Cabin. It wasn't right. The whole thing just wasn't right at all. It was good to think they could pull the wool over the women's eyes like that, but they shouldn't have to. They should be able to just say no to the women whenever they wanted. Davy was one of them, after all. Why should the women decide what happened to him? Willie shook his head unhappily. It wasn't for the likes of him to go changing the rules of Rightside/Wrongside, but somebody should. Somebody should do something.

He picked up a paperback and settled into his favorite chair.

****

"I just can't believe it." Jessie's voice was an awed whisper. She stood in the ruins of the Pennsylvania

Avenue Red Cabin's viewing room. Overhead, technicians on ladders strung new wires above the ceiling tiles. In front of her, the ruined one-way glass had been removed, and the empty framework exposed the men's waiting room. On this side of the framework, carpenters were measuring and making notes. The narrow men's room with its hard benches looked curiously naked and barren. Jessie felt that if she extended her hand across to the other side, it might disappear.

"All this," she whispered. "He did all this for me."

"Oh, for Milina's sake," Diana sneered. "He did it because he's crazy. The men have already locked him up, and we're going to make sure they throw away the key."

Diana was in a foul mood. As soon as she had this mess cleaned up, heads were going to roll, and one of them would very probably be hers. The only thing that had saved her so far was her quick execution of the emergency lockdown procedure. If she were really lucky that flawless lockdown would make the difference between losing her job and just being demoted to floor scrubber or something. Engrossed in her own dismal thoughts, it took her a moment to notice Jessie's tears.

Exasperated, she found a handkerchief. "What's the matter with you?"

Jessie was still staring at the empty framework, unmindful of the tear that slid silently down her cheek. "They put him in jail?"

"Of *course* they put him in jail. Did you think they were going to give him a medal for shutting down their Red Cabin? And besides, we insisted on it."

Jessie turned toward her sister, wiping away the tear as she did so. Jessie was in the first blush of pregnancy and looked radiantly beautiful through her tears. "All he wanted to do was see me. Is that a crime?"

"Yes, it most certainly is a crime," Diana returned. "And you know that as well as I do."

Jessie sighed. "It's my hormones, right? That's what the doctor keeps saying."

"And she knows what she's talking about." Diana went over to her sister and put both hands on her shoulders. "Sis, I've worked here a long time. There isn't much I don't know about women and men. This *connection* you feel with Davy isn't natural. It isn't *normal*. Just dry your eyes and go home and chalk it up to hormones. Why don't you work on the baby's room? I could come over later. Maybe we'll go shopping." She raised her eyebrows hopefully, but Jessie shook her head.

"Can I tell you something?"

"Anything, honey, what is it?"

"When I think about the baby—fixing up her room and imagining what she'll look like—sometimes I feel like Davy should be there too. I feel like he should be sharing all this with me. He should be a *part* of it."

Diana dropped her hands from her sister's shoulders. Her expression went from sisterly concern to quick disgust. Unconsciously, she wiped her hands across her skirt. "Jessie, that's sick. Have you talked to your doctor about this? Does Mom know? How long have you felt like this?"

"No, no, and ever since I found out I was pregnant." Jessie frowned. "I'm a nurse, and I know as well as you do that it's abnormal. But I can't help the way I feel."

This was getting scary, Diana thought. What was happening to her little sister? "Honey," she said softly, "I think it's real important that you tell your doctor about these feelings. Maybe she can give you a pill, something to stop them."

"Stop them?"

"*Yes!*" Diana was getting more and more frightened. She studied her sister's face. In spite of her healthy glow, there was a foggy, discontented look in Jessie's eyes.

"Promise, honey," Diana begged. "Promise you'll tell your doctor. Believe me, you don't want to go through your pregnancy feeling like this. It's dangerous."

Jessie sniffed. "You're right. Davy can't really be a part of it, I know that, but if I could just *see* him again—"

"You won't," Diana said shortly. "He's barred for life, and he's in jail. Apparently, they have a primitive justice system in Wrongside, and a sheriff has to wait for a judge to come to town and punish Davy, but it'll be done. I'll see to it." She made a quick cut-off gesture with her hands. "You already have what you needed from Davy. That's an end to it."

Jessie nodded slowly. That wasn't an end to it, as far as she was concerned, but it would do no good to argue with her sister. She left the Red Cabin and wandered disconsolately down the street.

New Washington was more modern than Wrongside Cody, and certainly cleaner. There were stone buildings and neatly paved streets instead of

Cody's brick and wooden storefronts and dusty lanes, but it was curiously barren on the right side of the Border Fence. No flower beds marred the smooth symmetry of the green lawns, and no statues or fish ponds cluttered the city parks. Women had no time for foolishness.

Jessie sat on a bench to watch some children playing ball. Surreptitiously, she touched her stomach. Soon her daughter would be playing ball, too. At the other end of the bench sat a young girl. She was watching the children with what Jessie interpreted in some confusion as barely contained anger. The girl's dark hands twisted restlessly in her lap, and her lower lip was raw and chewed. She looked familiar.

"Excuse me," Jessie said. "Is something wrong?"

The girl jumped and looked over at Jessie with a start. Jessie caught a glimpse of deep, churning violence in the girl's eyes, then her eyes cleared, and she just looked guilty, like a child caught doing something shameful.

"I—you don't—what?"

"I said, is something wrong?" Jessie leaned over to touch the girl's hand. "You look upset."

The girl took a deep, steadying breath. She pushed short, curly black hair off her forehead and shook herself slightly. "No, I'm all right, really." The guilty look had been replaced. Now the girl looked embarrassed. Jessie was intrigued. She loved a good mystery.

"If you want to talk about it," Jessie suggested quietly, "I'm a good listener."

The girl shot Jessie a startled look from beneath heavy, troubled eyebrows. "Talk about it?"

"Yes," Jessie encouraged. "I'm a nurse. You can talk to me about anything."

The girl's face cleared. "That's why you look so familiar. You were there. At the hospital."

"Oh!" The memory came back in a rush. The girl's name was Tenosha. Jessie remembered how hysterical she'd been when the baby turned out to be male. She remembered cleaning the baby later, playing with his tiny, grasping hands, and thinking that someday she'd have a baby of her own. Secretly, she touched her stomach again and offered the silent prayer of Rightside women. "*Please be female.*"

"I remember you, too, Tenosha," she said aloud. "My name's Jessie." She hesitated. "I really hate to say this—it sounds so trite and insincere—but I guess there's nothing else to say." She took Tenosha's hand. "Better luck next time."

Tenosha shuddered. "There won't be a next time. I'll never go through that again."

Jessie had heard it a hundred times. Women who had male babies were always so disgusted by the experience that they swore off pregnancy for life. But somehow, a year or two down the road, they usually changed their minds.

"Let it ride for a while," Jessie said. "You might feel differently later on, or you might not. You don't have to make any decisions right now."

But Tenosha shook her head decisively. "No. It wasn't just having the baby. I knew the risk when I got pregnant. Sometimes you lose. It's all this other stuff I can't go through again."

"All what other stuff?"

Tenosha's guilty look was back. She hesitated, and

looked at Jessie almost shyly. "I guess I could tell you. You're a nurse, after all. My doctor says it happens sometimes. She's giving me medicine."

Jessie smiled encouragingly.

Tenosha took a deep breath. "It's called post-partum depression."

Jessie nodded sympathetically, trying to show by her attitude that Tenosha's revelation was nothing unusual. "You'll work through it," she said. "The pills help."

"Well, they help me sleep," Tenosha said. "I get headaches, but at least they keep me from having those nightmares. When I'm awake, though…" Her voice drifted off, and she looked back toward the ball-playing children. A frown gathered on her forehead.

"What happens when you're awake?" Jessie prodded.

Tenosha turned her attention reluctantly back to Jessie. She was still wearing the frown. "I've been seeing a psychiatrist too, but I haven't been able to admit this to her." She hesitated, then blurted it out. "I get so *angry*."

"Angry?" Jessie was confused. "Angry about what?"

The look in Tenosha's eyes was suddenly bleak, as though she knew how unacceptable her feelings were. "I get angry," she said slowly, "about women who have female babies. Why should *they* be the lucky ones? Why should *they* have what I want? And you know what else?" Tenosha's voice was tight, her face thunderous with suppressed anger.

"Where's *my* baby?" she cried. "I had a baby too. I *saw* him! I didn't want to, but I did. And now I can't stop thinking about him. Where is he? Why didn't I even hold him?" A storm of tears burst through her anguished questions.

The girl shuddered and gulped, trying to get control of herself. Jessie was silent, because she knew there was more coming.

"Sometimes I look at women with baby carriages or baby sacs, and I think how easy it would be to-to—"

"Grab the baby and run?" It happened, Jessie knew. There were stories on the news, maybe a couple of times a year, of women who'd had male babies and just gone crazy. Unable to process their grief, they snatched someone else's baby. They were always caught, of course. Rightside wasn't that big, and no one could hide a stolen baby for long. There were mental health centers that dealt with just this problem. Usually, in spite of treatment, the women were never able to bring themselves to get pregnant again.

Jessie grimaced. Her heart went out to the girl, but there was nothing she could say, nothing she could do to make Tenosha feel any better. It was a cruel fact of life. When you had a male baby, the only thing you could do was forget about him.

Forget about him. With a wrench, Jessie realized that she and Tenosha were not so different.

"You sound as frustrated as I feel," Jessie admitted softly.

"What do you mean?" Tenosha asked. Her tears had subsided into gasps and sniffles.

"I'm trying to forget someone, too."

Tenosha wiped at her streaked face and drew a shuddering breath. "You are?"

Jessie watched the children, still playing their

carefree game of ball, as she talked. All the weeks of frustration and longing poured out.

"Diana said he'd been *shot*," she said. "He was on crutches and had bandages and stitches everywhere. What happened to him?"

"You'll never find out." Tenosha shook her head. Her eyes were wide with the enormity of their shared plight. "And neither will I."

Jessie ran her fingers through her hair and stood up suddenly. She paced in front of the bench with quick, jerky steps. "Sometimes," she began. "Sometimes, you know, I feel like—"

Tenosha looked up at her. "Feel like what?"

Jessie hesitated, then shrugged her shoulders in a what-the-hell gesture. It was illegal. Maybe it was even treasonous. She said it swiftly, letting the words spill out unrestrained. "Sometimes I feel like I can't settle for that."

She looked at Tenosha, daring her to be shocked. When the younger girl didn't respond, she elaborated.

"Just because the laws of Rightside say we can't have any contact with the men, why should we accept that? What's to stop us from contacting the men anyway?"

Tenosha's mouth dropped open. Unconsidered possibilities flitted through her eyes. She started to speak once or twice, then stopped as a new possibility occurred. Finally, she shook her head.

"I wouldn't know how," she admitted.

"Maybe not," Jessie said quietly. "But I would."

****

The girls didn't wait long to implement Jessie's plan.

"Stop fidgeting," she ordered Tenosha the next afternoon. "This has to look casual like we're just stopping off at the end of our shifts."

Tenosha pulled nervously at the tight bodice of the nurse's uniform Jessie had given her. She still had extra post-pregnancy weight, and the jumpsuit was uncomfortable. "I hope you're sure about this," she muttered.

"I'm sure," Jessie said with a confidence she didn't really feel. "I've done it before, for official reasons, and no one's ever questioned me."

Casually, they sauntered across the obstetrics department to the Transfer Room.

Tenosha slowed as they approached it, awed to inaction.

"Don't dawdle!" Jessie ordered. "We can't let anyone see us hanging around outside. It's just a Transfer point!"

"I-I've never been in one before," Tenosha whispered.

"Not even in school? On a tour?"

"Well, yeah, I guess, maybe. A long time ago."

"Then just think of this as another tour," Jessie said briskly. "Come on."

She swept through the door, and Tenosha had no choice but to follow.

"Let me do all the talking," Jessie muttered as they approached the desk.

"Don't worry."

The desk clerk stood up to greet them with a smile. "Jessie! No babies? What do you need?"

"No babies today, Sashi, just a note. I thought I'd give you a break, seeing how overworked you are, and deliver it on my way home. This is Tenosha, by the way. She's new."

"Hi, Tenosha. Jessie taking it easy on you?"

"No," Tenosha stammered, too nervous to lie. "She's been pretty rough on me, as a matter of fact."

Sashi laughed. "Good for her. Only way to handle you fresh ones. Hey, Jess, what's the scoop on your sister? She's in some deep shit."

"Not so deep she can't dig her way out," Jessie said lightly. "She had to lock down, I guess you heard. Some man tried to punch his way through the mirror, but she handled it. No one was hurt. The worst part is making everyone go to out-of-town Cabins till the men here learn their lesson."

"Men." Sashi dismissed the whole race with a disinterested wave of her hand. "Who needs 'em? You'll never catch me in a Red Cabin." She looked at Jessie speculatively. "I could show you some things the men never heard of, if you're interested."

Jessie shook her head gaily. "No thanks, Sashi." She patted her stomach. "I'm going to be busy with Baby here, for a while."

Sashi smiled. "Congratulations, Jess. But you can't blame a girl for trying."

The three women laughed, Jessie with joy, Sashi with regret, and Tenosha with every nerve in her body jangling painfully. How had she let Jessie talk her into this, anyway?

"So what's in the note?" Sashi said suddenly, back to business.

Jessie waved a hand dismissively as she handed the note over. It was just a single sheet of paper, folded in half. Tenosha wanted to put it in a sealed envelope, but

Jessie said no.

"A sealed envelope would attract more attention, make them curious," she said. "This way, they'll think it's not important enough to inspect."

As Sashi took the note from her hand, Jessie hoped with sudden desperation that she hadn't been wrong. This was the crucial moment. If the clerk decided to open the note and read it, she and Tenosha would be getting another tour real soon, of the city jail.

"It's not a rush or anything," she said now. "We got blood work back on the male who was sent over this morning. He has some signs of kidney disease, and the men are going to have to get a doctor to look at him."

"Poor kid," Sashi said automatically, turning the note over in her hands. "If he'd been female, we could have cured it."

"Yeah." Jessie couldn't take her eyes from Sashi's hands. From where she stood, she could read part of the first line of her carefully composed note: *Give this note to Davy Re—* All Sashi had to do was look down.

"Who knows if the men can even treat kidney disease," Jessie continued, trying to hold Sashi's attention. "I mentioned in the note that we're available for consultation. They may write back, asking for help."

"Okay. I'll be on the lookout." Sashi took the note to the side of the room, opened the big metal Drawer, and dropped it in. Then she closed the Drawer and sounded a buzzer. "Do you want to wait and see if there's an answer? We've got coffee in the back."

Jessie shook her head and tried to keep the relief out of her voice. "No, it's late. If they want anything, it can wait until tomorrow."

"Good enough. Hey, take care of that baby, now. Tenosha, nice to meet you."

"You too," Tenosha managed in a croak. Jessie pulled her out of the door.

"We did it!" she cried as soon as they were outside. "We did it. We sent Davy a note!" Jessie spun around gleefully, hugging herself. She looked up at the tall, spotlighted Government Building in the distance and thumbed her nose at the entire body of Rightside law.

"It's us against the world, Davy," she said solemnly. "Us against the world." And as she said it, she touched her stomach protectively.

Tenosha watched this display solemnly. "Are you sure Davy can tell us what happened to my baby?" she asked.

Jessie nodded happily. "I think so. Every baby is given to its father, and your baby's father probably lives right there near the Cabin somewhere. All I'll have to do is give Davy its birthdate. He ought to be able to tell us which one of his neighbors got a baby that day."

Chapter 14

Across the Border Fence, Old Willie opened his Transfer Drawer. The women didn't usually send stuff over at this time of day. Thank Yong it wasn't another baby. The one that came this morning had worn him out with its fussing and crying, and on top of that he'd had to deliver it to the Clingmans, way down south of town. Now his bad leg was singing hallelujah and was liable to keep him up all night. Damn, but he needed a truck!

Willie frowned down at the single piece of paper lying in the bottom of the drawer. What the hell did they want now?

He read the note through once, then carried it over to the window to read it again.

Give this note to Davy Redwolf, it began.

If I get an answer, there'll be two gold coins with my next note. Davy, I have to know if you're all right. All I heard is that you were shot. I miss you, and I love you. If you're all right, send back a note addressed to Jessie Sandova that says this: 'Please advise on proper medication for this type of infant kidney disease.' I'll write back. Love, Jessie.

Willie had to read it through a third time before it sunk in.

****

This is from that woman. he realized. *That woman Davy wrecked the Cabin for.*

Willie's first impulse was to drop the note back in the Drawer like a hot potato, but mindful of the security camera, he slammed the Drawer closed and stepped back out of camera range.

An hour later, he was still afraid. He sat at his kitchen table, head in his hands, the note spread open between his elbows. What to do? That was a puzzler. His first instinct was to burn the damn thing in the stove and forget he ever saw it. He'd bet anything that none of the other women knew Jessie had sneaked that note over here. If he burned it, who would she tell?

His second instinct was to wonder about the gold coins. If these two kids started sending love letters back and forth, it wouldn't take him long to save up for that truck.

Oh, but what kind of trouble could he get into for that? Willie was damn lucky to be the transfer man at all. He'd only gotten the job by the skin of his teeth, and with a lot of help from Bally. If he lost it now he might's well walk out onto the Plains and set down and die. Age was not kind to childless old men in Wrongside.

Willie concentrated hard. If he got caught passing personal notes from a woman to a man, what would happen? The men might not even care. They'd think it peculiar, maybe, but in the end, they'd shake their heads and smile. Everybody had a soft spot for a good love story. The women, now, that was the thing.

The women would care plenty. They even had a law about it. Willie had been made to memorize a bunch of them when he started the job: "No transfer agent shall transfer items of a personal nature." The only punishment was loss of the job, but that was the punishment Willie couldn't afford to take. There were sixteen ways to Sunday he could lose his cushy position, and this was most definitely one of them.

No, it was too risky. Willie had to look out for himself first. That was certain. No one else would. Willie got up and took the note to the stove. He opened the door, then paused to look at the words one more time.

"Two gold coins," he read aloud. Two gold coins. Not a fortune, but not to be sneezed at, either. And not to be dismissed without careful consideration. He could get a decent used truck for less than two hundred, and he had more than half that saved up.

Willie closed the door of the stove and sat down with the note to think some more. He wasn't the smartest man in Wrongside, but as Bally said, he could see through a brick Fence in time. Willie was a slow thinker but a careful one.

In his mind, Willie walked around the problem cautiously, studying every angle. If he took the coins and passed the notes, how could he get caught? That was an interesting question. First, there was Jessie. Willie knew a little bit about women, and this Jessie sounded like a real rebel. No woman he had ever had contact with would want to send a personal note like that. Jessie was probably a loner, he decided, who would keep her illegal doings close to her chest. That kidney disease business, for instance, sounded like a code to him. No, Jessie wouldn't give him away.

Then there was Davy. Just a kid, and a reckless one at that. If he got a note from a woman, who would he tell? His father, probably. Bud, maybe. Now, what would they think? Tom would be afraid, that was certain. He knew how close Davy had come to being killed on the Plains, then lynched in the town. He wouldn't want his son to go begging for any more trouble. But was Tom a danger to Willie? Probably not. Now Bud. Bud was a stickler for the law, all right, but he wouldn't go against his own kind. He wouldn't rat on Willie to the women.

Okay. Willie could see the answer clear and plain, and it was scaring him a little bit. There were only two questions left: Did he have the balls to go through with it? And: how bad did he want that truck?

Willie stood up, put the note in his pocket, found some books and a jacket, and slipped silently out of the cabin.

****

Davy lay in his narrow bunk. The builders of the Cody jail had wasted no effort on amenities. His cell was a small, square room with whitewashed walls and a single barred window and door. A slot in the metal door served to pass food trays in and out. There was a cold water sink in one corner and a metal toilet in the other. Besides the bunk, there was one small table and a straight-backed chair. The walls held the usual assortment of obscene cartoons and limericks, but Davy hadn't read them. Instead, he stared at an oval water stain on the ceiling above his bunk. If he squinted just right, the stain almost reminded him of Jessie's face.

He could hear Frank and Chad Gibson arguing down the hall, hissing back and forth between cells in furious whispers. They knew there were other prisoners in the building, and they didn't want to be overheard. Davy didn't really care. His healing bullet wounds had begun to itch maddeningly, and the broken leg still throbbed with every beat of his heart.

He was waiting. Waiting for his shattered body to knit itself together. Waiting for the judge to show up and pronounce his doom. Waiting to get out of there so he could find a way to contact Jessie.

"—come after us!"

The Gibsons' argument had escalated, and Davy could hear snatches of it.

"Use your head, boy! Trask springs us outta—hide up north—never find us."

"But Pop, what about—"

"Shhhhh! Not so loud!"

The heated whispers continued. So the Gibsons were planning a jailbreak? Davy couldn't bring himself to care. He turned carefully onto his good side and continued to wait.

Bud's voice came from the cell door. "Visitor for you, son." With a heavy clank and a bang, he opened the door, and Old Willie, of all people, came in.

"I brought you some books," Willie began nervously. His heavy-lidded eyes slipped from Davy to Bud and back again. Bud stood in the doorway with his arms folded, making no move to leave. Davy didn't bother to sit up.

"I know how much you like reading," Willie continued, "and Tom told me you was gonna be here a couple weeks, so I brought you these here." He held out two paperbacks. Davy frowned at them. He hated to read. He shifted his head as though to turn his face to the wall, but Willie's next action caught his attention.

With his back to Bud, Willie was holding out the books in one hand. The other hand touched a slip of paper that jutted from the top book. Willie looked at him significantly and nodded his head once. Davy nodded back. He swung his good leg over the side of the bunk, dragged his bad leg after it, and sat up. He reached out with his left hand and took the books, turning them sideways so Bud wouldn't see the piece of paper.

"Thanks, Willie," he said shortly. "I'll read them."

Willie gave a gusty sigh. "I'll be back in a couple days. Bring you some more." He limped out of the cell, past the lawman, and up the narrow hallway. "Thanks, Bud. I didn't think you'd mind."

"Why should I?" Bud grunted. "Kid wants to read. He can read." He slammed the metal door and left Davy alone again.

Davy snatched the note out of the book. He couldn't imagine who'd be sending him secret messages through Old Willie. He read the note through.

"*Jessie!*" he breathed. Jessie. He rubbed his thumb over her name as though he could use the word on the paper to invoke the living, breathing person. The feeling that suddenly welled up inside him was too big to hold. He struggled up out of the bunk and stood swaying on his good leg, breathing fast and hard and ignoring the pain it caused in his chest. He hugged his good arm around himself and closed his eyes, trying to imagine how Jessie would feel. He brought the note up to his lips and kissed it.

"I love you," it said. "I'll write back."

"She loves me," he whispered to his empty cell. "Jessie Sandova loves me." Eagerly, he dragged himself to the cell door.

"Bud!" he yelled. "Hey, Bud, come back here!"

No answer. He rattled the bars on the door. "Bud!"

he shouted again. "I need you back here! I gotta send a message!"

"A message?" The querulous reply hadn't come from the front of the building but from the back, where the other cells were.

"What's so mother-lovin' important that you gotta send a fucking *message* about it tonight, kid?"

The voice belonged to Frank Gibson, Davy was almost sure. Immediately, he backed away from the door. Stumbling over his bad leg, he fell onto the bunk. He held his breath. Had Gibson recognized his voice? Davy had a bad couple of minutes, listening to Frank rant and rave.

"Hey, you up there, answer me! I know you're there, shithead! If you can talk to Bud about your *important* message, you can damn well talk to me! What do you need that stinking lawman for, anyways? Let us in on it, huh, kid? Tell us all your problems!"

The more Davy listened, the better he felt. Frank didn't know who he was shouting at. He was just bored, picking on a kid he couldn't even see. Another prisoner started to grumble.

"Shut your head, Frankie! Trying to sleep."

"Hey, *can* it up there, asshole!"

Frank's monologue eventually faded to angry muttering. No one had come to investigate. Bud had evidently gone home for the night, and the deputy was out somewhere. Davy pounded the bed in frustration. Now he couldn't send his message to Jessie until morning. He'd give it to Bud, and Bud would—

Wait a minute. Davy made a face at himself in the dimness of the cell.

"Stupid," he said out loud. "Stupid, stupid, *stupid.*"

Willie was the one he had to give his note to, not Bud. The lawman would tell the women, sure as sunrise. And Willie wouldn't be back for two days, he'd said so. Davy considered asking Bud to get Willie back here tomorrow morning, but he reluctantly discarded the idea. It looked too suspicious.

Willie must have decided the gold coins were worth the risk, so Willie would be the one. The only one. Davy couldn't tell anyone else about this, not even his father. He eased down onto his back in the narrow bunk and propped his bandaged leg on Willie's paperbacks. He tilted Jessie's note toward the window, so he could read it again.

****

Two days later, Jessie's note was creased and thin from handling. Davy read it hundreds of times a day, although he'd memorized it long ago. He slept with it inside his shirt, next to his heart.

The prudent thing to do was get rid of it, Davy knew. He should have torn it to shreds and put the pieces in the toilet, but he couldn't bear to. The note was the only thing Jessie had ever given him. It was his only link to her, the only thing that gave him any hope. So he kept it, using it to make a faithful copy of the magic words: "*Please advise on proper medication for this type of infant kidney disease.*" He wrote them on a blank page torn from the back of one of Willie's books.

He was standing one-legged at the door of his cell when Old Willie limped down the long jail corridor with new books.

"*Cripes,*" Davy thought, watching him, "*am I gonna walk like that, like a gimpy old man? What'll Jessie think?*" But this vain thought vanished when

Willie simply pushed the new books through the bars of the door. Davy pushed the old ones, which he hadn't read, through to Willie. His note was barely visible, tucked between the pages of one of the books. Willie nodded once.

"Hope you liked them," he said shortly. He didn't lift his head to meet Davy's burning gaze.

"Reading's real fine," Davy said in a rush. He had rehearsed these words a dozen times, wanting to get them exactly right. "I hope you'll bring me more of these books. Maybe you could come by every couple days."

Willie nodded, still studying the floor. "Bud won't mind," he said.

****

Vice President Kai Makele sat quietly behind the podium in the cavernous Congressional chamber, listening to the debate. Alanna had decided to make herself scarce this morning to let the lawmakers talk themselves out, so Kai was presiding. She could feel fear in the room, swirling around the feet of the lawmakers like a sly wind that threatened to blow into a gale at the first opportunity.

The attack on the Pennsylvania Avenue Red Cabin had galvanized the country. Nothing like it had happened in anyone's memory. It was the sole topic of conversation and had been for a week. Alanna had given top priority to the problem of security in all Red Cabins.

The Constancy Party chairwoman was speaking from the floor. Haranguing, rather, Kai corrected herself. The woman was nothing if not tenacious.

"I repeat," she said now, "what are the members of

145

the Fidelity Party planning to do about this? Do they even have a plan? I submit to you that they do not! They would leave us to be *savaged* by the men at any time!"

The undercurrent of fear eddied a little higher. Kai felt its cold breath about her ankles, and she shivered. It was time to stop this. She stood up and quickly took the floor.

"Ladies, please, a little restraint," she said soothingly. "Somehow, I can't imagine savage men running rampant through New Washington." She was relieved to hear a few isolated chuckles.

"Madam Vice President, maybe you need a little more imagination," the chairwoman said darkly. "I shouldn't have to remind you that the very thing you're treating so lightly almost became reality last week. Davy Redwolf came this close"—she held up thumb and forefinger for emphasis—"to breaking through into Rightside. How could we have handled it if that man had succeeded?"

"Man?" Kai broke in quickly. "Man? You must not have been paying close enough attention. Davy Redwolf is an eighteen-year-old boy. A child. He only had sex for the first time three months ago. At the time of the attack, he was injured and half out of his mind with pain. We were never in any danger."

The mood in the chamber was swaying back and forth like a pendulum. When Kai spoke in her quiet and reasonable tone, the legislators nodded sagely. They settled into their seats a little more comfortably. They were women, after all, mistresses of the planet. The men were inconsequential.

But when the chairwoman spoke, the same women

stirred restlessly. They had long memories, and they remembered stories of the Territory Wars when their grandmothers were not mistresses of the planet, and their grandfathers were not inconsequential. Then the women shot nervous glances back and forth and whispered in uneasy undertones.

The balance of power swayed right along with the mood. Kai's Fidelity Party might have placed Alanna in the presidency, but they only held power by the tips of their fingers. The still-strong Constancy Party had a potent orator in its chairwoman. Each time the pendulum swung toward Constancy, Kai could feel that power slip a little further through her fingertips.

"Never in danger?" the chairwoman shouted now. The whispers grew louder. She stepped out into the aisle and strode a few paces toward Kai at the podium. She used her forefinger as an angry counterpoint.

"Kai, I have one"—*stab!*—"simple"—*stab!*—"question"—*stab!*—"for you. And I demand an answer." She paused, and the legislators stopped their whispering. Every pair of eyes was riveted on Kai.

She drew herself up dramatically and pitched her voice low. Every ear strained to hear. "Exactly how much are women's lives worth to the Fidelity Party?"

Kai hesitated several seconds, taking a sip of water to cover the pause. *Milina, let me get this right,* she entreated silently.

"Women's lives," she began slowly, enunciating each word, "are worth everything, not only to the Fidelity Party, but hopefully to the Constancy Party as well. That's why we have the Border Fence. That's why the Red Cabins and the Transfer Cabins are equipped with every imaginable safeguard. Let me remind you how well we're protected from the men." *The savage men,* she thought, suppressing a sudden urge to giggle.

"The Border Fence itself, all hundred miles of it, is electronically fortified and monitored twenty-seven hours a day, seven days a week. No one on either side can touch it without sounding an alarm. High drone camera surveillance is a regular daytime routine and extends a full mile on the wrong side of the Fence."

Kai was warming up to her subject. She had the full attention of the room. Women always loved to hear about security arrangements.

"The North and South Fences run perpendicular to the Border Fence at each terminus, no less strong and protected than the Border itself. Both of them end three miles out into the Western Ocean, an amazing feat of engineering. We know, through constant surveillance, that only a few men travel as far as the ocean, and no one lives there.

"Inside the Transfer Cabins, the Drawers and Doors are monitored by sound and video cameras. The Doors have buffers, just like the Red Cabin doors. The men can put nothing through until we inspect and approve it.

"The Red Cabins—" Kai paused, trying to gauge the mood of the room. The women were still with her, but they hadn't forgotten the opposition, standing defiantly in the aisle. Kai deliberately injected more reassurance, more reasonable calm, into her voice.

"—are safe. I think we just had ample proof of that. The Constancy Party asks how we would have handled it. Ladies, we *did* handle it. The emergency lockdown worked exactly as planned. Every woman in the cabin got out safely. We did stop the intruder. We did bar him from the Red Cabins for life. We did force the men to incarcerate him."

"What's happening now, Kai?" a legislator broke in rudely. "You say the lockdown worked, and maybe it did, but what are you doing to make sure we never need it again? What is the Fidelity Party doing to assure our safety?"

As predictably as a fine clock, the mood of the chamber swung back toward Constancy. Questions came from all around the room.

"Yes, what are you doing?"

"Constancy is right. We need more safeguards."

"Maybe we should limit the men's access to the Red Cabins."

"What about it, Kai?"

"What's the Fidelity Party position?"

Kai turned her head sharply to catch the origin of the last shouted question. It had come from the near left, she thought. She scanned the first two rows. A leading Constancy member looked back at her smugly. Of course, it would have come from her. Well, two could play that game.

"First," Kai cut in, "let me emphasize that this should not be a partisan issue. It's too big for that. The Constancy Party *must* take some interest in the problem." Skillfully, Kai had tugged the wildly swinging pendulum back in her direction. With a few well-chosen words, the Constancy Party was now seen as irresponsible and uninterested in solutions.

"And second, let me update you on the situation at the Pennsylvania Avenue Red Cabin. Diana Sandova is administrator there. Most of you know her. She and her staff have been holding round-the-clock meetings, and

149

she has personally briefed the president several times. Besides the obvious repairs, one of the most important things they're working on is a full security update using the latest technology. In fact, I can announce to you today that the administrator will be here Friday. She's going to present her report to the full chamber. I hope you'll all make an effort to attend."

Kai looked around the chamber. She had said all there was to say. If there was one thing a good politician knew, it was when to stop talking. "Any questions?"

No one spoke.

As the session broke up, the Constancy chairwoman lingered for a few moments, watching Kai as she gathered up papers and spoke to another legislator. Interior Secretary Maud Adams brushed past Kai, and the chairwoman hurried to catch up with her.

"Meeting still on?" she asked softly.

Maud turned her head and nodded once, briskly. To anyone watching, it would have seemed as though the two women were saying goodbye. Without missing a beat, Maud peeled off and swept down a side hallway.

****

Ten minutes later, a small group of women sat down in a private, out-of-the-way conference room. All had arrived quietly and casually.

"It's beginning to happen," the chairwoman said with satisfaction. "Your precious Fidelity Party is going downhill fast."

"And I couldn't be happier," Maud said with a nasty, sharp-nosed grin. "The Fidelity Party started down that hill when Alanna took over. If they'd had the good sense to choose a more fitting presidential candidate—"

"Someone like you, perhaps?" The Constancy Party leader's voice was deceptively gentle.

Maud widened her nasty smile. "Let's just say that if they had, I wouldn't be helping you now."

"I believe that," she said simply. "But now let's get some work done. She nodded in turn to Maud, their spy; to three others; and to the last unwilling accomplice. "The five of us must never lose sight of our main objective. We want Alanna Olaffson out of office. The sooner, the better. With the speed of her reforms, it can't be long before she turns her attention back to smuggling. I'm told that Kai has already commissioned a special investigation of illegal commerce between New Pittsburgh and Bozeman.

"And that, ladies, would spell disaster for our pocketbooks, not to mention our political careers. This debacle at the Red Cabin has been a lucky distraction. It will hold their attention for weeks, and by the time they get around to chasing smugglers again, we'll be ready."

The fifth woman spoke up hesitantly. "What does that mean, ready? You wouldn't really—?"

The party leader shook her head. "That's only a last resort, dear, believe me. No one wants it to go that far, but we have to be prepared for any eventuality. If our luck continues to hold, we may not need your help at all."

"Then maybe I should go, let you get on with your plans. I don't really need to know the details, do I? I mean, should I? I am still a member in good standing of Fidelity."

"So am I, you silly goose," Maud said impatiently. "And if the precious Fidelity Party had done right by us, we wouldn't even be here."

"It wasn't like that for me." The woman's tone was aggrieved. "It wasn't the party's fault. You *made* me come! I didn't want to. If it hadn't been for Mama needing money, I would never have agreed to the smuggling."

"You did agree to it," the chairwoman said shortly. "And you are here, albeit somewhat reluctantly. Now have the good grace to accept the situation. Sit quietly and listen. The Red Cabin incident turned out to be a good beginning for us, but now we must keep the pressure steady. We're going to engineer a small, discreet series of incidents that will show the women of Rightside how incompetent their president is. We'll build a case against her slowly and solidly, and when the case is strong enough, our work will be done. Congress will call for a new election, and Alanna Olaffson will be driven out of office."

Maud shuffled through her notes. "Now, we've come up with some ideas."

A thoroughly frightened Giulia Saracco sat and listened.

****

Alanna read through her short list of topics prior to the monthly teleconference with Commander Sherman in Wrongside. As always, Kai sat out of sight to her left.

"Good afternoon, Commander."

On the video screen, Sherman nodded. "Madam President."

"Let's talk about the attack on the Red Cabin up north." Sherman didn't know, of course, that the Cabin in question was located in Rightside's capital city, just as she was.

"Don't know much about it," Sherman answered. "Cody's pretty far from us down here in Jackson Hole. My lieutenant up there tells me the sheriff jailed the boy according to your order, but a local mob took him out and hung him." As far as the commander and his lieutenant were concerned, this was the truth. Neither had bothered to check Bud's story.

"That's what we were told," Alanna replied. "I'm glad you can confirm it."

"Ma'am, the men up in Cody have been pretty riled up, not being able to visit a Red Cabin. Any idea when things might get back to normal?"

"When we're ready," Alanna said firmly, "the supervisor of the Cabin will be informed. It shouldn't be longer than a week. You might inform your people that each Red Cabin will close temporarily in the coming months for maintenance and upgrades."

The Commander clamped down on his anger. Maintenance and upgrades? The women wanted more security, that's all. A Wrongside kid had ruffled their precious feathers, and now they were scared. Why, if the kid hadn't got himself lynched, damned if Sherman wouldn't have given him a medal. Upgrades. Shit.

"Enough of that, though, Commander. Tell me how our new medication supply plan is working out for you."

"Well enough," he conceded. "Three of the smugglers are behind bars, and the rest of them are in hiding, not doing much. The new supply chain seems secure. Our doctors aren't complaining of unexplained shortages of drugs, for a change."

"I'm glad. We're working hard to break the

smuggling ring over here, and I hope I'll have good news for you soon. If our task force is successful, the smuggling problem will be over for now."

"For now. Always seems to crop back up eventually."

"You would know," Alanna commented. "How long have you been in power now?"

The commander allowed himself a small inward smile of satisfaction. He knew the Rightside president's term was limited to three years. They didn't hold with that in Wrongside. He'd made sure of it.

"Going on eleven years now, ma'am. Wrongside seems to be happy with me, has no reason for a change. Not that I'd make it easy for them, but they're content. I don't want to brag, you understand, but things have been better here since I took over. The economy's improved a bit, high school graduations are increasing, and art and culture are on the upswing. We even have our own symphony orchestra now."

Alanna was shocked but didn't show it. "I'm glad to hear it, Commander. You're doing good work. I'll need to sign off now. Talk to you next month."

"Ma'am." Sherman clicked off his screen. This new president of theirs was high-handed as all get out, but then, they all were.

****

At yet another meeting, across the wide, empty plaza that separated the Government Building from the Pennsylvania Avenue Red Cabin, Diana Sandova unconsciously echoed the Constancy chairwoman's comment.

"Sydney and I have come up with some ideas," she said slowly. Her voice was gravelly with fatigue, and there were circles under her eyes. Man, she was tired. When this was over, for better or worse, Diana was going to farm out the kids and sleep for a week. It would feel so unbelievably good to sink her aching head into a soft, white pillow and forget the very name of Davy Redwolf.

But before she could afford to forget about him, there was a lot of work to do. Diana squared her shoulders, gathered what strength she had left, and stood up. She moved to a chalkboard set against one wall of the Cabin's training room. Swiftly, she sketched the outline of a typical Red Cabin meeting room. Women's door, men's door, bathroom door. Bed, nightstand, table and chairs, video camera, alarm box. She turned and looked at her staff.

They'd all been run ragged in the last few days, under the gun to come up with new security arrangements for the Red Cabins after Davy's attack. They looked as fatigued as she felt, but Diana was too tired to muster up any sympathy for them.

"You all know the standard security procedures," she began. "Let me give you the new—"

At that point, Diana was interrupted by a knock on the door. "Come in," she sighed.

She straightened up, surprised when the president and vice president walked through the door. "Ladies," she said, trying to inject some welcome into her weary voice. "Come right in. Have a seat. Can we get you anything? What can we do for you?" Inwardly, she was puzzled and a little resentful. What did they want from her now? Didn't they know she was already doing everything humanly possible?

"Relax, Diana," Alanna said with a warm smile.

"And please, since we've been working together for days and it isn't over yet, call me Alanna."

"And I'm Kai," the vice president added, pulling out chairs for the president and herself.

When they were seated, Alanna continued. "This isn't an official visit. I've just announced to Congress that you'd speak to them Friday on new security arrangements. Kai and I decided we'd like to come over this afternoon and get a preview if we could."

Diana mustered a smile. "Of course. We were just finalizing the new plan. It'll be a lot of work to put things into place, but I think we can open the Cabins again on a limited basis in two weeks."

Alanna nodded her approval. "That'll be about right. It's just enough time to show the men we mean business without making them so frustrated they decide to take action."

No one asked her what action she thought the men might take. It hadn't escaped any of the Red Cabin employees that Davy was only eighteen and injured at that. If full-grown men were to try to break through a Red Cabin to the women's side, the results would be quite different. At all costs, they had to make their Cabins impregnable.

"If we like the results," Diana continued, "we can implement the same precautions at every Red Cabin." This was the important part, as far as Diana was concerned. If her and Sydney's new security plan found approval and became the standard for every Cabin, it just might be enough to save their jobs. She plunged in.

"Sydney and I came up with this last night," she said, generously handing out credit, "and the rest of the staff has been throwing in ideas. We were just about to put it all together." She turned back to the chalkboard.

"Now, our basic problem is that the old security system has been breached. No one has ever had to lock down before, and now that we have, we must assume that every man in Wrongside knows about it. If we had to do it again, we couldn't count on the element of surprise long enough for all the women to escape.

"So the challenge has been to come up with something entirely new that the men won't expect." She paused and smiled. "Syd, tell them about some of our first ideas."

Sydney laughed, a rusty, unused sound. "We thought of everything, ma'am. Any crazy idea you can think of, we had. Electric eyes, gates that come out of the ceiling, force fields, you name it.

"The problem with all of them was that we couldn't absolutely predict where the women and men would be when the gates came down or the force fields formed. It would be way too easy to catch a woman on the wrong side and a man on the right side. We needed something foolproof that would give every woman in every room instant and absolute protection from any man."

Alanna shivered as she listened, unpleasant images forming in her mind. Her grandmother had told a few stories of the men's Territory Wars. Rape was extinct in Rightside, but not forgotten. It was their job, they in this room, to make sure it never reared its ugly head again.

"So what's the answer?" Kai asked abruptly. Alanna could tell by her tone that images had formed in her mind as well.

"Gas," Diana said simply.

"Gas?" Alanna and Kai gave each other blank looks.

"Diana thought of it," Sydney said generously. "We asked a medical researcher if it would be possible to adapt a surgical anesthetic to work for security, and she said yes."

"Every meeting room would have an inconspicuous nozzle," Diana explained. "We could make it look like part of the sprinkler system. All the rooms on the men's side would have one, too. We could just close each Red Cabin in turn, for "maintenance," to install them. In the event of trouble, we just introduce the gas into one room or all the rooms. Women, as well as men, would be rendered unconscious in a matter of seconds.

"Then we go in with gas masks, remove the women, and lock up the men. When we're ready, a few minutes of oxygen will wake everyone up."

"And the best part about it," Sydney added, "is that the gas can be colorless and odorless. The men will never know what hit them. We can use it over and over again if we have to, and they'll never catch on."

Alanna slapped both hands on the table and grinned. "It's brilliant! Ladies, this is the best news I've had in weeks! Kai, what do you think?"

Kai was grinning, too. "I can't wait till Congress hears this. You couldn't have given us better news."

"Actually," Diana said, her fatigue forgotten for a moment, "I can. I got some news this morning that I haven't even told the staff yet." She looked around the table at the women. "The sheriff asked to talk to me this morning. You all know Bud Hopper. He told me that the men of Cody were so angry with Davy Redwolf for forcing us to close the Red Cabins that they dragged him out of jail last night and killed him. They hung him from the nearest lamppost. It's called lynching. Mob justice."

The women's faces registered shock and disgust. "Men," Amber said faintly. "They're so revolting."

"It's what he deserved," Sydney said with a shrug. "But you're right. It's revolting."

"I never expected them to carry it that far," Alanna said, not admitting she'd already gotten that news. "You told me Bud didn't even want to put the boy in jail at first."

"He didn't," Diana said. "But you know Bud. He's not exactly your typical man. The others weren't so forgiving. They saw Davy as their obstacle to the Red Cabins, so they got rid of him. Simple as that."

"Simple," Alanna echoed. "Well, I hate to admit it, but this makes it simple for us, too. Davy was the problem, and he's gone." She stood up and nodded briskly to Diana. "Congress can hear about this Friday, and you can reopen the Cabin as soon as you're ready." She swept out, Kai following.

Diana looked at her staff. "*We* can reopen? As soon as *we're* ready? Do you realize what this means?"

Amber laughed. "It looks like we keep our jobs, boss."

The meeting broke up with the staff in high spirits. The women filed out, chattering about dinner and a good night's sleep, and a better day tomorrow. As Diana gathered her papers, she reflected sadly that everyone on both sides of the Fence seemed to be happy about Davy's death. Jessie wasn't going to feel that way.

****

Diana called her sister later and invited her to dinner. When Jessie arrived, she was bubbling over with happiness, looking like she'd had good news.

"What's up?" Diana asked curiously, putting off the moment she'd have to deliver her own bad news. They were sitting at the dining room table and talking over the squabbling of Diana's daughters.

"Oh, nothing much," Jessie said airily, flipping her hair with one hand. "Things are just looking up, that's all." In her pocket, though she had no intention of showing it to her sister, Jessie had a note torn from the back pages of a book. She had just picked it up from Sashi at the transfer cabin and had promised to answer it in the morning.

"I'm glad," Diana said, searching her sister's face. "But are you sure there isn't something else? You look like that cat in the old storybooks who swallowed a canary."

Jessie ducked her head and gulped, looking as guilty as the proverbial cat. "Nothing, really," she said hastily. "I just feel better, that's all. No more morning sickness, no more morbid fantasies. And I made a new friend."

"Oh?" Diana settled back to listen. Her bad news could wait.

"Who'd you meet, Aunt Jess? Was it a doctor?" Trini, Diana's oldest, was mildly interested. She wanted to go to medical school in two years and was always pumping Jessie for stories about doctors.

"Sorry, kiddo," Jessie said. "This was a patient."

Trini returned her attention to her plate, and Jessie returned hers to Diana.

"Her name is Tenosha Hausen. I met her a few months ago when she came in to have a baby." She hesitated for a beat, and in that beat, Diana, and even Trini, understood that the baby had been male. No one would mention it again.

"Tenosha and I ran into each other by accident the other day and had lunch. It was fun. We're going to spend time together."

Diana nodded. Because the women of Rightside did not have husbands or boyfriends to occupy them, friendships with other women were important. "Spending time" with women was the accepted term for what might have been called "dating" if there had been any men in Rightside to date.

"I'm glad you're feeling better," Diana said.

Jessie waved a casual hand. "Nothing to worry about," she assured her sister. "Now, how about you? Still have a job?"

Diana laughed and launched into a recital of the afternoon meeting. Trini was fascinated to hear that her mother had been invited to call the president by her first name, and even little Sara paid attention.

After dinner, Jessie and Diana left the girls to fight over the last piece of vanilla cream pie and retreated to the living room. Jessie settled onto the couch with a cup of hot herbal tea, feeling the note crackle in her pocket as she did so. Diana put her coffee mug on a side table and sat down opposite. She began carefully.

"Sis, I was glad to hear you say earlier that you weren't having any more morbid fantasies. Is that really true? No more pining for Davy?"

Jessie looked her sister right in the eye. "No more," she promised. And it was true. She didn't need to pine for Davy when she had evidence of his undying love right in her pocket. "I'm looking toward the future now," she assured Diana.

"That's good." Diana drew a deep breath. "Because I have some sad news for you."

Jessie frowned. "What's the matter?"

Diana sighed, hesitated, then blurted it out. "Yesterday, the men over in Wrongside made a move against Davy. Their lawman says they blamed Davy for everyone being shut out of the Red Cabins. They took him out of the jail and killed him."

"Killed h—" Her mouth hung open on the final word, as though it had forgotten how to form the final letters. Her face was blank with shock, but behind the blank, her mind was working furiously. The note had come this afternoon. *The note had come this afternoon!* Sashi had said so! How could Davy be sending her notes today if he'd been killed yesterday?! He couldn't be dead. That was wrong. *She had the note in her pocket!*

But Diana didn't know about the note. The thought splashed into her racing mind like a bucket of cold water. Jessie closed her mouth with a snap, biting viciously on the side of her tongue. The pain and the unpleasant taste of blood put a halt to her frantic thoughts. The men must have had their own reasons for telling the women Davy was dead, and Jessie couldn't worry about them right now. If her secret correspondence with Davy were to continue, she couldn't afford to make Diana suspicious.

"Killed him," she said again, flatly. The words came out short and hard, like bullets. "Well. I'm sorry it had to end this way. He was only a kid, and he didn't deserve to die like that just for loving me. But it's over. He's gone, and we can all get back to normal. I have the baby to think about now."

"Oh, I'm so glad you feel that way," Diana said. Lines of anxiety smoothed out of her forehead, and she sank back in her chair. "I mean, I'm sorry too about Davy, but you're right. We can all get back to normal now."

Diana watched as her sister turned to say something to Trini in the dining room. It seemed she had been wrong. No one in Rightside, not even Jessie, was too upset about Davy's death.

Chapter 15

Bud knocked on Ricky's door and was happy to see that his brother answered. If he was lucky, Clyde wouldn't even be home.

"Hey, Buddy, what a surprise!" Ricky socked his brother on the shoulder and waved him into the house. "Come in, come in. Can you stay for supper?"

"Maybe," Bud said agreeably. "What's cooking?" So far, there was no sign of Clyde.

"Chili and corn muffins," Ricky replied. "Clyde's specialty."

Keeping his face friendly, Bud said, "Sounds good. Sure there's enough?"

"Always enough for my little brother, right, Clyde?" Ricky addressed this last to his partner, who'd come from the kitchen to see who the visitor was.

"Shoot, Clyde, you look like you just ate a persimmon!" Bud said loudly, moving into the hallway. He captured the smaller man's hand with a hearty shake, at the same time giving him a none-too-friendly squeeze on the shoulder. Warning Clyde to silence with narrowed eyes and a slight shake of his head, he crowded him backward into the kitchen. Ricky, sensing the tension between the two men, followed warily.

"I know I ain't exactly your favorite person," Bud continued, "but you could at least say hello. Offer me a bed for the night?"

Ricky didn't miss his man's sudden look of dismay. He'd have to make it up to Clyde later.

"Of course we have a bed for you," he said swiftly. "And we already invited you to supper. But what's the occasion? Do you have business in Jackson Hole?"

"Not business," Bud answered, "pleasure. I came down to buy another sculpture from Clyde's friend."

"Simeon?" Ricky was puzzled. "I didn't know you'd ever bought anything from him."

Clyde just snorted. He went back to his dinner preparation, slamming pots and dishes, but not so loudly that he couldn't listen to the conversation.

Ricky gestured Bud to a seat at the table. "And I didn't know you were all that interested in sculpture. Simeon's expensive, isn't he?"

Bud shrugged, and Ricky caught a trace of bitterness in the movement. "I ain't got any boys to spend my money on. And Clyde here got me interested with that *Mother and Child* piece. I bought a real pretty piece from him last month, and I got an appointment with him first thing in the morning to see some other stuff."

"*Other stuff!*" Clyde muttered from the sink. "Other *stuff*, he calls it. Wouldn't know fine art if he fell over it, and he thinks he wants more."

"Don't burn the muffins," Ricky interrupted sharply. "Remember, the oven's been acting up."

Ricky made a dive for the stove and pulled a smoking muffin tin from it. "They're *ruined!*" He groaned, shooting a black look at Bud as though to blame him.

Bud laughed. "Hell, just cut the bottoms off. It's what I do all the time."

165

Dinner was uncomfortable for Bud, though he tried not to show it, hiding behind the bluff, tough exterior he always presented to Clyde. It was equally uncomfortable for Clyde, who had never told Ricky about Bud's outrageous intrusion the month before. He had kept silent in the beginning because he was ashamed of himself for caving in and writing Bud's letter of recommendation to Simeon. Now, so long after the fact, he knew he could never tell Ricky how cowardly he had been. It made him resent Bud more than ever.

Ricky was tense all evening. He walked a constant tightrope between his brother and his lover, and it never seemed to get any easier. And there was some new undercurrent here that he didn't understand. Clyde seemed to resent Bud more than ever, and not just on general principles anymore. He acted as though he had a personal grudge. Ricky frowned, watching Clyde snipe at Bud on the subject of modern art. Clyde had never been any good at keeping secrets. Sooner or later, he'd get to the bottom of it.

In the morning, over coffee and leftover cornbread with wild honey, he tried to bring up the subject with Bud.

"A personal grudge?" Bud snorted. "Nah, Clyde never did like me. He's just carrying on like normal. Hey, listen, Ricky, try not to worry about it, huh? We have an understanding, Clyde and me. He hates my guts, and I think he's a miserable little twerp, but we both love you. End of story."

Ricky sighed and stood up. "Try not to worry about it. Yeah, right. Listen, Bud, I've got to get going. Can I drop you off in town?"

"Nah, I'll just take my truck. I'm headed back as soon as I see Simeon. I'm working tonight."

Bud didn't wait to say goodbye to Clyde. Jackson Hole was bustling as he drove in. It was almost summer now, and the trees were in full leaf. The city park was filled with raggedy wildflowers. Boys were headed to school, and men were headed to work. The munitions factory was in Jackson Hole, and that, along with the university and hospital, made the town Wrongside's most prosperous. Bud felt an energy here that was mostly absent in Cody. He stood a little taller and walked a little faster down the crooked street that led to Simeon's gallery. He imagined that he was getting closer to his daughter with every step.

"Well, Mr. Hopper! How nice to see you again!" Hasad was lavish in his welcome. It wasn't every day that he sold an expensive piece of smuggled art.

Bud laughed. "I ain't so formal as all that, Si. Call me Bud."

Hasad returned Bud's grin with one of his own. "Only my best friends call me Si, Bud, but if you're here to buy another sculpture, maybe you qualify."

Bud dipped his head in acknowledgment. "I'm here to buy. And not only that, I'm here to make you a business proposition."

Simeon raised his eyebrows and rubbed his hands together in anticipation. "I like you better all the time, Bud. I can see that we're going to be very good friends. Come back to my office."

Bud followed the dealer through his gallery, past the rich oils and watercolors that represented the best of Wrongside art. Clyde Wether paintings, Bud noted wryly, were still commanding good prices.

Behind the closed door of Simeon's private office, the two men quickly got down to business.

"I'm anxious to hear your proposition, Bud," Simeon began, walking around his desk. "I'd guess it has something to do with my private stock."

"You guess right," Bud said. He pulled a chair up close to the desk and sat on its edge. "I've been showing my new sculpture to a few friends up in Cody. Close friends, you know, men I can trust. They're real interested."

"Interested?"

"Very." Bud leaned both forearms on Simeon's desk and dropped his voice to a confidential level. "They're looking to buy, too. They want to know if maybe I can do some business with you, on their behalf."

Simeon pulled back slightly, and caution showed in his next question. "Why don't they come down to the gallery themselves? I'd be happy to show my stock to any friends of yours."

Bud shook his head ruefully. "It ain't so easy for them. One's an older fella, got a bum leg, and one's our only doctor. He can't just ride on down to the Hole anytime he wants. The other guy runs a bar there in town—he's pretty much stuck in place."

Bud had not, of course, shown his sculpture to Willie, Doc, or Bally. He hadn't shown it to anyone.

"But me, now," he continued, "I come down here all the time, what with business and visiting my brother and Clyde."

"You never told me, Bud," Simeon asked. "What kind of business are you in?"

"Transport," Bud said quickly, with no hesitation.

"I do a lot of transport between here and there." And it was true, actually. As sheriff, Bud spent a considerable amount of time transporting prisoners back and forth from Cody's tiny jail to the maximum security prison outside Jackson Hole.

Simeon nodded, satisfied with the explanation. "I think we can do business. Do you know what your friends are looking for?"

Bud shifted in his seat. This was where it might get tricky. Simeon trusted him now. Bud had to make sure he kept it that way.

"Well, Bally, he's ready to buy. I know his tastes pretty well, and he wants me to pick him up something today. The other two they ain't quite sure they can afford your prices. They want me to get a better idea of what's available. Maybe bring back a catalogue?"

Simeon shook his head and smiled indulgently. "Not for these pieces, Bud. Even a beginner like you should know that. The nature of this art is a little too delicate for general publication."

Bud nodded as though this was no surprise. "We kind of figured that, but I asked anyway. No problem. If you ain't got a catalogue, maybe I could meet your supplier."

Simeon started. "My what!?"

"Your supplier." Bud kept his tone casual. "The boys and me, we thought maybe if I could talk to the person you buy from, we could find out what all's available."

"You can find that out from me." Simeon glared at him. "There's no need for you to meet anyone else. You must realize I have to protect my sources."

Bud shrugged his shoulders. "You don't need to

protect them from me. Or my friends. We don't mean no harm."

"You may not," Simeon agreed smoothly. "Nevertheless, my supplier and I must be very careful."

Bud nodded. "I can understand that." He leaned forward again. "Let me be honest here for a minute. Me and the boys, we're just kinda curious, you know? It's been pretty exciting for us finding this new source of art. We don't get much culture up in Cody, and your little sculpture has turned us all on our ears. The boys, they're pretty much homebodies. I explained all that. Hell, Willie don't even go to the Red Cabins no more. But they want to know all about this supplier of yours, and they delegated me to find out."

Simeon looked shocked for a moment, then he pushed back in his chair and began to laugh. Bud was encouraged. At least he wasn't angry.

"So what we've got here," Simeon said between chuckles, "is a bunch of dirty old men who want to get their kicks out of meeting a female smuggler."

Bud grinned bashfully. "More or less, yeah. They want me to meet her, then go home and tell them all about it. But it's more than that, really. They want me to find out what she can get. Doc has a special order in mind, and I really need to talk to her about it."

Simeon shook his head, still smiling. He wasn't about to jeopardize his source to satisfy a whim. "You can't meet her. I understand why you'd want to, but you can't. Tell you what, though. If your friends can't visit me, maybe I'll take a drive to Cody myself. I've never been up near the Plains, and I've always wanted to go." He swung around and looked out of his office window, thinking through the idea. He smelled gold coins, a lot of them.

"There's no art gallery in Cody, is there? Not since old Dick Chen died? If no one's taken over his building, I can organize a temporary exhibition there, do some business. Hell, maybe I'll spend a few days, see about opening a Cody branch myself. I can bring a few of my special pieces, too, and hold a private showing for your friends." He swung back to face Bud, excitement in his well-kept face. "What do you think?"

Bud could see a big problem right off. His friends didn't know jackshit about the smuggled art, but he had to fall in. He mustered more enthusiasm than he felt.

"Mother love, Si, that's a great idea! The guys'll love to see more of your stuff. They'll be disappointed about me not meeting your supplier, but having you there to tell them about her will be just as good."

The men shook hands on the idea, and Bud picked out the least expensive piece in Si's special collection, still pretending it was for Bally. They shook hands again, and Bud headed home. All the way to Cody, he wrestled with two questions. How long would his savings hold out if he kept buying expensive art? Not much longer, he didn't expect. And did this plan of Simeon's to come to Cody do anything to further his quest to find his daughter? He didn't think so.

****

For his part, Simeon Hasad was pleased with the day's business. He left the gallery promptly at five and headed home. He was seeing Toller that evening.

Two hours later, showered and shaved, black hair gleaming softly over the collar of his snow-white shirt, he presented his appointment card to the clerk at the Teton Street Red Cabin.

"Again?" the clerk said rudely. He was a squat, muscled man who looked at Simeon's lean elegance with disdain. "What does she see in you?"

Simeon was in too good a mood to take offense. "Things you couldn't even imagine, trust me. Just tell them I'm here."

If Simeon's mood was sunny, Toller's was midnight black. "Don't look so cheerful. I only came because I knew you'd whine if I missed again."

"Oh, what's wrong, sweetie?" Simeon crooned. "Come here and let me fix it. I'll rub your shoulders. How's that?"

Toller allowed a small smile. She considered her lover's handsome face and his soulful eyes. He always reminded her of a good dog, happy and eager to please. "I guess that's really why I came. To see if you could lift this black mood I'm in."

"Why black?" Simeon took her canvas tote bag and set it aside. He drew her to the bed and coaxed her to sit, then knelt behind her and applied his skillful fingers to the knots at the back of her neck. "I brought you a whole bagful of pretty gold coins. That should put you in a better mood. That, and my extraordinary lovemaking." He dropped a kiss on her shoulder.

Toller laughed ruefully and stretched her neck to give him better access. "Well, I hope you didn't bring any more orders, because I've lost my best supplier."

"Oh, no." Simeon stopped his massage and sank down beside her on the bed. "Not the mommy sculptor?"

Because Toller wouldn't give him the actual names of her artists, Simeon had made up nicknames. The mommy sculptor produced exquisite mother and child pieces.

Toller nodded. "Her."

"Oh, damn." Simeon fell back on the bed. He didn't feel quite so elegant and sexy now. There were three orders for mommy sculptures in his shirt pocket, and he'd already spent the commissions on a few cases of smuggled Rightside wine.

"Is it temporary?" he asked. "Is she sick, or something? What'll I do with these orders? Maybe she has a backlog we can draw from."

"She got called up earlier this year," Toller said shortly. She was too upset to notice, for the moment, that she was talking to a man. Sometimes she almost thought of Simeon as a colleague. "And I've just finished selling off the backlog. We're shit out of luck for the next year, as far as her work is concerned."

"Called where?" Simeon was clueless. "Called what?"

"Oh!" Belatedly, Toller shot a glance at the security camera in a corner of the ceiling. She knew the Rightside clerks occasionally did random spot checks, and she was usually more careful. The light was off, thankfully. She shook herself and pulled her thoughts together. This was a dangerous game she was playing, and she needed to keep things in focus.

"Called up north. Her mother lives up there. She, uh, owns a gallery. The mother fell, and she broke her hip or something. There were complications. She had a heart attack while she was in the hospital, and all kinds of other stuff, and now Kiran—the mommy sculptor has to stay there and run the gallery. She won't have time for her own work."

Simeon stared blindly at the ceiling. "If we don't

have her work, I wonder if my customers would take something else. Maybe the granny painter's work or one of those small metal floral arrangements from the girly one. I think…" He trailed off, his mind clicking through possibilities.

He'd already dismissed the mommy sculptor, Toller could see. She breathed an inconspicuous sigh of relief. Thank Milina, he hadn't questioned her story. No man needed to know the details of Rightside's Guard, in which every woman was expected to serve a full year. Most girls did their Guard hitch right out of high school or college, but Kirannan, the sculptor, had put hers off as long as possible. At twenty-eight, she was out of time and had been called to military duty. Toller heard she'd already made sergeant.

Rightside women had never forgotten the Territory Wars that had almost killed off the original colonists, and they stayed ready to defend themselves if necessary. Men would never be allowed to endanger the women again.

Simeon was still murmuring to himself. Toller smiled. "We'll figure it out. Anything else to report?"

"Report?" He thought for a moment, then barked a short laugh. "Not unless you want to meet a sheriff from up north."

"What, pray tell, is a sheriff?"

"Lawman," Simeon said shortly. "It was a hoot, really. This hick sheriff got wind of the pieces you sell, and he thinks he's an art connoisseur. He's bought two, and he actually wants to meet you so he and his friends can get their jollies out of buying directly from a female version of me."

Toller snorted. "Fat chance. Si?" she leaned over

him.

"Hmmmmm?"

"Shut up." She claimed his mouth with a kiss. "Enough business. I want to see how fast you can fix my bad mood."

Chapter 16

Davy rolled onto his good side with a groan and folded half the stained pillow to cover his ear. The Gibsons were at it again. They'd been whispering and banging around their cells since lights out. A prisoner down the row was yelling for quiet.

"Shut your trap, Bonner!" Frank Gibson yelled back. "Fuck do I care if you're tired? What do you need to sleep for anyways? You gotta get up early for work?"

An obscene reply rumbled from the cell next to Davy's, and he heard the man thrash up out of his bunk. "Deputy!" the man bellowed up the hall. "Haul your ass back here, you worthless tub! Shut these two up, or I'll get you fired from this cushy job of yours!"

"Hee-ya, Bonner, you tell 'im," Gibson laughed. "Let's start us up a protest back here, get that worthless deputy's ass fired!"

The door between the sheriff's front office and the cell corridor crashed open. "What's going on back here?"

Even Davy could hear the uncertainty in Mikey's voice. Mike Tinson, Bally's gentle son, had never been cut out to be a deputy, but Bud did the best he could with the boy because he owed Bally too many favors. Davy knew Bud was gone for the night, down to Jackson Hole, and Mikey was in charge. Davy rolled off the cot, grabbed his crutch, and stood at the bars to see what would happen next.

Mikey didn't turn on the corridor lights, but left the door to the front office open. In the dim illumination, he walked down toward Davy's cell.

"What's wrong, Bonner? Why you yelling for me?"

"You gotta shut them damn Gibsons up," the man whined. "They're keeping all of us awake."

"Come on down here, pretty boy," Frank crooned. "See if you can make me shut up."

"Now, Frank," Mikey began. In the dim light from the office, Davy could tell how nervous the deputy was.

"Don't listen to him, Mikey," Davy whispered. "You don't wanna go down there. Just let them yell."

Rather than reassure him, Davy's voice seemed to goad the deputy to action. Mikey took a few hesitant steps, then straightened his shoulders and marched down the hall. Davy could just see him reach out to the bars of Frank's cell. "Don't…" he whispered again.

Too late. Davy watched Frank's arm snake out between the bars to grab hold of Mikey's shirt. Yanking the deputy forward, Frank slammed his face against the bars with a meaty thud.

"Chad!" Frank called to his son in the next cell. "Lemme swing him over to you. Check and see if he's got keys."

There was more rustling and a groan from Mikey, then Chad whooped with delight. "Got 'em, Pa!"

Davy heard clanking as the deputy's key ring rattled against the cell locks. From the sounds, he guessed they'd dragged Mikey into Frank's cell and slammed the door on him.

"Hoo-ee, weren't that a treat!" Frank chortled.

"Always wanted to lock me up a deputy. You stay right there, now, be a good boy."

Davy didn't even hear a groan. He hoped like hell Mikey was still breathing.

"Hey, Bonner!" Frank called, rattling keys. "Seeing how you got Deputy Mikey to come back here, I'll let you out, too, see if I don't. Ain't sleepy now, are you?"

Davy heard a nervous laugh from the cell next door. "Naw, I ain't, Frank. You spring me loose, and I'll never say a word against you again."

"You better not." Keys rattled again. "Go on now before I change my mind."

By the time Bonner had scrambled up the hall and Frank had stepped over to Davy's cell, the boy was back on his bunk, sitting pressed into the shadowy corner.

"You want out too, young'un? I'm in a real good mood all of a sudden." Frank peered through the bars.

"Let's go, Pa, we gotta get out of here!"

"Yeah, yeah." Magnanimously, Frank unlocked Davy's cell door and swung it open, keys dangling in the lock. "I'll leave it up to you, boy. How's that? If you got enough smarts to take advantage, you're free to go." He ambled out after Chad.

It took a few seconds for Davy's guts to unclench, then he eased himself off the bunk, stuck his crutch under his arm, and swung out into the corridor. "Mikey?" he called. "You dead down there?"

A moan answered him. The deputy was conscious, barely. He breathed heavily through a smashed nose, through blood sheeting over his face. Davy sat on the cot, dropped his crutch, and hauled Mikey up beside him. He pulled the pillowcase off the pillow, turned it inside out, and pressed it against the gash on the deputy's forehead.

"I gotta go get your dad, Mikey. You try not to pass out, okay?"

"No," Mikey gasped. "Look at you, Davy, you're worse off than me."

Davy shook his head. "Can't be helped. You just rest, I'll make it, and Bally can drive me home." He picked up his crutch again, stood, and set himself for the hike to Bally's bar.

****

When Bud walked into his empty office the next morning and saw Davy's note, he swore heavily.

Gibsons broke out, smashed Mikeys face in, took off. He's at Bally's. I'm home.

Now he had half a dozen more problems. Calling in the two off-duty deputies, he sent them to check on the Gibsons. They'd be long gone to the Plains, no doubt, but a check had to be made.

"If the other boys are there," he instructed the deputies, "chase them off to school. Take the baby and that little one to the Corral and then make a sweep of the bars, just in case. Make sure Mikey's okay at Bally's. I'll be at Tom Redwolf's, or back here."

Davy'd been expecting him. "I wasn't right sure what to do, Bud. I wasn't trying to run out on you, honest, but I figured I better get help for Mikey, then I just come home. Didn't wanta be in that jail by myself."

"I don't blame you, Davy," Bud said. He pulled out a kitchen chair and sat down. "You'd best tell me what happened, right from the beginning."

An hour later, Davy felt better than he had since the shooting. His leg was playing hell, and so was his sore shoulder, but at least he was out of jail for now. Bud had agreed to let him stay home as long as he promised to show up for the judge on Court Day. As soon as the pain pill he'd taken had kicked in, he'd stump on over to Old Willie's place.

****

Jessie, I'm outta jail for now, still have to see a judge, but it'll be okay. Can't wait to see you again, Jessie. I love you so bad. When them Cabins opens back up, we can talk to somebody and make it okay for me to see you. All my love, Davy

Jessie pressed the note against the bulge of her stomach. Davy didn't understand, but she did. Nothing was going to make the Rightside authorities change their minds about Davy. He'd never be allowed into a Red Cabin again as long as he lived. And since she didn't want to live without him, where did that leave her? She was hiding her feelings about Davy from everyone but Tenosha.

Jessie needed a plan. She had one in mind, but couldn't do it alone. First things first, though. She couldn't wait to write back.

Later that afternoon, toward the end of her shift, Jessie took a prescription bottle to the Transfer Room at the hospital. This would be her first try at sending "medicine" to the male baby who supposedly had a kidney condition on the other side of the Fence. Rather than pills, though, the brown glass prescription bottle held gold coins wrapped in a rolled-up note for Davy. The bottle's label specified it held one week's worth of pills to be crushed and given to the baby with milk. A urine sample would be required in return before another prescription was written.

180

The procedure was a little unusual, but not unheard of. Jessie knew of a few other male babies that were being regularly supplied with prescriptions from Rightside. She'd forged Dr. Goschalk's signature from the beginning, and could only hope no transfer clerk would ever check on it.

Casually, but as though she were a bit in a hurry, Jessie handed the bottle to Sashi.

"For the same baby, Sashi. Looks like these pills will be regular transfers for a while."

The clerk, too busy for chatting, reached out a hand for the bottle, her eyes still on a computer screen. "No prob, Jessie, just drop 'em off when you get 'em."

Jessie let out a breath she didn't know she'd been holding. "Will do."

The note had taken a lot of thought to get it just right. She couldn't upset Davy, but they had to start working on a plan. She wanted desperately to tell him about the baby, but she was afraid he'd go crazy again. Better to wait. She also had Tenosha to think about.

Davy,

All my love comes right back to you. Can you feel it? I can't wait to see you again, either, but it won't be as easy as you think. I'm working on a plan, but it'll take a while, so please be patient. You concentrate on healing. You'll need both your legs for what I have in mind. A friend is helping me. Her name is Tenosha, and she had a baby boy on February tenth. Do you know a man who got a black-haired baby boy on that date? Tenosha wants to know if the baby is okay, and if his father is good to him. Keep the plastic bag I put the note in, and seal your own note inside it. That way your note can stay dry because you have to pee in the bottle.

I said the doctors need to test a sample from the pretend baby. I fixed it for us to trade notes once a week. It's too dangerous to write more often.

All my love, Jessie

Chapter 17

Simeon stood with his hand on the doorknob, his heart beating heavily with anticipation. They'd had a dry spell here in Jackson Hole while their Red Cabins were closed for "maintenance." Everyone knew that meant new security measures after the to-do up in Cody, but no one had questioned the women on it. Safer not to.

It seemed a longer wait than usual, but as soon as the buzzer sounded, he turned the knob and walked through the men's door. He looked first at Toller, then snuck a discreet sideways glance at the security camera. It was recessed into the ceiling farther than it had been, but he could still see that the light was off. Simeon could only assume that was Toller's doing. She seemed to be a woman of some influence in Rightside.

He was right, though Toller had of course never admitted that. She'd slipped a few gold coins to the clerk in the viewing room. "You know the cameras always take the fun out of for me," she'd confided quietly. "I didn't even want one my first time, but they insisted. I can't enjoy sex if I know someone is watching. Can you do me a favor? Leave it off in my room?"

"Of course, ma'am," the clerk agreed, making the pieces disappear into a pocket. "We don't expect any trouble. The cameras are just on for a few days for insurance."

"Thanks, honey." Toller was more relieved than she admitted, even to herself. She didn't give a hoot about a clerk watching her have sex, but she needed privacy for this visit. She wanted to expand her illegal Wrongside smuggling business and had decided to take a dangerously exciting step to make that happen.

Now she smiled a slow, heavy, wanting smile at Simeon. It had been a serious dry spell for the women, too.

A long time later Toller walked out of the bathroom, indulging in a luxurious stretch that she knew highlighted her lush, well-kept body. She needed Simeon on tenterhooks for this conversation.

"Let's talk business." She sat on the edge of the bed, not bothering to pick up a robe or even a sheet. Idly, she reached out to trail a lacquered nail over Simeon's thigh. "I've been thinking about that sheriff of yours."

Simeon's mouth dropped open, but he shut it abruptly. He was walking a tightrope and couldn't afford to slip up.

She resisted an urge to check that the camera light was still off. Simeon might catch that, and no man needed to know about the cameras.

"It's safe to talk," she told him. "I made sure of that."

"Okay." He gusted a relieved sigh. She didn't suspect that he knew about the cameras, and they'd maneuvered safely into forbidden territory. "About you meeting one of our customers?"

"I'm willing," she said immediately. "He'll come to me, of course."

"You are?" He gasped. "You'd meet that hick sheriff who thinks he knows good art? That's dangerous."

She brushed aside his protest. "Don't you see? It's the perfect time. Rightside is still in an uproar. No one's thinking about anything but the Red Cabins and our security. You men are probably thinking about the same thing. No one's going to care if an enterprising businesswoman finds a new sales outlet."

Simeon forced himself to stay calm. "It's a hell of a stretch to call smuggling a sales outlet." He wanted no part of this deal. In the first place, it was damn dangerous. He didn't have any boys yet, and this was the kind of thing that could get him barred from the Red Cabins for life, like the kid up in Cody. And if that sheriff started meeting Toller, it would cut him out of the loop. She'd sell directly to those hicks up north, and where would that leave him? Did he dare protest?

Toller laughed. "I can practically see the wheels turning inside that handsome head of yours," she said. "Stop being so jealous." She waved a dismissive hand through the air. "Of course I'll cut you out, but so what? You'll still have the sales here in Jackson Hole. There's plenty of money to go around."

She stood up and reached for her clothes. "And Simeon, be happy with what you've got. I can take it away, you know. I like you, and we have great sex, but you're not that important now that I have another connection. Set it up for me, be a good boy. I'll see you again next week, and you can let me know when the sheriff will be here."

****

Simeon was seething when he walked out of the

Red Cabin. Who knew how long it would take that damn sheriff up in Cody to get back to him, then arrange time off to come to Jackson Hole to meet Toller. It all had to happen in a week. Simeon was not about to jeopardize what little profit he was still making from Toller.

****

Bud had to get off the fence. The next step of the cockamamie plan to find his daughter had been taken. He had an appointment to meet Toller Sheridan, the Rightside art dealer in Jackson Hole, in two days. Now, how was he going to handle the next step after that?

"Bally," he said, walking into the bar well before the Saturday night rush. "Need to talk to you privately."

Bally scanned the mostly empty room, then nodded to a table of poker players in one corner. "Let me set the boys up fresh, then we can talk down here." He jerked his chin toward the far end of the bar.

Bud ambled along the bar and got out a gold coin. Bally was a good friend, but everyone knew he didn't talk with a dry throat.

They were halfway through their first beers before Bud spoke. "I got a plan in mind," he began. "And it's complicated."

Bally took a deep draft. "I love a good story," he said. "Start at the beginning."

Bud took a deep breath. *Get off the damn fence*, he ordered himself. "Lately, I've been wondering if I might have a daughter." He had expected disbelief, mild shock, or even laughter. What he hadn't expected was Bally's thoughtful nod of understanding.

"I've had the thought myself," Bally admitted. "All these years, I've only ever got Mikey. No way of

186

knowing if any girls came out of all those Red Cabin meetings. Makes me sad, or lonely, or something, I dunno."

Bud nodded in his turn. "There might be a way. But we need help."

****

The meeting took place late Sunday morning, up on the Plains. Bud and Bally had decided they couldn't risk a public meeting. Bud took Doc Medina to an isolated dry wash north of Cody with the excuse that he wanted to show him where some medicinal herbs grew. Willie had deliveries to make that morning, and Bally offered to drive him, then with no explanation, he continued up to the wash.

"The hell you going?" Willie complained. "I got to get back, even if it is Sunday."

"We got a meet with Bud," Bally grunted, and Willie shut up fast. Whatever the sheriff wanted was fine with Willie.

Bud had a thermos of coffee, and the four men squatted on rocks placed around an ancient campfire site. Willie sat as far from the others as he dared. He didn't want to be involved in this, whatever it was, no, sir.

Bud told them his story, beginning to end, then waited for the questions and protests. He knew Bally was on his side. He just needed to satisfy the other two. The protests, predictably, came from Willie.

"Bud, you know I gotta keep my nose clean," he whined. "I can't be involved in a crazy plan like this. If I lose my job—well, Bud, you know how it'd be. You don't have any boys, neither. If I lose my job, what'll I do? Where'll I go? You've got to let me outta this, right now. Bally?"

"Hush for a minute, old man," Bally said. "Doc, what do you think?"

Medina looked from Bud to Bally, and back again. "I guess it's time to tell them my tale."

After Doc had recited the story of Milina and his abortive efforts to get to her, Willie was speechless. Bally just looked at Bud and nodded his head slowly.

"It's been seventy-one years things have been this way, but yours aren't the only stories I've heard just lately. I wonder if the system ain't starting to crack apart under the weight of its own stupidity. Whatever the women say, it ain't natural, never was. Not on old Earth."

"You've said it yourself," Bud reminded him. "It ain't only about the separation between men and women. We've talked about the stagnation in Wrongside, and how we could never match Rightside in manufacturing, or education, or anything. How keeping men and women apart was bad for the whole planet. If we can put just one little chink in the Border Fence, maybe I can find out whether I have a daughter. Maybe Doc could find out whether that woman really wanted to give him up. If we could just do those two things, it might inspire other people and things'll start to change for the better."

"What would you even do if you found out you had a daughter, Bud?" Willie was bursting with indignation. "What damn good would it do you?"

"Maybe I could meet her." Bud's intensity was fierce. "I have a daughter somewhere. I know I do. I want to meet her, look in her eyes, and know I'll leave someone behind when I die. Aren't you ever curious,

Willie? You and me, we might not be childless after all. Don't we have a right to know?"

"I don't have to know, Bud," Willie blurted. "Who cares if I have daughters? Why should it worry me?"

"Because they're *yours*, don't you see? Just because they're female doesn't mean we don't have a right to even know about them."

Bally weighed in. "He's not wrong, Willie. Them women been holding us down for so long we think that's the way it has to be. And it just ain't." He reached out a booted foot and slammed it against the rocks of the old fire pit, scattering flaky ashes into the air. "It don't have to be like this."

"And it's not just about babies, either," Bud continued. "I've read enough of your antique books, Willie, to know Earth wasn't the same as this. There were no Border Fences, no Transfer points, and for sure no Red Cabins. Women and men lived together, in the same houses sometimes, and they shared everything. There's no reason it couldn't be that way here. If I like a woman, if I want to be with her, I should be able to just go over to her house and visit her."

The very thought scared them all, even Bud. Could any of them dare to walk into Rightside? Could they find a woman's house and go to her without an appointment or anything?

Willie shuffled his feet in the dirt. "You're as crazy as them two kids," he muttered.

Bally reached out to grasp Willie's arm. "What kids?" he asked quietly.

Willie coughed. "Nothin'," he said. "Forget I said anything. It was just some kids talking, that's all."

"Who was talking?" Bally insisted. "What were

they talking about?"

Willie cursed himself for a fool. He was the transfer man, for Yong's sake. But he knew Bally wouldn't let up, and he knew Bud had a point, scary as it was.

"Babies," he muttered. "They're talking about babies. And I need me a goddamn truck."

They had to drag the story out of him. Bud was elated. Even Davy, who was just a kid, like Willie said, had been wondering. How many other men, all over Wrongside, wondered?

"Let's lay it out," Bud said. "Davy can't help us much right now, with his leg and all, but he's already got regular communication with his woman. It's another chink in that damn Fence. All we gotta do is figure out how to use it. When I talk to this art dealer, this Toller Sheridan, I'll buy a piece of art, then tell her I'm the sheriff. I've been chasing smugglers, I'll tell her, and now I've got proof she's involved. I'll threaten to turn her in to the Rightside sheriff if she don't do what I want."

Doc stirred. "You mean find out if we have any daughters."

"That'll get us somewhere, I figure."

Chapter 18

Davy lurched around the cabin, gathering supplies for Hud—diapers, a doll, an old blanket, bottles, and milk in a metal cooler. He added some knuckle bones for Hud to chew on since Pop said the kid was about to get his first teeth. Davy's leg still ached all the time, but he could stand it. Him and Jessie had a plan, and it was time to get started. His heart was bursting with the thought of it.

He limped to the window again. Tom had been gone to work for an hour already, but Davy had to wait for the moons to rise. *There it was.* While he'd been getting the baby's stuff together, the first full moon had finally swum into view on the horizon. *Now!*

In a sudden rush, he hauled the supplies outside and threw them into the bed of the truck, then went back for Hud. Slinging his brother under one arm, he maneuvered out the door and into the truck. Ropes were already tied around the bench seat, and he corralled Hud into them, tight enough so the kid couldn't get loose but not so tight he'd squall over it.

"Stay," he ordered the baby. "You been in the truck plenty. You know you can't move around in here." Hud could sit up pretty reliably, and the bones occupied him for now. Davy drove fast.

He had a particular spot in mind on the Plains. It took almost an hour to drive as far as he could up the rutted North Road. He turned east at the lightning-blasted tree he remembered, then bumped up a steep hill, which men called the Sleeping Woman, for another half-mile.

As he neared the Fence, he clicked the headlights off, swung the truck around in a half circle, and parked twenty feet away. This was the spot he'd found a year ago, on a hunting trip. It had just been creepy then, but now he could see exciting possibilities.

The truck was sitting on high ground here, well above the North Road. Below the truck the Fence sat in a natural gully. It was twelve feet tall and topped with razor wire, regulation for an area with no buildings, but he was far enough above it that Davy could just see over the top from his seat behind the wheel. On the women's side, there was a road running parallel to the Fence, with another road bisecting it.

"This is the place, Jessie," he whispered. "I know it'll work."

"Want to get outta these ropes, kid?" he asked Hud. The baby crowed obligingly. Davy grabbed his crutch and stumped around to the passenger door. Leaning against the side of the truck, he lifted Hud out and plopped him down into the truck bed against the back of the cab. Arranging the bones, a filled bottle, and the rag doll where Hud could reach them, he prepared for the next step.

He wasn't stupid. He knew he couldn't mess this up because if he did, no one in Wrongside would know where they were. Hud could—but he brushed that thought aside. He'd be careful.

Years ago, Pop had welded a step just in front of the fender on each side, so they could reach things in the bed more easily. He dropped his crutch into the bed, set his good foot onto the step, and heaved himself upward, twisting as he went. His butt landed hard on top of the side rail, and he almost overbalanced, but it worked. Hud gurgled his delight.

Moving carefully, Davy swung his legs, one at a time, over the side and stood up in the bed, this time leaning next to Hud against the back of the cab. Reaching through the open back window, he snagged the strap of Tom's binoculars, pulled them out, and set them carefully to one side on the roof of the cab.

Then, balancing his good foot in the window frame, he set his hands on the roof of the cab and hoisted himself onto it. For a few seconds, he felt like a landed fish, squirming on his belly and searching for leverage. Finally, he worked his good knee into position and was able to pivot until he was sitting upright.

Now, he thought, *we'll see*. Facing the Fence, he lifted the binoculars. *Yes!* He could see over the Fence. *Oh, Mother*, he swore. *I'm looking into Rightside.* Most of the view was through razor wire, but that was all right. He was looking at a gentle rise of farmland. He couldn't tell what kind of crop was growing, but he didn't care. A dirt road ran straight into the field from the paved road at the far side of the field. He couldn't see the Rightside base of the Fence, but it looked like the dirt road ran all the way to it.

Had Jessie found it? He'd measured the miles from the Cody transfer cabin as carefully as he could and described both roads in his last letter. It was perfect.

Davy reached into his shirt pocket and withdrew his slingshot and a stone. A note was already tied carefully around the stone. Aiming for the dirt road, he shot them over the Fence. Paper and rock shone in the light of the full moons. If Jessie was there, she couldn't fail to see them. He waited.

Did he hear a rustle? He couldn't tell. He wanted to call out but didn't dare. He waited. His bad leg was throbbing. He didn't dare to move.

"Davy?" It was barely a whisper.

"Jess?" He called back. "Jessie, is that you?"

"I'm here, Davy!"

"Oh, Mother! Mother, Jessie, I'm here, too! Can you get on top of your truck? Maybe we can see each other, is it safe? Are you safe, Jessie?"

"There's no one here. I came down this dirt road with the lights off. Wait a minute."

Davy heard scrambling sounds, then saw her shape through the razor wire. He whipped the binoculars back up, then started waving frantically. "I can see you!" he shouted, "Jessie, I see you!"

Jessie had her own binoculars. "Me, too! Oh, Davy, it's so good to see you, even in the dark."

"I got something to show you!" he called. "Wait a minute!" Swiveling again, he lay on his side. He hooked his good foot into the open driver's window for leverage and reached down to the baby with his good arm. "C'mon, Hud," he urged. "C'mon, grab my hand."

Hud reached up obligingly. Davy took hold of the baby's arms and heaved. Hud screamed with delight as Davy hoisted him into the air.

"Look, Jessie," he called over, "this is my brother, Hud!"

"Oh!" Jessie stared hard, entranced by the sight of a male baby older than a newborn. What a thing to see! She couldn't help but wonder whether her baby would be female or male. Seeing Hud trying to imitate Davy's wave, she could almost wish—"Davy, he's adorable, I'm so glad you brought him!"

He hesitated over the unfamiliar word. Adorable? Then he let it go. He had important news to share. "We got him on February tenth, same day your friend's baby was born. There were two that day like you said. Hud's got black hair and dark skin like us, and the other baby is blond and light-colored, like his pop. What color is your friend?"

Jessie gasped. "She's dark! Tenosha has dark skin too, and brown hair. Oh, man, Davy, your brother is probably Tenosha's baby. Wait'll I tell her! Davy, I'll have to bring her next time. Can you bring him again? What did you say his name was?"

Hud fell asleep eventually, then Jessie told Davy her news.

****

She couldn't settle down after her meeting at the Fence with Davy, so she spent the rest of the night thinking about an idea that had occurred to her when she saw Hud. What if her own baby was male? There was no way she was going to give it up, even knowing it would go to Davy. Could both of them go to Davy?

Was that possible? He'd told her before that he spent a lot of time in the north, where no one lived. On the Plains, he called them. She could empty her savings, take plenty of gold coins, get across the Fence somehow. Maybe they could build a house way up in the wilderness. Davy could drive to the nearest town once in a while for supplies. She'd plant a garden, and he'd hunt. They'd be so happy.

But what if it was a girl?

She'd go anyway. But she had to know.

****

It wasn't even difficult. Everyone was always busy in the hospital lab, and Jessie was a familiar face. She'd learned in school how to test for a baby's sex. It was illegal but sometimes allowed in cases where the baby's life might depend on a sex-specific problem. With placental cell samples she'd harvested from her own belly, she walked calmly into the lab, gathered some supplies, and set up the test. No one had enough time or interest to question what she was doing.

Chapter 19

Laran looked up from her breakfast when the back door opened. "Aunt Kai! Want a muffin?"

"Sure," Kai replied. "It won't change my bad mood, but at least it'll taste good."

"Why are you in a bad mood?"

Kai sighed. "Because the Constancy Party is trying to cause trouble again." She took a plus-size chocolate chip muffin and plopped into a kitchen chair.

"What is it this time?" Alanna demanded, sweeping into the room. "Snide allegations? Sabotage? Outright lies?"

"Wow," Laran observed. "The Constancy Party sounds really mean."

Kai and Alanna burst out laughing. "Now that," Kai admitted, "changed my bad mood."

"So which is it?" Alanna reached for the juice pitcher and poured a glass for her daughter.

"Sabotage. I just got a report from the chief engineer up at the dam."

"Oh, man." Alanna swore. "We got a status update yesterday, and everything was fine."

"That was yesterday. Today they're reporting trouble with one of the generator sheds. It looks, they say, like someone broke in through a window, took a hammer to the generator, and cut holes in the fuel barrels. A watchwoman heard the noise and investigated, and that's probably the only reason a fire wasn't set as well."

"The whole job site could have gone up," Alanna murmured. "It almost had to be someone from Constancy, didn't it?"

Kai nodded. "Given the nature of it, yes. They want people to see our dam project as badly run and inefficient."

"And remember, the Constancy chairwoman wants my job. I'd guess she's the ringleader of whatever's going on."

"We need to keep an eye on Maud Adams, too, even though she's officially Fidelity. She started out in the Constancy Party, after all. I've seen her whispering with Constancy members more than once lately."

"She doesn't have any reason to love me, either, since I've been so hard on her."

"Why are you hard on her, Mama?" Laran had finished her muffin and was slurping down orange juice.

"Because repairing the dam should have been her job, darn it. She's my Interior Secretary, remember? That's what Interior Secretaries are supposed to be concerned about, and she wasn't."

"So there," Laran said complacently, echoing a favorite family saying.

"So *there*," Alanna laughed. "I showed her, didn't I?"

"That's because you're the boss, Mama."

"I am," Alanna agreed. "Go brush your teeth, and we'll walk you over to school."

"I had a report from Security," Kai said.

"Oh, right, I forgot to ask you about it."

The Security Cabinet managed all the women's security operations. It oversaw maintenance of the Fences, coordinated with Red Cabin supervisors, and controlled the high-flying drone cameras that kept watch in Wrongside.

"It seems that Bud Hopper told Diana the truth. Men are talking about the lynching in Red Cabins all up and down the Fence. They're grumbling too, but the report says it's nothing serious. With the New Washington Red Cabin opening again, they're content."

"Give them sex, and that's all they need?"

"Pretty much. Remember what our grandmas always said, that men think with their penises."

Kai wrinkled her nose. "That's disgusting. But true." She stood up. "I hear Laran thundering down the stairs. Let's go, boss. You have dams to finish and enemies to watch here in Rightside, without worrying about Wrongside."

****

Giulia had been called to another secret meeting. She hesitated at the door to Maud's office. "Are you sure you need me?" she quavered. "I'm pretty tied up today."

"Have a seat, dear," the chairwoman said. "We won't take up much of your time. Maud, what do you hear from the dam?"

"Things didn't go quite as we'd planned. A watchwoman heard the noise and prevented a fire from starting."

"Man!" the other woman swore. "That won't even be seen as Fidelity mismanagement, just vandalism. No one was caught, were they?"

"Thankfully, no, but we won't use them again."

"What about the other ideas?" Maud asked.

"One is already underway," Maud replied. "In two days, there'll be a massive, spontaneous demonstration by unemployed construction workers on the Government Building lawn."

Giulia protested. "But most of them have gone back to work already. They don't need to protest."

Maud smiled in a way that made Giulia shiver. "Need is such a useless word in politics, dear. Haven't you learned that? Of course, they don't *need* to protest. That isn't even the point. The point is the negative publicity that the Fidelity Party will face. The newspapers and television stations will jump all over this demonstration just for the excitement. Dear Alanna and her party will fall back on facts and figures, but no one in Rightside will really believe them. All they'll remember are the protests."

"And our next big gun?" a co-conspirator asked.

"We'll save that until the furor over the demonstration dies down. It'll succeed brilliantly," Maud asserted. "It can't fail, and it will damage Fidelity so badly that they won't win a single seat in the mid-term elections."

"Bold claim," another woman said drily.

"See if I'm not right."

Giulia knew she shouldn't ask. It would be much safer to remain quiet. But she couldn't help herself. "What's the big gun?"

"I'm glad you asked," Maud sneered. "We're going to need your expertise on this one. You were Alanna's campaign manager, so the proof will have to come from you."

****

"I've been taking care of babies ever since I started nurse's training," Jessie told Tenosha. "Female and male. But seeing Hud the other day, I don't know. He stirred something new in me. He's almost a toddler, Tennie. He waved at me and smiled. He has his own little personality already, just like a regular baby. Imagine!"

"I can't wait." Tenosha sighed. "I stopped taking those post-partum depression pills, you know. I actually feel better without them. I'm not crazy. I'm going to meet Hud with a clear head and know I'm a mother."

The two were traveling north in Jessie's little aqua car, headed for the farm road where Tenosha would be able to look across the Border Fence and see her son for the first time.

"Tom, my baby's father—he doesn't know I'm going to see Hud, does he?"

Jessie frowned. "I don't think so. From what Davy said, Tom works at night."

"I wonder if I should talk to Tom myself. I could make an appointment and tell him I've seen Hud. Would he get mad, do you think?"

Jessie laughed. "Flummoxed is the word that comes to mind. Since when has a woman ever wanted to see her baby boy?"

"I wonder…Jessie, I can't be the only woman who feels like this. Can I?"

"Tennie, I can tell you that you aren't." She took her eyes off the dark road long enough to give her friend a troubled look. "My baby's a boy," Jessie blurted out. "There's a test you can do, an illegal test. I'm going to have a son, just like you did." She slammed her foot on the accelerator. The car shot forward. "And I'm not going to give him up."

Tenosha gasped. "How? You can't do that, I mean, how could you keep a *boy* in Rightside?"

"I'm not going to keep him in Rightside."

It took Tenosha a minute, but when she realized what Jessie was saying, she clapped a hand to her heart. "You can't mean it. What about the men? The men wouldn't let you live over there either, would they?"

"I doubt it." Jessie frowned. "I have this idea, though. Davy doesn't even know about it yet. I'm going to smuggle myself through the Fence before the baby's born, and Davy and I can live up on the Plains. That's what they call the whole northwest part of Wrongside. Hardly anyone lives up there, and we could build a little cabin, just the three of us."

"You mean you'd, you know, live *together*? With Davy? In the same cabin?"

Jessie grinned. "Shocked you, didn't I? Davy won't be able to believe it, either. Women and men haven't lived together since the first few months of the colony. But you took history in school, just like I did. You know that women and men lived together all the time on Earth. It was called marriage. Remember?"

"Sure, but that was back on Earth. Not here, not in Rightside."

"Nope, not in Rightside, or Wrongside, either. Up there on the Plains, though, who's to tell us we can't do it?"

Tenosha was silent for a full minute. "Man," she finally swore. "Oh. Man."

"I know." Jessie grinned. "It boggles the mind, doesn't it? Look, I think this is the road."

Tenosha's heart took a leap. She was going to

see—well, she might as well get used to saying it. She was going to see her son.

Jessie had already turned off the car's lights. She inched down the rutted farm track toward the Fence, using the light of gibbous moons. Thank Milina, it was a clear night.

"Okay," Jessie said. "Now we climb up on the roof. I brought a rubber mat this time, so it won't be so slippery. I almost fell off the first time."

"You brought the slingshot, didn't you? I can't wait to see if Hud likes the toy I brought him." She picked up the pink and white stuffed dog she'd bought nearly a year ago when she first got pregnant. They were going to try to shoot it over the Fence with Jessie's old toy slingshot.

"I'll bet five gold coins Hud's never seen a pink and white stuffed animal before. Remember, Davy said his favorite toys were deer bones." Both women crinkled their noses in disgust.

They threw the mat on top of the car and climbed up. Jessie had binoculars, and Tenosha held tight to the toy dog and the slingshot.

"I see him!" Jessie cried. "Davy!" she called, careful to pitch her voice just high enough to carry across the Fence.

"Hey, Jessie!" he called back, waving his good arm. "Did you bring your friend?"

"This is Tenosha. Do you have Hud? You brought him, didn't you?"

"Hang on." Davy leaned down, said something the women couldn't hear, then sat back up holding his brother. Boosting with his weak arm and lifting with the good one, he raised Hud as high as he could.

"Oh, Hud!" Tenosha breathed, tears already running down her cheeks. "You're so beautiful! Oh, you're adorable!"

Davy snorted. There was that word again. "Adorable" must mean something all tender and sentimental to the women, because now he thought Jessie was crying, too. Mother, women were strange.

Jessie, who had won awards for slingshotting, archery, and riflery at Scout camp, was able to shoot the toy dog straight into Davy's chest. Hud immediately grabbed it and put it into his mouth.

"That's so cute!" Tenosha cried. "Look, Jessie, he's just like a regular little baby! Oh, Jessie, there's really not much difference between girl and boy babies, is there?"

"Nope," Jessie agreed. "Not much difference at all. Hey, Davy, I've got some news. We're going to have a boy baby, too!"

"A b—b—did you say a boy? I'm gonna get a boy? Oh, mother, Jessie, I'm gonna get a boy!"

"No, silly, I said *we're* going to have a boy. Both of us. Together."

Davy was confused. "Well, sure. I mean, we both made him. But you won't get to keep him, will you? I'll get him. Baby boys go to their fathers. That's the law, ain't it?"

"Yes, of course. But we have to talk about it, Davy, and we can't do it by shouting over the Fence. I have a plan. I'll have to explain it all in a letter."

Davy hadn't heard anything after "Of course." *A boy! Wait'll I tell Pop!*

"Davy?" It was Tenosha. "Can you tell me all about Hud? Does he have any teeth yet? Can he clap his hands or wave bye-bye? Can we get him to wave? Wave to Mama, Hud! Is he crawling good? Does he try to talk yet?"

The women stayed for two hours and would have stayed longer, but Hud fell asleep again, and Jessie had an early shift at the hospital. Tenosha waved goodbye anyway and looked back, tears running down her face until long after the road was out of sight.

****

Davy, my heart,

I think of nothing all day long but you and our baby. I can't live with the idea of sending our boy to you and never seeing either of you again, so I've decided that I won't. You've told me all about the Plains, how no one lives up there, and it has a dirt road that goes all the way to the ocean, but no one lives there, either. Well, why couldn't we? I can get across the Fence. I know I can. You could build us a cabin, and we could live there, just us and the baby, and nobody would bother us. I have enough gold coins saved to buy us a truck. You could hunt for food, and I could plant vegetables. Oh, Davy, we'd be so happy. Will you do it? I know you could take our baby and forget all about me, but Davy, don't you love me as much as I love you? Can't we try? Write back soon.

All my love,
Jessie

****

"For Yong's sake!" Maud Adams swore. "Where in Rightside did we go wrong?" Trailing behind, Giulia opened her mouth to answer, then shut it again. Whatever she said would be wrong. Giulia wished that she had never agreed to any of this. Subterfuge was not her strong point. She was just a treasurer. Well, the treasurer for the whole of Rightside, but that wasn't her doing, either. Alanna had come to her, impressed by her resume. *And now look at me.* Guilt was beginning to consume her. *If Mama hadn't needed money…*

"Keep up, can't you?" Maud strode across Government Plaza as though a raging horde of men were after her. Giulia scrambled harder, huffing and panting. "Maud, I can't move as fast as you!" *What will she make me do this time? Would they really dare to—? But Laran's so cute and friendly, and I can't—*

"Oh, yes, you can!"

Giulia gasped, certain that Eli had somehow heard her thoughts, but the legislator just wanted her to walk faster.

"We need to get some damage control in place, and we need to do it right now! Faster!"

Up the front steps, across the rotunda, more steps, and into Giulia's office. She collapsed behind her desk, heaving and clutching her chest.

"Don't have a heart attack on me, you twit," Maud sneered.

Giulia flushed even more. "I don't even think you—you need me." She gasped. "You can just lock up when you leave, okay?"

"Don't even think about it," Maud warned. "Our third incident hasn't brought us the results we need, so it's time for the last gun. You're our front woman for that, Giulia, so stay put."

The leader of the opposition Constancy Party swept in. "Give me the details," she said. "Is it as bad as I think it is?"

"No, no," Maud insisted. "Don't worry. We have

zero liability. No one will ever know we were the instigators. But I have to admit that it didn't go as well as we expected."

"That newspaper reporter didn't come through, for one thing."

"I won't forget it, either," the chairwoman promised. "If she'd just taken the bait, we might have had better results."

"I don't understand why no one seemed to believe Alanna took bribes from the contractors at the dam," Giulia ventured. "I did everything you said, fixed the books, so it looked like she'd accepted money."

Maud shook her head. "She skated out from under it somehow. Nothing seems to stick to that woman. She's golden. People are beginning to see how the economy is improving, and I have to admit she's kept her promises about infrastructure."

"Oh, right, let's all stop and sing Alanna's praises," the chairwoman interrupted. "Can we get on with it, please? Damage control."

Maud sighed. "That'll be up to me, I assume. I'm officially Fidelity, after all. Let's see. I'll issue a statement, using a different reporter, of course." She gestured to Giulia. "Turn on your screen and type for me. Hmmmm. Okay: Recent allegations dogging President Olaffson might be seen as an attack on her integrity. As a longtime colleague and friend of the president—"

"But you aren't!" Giulia broke in.

"—of the president," Maud continued with a glare, "let me go on record to say I have complete confidence in Alanna, and we in Fidelity throw our total support behind her. Even members of the Constancy Party are showing their support…

"It's rough," she admitted, "but it's a start. I want to appear to support her without addressing whether she's guilty. I may have to renege later."

"Not so fast," the chairwoman said. "Your complete and total support might be needed after we fire that last gun. Have you heard the rumor? Alanna's going full speed ahead with the crackdown on smuggling. We have to divert her attention quickly."

Maud nodded. "Let's finish this statement first. Then we can load the gun."

The woman sighed. "Right. Should we throw something about bipartisanship in there?"

"Why not?"

Chapter 20

It was just two weeks later that the conspirators drew that last gun. Giulia Saracco, shaking in her boots, approached Laran on her way home from school. How had she ever gotten herself into this appalling mess? Maud kept telling her it was necessary. They had no other choice, since their other attempts at discrediting Alanna and the Fidelity Party had failed. No one would get hurt, Maud promised again and again. It would only be for a few hours. Giulia was trying hard to believe that.

Giulia didn't even notice that summer had finally erupted across Rightside. The trees were in full leaf, and the sun shone more often than not. Laran wore her favorite purple shorts with a polka-dot T-shirt and matching sandals.

"Well, hi, Laran. It's nice to see you. Don't you look pretty? Do you remember me?"

Laran squinted and thought. "Ms. Giulia, right? Aren't you the Treasury secretary?"

"Oh, you remember me, aren't you sweet? You're so sweet," Giulia said in a rush. Her hands were shaking, so she pressed them together. "Remember when I told you about my dog, Fluffy?"

Laran bounced a little. She loved to talk about dogs. "Oh, I do! I keep asking my mom for a puppy just like yours, but she keeps saying no."

"I'm sure your mom knows best." Giulia brushed sweat off her upper lip and forged ahead, desperate to get it over with.

"But Laran, I was sort of looking for you today because I remembered you wanted a puppy."

"Today? You were?"

"Because I have one. I mean, my next-door neighbor has one. He's a white poodle just like my Fluffy, and my neighbor has to give him away because she's sick. He's only a few months old, and I thought of you right away.

"He'd be perfect for a lonely little girl like you. When you come home from school and your mom's still working, your puppy would be right there ready to play. I wanted him myself, he's so adorable, but I'm hardly ever home. Fluffy is used to being the center of attention, and two dogs would be too much for me, anyway." Giulia ran out of steam all of a sudden. "Want to come and see him?" she finished lamely.

Laran really wanted to see the puppy. Maybe she could talk to her mom about how adorable it was, and how much the puppy liked her. It would like her, she was sure. She'd have to remember that the puppy's owner couldn't keep him because she was sick. Then mom could see how important it was.

"I'm supposed to go straight home after school," she said reluctantly. "How close is your house, Ms. Giulia?"

Giulia fluttered a sweaty hand. "Oh, just call me Giulia. We're practically old friends. I live a block away, on Potomac Street. Come on, my neighbor will be happy to bring him over to my house, so you can play with him. I can't wait for you to meet him. He's such a wonderful little guy."

"Do you think he'll like me, Giulia? Can he shake hands or roll over? He doesn't bite, does he? Are male dogs mean and aggressive, like the men? My friend Keiko has a dog, and she does all kinds of tricks."

"No, he's a sweet little thing. So cuddly. And that's what's wonderful about having your very own dog," Giulia gushed. "You can teach him as many tricks as you want."

****

An hour later, Alanna left a committee hearing with Kai. The Energy Department had just issued final approval to install windmills on some underused farmland north of New Washington. It was an important victory that signaled progress in her restructuring plan. The dam was almost finished, and the first windmills would be installed before winter. While Congress was in such a conciliatory mood, maybe she should bring up her ideas about senior housing. As their population grew, it had become a problem.

"Got plans for dinner?" she asked Kai. "I feel like celebrating, and I have a new idea for our next project. We could try the new restaurant Martha told me about. Apparently the chefs do most of their cooking right at the table, and they're very flamboyant."

"Not another project," Kai laughed. "I've heard good things about the new restaurant though, so I'll be glad to try it out. Give me an hour?"

"No hurry. I'll get Laran, and we'll pick you up at six."

Kai sketched a wave and peeled off.

Alanna was whistling as she rounded the

government building to her quarters. It had been a good day.

"Hey, Martha, what's going on here?"

"Not a thing," Martha said. "Did I miss something with Laran's schedule today? She's isn't home yet."

Alanna frowned. "I don't think she had anything after school this week." She pulled a pocket calendar out of her briefcase and flipped through it. "Nope, nothing written here. I wonder if she went home with Keiko? The two of them have been working on a science project they're supposed to have finished next week."

Martha shook her head. "I think she'd have told me or called. Should we worry?"

Alanna hesitated, then shook her head. "If she isn't at Keiko's, she probably stayed after school for some last-minute thing. I'll go up and call her teacher and Keiko's mom, just to make sure. Oh, and don't worry about dinner. We're going out with Kai."

Martha nodded.

****

Jessie left the laboring woman with quiet reassurances. "You're doing great. It won't be long now," she promised. "I'm going to see if the doctor's gotten here yet, and I'll bring more ice chips."

Jessie escaped the labor room, thankfully. What a whiner. Who cares if it's her fourth pregnancy and she's sick of waiting for a girl? She'll just have to take her chances, like everyone else.

Jessie knew it was a mean thought, but she couldn't help it. She'd been on tenterhooks all day, waiting for Davy's reply to her last note. They weren't due to meet at the Fence for another three days, but she'd expected to hear from him before that. Why hadn't he answered? Had he gotten cold feet? Did he want to back out? Didn't he love her? Maybe she'd better check at the transfer cubicle again.

"Hey, Jess!"

Jessie whipped around in the hallway, expecting her patient wanted her again.

It was Birdie, the young clerk from the Transfer cubicle. Her heart lifted. "Got another request on that baby?" she asked.

"Yeah, the poor kid. I never thought I'd feel sorry for a male baby, but it seems like he's really sick."

"Oh, don't worry, it's not that bad," Jessie rushed to say. She didn't need people at the hospital to start speculating about her non-existent male patient. "He's fine, just needs regular medication that the men can't supply. We've done it before."

Birdie nodded, handing over the empty bottle. "Sashi told me I could just give it to you since I'm visiting my sister anyway."

"Oh, you have a sister here?" Jessie asked, casually dropping the brown bottle into her pocket.

"Dannai Bergenfeld. It's her fourth time, so we're all crossing our fingers."

"She's my patient." Jessie smiled. "Come on, I'll take you in. She's nearly ready."

Less than an hour later, Jessie handed Birdie her brand-new niece. "Here, Auntie, hold our little sweetie for a minute while I take care of Mom."

Dannai's entire family was on hand for the event. Jessie was glad for their happiness, but she couldn't help feeling a little resentful, as well. In the first place, they were keeping her from reading Davy's note, and in the second place, why couldn't they have been happy for Dannai's other children? For the three boys she'd sent across the Fence? Jessie touched her stomach, feeling almost insulted on behalf of her son. Why did giving birth to a son have to be the worst thing that could happen to a woman? Why couldn't everyone be happy for a healthy baby, no matter what the gender?

Jessie finally extricated herself from the happy family by claiming she needed to get some paperwork finished. In a back stairwell that no one ever used, she took a deep breath and pulled Davy's note out of the specimen bottle.

Jessie, my love –

I do love you so bad, Jess, don't ever worry about that. I believe you love me just as much. I already love our boy too, and we're gonna have a good life on the Plains. I know just the place to build our cabin. I can make it real nice for us. I figure it don't make much difference where I live because I hunt up on the Plains all the time anyways. If you can get us a truck, I'll do the rest. Jessie, we're gonna be a new kind of famly. When we meet, let's talk about how to git you over here.

All my love,

Davy

Jessie pressed the note to her chest. Ever since she'd been pregnant, she'd felt as though she was on a roller coaster. One minute she was fretting about whether Davy loved her, and the next minute she was delirious because he clearly did. One minute she was thrilled to share in Birdie's family's happiness and the next minute she was resenting all women who sent their male babies across the Fence.

It couldn't just be the hormones that made her feel so unsteady. It had to be because she was doing something absolutely new and unprecedented. At least it was unprecedented in Rightside. Since the day the women of the Earth colony had first imprisoned the men behind a makeshift fence, no woman had done what she was about to do. How many women had wanted what Jessie wanted, but hadn't been brave enough or smart enough to attempt it?

Well. She was brave enough. She was smart enough. She already had the beginnings of a plan for getting through the Transfer Door. She'd need to get some things from the pharmacy, and she'd need Tenosha's help. She also needed to concoct a believable lie for her mother and Diana. She couldn't tell them her actual plan, because they'd call a psychiatrist and have her committed. Maybe she could just casually announce a two-week camping trip and leave it at that.

The most important component of her plan was that Davy loved her. They were going to make this happen. They were going to be a family.

Chapter 21

Major Louise Gallech, newly promoted head of the Rightside Guard's special forces, was as nervous as a nineteen-year-old in a Red Cabin. She had never been lead on such a big operation before. She had never even met the president.

"Ma'am," she ventured, "if you can just stay calm and tell me—"

"How do you expect me to stay calm?" Alanna erupted. "I can't be calm. My daughter's missing! Do you get that? She's missing. She's nowhere she's supposed to be! Maybe she was hit by a car. Did you check the hospitals? Has anyone searched the park, maybe she fell in the lake, or—" Wild-eyed, Alanna stopped talking. She sank onto the couch where Martha sat, wringing her hands.

Alanna's quarters were filled with women. Word had spread fast. Besides Alanna, the household staff, and the major, Guardswomen were swarming through the rooms, tearing everything apart, looking for clues. Another team was down the block at Keiko's house.

"—tell me," the major repeated gamely, "whether she might have gone to a different friend's house—or a relative's house. Is there another name you can give me?"

Alanna was staring at the floor, biting her fingernails, so Martha answered. "All of their relatives live out of town," she said softly. "As for friends, there's Viki Musiolowski on North Street and little Cindee Meadows on Constitution Avenue. But I don't really think she'd have gone to either place. I don't know." Martha's voice broke.

Kai burst into the room and addressed herself to the major. "The Guard colonel just checked in. She said she couldn't get hold of you."

Louise snatched at the phone on her hip, thumbed the screen open. "I've got the message. I didn't hear it. Let me answer her." She strode out of the room.

Alanna looked up. "Kai." Tears glittered in her eyes.

The vice president sank to the couch beside Alanna. "I'm so sorry, honey. We'll get to the bottom of this, I swear. Laran's fine. I just know it. She's a strong girl."

That broke the dam in Alanna's heart, and she sobbed. Everyone in the room struggled to stay calm.

The major strode back in. "We're going to start a house-to-house search," she announced. "We'll begin at the school and spread out in all directions. Randi." She gestured to an officer. "Take the route the president gave you, form a squad, and move out. Another detachment will meet you at the school. I want you to start your search at the houses overlooking the plaza. Maybe someone saw something."

Half an hour later, Randi caught the first break. She called in to the major, still at the Executive Building with Alanna. "Ma'am, we have a witness who saw Laran at about three fifteen. Hilary Tarburner, 27 Schoolhouse Street. She likes to watch the girls going to and from school every day. She's pretty old but sharp. She knows Laran by sight, has seen her with her mother. She says Laran stopped on the Plaza to talk to a legislator. Washburn doesn't know the woman's name but says she's dark-haired, short, and heavyset. She's seen her on television."

"Dark hair, heavyset, legislator, television," Kai murmured. "Major, tell them to show the woman a photo of Giulia Saracco, the Treasury secretary. Maybe she knows where Laran was headed."

As soon as the first officer rang her doorbell, Giulia burst into tears. She was still sobbing, unable to talk, when she was brought to the police station. It didn't occur to her to lie.

"It was wrong of me, I know it, but Mama needed money! That's the only reason I listened to them. I had to help my mama. You see that, don't you? You can understand that. I would never hurt Laran. I thought we were just going to give Alanna a fright, I swear. She was just supposed to be distracted."

"Who was supposed to be distracted from what?" the major asked softly. She sat at her desk, across from the sobbing secretary. Kai, who had come in to observe, sat unobtrusively in a corner. Two Guard officers stood at the door.

Giulia looked up, tears streaming down her face, white with shock and fear. "From the—oh, I don't even know, I can't think about it! Just lock me up and throw away the key, but don't tell Mama!" She burst into fresh wails. "Don't tell Mama what I did!"

"Where's Laran?" the chief insisted. "Tell us that, and you can rest for a while."

"They took her," Giulia sobbed. "They wouldn't tell me where. But I told them not to hurt her. I'm sure they won't hurt her."

"Who took her? Who won't hurt her?"

It was a long night. Between sobs and self-recrimination, Giulia slowly gave up what she knew.

The major moved fast. Before Giulia had cried herself to sleep in a cell, three teams were assembled. Team One, headed by the major herself, would go after Maud Adams, thought to be the mastermind in charge. Team Two would slip out to surround the Constancy chairwoman's house. Team Three was headed by Kai Makele, who had talked herself onto the operation using her status as a Reserve Guard captain. The major didn't entirely approve of that, thinking Kai was too emotionally involved, but this was no time to complain. She decided to accept Kai's help and be grateful for it. Kai's team would sweep up the other conspirators.

****

By daybreak, the net was closed tight, but Maud Adams, who'd learned of Giulia's arrest, slipped through minutes ahead of the Guard. She was speeding north in a car registered to a fictitious name, on the run with her victim in the back seat.

Laran, hungry and frightened, was using her fear to fuel a righteous anger. "My mom's gonna lock you up and throw away the key," she threatened the woman in the driver's seat. She knew the woman was a legislator but had never met her or heard her name. "I know you just took me to make trouble for my mom. You better get me back home before she catches up with you. If you don't, I'll escape. I know what you look like!" she shouted. "I know this car's license number. I memorized it! When I get away from you I'll find a Guard officer and you'll be sorry. You'll be sorry you ever messed with me and my mom!"

"Oh, I'm real scared," Maud mocked. "You're a pretty tough little kid, aren't you? What makes you think you can get away from me? Are you going to beat me up? Just try it, girl. It'll give me an excuse to slap you silly."

Laran crossed her arms and held onto her anger. "Just you wait," she repeated. "You can't get away with this."

****

The news of Laran's abduction by members of the Constancy Party was all over Rightside by morning. It was all anyone could talk about. Jessie, getting ready for her shift at the hospital, watched the news with a growing sense of urgency. She felt sorry for Alanna, remembering how nice she'd been at Diana's Red Cabin and genuinely concerned about Laran. But at the same time, Jessie sensed an opportunity that shouldn't be missed.

This might be exactly the right time for her plan. Before she left for work, she called Tenosha.

****

Lulled by the drone of the car, Laran had finally fallen asleep near midnight. When she woke, it was morning and the car was still moving. She sat up and looked through the windows, seeing nothing familiar. It was a pretty place, way out in the country with big fields of corn. She didn't see any houses, though. "Where are we?" she mumbled.

"Almost there." Maud's voice was dry with strain and exhaustion. It was getting hard to think, to plan. She'd taken a random, circuitous route north, consuming hours and accomplishing nothing except, perhaps, to throw off pursuit.

"You better hurry," Laran said, "'cause I have to pee."

"If you wet yourself in this car, you'll be very, very sorry."

"And I'm hungry!" Laran shouted. "So hurry up!"

Maud slammed on the brakes, and the car screeched to a halt in the middle of the empty road. Laran, who'd unfastened her seat belt to lay down the night before, tumbled into the foot well and shrieked her indignation.

"Shut up!" Maud bellowed. "Shut up that caterwauling right now!" She reached over the seat, grabbed at the back of Laran's shirt, and hauled her up. "You're not even hurt, you little brat. Now listen to me. I won't take any shit from you today. You'll do what you're told, when I tell you to do it. Have you got that?" She gave the kid a hard shake to emphasize her orders. Laran burst into tears, and that satisfied Maud for the moment. "Put your seatbelt back on. We'll be there in ten minutes."

Laran wanted to ask where "there" was, but she didn't quite dare. She was hungry, thirsty, and scared, and her bladder was about to burst. Where were they? Where was the woman taking her, and why? *Where's my mom?*

Maud let off the brake and got the car up to speed again. She could only hope the safe house hadn't been compromised. That idiot Giulia hadn't known about it, but the others did. Maud had to assume they'd been picked up since they hadn't checked in with her on schedule. She was alone in this now. She needed sleep and time to think, but she'd have to get the kid locked away first. And fed, she supposed sourly.

****

Once the idea had popped into her head, Jessie's brain had gone into high gear. "This is the perfect time," she'd told Tenosha on the phone. "All Rightside is consumed with the news about the president's daughter. No one will think about Fence security for days till she's found, and this is my chance. I'm going through. I'll think of some way to send Davy an extra note this morning, then I'll say I've got a stomach bug or something and go home. It'll take all day, I figure, to get my savings out of the bank and pack some things, talk to my sister, then tomorrow you're going to help me smuggle myself across. I'll have a plan by then. You can get the day off work, can't you? You can help me?"

"Um. Yeah?" Tenosha agreed. "I guess if you think I can do it, then I can. But are you sure? Are you really going over to Wrongside? To stay?"

Jessie took a deep breath. She thought of Davy. Of their baby. "I'm sure. Gotta run now. Talk to you later."

****

Alanna hadn't slept all night. At mid-morning, she was still drinking coffee by the gallon, wild-eyed and exhausted at the same time. "Kai, I can't even blame Laran for going with Giulia. It's my fault. If I'd just gotten her a puppy when she asked…"

"Stop it!" Kai said. "There's no way we could have known what would happen. This is no one's fault but Giulia's."

"But we can't just sit here! What should we be doing? Don't you have any idea what to do next? Any?"

Kai, sitting across the kitchen table, was just as tired but holding herself together. She wouldn't fail Alanna, or Laran. "We all need rest, honey, but the hunt hasn't stopped. The backup teams are fresh and working hard. By the time the first teams are ready to take over again, we'll have new leads. We already know what kind of car Maud was driving last night. Guardswomen all over the country are searching for that car. She either has Laran or knows where she is. By the time you wake up, we'll be back on duty and heading out to rescue Laran."

"Wake up?"

Kai got up, moved around the table, and urged Alanna to her feet.

"Yes, honey, it's time to sleep now. You'll need to be rested and wide awake when we bring Laran home."

They would find Laran, Kai promised herself as she handed Alanna over to Martha. She poured more coffee into a go-cup and headed out the back door. They would.

Chapter 22

Kai was wrong. Maud's car had been spotted briefly at mid-morning, north of New Cleveland, but no one had seen it since. She'd gone to ground somewhere, probably with Laran. The Guard was expecting a ransom demand and recommended they all stand down till more information came in.

Kai hadn't settled for that. She'd commandeered a car and driver and sped up the highway with Louise. They were on a first-name basis with the major by now.

At noon the two were sitting in a bland conference room at the New Cleveland Guard station, still arguing about the standdown. "I can keep up the search with a small team, whoever's willing to stay with me. We'll start another house-to-house search here. I need to be moving, Louise. I can't just sit and wait."

"Sometimes that's the best choice, Kai," Louise insisted, "especially when your team is exhausted and out of options. You haven't slept in thirty-six hours. Neither have they. And you know we can't keep going indefinitely."

Kai sighed. "You're probably right. I should trust the process and let things develop. I know that. And I know I'm exhausted. We all are. I'll try to get some sleep after I call Alanna. I all but promised her we'd have Laran back by the time she woke up. She must be awake by now, and I should…" Kai waved a hand, too tired to finish the sentence.

"Why don't you let me do that?" the major suggested. She stood to signal the end of the meeting, and everyone stood with her. Discreetly, she motioned for an officer to take Kai out and find a bed for her.

Louise waited until she was alone in the room, then reached for a telephone. She hadn't slept either, but she was used to it. She was also a good many years younger than the vice president.

****

Maud had set an alarm, and was jolted awake by its strident clang after only three hours of restless sleep. She checked on the kid first. Laran was still sleeping in the locked bedroom they'd prepared for just this emergency scenario. A bathroom adjoined it. All the windows were securely locked and barred. Maud had left a bag of apples, some Guard ration bars, and water. The kid had everything she needed and could be safely ignored.

She needed to think rationally. She made a cup of coffee and unwrapped a ration bar for herself. Sitting alone in the safe house kitchen, she first allowed herself a moment of despair. Their plan had gone wrong almost from the start. It had been a bad mistake to use idiotic Giulia Saracco. They should have threatened the woman's mother, she now saw, instead of giving her money. Because of the idiot, they'd been revealed as the kidnappers almost immediately. The others almost certainly in jail by now, spilling their guts.

She couldn't stay at the safe house, that was clear, but it was only one of her problems. The plan had been to lock the kid in Maud's basement, never letting her see their faces. They would all have remained in New

Washington, sowing confusion, discord, and mistrust among the members of Congress. They'd have been able to keep attention on the kidnapping—and on Alanna's incompetence—for days while their smugglers moved as many shipments as they could through the Fence. They'd maximize profits while they could, then lie low afterward while Alanna fought to stay in power.

"She can't even keep her own family safe!" they would have trumpeted from the Congressional floor. "Women of Rightside, how can we continue trusting her to lead us?" A vote of no confidence would have been called, and that would have been that. Laran would have been released eventually, and idiot Giulia would have taken the blame and the fall. Kai would have had a convenient accident. Nothing fatal, of course, but nearly so. Then the way would have been clear for Maud, as a faithful Fidelity member, to move smoothly into Alanna's place as leader of Rightside. None of that was possible anymore.

"And now look at me," Maud muttered, "alone and in the wind with the brat, who's seen my face." No one was free to direct the smuggling operation, either, and when her team's assets were seized, which they surely would be, irregularities would trigger even more jail time. Not that Maud cared about that since she had no intention of going to jail; more importantly, she couldn't access her cash.

But there was no time to wallow in regret. She had to move. It was probably only a matter of hours before their location was discovered.

****

On the other side of the house Laran was awake

226

and working on her escape. The doors were locked, and the windows were barred, but she was going to get out if it killed her. No way would she stay here and let that woman tell her what to do. She wasn't gonna wait to be rescued, either. She was the president's daughter, and she was as brave as Milina.

She let her gaze wander over the room, around the door frames, over the walls, the ceiling. *Suspended ceiling*, she thought. That's what it was called when there were metal rails holding up big squares of ceiling tile. *This is just like the ceiling in Keiko's basement!*

It was an exciting thought because of the story Keiko had told her once about the ceiling in her basement.

There were lights above the ceiling, she remembered, and some of the tiles were see-through so the light could shine down. Once, Keiko had told her, her mom had popped one of the see-through tiles loose so she could change the light bulb. They just pushed right up, Keiko said, because there were no nails or anything.

"But as soon as she lifted the tile," Keiko had whispered dramatically, "a piece of snakeskin fell out— like a snake sheds its old skin? But there was no snake!

"And Mom freaked out big-time over that, 'cause where was the snake? It could have been anywhere, and Mom was practically in hysterics. She called an exterminator and everything, but they never found the snake. She says she still has nightmares that it'll slither out of her closet, or out from under her bed or something."

Laran wasn't afraid of a snake crawling out through the ceiling tiles, but she did wonder if a little kid could go where a snake had gone. Maybe if she climbed up on the dresser, lifted one of the tiles, and got up on those rails, could she crawl right over the wall into the next room? Maybe the door of the next room wouldn't be locked. Maybe she could—

****

Maud came in after loading the car with supplies and heard a thud from the back of the house. The kid was awake. Shit. She stomped back the hallway, key in hand.

"What are you doing in here, you miserable brat?" Maud threw open the door to see Laran's bare, skinny legs dangling from a hole in the ceiling. Overcome with rage and frustration, Maud rushed into the room and made a flying leap upward. Grabbing at Laran's legs, she yanked them down, heedless of the consequences. They crashed to the floor, Laran squirming to get free before they'd even landed.

Screaming obscenities, Maud lashed out, slapping and pummeling Laran into whimpering submission. By the time she'd worked out the worst of her rage, the kid's nose was bleeding, both eyes were puffing, and snatches of her hair littered the rug.

"That," Maud gasped, "is what you get when you make me mad. Not a word!" she added when Laran opened her mouth. "Not a damn word." She jerked Laran to her feet. "Not one damn word. Come with me."

By the time one of the co-conspirators traded the location of the safe house for a lighter jail sentence, Maud had been on the road for three hours. Laran was finally asleep, snuffling through a nose that was, Maud had to admit, probably broken. She'd seen little traffic on her chosen route so far, but that was about to change. She'd find a place to lay up soon, wait for dark, then ghost her way back into New Washington. There was still no better place to hide the brat and herself than her own basement. It would have been searched by now, crossed off the list.

She'd lay low for a week or two, let the worst of the womanhunt blow over while she worked out a way to disappear, tossing the brat out of the car somewhere along the way. It galled Maud to admit how badly their brilliant plan had failed. Their political careers were finished. Idiot Giulia and the others would languish in jail for years. Maud would spend the rest of her life in obscurity, scratching out a meager living instead of living her dream of being the one in control.

"There," she muttered, checking that no one was behind her before she pulled off the road onto a farm lane. Out of sight of the road, Maud backed into a copse of trees, locked the car doors, put the keys in her pocket, and racked back her seat to try and rest.

* * * *

When the sun hit the back seat of the car just before sunset, Laran woke up. She was thirsty again but too nauseated to be hungry. Her nose hurt like fire, and her eyes were puffy and sore. There was dried blood all over her face that smelled bad and was unpleasantly sticky. She had to pee again, too.

The woman's head was only a few inches from Laran. She seemed to be asleep, but Laran didn't want to find out. She eased carefully into a sitting position and tilted her head back to look around through the bottoms of her swollen eyes. They were in the country again, not even on a road. The car was surrounded by trees.

Why had they left the house? Maybe it was because of her, Laran thought with some satisfaction. The woman must have figured Laran would escape, so they were going somewhere else. She hoped all the woman's plans were messed up now, messed up so bad that she couldn't figure out a new one. *She'll get tired of driving me around*, Laran guessed, *and eventually, she'll just have to give up and throw me out of the car somewhere.*

She could deal with that, Laran decided. She'd been on camping trips with the Junior Scouts, and she could find her way home by looking at moss on the trees or something. When she got back to New Washington, everyone would be amazed. She'd be on TV, and her mom would be so proud of her.

Laran sighed. It was a nice daydream, but what about right now? She still had to pee, her nose still hurt, and she was still locked in the car with the crazy woman. She reached toward a door without much hope. Yep, it was locked. Leaning forward cautiously, she could see the empty slot where the car keys were supposed to be. If the woman didn't wake up soon, she decided, she'd have to accidentally kick the back of the seat to wake her up.

Chapter 23

"She was wearing a polka-dot shirt!" Kai reached out to take the torn scrap of polka-dot material from Louise. "This must be from Laran's shirt. But how did it get up there?"

The two of them looked up at the ceiling of the back bedroom in Maud's safe house. One of the tiles had been pushed aside. The scrap of material had been caught on a junction of support rails.

A woman in a Guard uniform who'd been crouched at the foot of the bed stood up. "Ma'am?" she addressed Kai. I'm Chetta Elton, crime scene investigation. I've got experience reconstructing crime scenes, and I have some ideas if you'd like to hear them."

"Of course," Kai said. "Let's hear from the expert because we're both clueless."

The Guardswoman walked over to the door. "I'll start here. The door has been opened and closed normally, no sign of tampering. There's a pretty sturdy deadbolt here, unusual for a bedroom, and these windows are barred. None of the others in the house are."

She moved to a desk and chair. "Take a look here at the half-empty bottle of water and pile of ration bars. This bag of apples has been opened, and there's a core in the wastebasket along with a bar wrapper. We can confirm with DNA testing on the apple core and water bottle, but I'm fairly sure already that this is where Laran was kept."

Kai and the chief nodded. "The scrap of material confirms that, too, but I still don't know what it was doing on the ceiling."

"There's no sign that Laran was tied or handcuffed, and it wouldn't have been thought necessary in a locked, barred room. I'm guessing the girl knew something about suspended ceilings."

Light dawned, and the major grabbed Kai's arm. "That's it! She must have known there would be open space above the ceiling. She could have climbed up on the dresser, moved a tile, and gotten into the crawl space. Her shirt must have caught on a rough edge of the rails."

"If that's true," Kai answered, "where is she?"

"I expect the Adams woman discovered her, pulled her down, and took off. She must have known we'd find this place eventually, anyway. And there's one more thing." The woman returned to the foot of the bed and pointed out a stain on the carpet.

"This is blood, I think. Not much," she added hastily as Kai gasped. "There are only a few drops. I see two possibilities. Laran may have cut herself as she tried the escape, or the kidnapper might have slapped her, caused a nosebleed."

"I have to sit down." Kai sank to the bed, shaking. "Is there any way we can keep that last idea from Alanna? She doesn't need to hear about drops of blood that might belong to Laran."

"She doesn't need to know," Louise agreed. "Obviously, the kidnapper is long gone. I'm not sure what our next move should be, but I've got a glimmer of an idea. Let's get some food ourselves, and we'll brainstorm."

Chapter 24

Parked outside her sister's house, Jessie tried a deep, calming breath. Her heart was racing, and a thousand different ideas clanged in her head. Her medical supplies and clothes, plus a few baby clothes, were ready in a backpack, and money was already secreted in the bag she wore cross-body above her midsection. It was a good thing, she thought distractedly, that she was going across the Fence now, before she was too heavy and ungainly in the last stages of pregnancy.

"Stop thinking about the Fence," she ordered herself. "You're not even going anywhere near the Fence, as far as Diana is concerned. You're going camping. You're going on a long camping trip with Tenosha, up north. We'll be back in a week." She got out of the door, took another deep breath, and started up the sidewalk. "In a week," she muttered. "That's all. Just a week for an innocent camping trip before the baby gets here."

She wasn't proud of lying to Diana, but with only a day to prepare, she hadn't been able to face telling her the truth in person. She had written a letter, though, explaining things more fully, and mailed it. Diana wouldn't get it for a few days. Jessie got out of the car, gave her sister's doorbell a token push, and opened the door.

"Oh, Aunt Jess, I want to go, too!" Trini exploded as soon as Jessie announced her plans. Trini turned to Diana with a pleading look. "Mom, can I go with Aunt Jessie? You said I could sometime, remember? Please, please?!"

Jessie had a bad moment when Diana laughed. If she had to take her niece their plans would all be for nothing.

"Of course you can go along, baby, on two conditions."

Trini bounced on the couch. "What are they? What are they? I'll wash dishes for a month straight and make your bed every morning."

"Wait till next time," Diana interrupted. "I did say you could go sometime, but you can't miss the leadership retreat. It starts in two days, have you forgotten? That's the first condition, that a camping trip doesn't interfere with your other commitments. The second condition is that Jessie invites you before you ask. She's going with her friend Tenosha this time, and maybe they don't want a teenager for company."

Jessie put her arm around a crestfallen Trini, and was careful to keep the relief out of her voice. "Of course we'd want you along," she lied, "but your mom's right. You were lucky to be invited to the retreat, and you can't just blow it off for a camping trip. Next time, I promise."

The guilt set in as soon as Jessie said her goodbyes and walked out to the car. Would there be a next time for Trini? Jessie didn't know if she'd ever leave Wrongside, once she got there. It was possible she'd never see her Rightside family again.

Searching her heart, Jessie knew that in spite of her

guilt over lying, in spite of her sadness at the thought of all she was leaving behind, she had no misgivings. This was the right thing to do. She and Davy and their son had to be together, to make a new family, and she'd give up anything to make that happen. Even her old family, if necessary.

Back at home, Jessie drove her car into the garage, something she rarely did. She pulled down the door, locked it, and went into her house. Everything was prepped for an indefinite absence. She'd cleaned out the refrigerator, set the climate controls for summer, and left every room in order. She changed quickly into sturdy hiking pants, filling the pockets with a compass, waterproof lighter, flashlight, and first aid kit. She added a belt with a loop for a water bottle, a loose, long-sleeved shirt, a hooded waterproof jacket, and the cross-body bag. With no hesitation she slung her backpack over her shoulders, walked out, and locked the front door behind her.

The sun was just disappearing over the horizon, but Rightside's small moons had already risen and would provide some light for her three-mile hike to Tenosha's apartment. From there, it would be a shorter distance to the hospital. Jessie set off at a good pace, thumbs hooked through the straps of her backpack. She breathed in the balmy night air, feeling good, feeling healthy. Baby Boy, as she'd been calling her son, seemed to like hiking.

The first stage of her journey to Davy took just an hour. "Everything's set, Tennie," she announced when Tenosha answered the door. "When I got to work this morning, a male baby had just been born, so I snuck a note inside his blanket for Davy. He'll have gotten it by now and will meet me when I get across the Fence."

She followed her friend back to the kitchen where Tenosha had been filling a bag with homemade cookies.

"Wow, those look good. Wish I could taste one."

"Here," Tenosha said, handing Jessie a smaller bag. "These are the plain ones for us."

Jessie didn't hesitate. "Mmmmmmmmmm! I guess I didn't think about dinner. I was way too excited. I did eat lunch, though, at the hospital cafeteria. I arranged for a week's vacation, then asked to leave after lunch so I could get ready for my trip. We were slow, so no one minded. I hit the supply closet before I left, so I've got everything I need for when Baby Boy arrives." She giggled. "Davy won't know anything about that, I guess. I'll have to coach him when the time comes."

Tenosha, remembering the harrowing experience of her own labor and delivery, shivered.

"Jessie?"

"Mmmm, what?"

"I've got to ask you something."

"What is it?" Jessie still munching cookies, wasn't paying much attention to Tennie. Her mind was too busy ticking through details of her plan. She pulled off her backpack and started searching its zippered pouches. Had she remembered to bring antibiotics, in case of—?

"I want to come," Tenosha burst out in a rush.

"Well, yeah, you have to come, remember? I'll need your help."

"No, I mean I want to come to Wrongside with you."

Jessie stopped her search. "You want to *what*?

Why? What possible reason could you have to—oh." Jessie let her backpack slip to the floor. "It's Hud, isn't it?"

Sudden tears slipped down Tenosha's cheeks. "I have to hold him, Jessie. I can't just look at him from a distance, with the Fence between us. I have to hold my son. You should know…"

Jessie nodded, tears in her own eyes. "I do know, Tennie. I do. But have you thought about the consequences? I don't know if I can come back. I might never see my family again, but it's a chance I'm going to take so Davy and I can choose our own lives. It'll be a new kind of family, with a mother and father right there together with their baby from the very beginning." Her breath hitched. "I don't know if I can come back. You've got your life here with your mom and your sisters and nieces. You could try again, maybe have a girl of your own."

Tenosha shook her head. "So could you. Would that be enough for you? To have a girl next time? Don't you see, Jessie, now that we know about our sons, we can't live without them. There's got to be something unnatural and wrong about that, I know, but we can't deny that we both feel this way. We have to be with our sons, and I'm coming with you."

Jessie nodded and reached out to hug her friend. They clung together, with Baby Boy between them, and gave in to the tears.

Tenosha eventually pulled back and wiped her face. "I packed a bag already and told my mom I was going on a camping trip with you. Okay?"

Jessie took a deep breath, then nodded. "Okay."

****

Bud wiped his hands down the sides of his pant legs. He was in the buffer between Wrongside and a meeting room, waiting to be admitted. On the other side of the door, if all had gone as planned, was the art dealer who could give him information about his daughter. He had to handle this right. The buzzer sounded. He reached for the doorknob, turned it, opened the door, and walked through.

Though they were in a Red Cabin, neither Bud nor Toller was thinking about sex. This was strictly a business meeting. Toller must be used to that idea, but Bud's head was still reeling over the idea of doing business with a woman. Should he shake her hand? Again, he wiped his right hand surreptitiously against his pant leg. He waited for her to speak first.

"Bud Hopper?"

He nodded. "You're the art dealer?"

It was her turn to nod. Without extending a hand to him, she moved to the snack table against one wall. "Have a seat, and we'll get down to business."

Bud cleared his throat. "Of course. Right." He jerked himself forward with an effort and managed to sit down without knocking over table, chairs, and all.

"Don't be so nervous. We're perfectly safe here."

Bud didn't dare look at the camera while she was watching. He'd have to trust the woman. She'd be in just as much trouble as he would, after all, if they were caught.

He pulled in a breath and willed himself to calmness. "I have money," he said, "and I'm ready to deal." In his pocket was a bag filled with every gold coin he owned, plus a generous amount from Bally and a somewhat smaller amount from Doc. Willie had insisted he couldn't spare any coins.

Toller smiled, but there was nothing friendly in her face. She opened a capacious bag. As she dug into it, Bud risked a swift glance into a corner of the ceiling. The camera was dark.

Toller took out four paper-wrapped packages and unrolled them to display four small sculptures. Bud drew in a sharp breath. Toller grinned again. "Beautiful, aren't they? There's no market for sentimental pieces like these in Rightside, Simeon probably told you."

Bud put out a tentative hand. "Can I?"

She nodded, and he picked up the first piece. It was from Kirannan, the mommy sculptor, one Toller had held back from Simeon. A tiny female child stood under an umbrella, laughing. She held one hand away from the umbrella's shelter as though to catch a drop of rain. Bud cradled the piece in his rough hands.

"I'll take this one myself," he said hoarsely.

In just half an hour, their business was concluded. Bud's money bag was down to its last few coins, but he'd managed the bargaining well enough to purchase all four pieces. He started re-wrapping them.

"You might as well take them out in this bag," Toller said, tossing it to him. "No one will question you on the other side, will they?"

"Naw," Bud said distractedly. "No one much cares in Wrongside."

"I suppose you don't," she murmured. She looked at her watch. "We'll need to stay here a while longer, I think. If we were doing ordinary Red Cabin business, we wouldn't be finished yet."

Bud sat up straighter. He'd been counting on this. "Just as well, Ma'am. I've got something else I'd like to talk to you about."

"More orders? We can't meet too often, of course, but I'll set up an appointment in about a month."

"Not orders," Bud began. "Well, I mean, yeah, that's great, the guys and me definitely want more sculptures, but I've got another problem you can help me with."

"I doubt that."

Bud waged a short mental struggle with his nerves, reminding himself that he was a lawman. "First, I should tell you something Simeon don't know. I'm a sheriff."

"Sheriff?" Toller was clearly unfamiliar with the word. "What's that?"

"I represent the law. I keep the peace, see the law is respected, arrest people if necessary."

Toller barked a laugh. "And you want to arrest me? For smuggling?" She snorted in an unladylike manner. "You said the men wouldn't care much."

Bud shook his head. "We don't. We ain't got no actual laws against buying Rightside art. This ain't even strictly smuggling since I paid you, the rightful dealer, for the pieces fair and square. It's just a business transaction, according to Wrongside law."

Toller gaped at him. "But even if you didn't get in trouble, why would you cause trouble for me? You don't even know me or care about me. All you'd do is lose your source of Rightside art. Why would you want to do that when you've just found me?"

Bud forced an easy grin. "You're right. I don't want to get you in trouble. I got another agenda altogether, and this" —he waved his hand vaguely at the bag of sculptures—"is just leverage. If you'll do me a small favor, we can continue our business as long as it's profitable for you, and as long as our money holds out."

"Small favor."

Bud nodded. "I need one piece of information that I can't get no other way. I got to sneak around the corners of Rightside law, and I figure only a woman can help me do it."

Toller sighed. "I can live without your business, you know. I should just give you back your coins, take the sculptures, and walk out of here."

Bud cringed inwardly. He had no choice but to keep going.

"You won't," he declared with manufactured confidence. "Simeon told me the arts are in a decline in Rightside, and your gallery's in trouble. He said you can't pay your mortgage with what you make from the women, and you need our business to survive."

Bud watched the anger building in her and hoped he could finish before she called security and got him warned off for life.

"Just hear me out, Ma'am," he said hastily. "I want one little favor, then I'll never ask again. Like I said, we can continue to do business, and you can forget I ever said I was the law."

"Name it," she said through gritted teeth.

"I want to know if I have a daughter. I've only ever been to the Cabin here in Cody, so you wouldn't have to search everywhere. You women must keep track of who the fathers are. You could just look for my name in a computer file or something."

Toller slammed a palm down on the table. "That's crazy! You're Yong crazy, Bud Hopper. What in

Rightside do you think you'd do with that information? What would you get out of knowing if you have a daughter? You'll never meet her. Never."

The words cut deep into his heart, but Bud masked it as well as he could. "I know that. Believe me, Ma'am, I know. But having the information, well, it would give me peace of mind. I ain't got any boys, you see, may never get any. Knowing I had a daughter in the world, that I'd leave someone behind when I die—well, that'd give me comfort."

Toller stared at him. "You are crazy."

****

Leaving the Red Cabin, Toller tried to think of a way out of this. In the end she'd promised to try to help him, knowing it would be nearly impossible. Even if she could get the information, how could she justify giving it to a man? It was against the very code of women, their most basic code of survival. No woman ever gave a man information. It was beyond dangerous. The only things a woman freely gave a man were unwanted sons.

An equally dangerous thought wiggled its way into her mind. There was always her cousin Serena, who worked at the New Atlanta Red Cabin and probably had full computer privileges, but at what cost to both of them?

Chapter 25

Jessie and Tenosha headed to the hospital. Tenosha fretted all the way there. "What if they're busy? What if they don't want the cookies? What if someone else comes in?"

"They're always up for goodies." Jessie refused to allow any glitches to her plan. "And things were slow in the maternity ward when I left this morning. They probably still are. Babies kind of run in batches. I just hope I didn't overlook anything. Come on, let's do this."

On their way to the Transfer Room, Jessie stashed their backpacks in a supply closet. They walked into the cubicle, chatting casually. Jessie was carrying the bag of cookies.

"We come bearing gifts!" Jessie called gaily. "Look what one of the grandmas just dropped off. Fresh-baked double chocolate chunk cookies! I snagged some for you guys on my way out."

"Chocolate chunk?" Sashi moaned. "Jess, I'm your slave for life!"

"Did someone say cookies?" Birdie came out of the back office, grinning. "We've been bored stiff tonight. You couldn't have picked a better time."

"I just told Tenosha that babies come in batches, and you'd probably be slow all night and glad for some company. Hey, got any coffee to go with these?"

"There's a fresh pot," Birdie said. "We'll have a party!"

Jessie watched as Sashi bit into one of Tenosha's special cookies. "Eat all you want," she encouraged. "We've had ours."

****

Maud was exhausted by the time she pulled into her underground garage. She lived on a hillside above New Washington, where most houses had basements. Beyond the garage, her basement extended back into the hillside with only small, ceiling-level windows. With some minor security upgrades, it made the perfect hideout.

She left Laran locked in the car while she went cautiously upstairs. She'd been right. There were ample signs of a search. Fingerprint dust was everywhere, and closet and cupboard doors had been left ajar. She could see crime-scene barricades through the windows of the front and back entrances. She threw the inside bolts on both doors and made sure all the curtains were drawn.

Back in the basement, she dragged Laran out of the car and pushed her unceremoniously into the basement room the conspirators had intended as Laran's original holding cell. Locked shutters covered both windows. The room held a bed, a table, a chair. A small refrigerator contained enough food and water for a week, and the kid had access to an adjoining bathroom.

"No one can hear you," she assured Laran and locked her inside.

****

Laran fumed. The anger was still working to keep fear at bay, but not as easily as it had the day before. She worked up a fresh spurt of indignation at having her escape plan foiled. There weren't any suspended ceilings in this room, but she figured the kidnapper would have to come back sooner or later. Maybe she could hide behind the door, find something to hit the woman with, and then run out. Maybe.

****

In Rightside, the entire country was still galvanized by the kidnapping. Photos of Maud Adams were all over the news, and every woman in the country was on alert.

The theft of a child happened occasionally. Women had been known to go quietly crazy when they couldn't manage to bear a daughter. Eventually, their grief and desperation erupted into the uncontrollable urge to steal someone else's daughter. Such women were always caught and put safely away in a prison hospital.

This, however, was no ordinary child theft, and the Constancy Party was being universally reviled for the despicable crime. It might never recover, Kai was beginning to realize.

Still in New Cleveland with Louise, Kai was on a conference call with Alanna. Her boss had pushed the initial panic and irresolution aside and was thinking clearly again, Kai saw. She decided to tell Alanna about Louise's idea.

"Far-fetched as it seems," she said to Alanna's image on the phone screen, "the chief thinks Maud might have gone back to New Washington."

Alanna was still haggard but calm and focused. She nodded now. "I hadn't thought of it, but I can see some logic in that, myself. The Guard have already searched this city from top to bottom and are starting to spread out across the country. Maud might have decided to slip back home while attention was in New Cleveland."

"Home?" Kai mused. "Do you mean literally? Could she have gone back to her own house?"

Alanna gathered herself, forcing her spine upright and raising her chin. "I'll take out a squad myself. We'll hit it again."

"It isn't likely she'll be there," Kai mused. "Maud may have had more than one safe house, or she may just be on the run, not even thinking clearly. There's so much farmland up here, not to mention the National Forest in the northwest. She could get lost in an unpopulated area pretty easily."

"I still want to raid the house again," Alanna insisted. "If it is where she's headed, could she have gotten there already?"

"We don't know how much lead time she would have had before we arrived this morning. If she did go home, she would take back roads, a roundabout route. And she probably had to stop to rest at least once. Best guess? She's still on her way."

"Then we'll wait until tomorrow," Alanna decided reluctantly. "I'll set a watch on her house now. If she's seen, we'll give her a few hours to settle in, then surround her."

"We'll start back now," Kai decided. "Let's have the major plan the operation."

Alanna nodded. "At least we have a new idea, and a direction to go from here."

"Try to get some rest," Kai urged. "You'll need to be fresh for the raid."

****

In Wrongside, life was still going on as usual. Hud was learning to wave bye-bye. Davy had discarded the crutch and was limping along without it. He was alternately thrilled and panicked at the thought of Jessie's impending escape to Wrongside.

Over at the sheriff's office Bud was working late, trying to finish some paperwork on Davy's case. The judge would be in town tomorrow. Frank and Chad Gibson were still on the lam, and Bally'd been feeding the younger kids for weeks.

Bud gripped his pencil. He was no writer, but he had to lay everything out right to keep Davy free and walking around instead of locked up just for making the women mad.

At the Transfer Cabin, Willie got up from his comfortable chair on the front porch. He'd heard the bell for the Transfer Door, so that meant something big that wouldn't fit into the Drawer. Inside, he pushed a hand truck over to the door. Probably computers or such, he thought, rolling the door up on its tracks. Doc had said he was expecting a—

"I'm Jessie," said the woman who stepped through the door. "You must be Old Willie."

Willie cried out his shock and fear and stumbled back. A woman in his cabin? *Here in his cabin!* "What the—? How? What are you *doing* here? I ain't done nothing, not nothing, woman. What do you want with me? How do you know my name? What the mother-loving hell's going on here?"

She was kinda short and had an odd little beer gut, sticking out high and tight. He'd never seen a woman with a gut like that. Hell, he hadn't seen a woman at all in maybe five years or more. He'd been well shut of them, he figured, and now there was one standing right in his own cabin. His own *Wrongside* cabin.

He shook his head. "This ain't right. It ain't right at all. You shouldn't be over here." He was babbling now, but he couldn't stop. "You can't be in Wrongside. Did you say Jessie? Are you Davy's Jessie, the one's been sending him notes and bottles and such? I could have lost my job any time over your damn foolishness, and I'm an old man. I need this job, and you—you—"

He hadn't even noticed the second woman till she stepped through the door, and now there was *another* one in his cabin. Willie's world was reeling. He couldn't think. The first one was talking, but he couldn't even hear her, couldn't make sense out of anything. They were in his *cabin*, for Yong's sake.

"I said *listen* to me for a second, Willie. You're not in trouble. No one in Rightside knows we're over here. No one saw us come through the Transfer Door, we gave sedatives to the clerks, and we set a timer to turn off your security camera for ten minutes. It's late. It's dark outside. All you have to do is tell us where Davy lives, and we'll leave. You're safe."

"You know Davy, don't you?" the other woman asked. "Do you know his father, Tom? Tom has a baby, doesn't he? Do you know Hud?" The woman looked at him like she wanted an answer, but Willie shook his head dumbly. "The baby?" she prodded. "Do you know about Tom's baby?"

That shook an answer out of him. Willie drew himself up a little and took a deep breath. "I'm the transfer man," he said, assembling what dignity he could. "Of course, I know about Hud. I picked him up outta the transfer drawer the day he was born, didn't I? I know about all the babies. I record them, name them, take them to their fathers. Babies go to their fathers, and

I'm the one who does that. I'm the transfer man."

"You gave Hud his name?" The woman seemed confused, for some reason. "Why?"

"It's my job. I'm the—"

"Yeah, yeah, you're the transfer man," Jessie interrupted. "We got that. Listen, Willie, all we need is for you to point the way to Davy's house. It isn't far, is it? Just tell us which way to go."

He didn't have to. Out in the front room, Willie's screen door burst open, and Davy limped through. "Willie? You here? Willie, I'm expecting—Jessie!"

****

Though they'd talked over the Fence just a few days earlier, Jessie and Davy ran for each other like waves running for shore, crashing together in a tangle of arms and hands and lips. Tenosha, standing behind Willie, could swear she heard bells ringing a cacophony of celebration as the lovers' lips finally touched again.

She couldn't turn her eyes away from the sight. Hours might have gone by, Tenosha thought, but it was probably only a few minutes before Jessie disentangled herself and turned. Tears, happy tears, streamed down her cheeks. "Tenosha, this is Davy!"

Tenosha laughed through her own tears. "I recognize him, even up close. Hello, Davy."

Without letting go of Jessie, Davy stuck out his hand in automatic welcome. Tenosha looked down at it. Women didn't shake hands with *men*, she thought, with some distaste, only with each other. Davy must have come to a similar conclusion because he withdrew his hand and wiped it self-consciously on his pant leg.

"Yeah, hello, uh, Tenosha. Thanks for helping Jessie. I didn't know you was coming, too."

"Neither did I," Jessie laughed. "It's a long story." She looked over at Willie. "Listen, can we go now? I think we're making your transfer man nervous."

Davy wasn't looking at Willie, though, Jessie realized. He'd just noticed her stomach. He touched it lightly, reverently, with one finger.

"This is the baby?" he whispered.

"It is." Jessie lifted his finger and repositioned his entire hand to the other side of her belly. "Leave your hand here for a minute. *There*. Did you feel that?"

Davy snatched his hand away as though it had been burned. "What was that?"

"He's saying hello." She smiled. "He's saying hello to his father."

****

Willie retched, but had just enough sense to stifle the sound. He couldn't even think of how many ways this was unnatural and wrong. He'd seen plenty of pregnant animals before, sure, but a pregnant woman? Oh, Yong, he had to get these batshit people out of here. Behind him, the other woman stirred.

"Jessie, we need to get moving. Remember, you have to be out of sight, up on the Plains, before morning."

"You're right," Jessie sighed. "Can we stop at your house first?" she asked Davy. "Tennie needs to see Hud, and we can explain everything."

Old Willie stirred, almost spoke, then changed his mind. Good, they were leaving. He had an awful suspicion why the women wanted to see Hud, but he didn't want to know if he was right. If he could just get them out of his cabin...

"Willie," Davy said. "Nobody needs to know we

were here, right?"

"Right." Willie nodded vigorously. "Time you're out the door, I'll forget I saw any of you. I been sitting here by myself all this time, no transfers or nothing. Been out on the porch, in fact, never came inside at all. I'll probably fall asleep out there."

"We get you." Davy smiled. "Thanks, Willie. For everything."

"Sure," the old man said uncertainly. "Sure, Davy. Uh, good luck. To all of you. I guess."

Jessie drifted toward the front screen door, arm in arm with Davy. The other woman gave Willie a short nod and started after them. Before they reached the door, Willie limped up behind them and slapped at the switch to turn off his porch light. He watched them ease down the porch steps, turn left, and disappear into the night. He breathed a gusty sigh, shook his head, and sat back down with his book. He could write a damn book after all this.

****

Tom was moving around his kitchen, packing his lunch for work, when the front door opened. Davy must be back, he thought. "I fed Hud already," he called out. "He's in the bedroom, probably getting sleepy by now."

"Pop?" Davy's voice sounded strange. Tom had grown used to his moods lately; wild excitement, followed by depression, followed by nervous pacing, then more excitement. But this sounded like something different. He wiped his hands on a dish rag and walked out to the front room.

"What's wrong, son?" He saw what was wrong right off. Tom might be slow and old, but he understood immediately what had been causing his son's strange and unwelcome moods.

"You're that Jessie," he said flatly, eyeing the woman who was holding Davy's hand as though she'd never let go. His gaze moved past her to the other woman, a woman he knew.

"And you're Tenosha. I recollect you from the Red Cabins, maybe a couple years ago? What're you doing here, with her?"

Tenosha stepped forward, twisting her hands. Her face held hope and fear, and maybe a dozen other emotions Tom couldn't recognize. What the hell did she want?

"I came to see my son. I want to see Hud."

Tom stepped back, instinctively blocking the path to the boys' bedroom. Shock drained his face of all confusion, all suspicion. He forgot about Jessie. How in hell had this woman got here, and what did she think she was gonna do, steal his son?

"He ain't yours. You might of birthed him, like a cow or a dog, but he ain't. Hud is *my* son. Mine. That's all."

"I know that," Tenosha hastened to say. "I know fathers keep their sons. I just want to hold him." Ready tears started into her eyes as she sobbed out her request. "I just have to hold him, Tom. Please? I carried him for nine months, and I gave him away. If I could hold him, just for a little bit, please?"

****

Davy and Jessie watched, breath held. That could be us, both were thinking. We have a son together, too. We both made him, the two of us. Davy dropped his hand to Jessie's stomach, wanting to feel his son move again.

Tom stirred and dragged a hand over his face. He still stood foursquare in front of the door to the boys' room. "You got no call to come here. You women got nothing to do with our sons." He looked, for the first time, at Jessie's protruding belly. "That your baby? Or Davy's? Do you know which?"

Jessie nodded. "It's a boy. That's why I came here, so Davy and I could be together, raise our son together."

"Women don't raise boys," he insisted. "That's the way it is. That's the way you women made it be, years ago. Tenosha, you ain't taking my son."

"I don't want to take him from you," Tenosha insisted. "We have a place. Well, Davy and Jessie have a place, up north, where we can see over the Border Fence. Davy brought Hud there so I could see him, but it was too far away. As soon as I saw Hud, I knew I had to hold him, at least once, so I came with Jessie."

Tom glared at his son. "Wasn't Davy's right," he declared.

Hud picked that moment to crawl out of his room and around Tom's legs, attracted by strange voices. He plopped onto his butt in front of his father and raised both arms to the women, gurgling a welcome.

Davy laughed, breaking the tension. He scooped up his brother and turned to Tom. "See, Pop, he wants to meet Tenosha. Can't she just hold him for a minute?"

Tenosha didn't give Tom a chance to answer. Stepping forward swiftly, she held out a hand to the baby. "Hi, Hud, it's me. It's Mommy, remember me? Did you see me at the Fence? Did you like the toy I brought, huh, baby?" She held out her other hand and wiggled her fingers. "Can you come to Mommy, Hud, can you?"

She shot a look to Tom, who stood frozen, shaking his head. "*Please,* Tom."

Though he tried not to, Tom couldn't help seeing the naked longing in her face. He remembered her face from the evenings they'd spent together in the Red Cabins. It had been good times for both of them, he'd believed, until she stopped making appointments. Now he knew why.

Hud leaned away from Davy and held his arms out to Tenosha, ready to embrace this stranger who smelled so good, nothing like his father and brother. Abruptly Tom waved an angry hand, coughed, and turned away. Tenosha gathered her son in.

****

Months of fear, confusion, anxiety, and finally, anger melted away. Tenosha understood that this was the answer to all of it, right here in her arms. This was right, she realized. This was good. This was the way it was supposed to be for a mother and her child, no matter what. She turned, eyes shining, to Tom.

"He's beautiful," she choked out. "He's so beautiful. Thank you, Tom. Oh, Tom, thank you, thank you!" She buried her face in Hud's wild, curly hair, sobbing and laughing, shoulders heaving. Hud patted her arm.

****

Jessie turned into Davy's shoulder, not wanting to intrude on the moment. Davy looked at his father, neither ashamed of their own tears. Tom pressed his lips together and nodded. He couldn't hate anyone who loved his son, be she a woman or not.

****

Tenosha rocked Hud and put him to bed, then sat down to watch him sleep. The other three left her to it and sat around the kitchen table to talk.

"We'll take you to work," Davy explained to Tom, "then I need your truck just for the night. We're going to the Plains. I got a place up off the North Road where we can camp. Once I get Jessie settled, I'll come back in time to pick you up. Then we got that hearing with the judge. If it goes okay, I'll head to Mike Dannon's after. Gonna buy his old truck. Jessie brought enough money."

Tom shot her a look. "You're planning to stay, then? On the Plains?"

Jessie nodded. "I'm a nurse. I brought all the supplies I'll need for the baby, and we'll make a home up there, the three of us. Davy tells me Wrongside has no laws against that."

"Not yet they don't," Tom agreed. "What the law will do when it finds out about you, I can't say."

"I don't figure Bud'll mind," Davy said. "But you won't tell him yet. Will you?"

Tom looked at his son. "No. I won't tell him. What about her?" He jerked a thumb toward the bedroom.

"She's going back tonight," Jessie promised. "She just needed to see Hud and hold him one time."

"That's what I thought this morning, but it isn't enough." The three looked up to see Tenosha in the doorway of the kitchen. "I can't leave Wrongside. This is where Hud is, so I have to be here, too. At least for now, if Jessie and Davy will let me stay with them. Tom?" She looked at her son's father. "Would you let me come down to town once in a while, to see him? I won't cause any trouble, I promise. I could come at night. No one would ever find out."

Tom scraped his chair backward and stood up. His hands clenched and unclenched, and he shook his head. "What right—?" he started but couldn't finish. He knew, even in his narrow and hidebound view of the world, that Tenosha had rights he never would have imagined, if she hadn't turned up in his living room. She was as much Hud's parent as he was, and he knew the strength of his own love. Hers must be just as powerful.

He turned away. "We'll see." He walked out the kitchen door into the night.

Tenosha looked at Davy. "What does that mean? Will he let me?"

Davy grinned. "When he says he'll see, that generally means he'll give in. And yeah, sure, you can stay with us at the camp." He turned to his Jessie, still marveling that she sat here beside him, in his kitchen, in Wrongside. "I packed some stuff. Are you ready to get going?"

Jessie jumped up. "Do you guys have a bathroom? A regular one, like in the Red Cabins?"

****

The next morning Bud cleaned his kitchen, socked two pans of cornbread into the oven, and started frying bacon. He had company coming.

Ricky and Clyde had left Jackson Hole at dawn, packed up for their annual camping trip to the Plains. Clyde would paint, and Ricky would fish. They always stopped at Bud's on the way.

Bud stepped onto his front porch to welcome them. "You've got a beautiful week for it, looks like," he commented. Ricky bounded onto the porch and gave his brother a quick hug.

"We look forward to this all year," he enthused. "My classes are done for the summer, Clyde's got fresh canvases, and I've got a new fishing rod. Let's start this vacation off right. You did make Pop's cornbread, didn't you?"

"For you? Absolutely, come on in." He ignored Clyde, who ignored him in return. Ricky pretended not to notice, and they headed inside for breakfast.

Chapter 26

Maud woke up early after a fitful night's sleep, with a new plan. She'd thought of the perfect way to get rid of the brat. She dressed quickly, then dragged a dozen shoe boxes out of her closet, exposing a floor safe. She hated to part with her emergency money, but this was damn sure the biggest emergency she'd ever faced. She'd probably need every coin.

First, she found an envelope, wrote a short note on the outside, put a few coins inside, and sealed it. She shoveled the rest of the money into two sturdy canvas bags. To the smaller one she added her mother's jewelry, the few pieces she herself owned, and some clothes. She wouldn't be returning here. When the car was loaded, she came back for the brat.

"Leave me alone," Laran whined, burrowing deeper into the bed. Her nose still hurt, and she wanted her mother.

"I said, *up.*" the woman shouted. "Get dressed. We have to go. If you're not ready in five minutes, I'll break your arm, too."

Laran sat up reluctantly. "I need clean clothes."

"Too bad. Five minutes." The woman swept out of the room, muttering to herself.

Wrinkling her nose, Laran shrugged into the clothes she'd worn to school two days earlier. When was this gonna be over? She'd already missed a spelling test and a field trip to a pony farm. How much longer would it take for her mom to find her?

"Now, listen." The woman was back, grabbing at Laran's arm to drag her from the room. "I'm going to disappear. You're not going with me. I can't drag you around anymore. I'll take you to a place where you'll be safe for a while until Alanna finds you."

Laran struggled to keep up. "You're taking me home?"

"No, you stupid brat, I said a safe place. I need time to get out of this town before you can go home."

"What town? Where are we?"

"New Washington. Get in the front seat."

"We're in New Washington?"

"Not that it'll do you any good. I want you down on the floor. Don't raise your head, or I'll smack it down again. Be quiet, be still, and you won't get hurt. We'll only be in the car for a few minutes."

Laran crouched on the floor of the front passenger seat, unwilling to risk another beating. She hoped the traffic would be bad this morning. If the woman got distracted, maybe she could wave her hand out the window or something. Maybe a Guard officer would see her hand, and she'd get rescued, and her mom would be so glad that she wouldn't even be mad because Laran had gone with Giulia.

It was still early enough for traffic to be sparse. Maud had jammed a ball cap over her head and wore her largest pair of sunglasses in spite of the foggy morning. She'd also smeared mud across her license plate. It would have helped, she thought sourly, to know more details of the smuggling operation she'd run with the others for the past two years. But everyone had agreed they do everything on a need-to-know basis. It had seemed like a good idea at the time. Too late to worry about it now.

She drove straight to the Pennsylvania Avenue Red Cabin. Approaching an alley on the far side of the Cabin, she leaned forward, craning her neck, then wheeled in.

As the car turned left, Laran snaked a cautious hand up to the window. The crazy woman's head was turned away. Without moving her arm, Laran waggled her hand back and forth, then used one finger to trace an 'L' on the foggy window glass. It was all she had time for.

Maud turned into a small parking area. "Good, no one else is here this early." She looked down at Laran. "Remember what I said. Be quiet. If one word comes out of your mouth, you'll be very, very sorry. Come with me." She dragged Laran out through the driver's side, slammed the car door, and pulled her quickly up two steps and through a door. Laran wondered why they were going into a Transfer Cabin but was afraid to ask.

****

A single disgruntled clerk womaned the counter. She was old, which Maud counted as a plus. The clerk looked up, already irritated by the harried stranger dragging a child. It was close to the end of her shift, and this had better not take long. "Help you?"

"Look at this," Maud ordered. She dropped a heavy canvas bag on the counter.

The clerk pulled the bag toward her. "Where's your paperwork?"

"Look in the bag."

Opening it, she gasped. It held more gold coins than she'd ever seen in one place.

"They're yours. All of them, in return for no questions and no paperwork."

The woman tore her gaze from the glittering coins long enough to give Maud a questioning glance that held just a touch of greed. Maud smiled. "No one will ever know. Turn off your Door cameras and put this kid through the Transfer Door."

"Kid?" The clerk looked at the bedraggled child whose head barely cleared the counter. The child's face, the clerk realized, had been all over the news for days. "But this, isn't this—?"

"Don't say it," Maud advised softly, "and then you'll never have to know for sure." Without taking her eyes from the clerk's, she dug a hand into the bag and sifted the sparkling coins through her fingers.

It didn't take long for the clerk to quell her conscience. What did she care? The kidnapping had nothing to do with her. She pulled the bag to her side of the counter. Now she could retire to New Miami.

Maud pulled Laran around the counter and handed her prepared envelope to the clerk. "Send this through first. When the man rolls his Door back down and signals, we'll put the kid through."

****

Laran was starting to panic. She knew what a Transfer Door was for. Her class had taken a field trip just a few months ago. They were going to send her to Wrongside. Wrongside, where all the men lived. How would she ever get back to her mom from there? She watched the clerk roll up the Door, put an envelope on the floor inside, and close it again. *I bet there's more*

262

money in that envelope. I can't go in there when the Door goes back up. I can't. "No!" she screamed, yanking her arm free from the crazy woman's grip. "I'm not going in, you can't *make* me." She scrambled back around the counter, skidding a little on the slick tiles, and made it all the way to the entry door before Maud caught her again.

"What did I tell you?" Maud bellowed. "What did I tell you about being quiet?" Two days of broken sleep, hours of driving, fear of being caught, and anger over the failure of their brilliant plan had the legislator at a breaking point. Screaming her frustration, she slapped Laran across the face, forward, and then back. Forward again, and back again. "Shut! Up!"

Whimpering and half-dazed, Laran didn't resist.

****

Over in Wrongside, Willie answered the bell for the Transfer Door. He was still expecting Doc Medina's computers, but when he rolled up the Door the small room was empty. He'd just reached up to close it again when he noticed the white envelope on the floor.

"What the hell?" He bent over to pick it up, grunting with the effort. Absent-mindedly, he walked out, rolled the Door back down, and slapped the all-clear button. The locks snicked shut. He noticed the envelope's heft even before he saw the writing.

The coins are yours.

"Coins?" Willie shook the envelope. Sure enough, the jingle of gold made him smile, then on second thought, frown. "Not again," he muttered. "What've I gotta do now?"

Pocket them and tell no one. Take the kid out where there are no people and dump it.

Willie looked back at the Door as though it could answer his questions. "What kid?" he asked it. "Why aren't you sending it through the Drawer, like always? Why do you want me to dump him?"

The signal bell rang again. "Women coming through to Wrongside, where they got no business. Now sending babies through the Transfer Door with bags of gold and bossy instructions." Willie complained out loud, reaching for the Door handle. "What's got into all the damn women, anyways? I can't just dump a baby in the wilderness. They're crazy."

Expecting a newborn, Willie staggered backward and fell against the door frame when he saw a small child instead. It was a small female child, he realized at once. What did they call 'em? Girls, that was it, from the old books. They'd sent him a girl.

"For Milina's sake," he whispered. With the ease of long practice, he shot a sideways glance at the security camera. No green light. Someone had turned it off to hide what they'd done.

Laran was huddled in the far corner of the small room, near the Rightside Door. Still dazed from the beating, she didn't register the opening of the Wrongside Door until Willie spoke. Her head flew up.

Willie stepped toward her. She shrieked.

"Get away, get away! Don't touch meeeeee!" Sobbing hysterically, she jumped up and pounded on the Rightside Door. "Help! Somebody help me!"

"Take it easy, kid. Girl. You're a girl, right? Hey, I ain't gonna hurt you, kid. Take it easy."

Willie's deep voice scared her even more than his size or the hair on his face. He sounded and looked like a big ape or something from the zoo.

"Don't touch me! Help, somebody, help!"

"You can't open that Door, you know. They have to do it from the other side. Listen, stop screaming, can't you?"

Laran, sobbing, put her hands over her ears. "Don't talk to me! Don't look at me. Go away!"

Willie had little experience with children, less with women, and none with girls. He backed out but left the Wrongside Door up.

Standing in the middle of his kitchen, he was at a loss. He looked down. The envelope full of gold was still in his hand. Absently, he opened it. "Now I can get me that truck," he told the kitchen.

It took almost half an hour for the girl to cry herself out. Willie was thankful for that, at least. He sat at his kitchen table, still in a daze of indecision. Part of him— a big part, he had to admit—shrank away from the responsibility of this child. There had to be something seriously wrong and illegal about sending a girl child over here, and that had to be all mixed up with the two women who came through yesterday.

Why, all of a sudden, was this happening? He couldn't afford to be involved. No, sir, he couldn't. He needed this job, and that was all there was to it.

But she was just a kid. Willie had never wondered about his paternal instincts before, but now he guessed he must have some, even for a girl. He wasn't gonna let her come to any hurt, and he'd do his best to see she got back to Rightside. He wouldn't, of course, mention them other two women to anybody.

He sure wasn't gonna take the kid up to the Plains and dump her, like the note said. So what came next? He looked at the envelope again and shook his head.

Hell, if he knew.

A small sound made him look up to the kitchen doorway. The girl stood there, most of her body out of sight around the door frame. Only her small, bloody face peeked into the kitchen. "Can I have something to eat?" she asked.

Willie stirred. "I got bread and jelly. That do you?" She nodded.

"Well, don't be scared, okay? I ain't gonna hurt you. My name's Willie. What's yours?"

"Laran," she whispered.

Willie cleared his throat. "You know you got blood on your face? Did somebody hit you?"

The small head nodded once.

Yong, what did them women do? Willie thought. *What did they do to the poor kid?* He cleared his throat. "Why don't you go on back the hall there, to the bathroom. You can clean up and wash your face while I get you some vittles. You like milk?"

The girl nodded, then skedaddled down the hall.

****

Laran was already unbuttoning her shorts when she ran into the bathroom, but what she saw there brought her up short. There was a toilet, that was the important thing, so she ignored the rest for the moment. When she was finished, she reached for the seat lid, but there wasn't one. Shrugging, she flushed and turned a slow circle to inspect the room.

Next to the toilet, a big white thing that was sort of like a sink hung on the wall. It had a faucet handle but no soap, so she turned to the other sink, which looked more or less normal. There wasn't any bathtub, either. There was just a shower stall, which didn't seem right.

How did he bathe his babies? She'd have to ask him if he had any. She'd love to see a male baby.

****

After he'd fed her two jelly sandwiches and all of his milk, the kid looked a little better to Willie. Her face, cleaned of the blood, was only a little swollen, but both of her eyes were black. He figured her nose was broken, and there was a cut on one eyebrow.

"I ain't got a clue what to do with you," he ventured.

"Let me go back through the Transfer Door," she said immediately.

He shook his head. "It don't work that way. I can't open the Door at all from this side, they have to do it over there, in Rightside. From the looks of things, they ain't gonna want you back over there, anyways."

"There was money in that envelope, wasn't there?" Laran's eyes were serious and too knowing. "They paid you to take me, so my mom couldn't find me."

Willie didn't want to answer that. "There was a note on the envelope. It said to take you out in the wilderness and dump you." Willie hesitated. "How'd you get in this fix, girl? How'd you get separated from your, um, your mother, and why don't the other women want her to find you?"

If the man wasn't going to admit about the money, Laran sure wasn't going to admit her own mistake that had led to the kidnapping.

"I think it's because my mom is the president," she said instead. "Lots of people don't want her to be in charge of Rightside, so maybe they thought they'd get her to quit if they stole me."

"President?" Willie echoed. "In charge of the

country? Is that like her being the commander? He's the guy in charge of Wrongside."

Laran brightened a little. "Commander Sherman, yeah! My mom talks to her—him—sometimes, on the computer. Hey, can we go see him? I'll bet he could make them let me back through the Fence. Can we go, Willie, please?"

Willie reared back in his chair and shook his head. "The likes of me, talk to the commander? No, that ain't gonna happen. Tell you what I should do, though, is go see Bud. He's the sheriff around here, and maybe he can take you to the commander."

Laran yawned. "Okay, I guess. What's a sheriff? When can we go see him?"

"You can't go outta this cabin," Willie declared. "It's broad daylight. What if somebody saw you? No, you stay here, and I'll go get Bud. He'll know what to do. I can't go till this afternoon, though," he remembered, "on account of today's a court day. The judge is here to see about Davy."

"Who's Davy?" Laran asked, yawning again.

"Just a kid who's in trouble, like you. Listen, Laran, seems like you're gonna fall asleep any second. Why don't you, uh, take a nap or something, and I'll bring Bud by here later."

"Okay," Laran agreed sleepily. She slid from the chair and followed Willie back to a tiny bedroom. There weren't any sheets on the single bed, but Willie pulled a quilt and pillow out of a cupboard.

"Willie?" she asked, crawling under the quilt without even taking off her shoes. "Do you have any kids? Any babies? I wanna see a male baby before I go home."

Willie snorted a laugh and sat down on the edge of the bed. "Girl, happens you're in baby central. I'm the transfer man, you know."

"You're the what?"

Willie started to tell her about his job, but the poor kid was fast asleep before he'd got two sentences out. He sighed, heaved himself up, and closed the door gently on his way out. He hoped for a baby or two today, so he could show Laran, but he didn't want the bell waking her up.

****

Bud slapped Davy on the back and practically knocked the kid over. "Sorry, Davy, just glad about this, that's all. Seems like the judge was on your side from the beginning. When he heard the whole story about the Red Cabin, laid out plain like that, there was no question he was gonna let you off."

Davy stumped alongside Bud and Tom, who carried Hud, as they walked out of the courtroom next to the sheriff's office and jail. He was glad to be clear of trouble with the law, all right, but he had places to go and things to do. He wanted to get back to Jessie before dark.

"I appreciate everything you done, Bud. Not everybody would of stood up for me like that. I think I'm gonna head outta town now, go up to the Plains for a while."

"I don't blame you, Davy, but be careful. The Gibsons are still up there somewhere."

Davy nodded. "I got me a place where I camp. It's pretty well hidden, and I won't stray far."

Bud stopped in the dusty street and reached out his hand. Davy shook it gratefully, and they parted. Bud had things to do, himself.

Half an hour later, Hud was at the Corral, and Tom was asleep for the day. Davy was negotiating with Mike Dannon for his old truck, and Bud was on his way to Jackson Hole.

****

"Gettin' some afternoon nooky, are ya?" The Red Cabin clerk grinned.

Bud hid his nerves. "Seems like."

"Have a seat, then. I'll tell them you're here."

Bud waited half an hour before being buzzed into Room 2.

"Afternoon, Ma'am." He nodded.

Toller didn't reply. "I've decided to help you out. Not because I'm afraid of what trouble you could cause me, but because this is all pretty unimportant. What do I care about your legacy to the world? I need your business. You know that. So let's do business with no more silly ultimatums."

"Fine with me. You got my answer?"

She waved a dismissive hand. "Eight years ago, a woman named Olaffson had a daughter by you. That's the only one my contact found."

His careful composure forgotten, Bud staggered to a chair and fell into it. "I really—I really do have a daughter? She's real. She's mine?" He looked up at the woman with disbelief, hope, and longing mixed on his face. It disgusted Toller.

"No, you idiot, she's not yours, she's Olaffson's. She's a Rightside woman, and you have no claim on her or her daughter. Never forget that."

Bud was too dazed to hear the rebuff. "Eight years. She's eight years old already, and I never knew." He jumped up again. "Is Olaffson the woman's last name? What's her first name?"

"First names weren't in the file," Toller lied smoothly. "Only initials, and hers was A." She might be halfway to being a criminal, Toller admitted, but she wasn't going to betray a Rightside woman—especially not the president—to this man. He might have recognized a first name. He didn't need to know about the kidnapping, either. That was Rightside business.

She turned away and rummaged in the bedside table for an appointment card. "I'll give you another appointment in a month, then I'm leaving. Just tell your clerk I was called away. And Bud," she warned, "come with plenty of gold next time, or I'll tell my clerks you slapped me."

Bud didn't hear that, either. *A daughter! I'm not childless, I have an eight-year-old daughter!* He picked up the card and stumbled from the room.

****

"Bud, I been lookin' for you all damn day." Old Willie huffed up to Bud's truck, carrying two bags of groceries. "Lucky I seen you driving into town."

Bud forced himself back to reality. "Trouble, Willie?"

The old man heaved a gusty sigh and shifted his grip on the bags. "You might say that, Bud. C'mon with me, I'll show you."

Chapter 27

Kai and Alanna were at the Guard station again, sifting through new reports in Louise's office. A second raid on Maud's house had yielded information but nothing really useful. The woman had been there again, as the chief had predicted. An open, empty safe had been discovered in a closet, and more clothes and food were missing. Laran's fingerprints had been lifted from the basement bedroom and bathroom.

"So close," Alanna murmured. "She was right here in town. How long ago? And where are they now?"

Kai shook her head and dropped the fingerprint analysis. "It's so frustrating! Why didn't anyone see them? Why aren't there any leads at all? Maud can't be that good."

Louise burst into the room, waving more paperwork. "I've got something!"

Alanna jumped up. "Did someone see them? Did someone see Laran?"

"Maybe." The major took a chair and motioned for Alanna to sit again. "It's a small thing that might not have much meaning, but we're already acting on it."

"Tell me," Alanna begged.

Louise didn't waste any time. "At about five thirty this morning, a commuter on her way to work saw something odd near the Pennsylvania Avenue Transport Cabin. She didn't get a license number, but it was a green car, scrape on the right rear bumper. It turned into Transport Alley next to the Cabin."

"To the Transfer Door?" Kai interrupted. "I've been back there once or twice, there's nothing except the parking lot and a loading dock for the Door."

"Correct. As the car turned into the alley, this commuter had a good view of the front passenger window. She saw a hand come up, a small hand, and start waving. She said it looked like whoever was waving was down in the passenger footwell. After the wave, the hand's index finger traced the letter "L" on the window.

"The woman didn't think much of it at first. Maybe some kid was playing around, but the "L" bothered her after a while, so she's just now reported the incident.

"I've sent one team to the Transfer Cabin," she finished, "and another to canvass the area."

"L," Kai repeated. "L for Laran, it has to be. Alanna, Laran was in that car. She must have been!"

Alanna reached over to clasp her hand. "Kai? Did she send my baby to Wrongside?"

Kai's round, earnest face blanched. She hadn't gotten that far in her thinking, but Alanna obviously had. "No, honey," she said immediately, "don't even think that. What reason could she have?" She shot a worried glance to Louise, whose face was suddenly as white as hers.

Louise shook it off fast. "We won't go there. Ma'am, we won't even think that, not without evidence. No Rightside woman could do that. There must be a simple explanation. Maybe she had to pick up a delivery, something she needed."

An officer stepped into the room and nodded

toward the telephone on the chief's desk. "First team calling in," she said shortly.

Louise pressed the speaker button. "Go ahead?"

A voice, tense with suppressed emotion, reported. "Chief, we've just left the Transfer Cabin. Shift changed at six, so we're headed to the home of the night clerk. The workers here now tell us the night clerk was acting strange, made some mention of being ready to retire."

"Bring her in," Louise ordered. "Don't even stop to ask questions, just bring her here."

"Got it."

She punched off the call. "Progress," she said. "It's progress. We'll know something soon."

****

Jessie ran up to the truck as soon as Davy pulled in. "Oh, I missed you!" she cried. "Isn't it wonderful, though, Davy? Whenever I miss you from now on, all I have to do is remember that you'll be home soon. No more waiting for days and days."

Davy grinned down at her. "Our home," he said. "Yeah, you're right. Even a camp on the Plains is way better than a Red Cabin."

"I guess it went okay with the judge?"

Davy nodded. "I figured it would. The sheriff said once we laid it all out, everything that happened, the judge would have to let me go, and he did. He don't like the Rightside rules any better than anybody else."

"Including me," Jessie agreed. "Come on, see what we did with the camp while you were gone. Did you get the groceries, too? I'm starved, and so is Baby Boy!"

****

Bud took Willie's grocery bags. He'd been headed

to Bally's to spread the news about his daughter, but the old transfer man, limping home from the store, might as well be the first to know.

"Willie, I just had some good news. It's the best news, you might say. Remember the plan for me to meet Toller, that art dealer woman, a couple weeks ago?"

"Yeah." Willie, sunk in his own problems, wasn't listening much.

"I saw her again just now. You remember. I wanted to get her to tell me whether I had a daughter."

"Yeah, so?"

Bud stopped in the street. "I do."

"You do what?" Willie asked.

Bud surprised him by dropping the bags and grabbing both of Willie's shoulders. "*I have a daughter!*"

Willie's mouth dropped open. This was just too much. It was too damn much. What was happening to the world?

Bud didn't notice his discomfiture. "Isn't it great? I can't wait to tell my brother. I can't wait to tell everybody! Don't you see, Willie, Ricky and me aren't alone in the world, after all. I have a child!"

"You have a daughter," Willie corrected automatically. "And yesterday, I'd have said you didn't have a chance in hell of ever meeting her, but now I'm not so sure."

"What do you mean?"

Willie picked up the bags and started walking again. "C'mon with me."

At the Transfer Cabin, Willie dropped his groceries on the kitchen table and gestured Bud down the hall.

"This way." He eased open the door of the extra bedroom and stepped back. "She got put through the Transfer Door this mornin'."

"She?" Bud stepped into the room, then stopped short and the sight of the very small, very female child hunched under the quilt. He threw Willie a wild look, but Willie just waved him out of the room and closed the door again. He led the way back to the kitchen.

"I don't want to wake her up, she looked fair tuckered when she come through, and somebody's been beating on her, poor kid. I think her nose is broke."

"Willie, for Yong's sake, what's going on here? She came through the Fence? The mother-loving *Border Fence*?"

Willie nodded. "Kinda puts a hole in the world, don't it? A big new hole with nothin' normal or right about it?"

Bud sank into one of the kitchen chairs. "Start from the beginning, Willie, and tell me everything."

Willie didn't tell the sheriff everything, not by a long shot, but he did recount the story of Laran's arrival just as it had happened. He even showed him the bag of money.

"I ain't taking her up to the Plains, goes without saying, but Bud, what are we gonna do with a little girl? It ain't safe to keep her. She wants me to take her to the commander, says her mother knows him, and he'll see she gets home."

Bud considered that. "I guess it makes sense," he admitted. "If her mother really is the head of Rightside, it stands to reason Sherman might help her."

"The kid says they talk on a computer, somehow."

"It'd be hard to drive her all the way down to

Jackson Hole. If any of the men got wind of her, they'd panic for sure. What if the commander wouldn't see us? What if he's not even there? I couldn't hide her with Ricky. He's away on a camping trip."

"What do you think, then? Could we send her back through a different Door?"

"Might be dangerous," Bud mused. "For one of the women to give you that many gold coins to get rid of Laran, she had to be desperate. We don't know the situation in Rightside. There might be a revolt, or something, for all we know. We can't be sure they wouldn't just kill her if we sent her back, even through another Door."

The two sat silent for a few minutes, turning over possibilities. Hide her with Ricky, Bud had said a minute ago. He could still do that, couldn't he? Hide her up at Ricky's camp, then come back and see what was to be done. Bud stirred, ready to put his idea to Willy, but was stopped by a small noise from the hallway.

"Willie? Where are you, Willie?"

Bud watched the girl start into the kitchen, then stop in confusion at the sight of a stranger.

"It's okay, Laran," Willie hastened to say. "This is Bud, the sheriff I told you about. He's gonna help you."

Brown eyes looked into brown eyes as man and child considered each other. Laran saw the second man of her life, smaller than Willie but with the same hair on his face. Bud saw a tiny female, the first of his life, with spiky blonde hair and slightly slanted eyes.

"Do all men have hair on their faces?" Laran asked into the silence.

The men laughed. "Yeah, we do," Bud told her,

"but some of us shave it off."

Laran nodded. "Like Mom shaves her legs."

Bud's eyebrows went up in shock. They must, he realized, because he'd seen some women with hair on their legs and some without.

"Imagine that," Willie managed.

Laran moved on to the larger question. "Can you take me home?"

Bud nodded, charmed by her small face and direct way of questioning. *Is my daughter like this? Is she just as pretty and smart?* He couldn't help but wonder.

"It won't be easy," he told her. "And we can't take you since men can't go to Rightside, but yeah, I think we can send you back there before too long. I was just thinking about the best way to contact the commander and what we should do with you in the meantime."

"Can't I just stay here with Willie?"

The old man stirred. "It ain't safe, girl. Lots of people come in and out of here since it's a Transfer Cabin. We better keep you a secret for now. The other men might not like having a little girl in Wrongside."

"I was just thinking about Ricky," Bud said. "Before, I told you I couldn't hide her with Ricky because he's out camping on the Plains, but why couldn't I take her there? It'd be safe, no one would see her, and I could drive down to the Hole tomorrow, try to get in to see the commander."

"Who's Ricky?"

"My brother," Bud said. "Uh, that is, I guess, like if your mother had two little girls. Does she?"

Laran shook her head. "I keep telling my mom I want a sister, but she just laughs and says maybe someday."

Bud grimaced. It was easy for them, he thought resentfully. They could decide whatever they wanted when it came to babies. He shot a glance at Willie and saw the same resentment there.

Laran didn't pick up on it. "I like camping," she said slowly. "I went with the Scouts once, so I guess that'd be okay. Can Willie come?"

Their departure was delayed when Laran suddenly got one of her wishes.

"Hear that bell?" Willie said with a grin when the chime sounded. "That's the signal for a baby. Rightside's sending us another baby boy. Come on with me, Laran. You can help me see to him."

He let her pull open the Transfer Drawer, and all three of them looked down at the newborn.

"But he's just like a regular baby," Laran said, disappointment on her face.

"What did you think, he'd have hair on his face already?" Willie grinned. "Let me show you how to pick him up safe, then you can hold him."

*****

They left an hour later in Bud's truck with Laran curled up flat on the seat until they were out of town. Willie, to her disappointment, had stayed behind to deliver the baby to its father.

Laran was fascinated by the windswept Plains. "There aren't any trees anywhere," she marveled, "but you've got so many more flowers than we do! It's so pretty here. And I love tumbleweeds! I want to take one home. We have show and tell at school. Nobody's ever seen a tumbleweed before."

Bud looked around, seeing the landscape through her eyes. It really was kind of pretty, he guessed. Like her. He kept sneaking glances at Laran, wondering if his own daughter looked so fragile, so tiny.

"How old are you?" he asked abruptly.

"I'll be nine next month," she answered, stretching to look at the sudden rill of a creek next to the road. "I was hoping I could get a puppy for my present, but now I guess not." Realizing she shouldn't have said that, Laran added, "What's your brother like?"

"Ricky? Well, he looks like me, I guess. He's a history teacher at the University, and he likes to fish. That's what he's doing up on the Plains this week. He's with his friend, Clyde, who's an artist. Clyde's going to paint pictures while Ricky fishes."

"Will they like me?" she asked in a small voice.

Bud grinned. "They'll be shocked to pieces, tell you the truth. Nobody in Wrongside has ever seen a little girl, remember? But you're so cute and friendly that they'll have to like you, just the way me and Willie do."

"Do they have hair on their faces, too?"

Bud laughed.

Chapter 28

It didn't take long for Louise to get the truth out of the transfer clerk. The major was in too much of a hurry to be patient. She'd actually smacked the clerk a good one on the side of her head to encourage her to talk.

"All right!" the clerk said angrily. "All right, yes, there was a girl. A dirty little kid with blood on her face. She tried to run, once, but the woman caught her. She put her through the Door with a note and some money. Does that satisfy you?"

The chief's mouth dropped open. She had been afraid of this, had tried to think of any other reason why Maud might have gone to a Transfer Cabin. This was her worst fear, realized. "You actually sent a child to Wrongside? *To the men?*"

"*I* didn't," the clerk hastened to say. "The other woman did. And she sent plenty of money, the bag was heavy. The men probably won't hurt her with all that money. And I don't know what the note said, so don't even ask."

"You sent her to the *men*," the chief whispered. "You knew what they could do to her, and you still sent her." She dropped into a chair, unable to stand under the weight of sudden dread. Violent, visceral images of fire, fear, and rape rampaged across her mind.

"You're a woman," she said to her prisoner, "just like I am. How could you do this to a child? A child!"

She shook her head. "We have to go over there. We have to find her, and fast." Abruptly, she leaned forward and dropped her head to her knees, hands over her face. "Oh, Milina," she moaned. "How am I going to tell the president? How am I going to tell Laran's mother?"

"I didn't do it," the clerk repeated mulishly. "It was that other woman. Blame her." She shifted uneasily. "Not me."

****

Laran and Bud were singing, having discovered that they knew some of the same songs. "Old MacDonald" was their favorite so far. Bud's truck rumbled up the North Road until it curved east to Bozeman, then turned onto a narrow track that led west to the river. Bud and Ricky had often camped up here with Pop.

"We used to sing all these songs around the campfire at night," Bud told his passenger. "Hey, do you know the one about the watermelon?"

"What's a watermelon?"

"Nobody knows for sure. It was some kind of food they had back on old Earth. Must not be anything like it here."

"Oh, look! What are those?" Laran was bouncing in her seat, pointing to a small herd of buffalo on the horizon.

"Did you ever eat buffalo steak?"

"Uh-huh. We make buffalo burgers too, but I like cow burgers better."

"Well, those are buffalo. And look over here on my side," Bud said, slowing the truck. "Down in that brush. Can you see anything moving?"

"No. Wait, I see them! What are they? Oh, they're so pretty!"

"Those are deer. We're lucky to catch a sight of 'em. I guess there aren't many hunters out this way, so they aren't too spooked by my truck. And look up ahead. Here's the river already."

They followed the wild Missouri for a few miles, past several sets of rapids and a long, shallow waterfall. Laran wanted to get out and wade, but Bud told her it was too dangerous.

"There are bad currents here that you can't see. Some fool kid drowns right along here most every spring. On ahead, though, where we camp, the water gentles down, and you can swim."

"Goody," Laran said, then frowned. "But I don't have a swimsuit."

Bud looked sideways at her grimy shirt and shorts. He didn't know that word, swimsuit, but it didn't matter none. "You can prob'ly jump in the water with those clothes on. They need a wash, anyway."

Laran started to wrinkle her nose, then stopped because it hurt. "I'm awful stinky," she complained. "The crazy woman wouldn't give me any new clothes. Maybe Ricky and Clyde have some I can wear. Do they have kids as little as me?"

Bud guffawed. "Those two ain't got any boys. But they'll maybe have an extra T-shirt you can wear for a dress. Here we are." He pointed ahead. "See the tent under those trees?"

****

Ricky registered surprise and pleasure when he recognized his brother's truck. Clyde, predictably, registered dismay. *Wait'll he sees who I brought*, Bud thought, grinning.

"I don't recognize the boy," Ricky said to Clyde. "Maybe Bud brought one of his neighbor's kids for the fishing." The two of them had just built up the campfire to start supper. Ricky was wrapping potatoes to roast. Clyde was cleaning fish. "Good thing you caught plenty," he muttered under his breath.

"Hey, Buddy!" Ricky called, waving from his seat at the edge of the riverbank. "C'mon over. We have a whole mess of fresh fish!"

Bud and Laran walked over to the campfire, and Ricky stood up, smiling a welcome. Clyde barely registered their arrival. "Who's this little guy, Buddy? Hope he's hungry."

"I'm not a he," Laran said indignantly. "I'm a she."

Ricky stopped in his tracks, and Clyde's head jerked up. Both men thought at first it was a joke, some trick Bud was playing on them. Then they looked more closely at the child holding Bud's hand.

Ricky turned his head toward Clyde without taking his eyes from the child. "I don't think—"

"No," Clyde decided, shaking his head. "What are you trying to pull, Bud?"

"Pull?" Bud was grinning like a polecat at their confusion. "Don't know what you mean, Clyde. I'd like you to meet my new friend, here. Her name's Laran, and I'm afraid she's in a mite a' trouble."

"She," Ricky repeated. "Bud, you can't mean that this child is—"

"I do mean, Ricky. There's trouble over in Rightside, and Laran took some hard hits over it. She was pushed through a Transfer Door this mornin', and I brought her up here to keep her safe."

"You're a woman!" Clyde gasped, jumping up to get closer to Laran. He stared at her, mouth open in shock, hands fluttering wildly. "I've never seen an actual woman, and now there's one standing right here in our camp."

"Don't get so excited, there, Clyde. She's only nine. She's called a girl, not a woman."

"A girl," Ricky breathed. He couldn't take his eyes off her.

Laran, squirming under their stares, looked down and dug the toe of her dirty purple sandal into the dirt.

Bud squeezed her hand. "Lighten up," he told Ricky and Clyde. "Give the kid a break. She's had a rough couple a' days. How soon's supper? We're both starved."

Ricky jerked back a step and shook himself. "We're being rude," he said and pasted a smile over his shock. "Welcome to camp, little girl. We'll have supper ready before you know it. Maybe Bud can show you the river while we cook."

Clyde returned to the half-cleaned fish with lightning speed. Ricky, realizing why he was in such a hurry, smiled indulgently. He gave Clyde a shove. "Go," he said. "Sketch."

Clyde shot into the tent and returned with a sketch pad and pencils. He climbed onto a flat rock above the river and started drawing with long, fluid strokes. Laran was just below him, wading cautiously through the shallow water. Bud splashed a little water in her direction, and she squealed.

"What a face!" Clyde murmured. "Those angles, and this light is perfect!" He finished one drawing, flipped the page, and started another. Laran was bolder now, splashing back at Bud and venturing out to deeper water. She stepped into a hole, sank, and came up sputtering. Bud laughed, and picked a trailing water weed out of her hair.

Too bad Bud doesn't have any boys, Clyde thought idly. He'd make a good father.

While the two played and Clyde sketched, Bud was formulating a vague plan. He'd go to Jackson Hole tomorrow, all right, but if he did get in to see the commander, he'd lay down some rules first. He'd agree to lead the women to Laran when they came looking for her, but he'd damn sure ask a favor first. He nodded in satisfaction while he splashed more water at Laran. He'd make them arrange a meeting between him and his daughter.

Chapter 29

Kai had been afraid Alanna would melt into hysterics, but she'd underestimated her friend. Alanna was as cold as ice. "I'm going," she stated. "I'll assemble a squad of Guards and go through the same Door. She can't have been taken far."

Kai nodded. "I'll be right behind you with a second squad."

"We'll need to spread out," Louise added, "once we get to Wrongside."

"We have maps," Kai remembered. "The Security Department maintains street maps of the Wrongside towns. Let me make a call. I can have them here in fifteen minutes."

The major stood up. "I'll put my teams on alert and talk to the colonel."

Alanna nodded. "I need to make some calls." She shot a look at Kai, who nodded.

****

Commander Sherman couldn't remember a Rightside president ever contacting him outside of the monthly conference. The woman, when she came on the screen, looked awful, like she hadn't slept in days. Was there trouble in perfect, superior, well-controlled Rightside?

"Madam President? Is there a problem?"

"We've had trouble," she admitted. "But it had

nothing to do with Wrongside, until this morning. There's been a child kidnapping, and when our police started closing in on the kidnapper, she evidently panicked and put the child through a Transfer Door that opens into your town of Cody. We're about to send a squad of Guards through the Door to retrieve her, and I decided you should be informed."

"Th-thank you," Sherman stammered. "I should go up there myself to oversee the situation. I'll contact Cody law enforcement and order their full cooperation."

"Appreciated, Commander. I'll keep you informed." She clicked off.

Sherman sat back and steepled his hands. Well. They really did have trouble in tight-ass Rightside. He'd be happy about that—serves them right—if it weren't for the little kid. Poor thing. What would the hicks up in Cody do with a female child? He reached for the phone.

"Get me the sheriff's office in Cody," he ordered. If he acted fast, he could have that kid safely corralled and ready to hand over when the women came busting through the Door. It couldn't hurt to have the president indebted to him.

"This is Commander Sherman speaking," he barked when his call was connected. "I need to speak to your sheriff."

"C-c-commander? Um, yes, sir. Yes, sir! Sheriff Hopper had business up on the Plains, said he'd be back late tonight. C-c'n I take a message, Commander, Sir?"

****

Alanna called Claire Boudreau next, her Security secretary. "Claire, I know I've asked a lot of you these last few days, but I need you to hold the fort a little longer. I'm going to be incommunicado for a while."

"Is there news of Laran?"

"There is," Alanna said, unable to hide the tremor in her voice. "Maud put her through a Transfer Door."

"Wrongside!" Claire gasped. "She sent her to Wrongside? Oh, Alanna, how could Maud, even Maud, do that?"

"She did it. Claire, I'm going through after her. Kai, too, and the Guardswomen."

"Are you sure? Is that wise? Oh, Alanna, we can't lose you and Kai, too! Rightside needs you too much. I need you too much."

"I'm sorry, Claire, but we have to do this. Laran needs us more. I'll be in touch when I can."

****

"We have to make a more solid plan before we go through," the major said when the three women assembled again, with the addition of the Guard colonel. "If we rush through the Doors with insufficient prep, what will we find on the other side? We don't even know if the men have a Guard."

"Yes, we do," Alanna said.

"What?"

Alanna hesitated for a beat, then answered. "This isn't general knowledge, and I'll appreciate your discretion, but the government keeps quiet, clandestine track of Wrongside. I'm in regular contact with their head of state, their commander. I've just called him to alert him to the problem. We also have the drone cameras."

Kai settled back in her seat. "We know they have no regular standing Guard. No one is required to report for one-year service, as we are."

"But-but don't they have—well, wars?" Louise asked. "Against each other? Don't they fight all the time?"

"Surprisingly, no. There are regular clashes, of course, since they're men, but nothing you'd call a war. And those clashes have actually diminished since Sherman's been in power. In my opinion, the lack of conflict is more an organizational issue than anything else. The men can't get along, but they're too lazy and incompetent to do anything about it. Still, they're volatile and easily roused."

"Why doesn't the public know any of this?" Louise asked.

Kai deferred to Alanna.

"I'm not sure," Alanna admitted. "I guess because that's the way it's always been. We pushed the men out of our lives, out of our minds, seventy-one years ago, and we never let them back in. The only reason we even keep tabs on them is for safety's sake, just in case."

"So what can we do with this information? How can it help us get to Laran?"

"I've got an idea," Alanna replied. "This discussion has reminded me of what I know. As much as I want to burst through that Door and take back my daughter, it's probably not the best idea. It might stir them up too much, and we could be overwhelmed. We need to do this covertly, so those lazy and incompetent men won't even notice we're there."

"Covert ops." The Guard colonel stood up. "One of my best new officers has an aptitude for that. She's right outside." The woman walked out of the room and was back within two minutes, followed by a young woman.

The new arrival saluted the room. "Lieutenant Kirannen Sobriski, third squad, special operations." Addressing herself to Alanna, she continued. "Ma'am, the colonel explained the op, and told me you've recommended using just a few people. I agree. We can outfit a team with weapons and soft clothes in less than an hour.

"Since your daughter wasn't put right back through the Door, we can assume the clerk over there took the bribe and kept his mouth shut. We should cross the Fence without involving the transfer clerk. It would be best."

Alanna and Louise exchanged glances. "Agreed," Louise said. "We'll have to leave earlier to get to the covert crossing point. Let's choose our team. Kirannen, you'll take lead."

"One condition," Alanna said. "Kai and I are on the team."

Kirannen nodded. "I remember how well you did on the smuggling mission last spring. You'll do well again." Everyone in the room nodded her head.

In the end there were six women, which Kirannen thought was a maximum. "Too many unfamiliar faces would raise suspicion."

Alanna, Kai, Louise, and Kirannen were four of them. The other two, introduced as Jo and Weezy, were privates. The women changed into shapeless cotton pants, baggy shirts and jackets, long-billed caps, and boots. Under the shirts, each carried a pistol and extra magazines. The Guardswomen had knives in their boots. All had radios, and they'd take rifles, as well.

They drove a few miles south of the city. It had

now been five and a half hours since Laran was put through the Door. Alanna had been preoccupied with planning the op, but now she was on tenterhooks again. In the back of the special ops van, Kai took her hand.

"We'll find her, Alanna. We will find her."

Alanna nodded tightly but didn't speak. Kai directed the car down a little-used gravel road, then an even smaller one. At the end of it was a small block storage unit surrounded by empty land. The closest buildings were a few hundred yards away, near the Border Fence.

Louise entered a seven-number sequence on a keypad next to the unit's only door. After everyone was inside, she quickly locked the door and led the team across the single room, filled with dusty crates and boxes, to a stairwell.

Twenty feet under the ground, the space opened out to an echoing garage. A dozen ratty old trucks sat there.

Understanding what was needed, Kirannen took over smoothly. "Each of you take a truck, and we'll head out immediately. We'll come up inside a garage in a mostly unpopulated area. We'll drive north again to the town, which is called Cody, and find a place to spread out."

"The radios are on a secure Guard frequency," Louise added, "and the colonel will be monitoring. We'll check in every half hour to start."

"I can lead," Kai offered. "I've had time to study the maps." Once everyone had chosen and loaded a truck, Kai steered toward a shallow ramp at the west end of the room.

The team was in Cody by late afternoon, seven

hours after they'd learned Laran had been put through the Door. They parked on an empty side street and disembarked, uneasily aware that they were the only women who had ever seen Cody. Kirannen transmitted their safe arrival to her colonel.

"Man," Alanna swore. "This is it?"

"It looks like those old Earth pictures of ancient frontier towns," Louise whispered. "It's so small and primitive. But look at all the flowers. Why do they plant flowers?"

Even on the side street, many buildings were equipped with window boxes filled with flowers. Tiny, faded houses straggled up and down the street in no particular order. Most had ragged vegetable gardens as well as flower boxes and some ornamental trees. No one in Rightside grew vegetables—or flowers, for that matter—unless they were farmers.

Few of the streets were paved, and there was no municipal lighting. The businesses were modest, with unlighted wooden signs and some wares in the dusty display windows.

"What's a barber shop?" one of the privates asked.

"Whatever I expected," Alanna said, "it wasn't this. But we need to get moving."

"Remember," Kirannen directed, "these are the same men we see in the Red Cabins. When you recognize someone, dip your head a little and turn it to the side. Try to make your voice low and hoarse, and don't do anything distinctly feminine, like sway your hips or touch your hair. Try to keep your hands out of sight. Try to talk like a man. Say ain't a lot."

They pulled out separately, agreeing to check in on the half hour. Kai left first. She had spotted a bar as she drove into town, so decided to start there. She almost turned around and walked back out, though, because Bally was behind the bar.

Bally had been her favorite for several years, back in her younger days. One of her daughters, if she remembered right, had come from Bally. How long had it been since she'd seen him? At least ten or twelve years, and her hair was gray now. Hopefully, he wouldn't recognize her. She took the chance and walked up to the bar with her head down. She looked sideways as though checking out the place.

"Beer?" Bally asked, making it easy for her.

She grunted assent, and he slid a filled stein in her direction. She took a sip, surprised that it tasted good. She took a good swallow and set herself to listen to the conversations going on around her.

A man stood at a table behind her, periodically hitching at his belt. "Yeah, you damn betcha I give him what-for. This ain't the Final Confrontation, I told the mother-lovin' fool, so don't be givin' me no orders."

Kai tuned him out when the old man next to her spoke. "New here, ain't'cha?"

"From out east," she answered.

"Sheridan?" He whistled.

"Yup."

"Never been," the old man said. "I don't get out much, bein' the transfer man."

Kai held herself still with an effort. *The transfer man*. "Yeah? Where's the Cabin?"

"Main Street."

Main Street sounded like it might be in the center of town, as the Pennsylvania Avenue Cabin was, but how could she know for sure? She'd just have to go with the flow.

"Yeah, been there four years now. It's a good job for a childless old coot like me."

"See a lotta action, do ya?"

Willie shifted importantly. As insecure as he was about his job, he took pains to brag about it, to make himself sound indispensable. He started with a heavy sigh.

"Some days them babies comes over like rain, and the Door goes up and down a dozen times. Other days I 'bout go crazy from boredom. Had me a chance to go fishin' this mornin', but then a baby came in, and y'know, there's a lot a' paperwork with that, then the little guy's gotta be delivered to his dad right off, and I gotta take supplies if he ain't had no boys yet.

"It's been hard, till now, on account'a I didn't have no truck." He took another slug of his beer. "But today I finely bought me one. Not a new truck y'unnerstand, but a good used one. No more walkin' for me, luggin' babies and goods all over town and way out past, almost to the Plains sometimes."

"So it pays good, bein' a transfer man?"

"Oh, hell no, it don't. Took me years to save up enough, but today was the day, finely."

Finally? Does that mean he didn't have the money yesterday?

"Yeah, Bally just give me a beer to celebrate. He's good that way."

Bally, hearing his name, walked down the bar. "Set ya up again?"

Kai looked down at her beer, surprised to find the glass empty. "Sure. 'Nother one for my friend, here, too, seein' how he's celebratin'."

Kai drank her second beer but didn't get much more out of the transfer man. At the half-hour mark, she grunted a goodbye and stepped outside into the dark. *They can plant flowers, but they don't put up streetlights?*

"I have a lead," she reported. "The transfer man bought a truck this morning, said he finally had enough money. Anyone else?"

Jo had overheard a man saying the sheriff had driven north with a child in his truck that morning. The man had wondered aloud about it, saying the sheriff was childless.

"Sheriff?" Alanna repeated. "That's Bud Hopper, right? We know Bud, but I'm not sure if that's a good thing or a bad thing at this point."

"Did anyone else hear a reference to the Corral?" Louise asked. "From what I can gather, it must be a daycare center. We could try there, as well as at whatever they have for a school. Maybe Laran's been hidden in plain sight."

"Good idea," Kirannen said. "Major, you go to the Corral, and I'll find the school, if there is one. Kai, go back and pressure the transfer man.

"That gives us three avenues to follow," she continued. "Let's put one woman on the road north. The other two can spread out a little farther into the countryside, looking for anything relevant."

"I'll follow the sheriff," Alanna said. "I think Laran's more likely to be out of town by now."

"We're set, then. Next check-in, one hour."

Chapter 30

The Gibsons, bored and restless after weeks of living rough on the Plains, had snuck into Bozeman and were laying low with Trask. Cousin Eddie was still in jail, the idiot, so they didn't worry about him.

Chad was so sick of the whole thing he was almost ready to go back to Cody and school, but he knew the law would scoop him up quick if he tried that. He wondered if he dared take off, go down south or somewhere, away from his old man, the smuggling, and Trask.

"So you reckon it's safe enough now if we go back to business as usual?" Frank was asking Trask. The three of them were sitting around Trask's kitchen table with a keg of beer. Chad didn't really like the stuff, but the other two were half-soused.

"Don't see why not," Trask drawled. "That fool sheriff's forgot about you by now. Long's you stay up here, outta his way, we can start running again."

"Guess I'll go collect up my boys if we're gonna be living here," Frank mused.

"Whatever." Trask wasn't interested in the Gibson brats. "I figure to go in town tonight and call my guy up north, tell him the pipeline's in business again. We'll start hauling them Rightside drugs right the hell down through Cody like we used to, be back in the money before you know it. Who's gonna stop us?"

Bud Hopper, Chad thought sourly. But he didn't say anything.

Trask, good as his word, left as soon as it was dark and was back almost immediately. "Git your ass off of that couch, Frank," he bellowed. "We got work." He rousted Chad, too, and the three of them set off north to pick up a truckload of bootleg drugs.

****

Alanna barreled out of Cody as fast as she dared, following one of Kai's maps. This was the North Road, which eventually connected to Bozeman, but there were dozens of smaller roads branching off of it. There was about one chance in a million, she figured, that she'd catch up with Sheriff Bud Hopper. But she had to do something. At least she believed she was headed in the right direction.

Unlike her daughter, Alanna was too focused to notice the beauty of the Plains. She sped past the same buffalo herds and tumbleweeds, the same sparkling river, without noticing. After the one-hour check-in, during which no one reported progress, she speeded up.

By the second check-in, Kirannen recommended all but one team member should follow Alanna. The transfer man had admitted to Kai that Laran came through his door but insisted he didn't know where she'd gone. As far as they could determine, Laran was not in Cody, but Jo would stay there to watch for the sheriff's return. They would build a leapfrog pattern and search each side road as they encountered them. Alanna chose a spot just outside Bozeman for their eventual rendezvous.

After the check-in, Alanna felt an even greater sense of urgency.

If she had ever been on the Plains before, she'd have known about washouts. Road crews came through from Bozeman or Cody occasionally to straighten them out, but no one had gotten to this one yet. A spring flood had taken out part of the road in the center of a bend that skirted a small gulch.

Unfamiliar with the higher center of gravity of the truck, Alanna couldn't control the skid as she hit the washout. The truck slid across loose gravel and dirt, caromed off a boulder, spun completely around, and thumped sideways into the gulch.

Alanna let out a yelp of shock as the truck came to a final halt. Her first thought was to call for help, so she reached for the radio. "Where are you, dammit?" Unhitching her seatbelt, she scooted across the tilted front seat, thinking the radio had probably fallen to the floor. Out the open window on the passenger side, she finally located it. It had been thrown through the window by the impact and was lying in pieces in a litter of gravel.

She clawed her way out of the truck and scrabbled up onto the roadway. Standing there, nursing a skinned elbow, feeling a thread of blood trickle down the side of her face, Alanna looked at her surroundings in dismay. She turned a slow circle.

"What the hell?" She groaned. "What the manly hell am I going to do now?"

She stood, literally, in the middle of nowhere. A brisk breeze harried clumps of brush across the road, and they were the only things moving. In the dim light from her headlights, she couldn't see a tree, a house, a vehicle, an animal, or a person. Disconsolately, she collapsed onto a handy rock.

****

Clyde, to Bud's surprise, had offered over supper to straighten Laran's broken nose. With his intimate knowledge of facial structure, he was confident he could improve it and keep her from developing an unsightly bump as it healed. Laran was game, so Bud had allowed it. Laran swore it didn't even hurt much, and she seemed pleased with the result.

Bud was sorry to leave camp, that was sure, but he had to get home, catch a few hours' sleep, then head for Jackson Hole first thing in the morning.

"When are you coming back, Bud? Will you bring my mom?" Laran seemed to like Ricky and Clyde, but she was anxious about losing Bud, the most familiar face.

"Maybe," Bud hedged, "but I ain't making any promises. I've gotta go clear to Jackson Hole in the morning, remember, and that's a long way off. I'll go to the commander, see what's best to do, and then come back here quick as I can. Maybe your mom will be over here by then, and I can bring her. Or maybe we'll just go back to town so she can meet you at the Transfer Door. Okay?"

"But can't I come with you?" she whined.

Bud, having no experience with the pleading whines of children, didn't know what to say. So he shook his head and stomped off to his truck. He sketched a wave to his brother and peeled out of camp.

Ricky walked over to put a comforting hand on Laran's shoulder. "Come back to the fire, honey. It's getting cold. Clyde's making popcorn."

Bud clicked on his headlights and drove slowly, watching for deer or buffalo. His thoughts were a hundred miles south. When and if he saw the commander he would start by reminding the guy of their recent clash with the women over the Red Cabins. Then he'd mention the trouble that must be goin' on over there to make someone put the president's daughter through a Door. Why should we help them out, he'd say, without getting something for our trouble? I've had this idea, see.

His headlights caught the glint of metal off the side of the road just before he saw a guy jump out to flag him down. He slowed to a halt and stuck his head out the window.

"Looks like you ran into some trouble," he observed. "Can we maybe pull her out?"

"Pull her out?" the guy echoed, clearly puzzled. "Pull who? Wait, Bud? Is that you, Bud?"

"Yeah, it's me," Bud answered, shouldering his door open and stepping out, "but who're you? Kind of dark out here."

To Bud's utter shock, the guy lunged forward to envelope him in a desperate hug. "Oh, I'm so glad it's you! It's me. It's Alanna!"

"What?" Bud might have thought he couldn't be any more shocked, but he was. "Alanna? Woman, what the mother-loving hell are you doing here? How can you be clear up on the Plains? In *Wrongside*?" The world was going crazy, had to be. Willie would have agreed whole-heartedly.

Alanna looked awful. He was used to seeing her as his well-dressed, perfumed, smiling partner of the Red Cabins. Now she wore shapeless old clothes, a ballcap, and boots. Boots! Her face and hands were dirty, and there was a trail of blood down one cheek. He looked from her to the wrecked truck and back again.

She mustered a rueful smile. "I know this looks crazy. There was a bad place in the road, and I skidded over the edge." She pulled off the cap, ran her fingers through spiky hair, and made a dismissive gesture. "It's a long story. I'm okay, really, and I was actually looking for you."

"For me?" Bud laughed. "All you had to do was make an appointment at the Red Cabin."

"I meant I was looking here, in Wrongside. You weren't in Cody, but we heard you'd gone up the North Road."

"We?"

Alanna looked past him to his truck, still running, headlights on, in the middle of the road. "Are you alone?"

Bud fisted his hands on his hips and frowned. Could Alanna be looking for Laran? Was she part of the law in Rightside, maybe, sneakin' over here in men's clothes to look for the kid? Or was she one of the ones who had put Laran through the Door?

Before he could make up his mind, another truck rolled up behind his. The driver propped an elbow on his open window and leaned out. "Want to get the hell out of the way, asshole?"

"Hold your water," Bud growled, and turned to walk back to the truck. He put up an arm to shield his eyes from the truck's headlights. "You got urgent business, do you?"

With a muttered oath, the driver cranked open his door and dropped out of the cab. Bud could just make out the sidearms holstered at the man's thigh, so he moved his right hand toward his own holstered gun.

A whisper came from one of the other men in the cab. "Trask, it's him! That's the sheriff, get back in here!"

Instead of returning to the truck, the man walked forward to get a better look, his right hand dangerously near the sidearm. Bud held steady, flicking his gaze from the man's eyes to his hands. With his left hand, he made a quick stay-back motion to Alanna.

"The sheriff? Out here in the dark, with just one skinny kid for a witness? Frank, I think we got us what you might call a golden opportunity here."

Frank Gibson came out of the passenger door, holding his rifle. He moved sideways to flank Bud. "Bad idea, Trask, bad one. I've seen him with a gun. But I'm with you."

Trask nodded. "Who's that there behind you, Sheriff?"

Alanna took two quick steps to the left. "Backup," she said grimly. "I've got my gun on your friend Frank, here."

Gun? Bud had time to think. *She's got a gun?*

"Chad!" Frank shouted. "Bring out your shotgun!"

Slowly, Chad pulled his gun free of the rack in the back window and got out. He stood uncertainly, shotgun barrel pointed at the ground. He wasn't even sure it was loaded.

Chapter 31

Fifteen miles south of Alanna and Bud, Kai pulled out of a side road and turned right. Following the pattern Kirannen had set up, she'd drive past the next three roads before checking the fourth. The side roads seemed to just meander into the brush, turning this way or that at random. So far, all the roads had come to dead ends, some at abandoned campsites. She'd found a man and some boys at one of the camps, and had made rough queries about a lost kid. They hadn't seen anything.

Wrongside was a mess, she'd decided, with no order to it at all. How did anyone ever find anything? Searching in the dark wasn't doing them much good now, either, Kai thought. Still, she'd keep going until she reached Alanna. They'd all keep going.

Her radio crackled, signaling another check-in. Without stopping, she thumbed the call button and reported her location. She listened as Kirannen, Louise, and the privates did the same, reporting no results. They waited a few beats, but Alanna didn't check in.

Kai stopped her truck and thumbed the radio again. "Alanna? We need a report."

There was nothing.

"She must be away from the truck," Kirannen decided. "We'll give her another ten minutes and try again. Let's keep moving, everyone."

****

With a violent sweep of his arm, Frank directed Chad to walk out farther. "Three against two, Sheriff," he cackled. "And I swear to Yong that one's a woman. I like them odds."

"Me, too," Bud called back. "So you better think about this, Frank. Would you rather be in jail, or laying dead on the side of this road?"

Trask pulled back the hammer of his pistol. All of them heard the faint click. "Come to that," Trask said, "maybe Frank'd be dead, but so would you."

Alanna eased backward to keep both Frank and the third man in her sights. The shotgun could do more damage to them, she realized. If it did come to it, she'd move fast, take out the man with the shotgun first, then swing her own gun back to Frank.

"Nobody needs to die," Bud answered Trask. "And I got no claim against you. You can get in your truck and go back the way you came. We'll take charge of Frank and Chad, here."

"Ain't gonna happen!" Frank shouted, crouching suddenly and raising his gun.

Bud drew and shot the rifle out of Frank's hands. Frank howled and dropped, grabbing his wrist. Trask's first shot kissed off the top of Bud's left shoulder, jerking him back in a half-circle.

Alanna aimed for center mass as she'd been taught years ago, but she was out of practice. Her bullet hit Chad high on one leg, and he flew backward, dropping his shotgun.

Trask retreated behind the open door of his truck and aimed again. Bud dove behind a boulder, then looked around frantically. "Take cover!" he shouted at

Alanna.

She was already moving right, slamming sideways into her tipped-over truck. She wedged herself between the truck bed and a cocked wheel and took aim at Frank.

Bud fired at Trask's legs, but his bullet skipped off the truck door's lower edge. Trask vaulted into the truck and jerked it into gear. "Frank! You coming?"

Still on the ground, Frank scrabbled backward toward his passenger door. Alanna got off a shot, but missed him by inches.

"Chad!" Frank shouted. "Can you walk?" The boy, who was in the open, yards away from Trask's truck, answered with a groan. Frank didn't hesitate. "Sheriff'll take care of you!" He hauled himself into the truck, slamming the door as Trask reversed, spun the truck around, and took off.

"I'll get you for this, woman!" Frank shouted back at them. "See if I don't!"

Bud stood, left arm held tight against his chest, and stumbled to the still figure on the ground. He kicked the shotgun away and dropped heavily to his knees. The boy was barely conscious. Blood pumped out of a ragged hole on the inside of his thigh. Bud pressed his good hand against the wound.

Alanna ran up to them. "Is he alive? Oh, he's just a kid! Bud, tell me I didn't kill him!"

"Artery," Bud gasped. Now that the fight was over, he realized that his shoulder was on fire, and his head was swimming. "Bullet must of nicked an artery. He's losing blood fast. See if—see if you can get my belt off."

Alanna reached for her own belt instead, and

ripped it out of the loops. She pushed Chad up onto his side, eliciting another groan, and together they got the belt under him. Chad gasped out a wavery scream as Alanna yanked it tight above the wound.

Bud forced himself to think straight. "Bozeman's closer," he decided. "We'll take him there. Get in my truck, bring it over."

Together, they got the boy stretched out on the front seat of the truck, with his head in Alanna's lap and his legs over Bud's in the passenger seat. By the time they were ready to go, all three of them were covered with Chad's blood, and some of Bud's.

"Do you have anything for your shoulder?" Alanna asked. "Will you be okay?"

Bud made an effort to sound normal, though he still felt woozy. "It ain't deep. Not bleeding much."

"Here." Alanna leaned forward and managed to struggle out of the baggy coat. "Bundle this up and press it down on your shoulder. I don't need you passing out from blood loss, too."

They drove in silence for a few minutes. Bud reached down to check Chad's pulse. He wasn't right sure what it was supposed to feel like, but it seemed weak to him.

"I can't believe Frank left him laying there," he muttered.

"That was Frank Gibson, wasn't it? From Cody?"

Bud shot her a glance. The only way Alanna could know Frank was because she'd met him in the Red Cabins.

"Yep, Frank's a real good one, ain't he? Left his own son bleeding in the dirt."

Alanna gasped and slammed on the brake. The

truck jerked to a halt in the middle of the dark road. Bud grabbed at Chad to keep him from sliding.

"What was it? I didn't see anything." He stopped. Alanna's face was as white as springtime snow, and her eyes, as she turned to him, were huge and dark with shock.

"Alanna, what's wrong with you?"

"This is Frank Gibson's son? His *son*? How old is he?"

Bud's mouth dropped open. "Hell, I don't know, fifteen, sixteen, maybe? Still in school, off 'n on."

Alanna groaned and dropped her head to the steering wheel.

Bud was clueless at first, but by the time Alanna raised her head to look at him with haunted eyes, he knew what she was going to say.

"He could be mine," she said, forcing out the admission. "I sent a baby to Wrongside sixteen years ago, and this boy could be mine. I might have killed my own child."

****

Bud directed Alanna to the Bozeman clinic and roused the doctor, an old man who was used to patching up bullet wounds in the middle of the night.

"This is a nasty one," he commented, loosening the belt around Chad's thigh, "but the boy's lucky you thought to truss him up. I can start a transfusion, clean out the dirt, find the bullet, patch the hole, he'll be good as new. Either of you his father?"

Alanna, who had settled the ballcap low on her forehead and shrugged back into her bloody, shapeless coat, opened her mouth, then shut it and let Bud answer.

"He's my prisoner," Bud said. "I'm the sheriff from down in Cody. Me and my deputy here had a shootout with some smugglers on the North Road. They left this one behind. Name's Chad Gibson."

"Gibson," the old man acknowledged. "I'll write it up. Let me start that transfusion, put a clean dressing on this, and I'll see to your shoulder."

Bud shook his head automatically, but the doctor insisted. When he'd finished bandaging the shoulder, he gave Bud a bottle of antibiotics and nodded over at Chad, lying on the next table. "You want to wait for him?"

Bud shook his head. "We've gotta get back to Cody. Tell your sheriff I'll call him later."

The doctor nodded and turned to the boy. Alanna looked back as they walked out. She'd had a good look at Chad under the lights of the clinic. His face was remarkably like her mother's.

Alanna followed Bud outside to the dark and silent street. A few lights shone from an all-night bar a block down. Bozeman was much smaller than Cody, she realized. It must be opposite Rightside's town of New Wheeling. They weren't far enough north for New Cleveland.

"I'm bushed," Bud admitted, "and hungry, and damn thirsty. Must be from losing blood. Besides that, woman, we got some talking to do. What say we go down to the bar there, find a quiet corner, and order some grub before we head south?"

"Grub? If that means food, I could use some, too." Alanna started down the street, forcing her thoughts from Chad to her missing daughter. She needed to decide how much she could trust Bud.

****

They stared at each other across the stained wooden table of a booth at the back of the Bozeman Bar. It was Alanna who spoke first.

"I came over here," she began, "to look for a child who'd been kidnapped, stolen from her mother. We've had some trouble in Rightside."

Bud grunted. "Figured that."

That surprised Alanna. "You did? Why?"

****

Now it was Bud's turn to decide whether he trusted Alanna. He thought of their nights in the Red Cabin, of their shared pleasure and their idle conversation. They were almost friends if that was possible. Whatever she was here for, he decided, it wasn't to do the poor kid harm.

"Because Laran's here in Wrongside."

"Oh, thank Milina!" Alanna gasped. "You've seen her? Is she all right? Where is she?"

"Safe. She got put through a Transfer Door yesterday morning, beat up some, and we got her hid safe."

"You hid her? Why? What do you mean she was beaten?"

Bud stirred and cut his eyes away from Alanna in warning. The barman had arrived with burgers and beers. After he'd gone, Bud spoke.

"She was scared spitless at first, but we—me and the transfer man—got her calmed down easy enough. She said a crazy woman snatched her and took off. They mostly drove around for a couple three days, stayed in a house for a while, then drove back to wherever the crazy woman lived. The woman smacked her around a little, broke her nose—" Alanna gasped, and Bud stopped for a long swallow of beer.

"—and blacked her eyes. Laran says she tried to get away a couple times, almost made it once, but the woman put some gold in a bag and drug her to a Transfer Cabin. She bribed a clerk and they pushed her through the Door."

Bud stopped abruptly. "You look like her," he realized. "Like Laran."

Alanna, too tired and relieved to hold back secrets, smiled and said, "So do you."

Chapter 32

Kirannen called a halt to the search two side roads short of the one that led to Ricky and Clyde's camp. "We've lost touch with Alanna," she apprised the colonel over the radio, "and we're all tired. We're not doing much good in the dark, anyway. It's only about two hours till sunrise. We'll pull over, try to get some sleep, then start again."

"Copy that," the colonel agreed. "Check in when you're on the move again."

"You might put that backup we discussed on alert," Kai added. "If we—when we find Laran, the men might not give her up willingly. If a fight becomes necessary, we'll need the Guard, especially if Alanna is in trouble, too."

"Noted. Get some rest."

****

Ricky and Clyde eased out of the tent early the next morning without waking their guest.

"She must really be exhausted," Clyde said, stooping to gather kindling for the campfire. "Just imagine, three days on the run, then she gets pushed over here to strangers. Her little head must be reeling."

"No more than mine," Ricky said. "Who'd have thought we'd be playing hosts to a frightened female? The two of us have never seen an actual woman, let alone a little girl."

Clyde squatted beside the remains of their fire and stirred the ashes, exposing a few coals. "You haven't even looked at my sketches yet," he complained. "I'd show you, but they're in the tent."

Ricky smiled. "If you thought you were a celebrity before," he predicted, "wait till Wrongside sees your sketches of Laran. You'll be more famous than Yong."

Clyde preened a little, then the smile fell from his face. "Oh, great," he said, looking over to the road. "Here's Bud back again. And he's got company." He sighed and stood up. "Guess I'd better whip up more pancake batter."

Ricky walked to the truck, not understanding why Bud was back so early. He must have changed his mind about trying to talk to the commander. His brother got out of the truck with a grin as wide as the Plains, holding one arm awkwardly across his waist. An unfamiliar man in baggy, stained clothes got out of the other side.

"Ricky!" Bud boomed. "Ricky, you'll never believe it! This is Alanna!" he gestured to Alanna, who pulled off her cap and stood uncertainly, teetering on the balls of her feet.

"Is she here?" the woman blurted. "Is Laran here? Where is she?"

Ricky stood rooted to the spot, mouth open in shock. Behind him, Clyde stopped dead, a bag of flour in one hand, a spoon in the other. Since they'd already met Laran, they realized almost instantly that this was another—another!—woman. Clyde dropped the bag, and flour exploded over his legs.

The woman stepped toward Ricky. "Where's my daughter?" she demanded.

He waved a hand toward the tent. "Sleeping," he managed.

Alanna ran for the tent, and almost immediately, the men heard a glad cry. "Mommy!"

Ricky tore his gaze from the tent. "Bud?" He shook his head once, twice, as if to clear it. "Buddy, what's going on? Where did you find her? Is she Laran's *mother*?"

Bud nodded, the grin threatening to split his face. "Ricky, I've got something to tell you, something real big. And after I tell you, I've gotta tell Laran somehow."

Ricky stepped forward and took his brother's arm. "What is it, Buddy?"

"Alanna just told me. I know her, you see, from the Red Cabins. We've seen each other plenty, going way back. She's probably the woman I've liked most, over the years. She came here looking for her daughter, and she just told me—"

Bud's legs buckled. He might have sunk right to the ground under the enormity of his news, but Ricky caught him. "Told you what, Buddy?"

Bud looked into his brother's brown eyes. "That Laran is my daughter, too."

They both sank to the ground. Behind them, Clyde looked uncomprehendingly down at his floury legs.

****

By the time a relieved and happy Laran walked out of the tent, dressed in one of Clyde's shirts and clinging to her mother's arm, the men had gathered themselves enough to sit down at the picnic table. Alanna, wiping tears from her cheeks, led Laran over to Bud.

"I told her you've got a surprise for her," she said.

She was breaking more than one Rightside law, Alanna realized. Other women would castigate her for it. But last night had irrevocably changed her view of women and men and children. She had almost killed her own child, and the depth of her feelings about that still scared her. Bud, she knew, must feel the same way about Laran, and he had a right to tell his daughter who he was.

Bud swung his legs over the picnic bench and patted a space beside him. "Set a minute, girl. I got a question for you."

"What's that, Bud? Clyde, we didn't miss breakfast, did we? I'm really hungry, and I'll bet my mom is, too."

It broke the tension, and they all laughed as Clyde jumped up, flustered. "I guess pancakes are off the menu," he blurted, "but we have leftover fish and cornbread. There's cheese, too, and um, eggs. I guess I'll just get busy with that."

"Thank you," Laran said and turned her attention to Bud.

"Have you ever," Bud began, "heard the word 'father'?"

"Huh-uh. Does it mean something in Wrongside?"

"It sure does, honey. Father means almost the same thing as Mother. If I had any sons—any boys—I'd be their father."

"But you said you didn't have any boys."

"I don't." Bud glanced up at Alanna, at a loss for what to say next. She nodded encouragingly. He pressed forward.

"But I'm *your* father, Laran, just like Alanna is your mother. You're her child, and you're my child, too."

Laran frowned. "I don't get it. You can't be my father. I'm not a boy. I'm a girl."

Alanna sat on Laran's other side and pulled her close. "Honey, I've told you how babies are made, remember? Women and men meet in Red Cabins to have sex, and sometimes women get pregnant. It takes a man to make a woman pregnant, and that man is the baby's father. Bud and I met in a Red Cabin, and we made you. Bud is your father, the same way I'm your mother."

"The same way?" Laran was dubious.

"You don't have to understand it right now," Alanna assured her. "All you have to know is that Bud cares about you the same way I do, now that he knows he's your father."

"Even before that." As Bud said it, he realized it was true. "I liked you the first time I saw you," he told Laran, "sitting in Willie's kitchen, all dirty, blood on your face." He smiled. "I cared about you then, too."

Suddenly Ricky clapped a hand to his forehead. "Wait a minute! I'm an uncle!"

"You're a what?" Alanna asked, startled.

"An uncle! I'm related to Laran, too, I'm Bud's brother. Laran, you're my—wait, what's the word? It isn't nephew, it's something else. Oh, I'll think of it, give me a minute."

Alanna smiled. "Niece."

Ricky threw up both hands. "Niece, that's it! Laran, come over here and give me a hug!"

Bud stirred. "I guess I never did introduce anybody. Alanna, meet my brother, Ricky. That's Clyde, Ricky's partner."

Clyde, hearing his name, sashayed over from the fire to put a proprietary hand on Ricky's shoulder. "We're together."

"Oh!" Alanna was nonplussed. "I didn't realize that men could be that way. Like women are, I mean, sometimes."

Ricky shook his head and enfolded his niece in a bear hug. "Women, too? It's a day for revelations, isn't it?"

****

A half-mile away, a truck roared by on the North Road. Frank Gibson, driving one-handed, was on his way back to Cody, bent on warning the men. That woman couldn't be the only one here in Wrongside. More had to be coming, too, and they best be ready.

Chapter 33

When Louise drove into the campsite, she saw four men and a child at a picnic table near a tent. She could smell food and fresh coffee. One of the men, seeing her, jumped up. With a shock, she realized it wasn't a man. It was the president herself, waving happily. Maybe that wasn't a male child, Louise thought. Could it be Laran? She jumped down from the truck, weapon drawn.

Alanna ran over to her, laughing. "Oh, put your gun away, Louise. We're okay. I figured you'd be showing up soon. I tipped the truck into a ditch a few miles north of here, and my radio was smashed. We're all right, though. Laran's fine. Want some breakfast?"

Relieved, Louise reached into the truck for her radio. "Second side road," she reported. "The president and Laran are here. All's well."

****

Kai was first to arrive. She stopped well back from the camp and came out of the truck with her gun drawn, covering the three men.

Laran ran toward Kai, calling a hello, but skidded to a stop at the sight of the weapon. "Aunt Kai?"

Kai moved her gun hand away from her body and beckoned to Laran with the other. "It's okay, honey. Come over here." She reached for Laran's arm and pulled the child behind her. "Get in my truck, Laran, and lay down. Keep your head down below the window."

"Aunt Kai, you're hurting me! Let me go. What's wrong?"

"There are three men over there! We need to get you safe."

"But I'm already safe!" Laran protested, trying to tug her arm free. "Bud's been taking care of me ever since I got away from the crazy woman!"

Kai stopped trying to push Laran into the truck, but she didn't let go of her arm. "These are *men*, honey. You don't know what they're like. We have no control, out here in the open like this. Where do they keep their guns, did you see?"

Laran yanked hard and finally got her arm free. "They don't have any *guns,* Aunt Kai, Ricky and Clyde are nice. Ricky taught me how to catch a fish, and Clyde makes really good cornbread."

Kai took a closer look at the camp. She could see Louise standing beside a campfire and talking to two of the men. Her hand rested casually on her holster, but she seemed to have the situation under control. Alanna was closer to the river, walking with Bud Hopper. Kai could swear they were holding hands. She'd never held hands with a man, but then, she'd never taken a walk with one, either. She was still trying to make sense of the scene when Kirannen drove in.

The lieutenant was out of her truck quickly, holding her own gun. "Good, you have Laran already." She took in the scene, frowned. "What's Louise doing? We need to get the president secure. Let's put Laran in the truck first, and—"

"Stop," Kai said. She holstered her gun and nodded her head toward camp. "Look at them. Really look at them. They aren't even armed. Louise is just having a conversation, and Alanna is walking with Bud, the sheriff. He's been one of her favorites for years. They know each other pretty well."

Kirannen snorted. "In the Red Cabins, sure, but that doesn't make you a man's friend. It doesn't mean you can just have a conversation with one, as you put it."

At the sound of another truck, they turned. Weezy, the Guardswoman, responded to the situation instantly, using her truck for cover, taking only seconds to aim a rifle with a fitted scope. "I can take down the one with the president on your order, Lieutenant."

"No!" Laran launched herself at the Guardswoman, knocking the woman off-balance in her fury. "You can't shoot Bud. He's my *father!*"

The obscenity left all three women gasping. Weezy froze in place, holding onto the truck bed for balance. Kai, who had been halfway toward accepting that the men were okay, moved forward, then stopped with a jerk. She wanted to grab Laran and throw her into the truck after all, but this was Alanna's daughter and Alanna was now running toward the sound of her daughter's angry shout.

"Laran, are you all right? Why were you shouting? Kai, why do you all have your guns out? No one's shooting anyone. These men aren't even armed." She didn't mention her own gun and Bud's, locked away in his truck because of Laran. Alanna glared at Kirannen. "Lieutenant, stand down!"

Kirannen holstered her gun immediately. The Guardswoman shifted forward onto both feet, laid her rifle carefully into the bed of the truck, and stood at attention.

Kai was still in shock. "Laran says—" she cleared her throat and started over. "Laran says that Bud is her—is her—"

"Father," Laran supplied. "He is, too. He told me so. Didn't he, Mommy?"

Alanna grimaced. "I meant to have Laran keep that to herself until I'd talked to you. But yes." She straightened up and took a deep breath. If she couldn't say it to her best friend, who could she say it to? "Kai, Bud is Laran's father. I told him, and he told Laran, with my permission."

****

Bud, Ricky, and Clyde had walked over in time to hear her admission. Bud's heart swelled. Alanna's words made him feel more like a man than he ever had, performing in a Red Cabin or wearing a sheriff's uniform.

"It's just like I said earlier, Clyde," Ricky observed to his partner. "This is a day for revelations."

It took more than a few minutes, but Ricky finally convinced everyone to sit down for a long-delayed breakfast. Clyde did more staring than eating, fascinated as he was by the women's faces. Ricky tried to keep everyone happy for Bud's sake, passing bread, commenting on the weather, chattering about the exceptional fishing.

Bud and Alanna just watched Laran with the all-encompassing relief of parents whose child was returned to safety.

It was the three other women who had the most trouble adjusting.

"Laws," Kai muttered into her iced tea. "We've

spent our entire careers working for the law, upholding the law, writing the law." She looked up at Alanna, anguish showing in her round, kindly face. "How many laws are we breaking right now, Alanna?"

"Kai? I've begun to believe that some of our Rightside laws are wrong. At the very least they're misguided. Let me tell you all what I did yesterday." *Was it only yesterday? Yesterday, that I shot my son?*

She recounted the shootout and her discovery that Chad Gibson might be her son. "He looks like my mother. It would take DNA testing, I know, to be sure, but in my heart I really believe he's mine.

"I don't know how he is today," she finished miserably. "The doctor, who seemed pretty competent for a man, said Chad would be fine. He's young and strong…and he'll be…he'll be fine." Alanna dropped her head.

She hugged Laran tight to her side. "Honey, I haven't told you this part yet, but you might have a brother. He'd be related to you, just like Bud and Ricky are related."

Laran nodded and took another bite of her cheese omelet.

Young Weezy obviously didn't get it either, but Kai, Louise, and Kirannen had each sent at least one male baby across the Fence.

"Think on it," Bud suggested, "when you're back in Rightside. Seems like you're all pretty powerful women over there. Think about how things could be different. Now that I've met Laran," he paused to smile at his daughter, "there's no going back for me."

****

They said goodbye to Ricky and Clyde right after

breakfast. Bud would accompany the women back to Willie's Cabin in Cody.

"I'll send you letters, Uncle Ricky and Clyde!" Laran called out the truck window. "Write me letters, too!"

"We will!" Ricky called back, waving madly. Without taking his eyes from Laran, he said to Clyde, "And how are we going to do that, exactly?"

****

It was a warm, breezy morning, promising heat later. Alanna could admire the wildlife this time, exclaiming with Laran over the herds of buffalo grazing along the road.

"It's so pretty here," Laran said. "Bye, bye, buffalo! Bye, bye, tumbleweeds! Hey, Mom, when can we come back to Wrongside? I wanna go camping and fishing again. It was really cool in the tent last night. We played shadow puppets."

"Shhh, honey, something's happening." Ahead of them, Kirannen had stopped her truck and climbed out, holding her radio.

"Ma'am, you'll need to hear this," she said, walking back to Alanna's truck. Ahead of them, the other three women were out of their trucks, too, scanning the surrounding hills. "Guard, say again."

Jo, who had stayed behind in Cody, was on the radio. "I'm making my way to you," she reported, "a couple of miles out of town. There's been trouble in Cody, and it's coming our way. I was in that bar on the main street, sitting in the back when Mike—I know him from the Cabins—burst through the door, shouting about another man who had just come into town, wounded. He said the man had been shot by a woman."

"Alanna didn't shoot him." Bud, last in line, had walked up to join the women. "I did."

Kai was thinking fast. "Alanna, you said Frank Gibson went north, but he must have turned around, gone past the fishing camp while we were all stopped there."

Bud nodded. "Between Mike and Frank, they're like to cause a panic. That's probably Frank's intention. Alanna, he said he'd get you. Wounded like he is, claiming you shot him, he can stir up the men something fierce."

Jo continued her report. "The wounded man came into the bar himself, started shouting that the sheriff had taken up with a gang of women, all armed and headed for Cody. Mike said he was going home to get his gun, and everyone else had better do the same. Another man said Willie and Hank should lock down the Cabins. Hold on, something's happening on the road behind me."

"Gang?" Alanna repeated. "What would he have said if he'd seen all six of us? An army?"

"Ma'am, I'm stopped at a small rise with a good view behind me. I can see a large cloud of dust. It looks like a convoy of vehicles."

"Get moving," Kirannen ordered. "We're at least ten miles north of you. Stay ahead of that convoy, whatever it takes. We'll scout a defensible location."

The five women stared at each other. All of them had served their time in the Guard. All had learned weaponry, tactics, hand-to-hand combat. All had prepared for this exact scenario, an attack by the men.

Alanna shot a questioning look at Bud. He looked down at Laran, then back up at the women. "I'm with you," he said with no hesitation.

Kirannen nodded to Louise. Both of them would be keeping one eye on the attacking men, and the other on Bud.

"This isn't a good place," Kirannen said. "We should keep moving. Bud, I think I remember seeing some high ground closer to Cody. Can we reach it?"

Bud looked around. "Three, four miles south."

"I'll call in for reinforcements," Louise said. "It's best now if the squads go right through the transfer door, as we'd planned originally. They can overpower whoever's there and follow the men north, box them in."

With a preliminary plan in place, the women set off again, Bud moving to the front of the line. When he got to the low hills Kirannen remembered, he stopped and walked back to Kirannen's truck. "Sleeping Woman," he announced.

"Sleeping *what*?"

"Woman," he repeated. "S'what they're called." He lifted his hand and outlined the shape of a reclining woman over the hills east of the road. "See?"

"No. Can we get up there with these trucks?"

"If we go around this next bend, there's a rough track. You can climb it, going slow. Goes right to the top of the far hill."

"Okay, lead us up."

****

"Did you hear that?"

"Mmmmm?" Tenosha, kneeling on the ground outside their rough log shelter, was trying to get Hud to wave to her. Tom had driven up with the baby for a visit to see if they needed anything. Far back in his mind, where he could barely admit thinking it, he'd also figured Tenosha might appreciate a chance to see Hud again.

"You can do it, honey," she encouraged, "wave to Mama. Hear what, Jess?"

"Trucks. What sounds like a whole army of trucks is coming up the hill. Can't you hear them?"

Tenosha cocked her head just as Davy exploded out of the shelter. Without a word, he ran to his truck, opened the door, and grabbed his shotgun.

When he looked at Jessie, all she could see was his fear. She knew that his worst nightmare was that someone would come for Jessie and take her and Baby Boy away. "Y'all get inside the shelter till I see what this is. Nobody ever comes up here. Why're they bothering us now?"

Hud squealed happily at his brother. Tom stood up and headed for his own truck. "I got my gun, too."

Tenosha scooped up the baby and ran with Jessie to the shelter. "Why didn't we bring guns?" she wailed. "They'll take me away from Hud!"

"They won't," Jessie insisted. "We won't let them."

****

When Bud topped the hill, he was surprised to see two trucks and a substantial camp. Looked like somebody was up here for a good spell. *Won't they be surprised,* he thought wryly, *when women start popping outta them trucks coming up behind me?*

He got his own surprise when Davy and Tom Redwolf walked onto the track holding guns. He stopped and left his hands right on the steering wheel while he leaned his head out the window. "Sheee-it,

Davy, you expecting bad company? Don't mean to bust in on your camp, but I got kind of a situation here." The Redwolfs lowered their guns but still didn't look best pleased to see the sheriff.

"We was enjoying this here hill all to ourselves," Tom said.

Bud jacked open his door and got out slow. "I'm real sorry about that, but—well, I might's well say it. I'm bringing trouble. You might wanta fade off down the back of the hill and stay there till we get things figgered out."

Davy stood his ground. "It's my camp. I got a right to be let alone."

"There's women right behind me, Davy. Women who think we hung you, remember that? These particular women might not know you to see you, but you best get outta sight anyway."

Tom gave his son a shove. "Get in the shelter. Now."

Kirannen's truck hove over the crest of the hill as the leather door flap dropped behind Davy. He rushed to Jessie and caught her in a one-handed hug. "It's the sheriff. He says there's a gang of women on their way up the hill."

****

Outside, Kirannen and Louise ignored Tom and the camp and went straight to the best south-facing vantage point. Weezy joined them with her scoped rifle. Tom and Bud watched the women point, argue, then seem to come to an agreement. Alanna and Laran walked straight to the men. Tom jerked back a step.

"My name is Alanna," she said. "And I'm sorry, we don't mean to cause you trouble."

"Then why are you?" Tom managed.

"We came to Wrongside, just six of us, to find my daughter. My child," she amended, gesturing at Laran. She explained the kidnapping. "Men from Cody didn't take our presence too kindly, and now they're after us. I'm not sure what their intention is, but until we find out, we need to establish a defense perimeter on this hilltop." She looked around the camp. "Maybe you'd better leave, head north until we get things straightened out."

Tom couldn't help a glance toward the shelter. "My family's here."

"Can you stand with us, Tom, you and your son?" Bud asked. "Guard our backs? Two more guns would help, and these women are just trying to get home. They ain't aiming to hurt nobody. We can put Hud in one of the trucks with Laran for safety."

"Me? Stand with women?" Tom was already shaking his head, but then he thought of the two women right behind him in the tent. He'd called them his family without even thinking. He gave Bud a short, reluctant nod.

****

As the women started working out a plan, Tom took Bud aside. "Davy and Hud ain't the only ones in the shelter," he admitted. "We got women with us, too."

Bud didn't have the energy to be surprised about that. He hadn't even slept since entering into this strange partnership with Alanna. The whole world seemed skewed to him now. If Tom and Davy had formed a similar partnership, what was it to Bud?

"I figure," Bud surmised, "one of them might be Davy's girl, the one he almost got hung over. Who's the other?"

"She's Hud's—" Tom let out a breath, then forced himself to say the word. "Hud's mother."

That did surprise Bud, but he didn't have time to indulge in curiosity. "You're gonna have to explain all that later."

"The women," Tom continued, "you might know 'em. Tenosha and Jessie. They're afraid these ones coming are gonna force them to go back to Rightside."

Bud nodded, recognizing their names from the Red Cabins. "They're probably right. But they can't stay in that shelter. There might be gunfire up here before it's all over. Let me talk to Alanna."

He pulled her away from a discussion with the others over weapons. "It's important," he insisted. "We need to settle it before the Cody men get here."

Alanna listened to him in dismay. "Other women are here?" She gasped.

Bud nodded. "I've just been telling myself that nothing makes sense anymore. It's all falling apart, somehow. Willie said the other day that there's a big hole in the world. He's right, far as I can see."

"I'm not sure what to do," Alanna admitted.

Bud's mouth dropped open. Women always knew what they wanted to do. How much more could his brain take? He forced himself to think, to take the lead.

"They can't stay in the shelter, and if y'all got more weapons, they'll help. Can you let them be when this is over? Leave them to stay in Wrongside, if they want? We got lots of room up here on the Plains. They wouldn't have to live in town with other men."

She took a deep breath. Things had changed in a deeply fundamental way, she knew, and there might be no way to go back. She could try to fight that or to embrace it. "Yes. Yes, I can."

Bud waved a hand toward the other women. "Won't they have somethin' to say about it, too?"

She gave him a wry smile. "Didn't I tell you? I'm Rightside's president. I'm the boss."

"Huh. I'd forgot Laran said that." Yong, but he needed sleep.

Chapter 34

A few minutes later Alanna and Laran came out of the shelter with Jessie and Tenosha, who was holding Hud. The other women looked at them askance but were too tense to ask questions. None of them noticed that Hud was a male.

"They're here on separate business," Alanna said. "We'll sort it out later. Kirannen, see that they're armed."

Tenosha handed Hud off to Tom. Laran, who had been warned to stay out of the women's way, ran over to be with the baby. "My name's Laran," she said politely, looking up at Tom. "What's yours?"

Louise had been in communication with her backup troops. "All we have to do," she said to the women now, "is keep control of this until our reinforcements arrive. They're already across the Fence, and ETA to this location is less than an hour. Bud tells me Cody doesn't have more than a few hundred men, and they can't all be headed this way. We'll be fine." She bit her lower lip, gave a sharp nod. "We'll be fine."

Kirannen got extra weapons for Tenosha and Jessie.

"You're trained?" she asked. Both nodded. Louise didn't even take time to ask their names.

One truck was detailed off to meet Jo, who was

still ahead of the men. Bud's truck was placed out of sight behind the shelter, tailgate facing south, to hold Laran and Hud in safety.

The rest of the trucks were spaced widely around the brow of the hill to provide cover for defenders. Louise and Kai started building rock piles between the trucks in a fall-back line. Davy slipped off with Tom to cover the north ascent. None of the women got a good look at him.

They didn't have long to wait before the two remaining trucks arrived. "Fifteen minutes behind me, at most," Jo reported.

Time slowed while the women built their rock redoubts. Kirannen ran through scenarios in her head, trying to form a response for every possible action by the men. Louise and Kai checked the deployments obsessively, searching for a better configuration. There wasn't one. Alanna fretted about the children. Jessie and Tenosha, assigned to a truck on the east side of the hill, whispered their worries.

"I haven't held a gun since I finished my hitch in the Guard," Tenosha said. "But to protect Hud, I'll do anything."

"When we get out of this," Jessie whispered back, "the president had better keep her promise. We're not leaving Wrongside."

Bud, shifting his sore shoulder to a more comfortable position, thought about potential injuries. He had a basic first aid kit. The women had better have more supplies. Davy worried about Jessie and Baby Boy. Tom hoped no one would come up the back side.

Laran, scrunched into the passenger well of Bud's truck, rocked a sleepy Hud. She'd played with babies before but had never been responsible for one. She knew that women and men had different shapes and hoped no one expected her to change Hud's diaper.

****

Below the Sleeping Woman, Frank Gibson slowed his truck and craned his neck to see the top of the hill. Yeah, that had to be them. He stopped and flagged the trucks behind him to a halt.

Some two hundred men gathered around him. He'd managed to rouse most of the town, and Frank felt good leading them, knowing they looked to him for direction. He waved an arm backward toward the hill. "They're up there, I figure. See all them trucks?"

"How many, you think?" Rollie Leon asked.

"There's a gang of them, for sure." Frank nodded. "Maybe twenty, thirty? Nothing we can't handle. We'll blow them out. They got no call to be here, shooting at folks." He raised his bandaged hand to get all the men's attention. "This look right to you? This look like it oughta happen in Wrongside, for a woman to just walk in and shoot a man? Shot my boy, too."

Bally shouldered his way to the front of the angry crowd. "Why are them women even here, Frank? Shouldn't we find out, before we start a fight? They got the high ground, after all. I don't think any of us are looking to die today."

Frank sneered. "You want to parley? Parley with women? You're a fool, Bally, didn't your granddad never tell you no stories? We got *guns*, this time around, and there's more of us. We can take these damn women easy, stand up to them, for once."

The rest of the men were on Frank's side, feeling strong and capable with their numbers and their weapons. This time, things would go in their favor.

Bally settled the argument by walking away. "I'm at least gonna ask. Don't shoot me in the back." He started up the track. Halfway there, he was stopped by a voice he recognized.

"Bally."

He looked up. "Hey, there, Kai. Never thought to see you here."

"Same goes."

Bally shifted to a comfortable stance and got right to the point. "Why are you in Wrongside?"

"We didn't intend to be. A child was kidnapped, an eight-year-old girl. The kidnapper pushed her through a Transfer Door to get rid of her. We came to retrieve her, that's all. We mean no harm to anyone in Wrongside, and we'll leave as soon as we can."

"You could of asked. Someone would've sent her back to you. Wrongside is men's territory, and you got no right to be here. We'll defend what's ours. Those men down there? They mean to blow you off this hill."

She craned to look around Bally. There were dozens of men gathered at the base of the hill, watching her. Seeing that many armed men in one place made her shiver. She hoped Bally couldn't see how nervous she was. "How many do you have?"

"They ain't mine," Bally was quick to say, "but a couple hundred, I guess. You?"

Kai sighed and shifted her hold on her rifle. "Not that many, but we have reinforcements coming up behind you. It's in your best interest to go quietly back to town."

Bally shook his head. "Not gonna happen. They're feeling good about this, spoiling for action. You gotta know, Kai, we been waiting seventy-one years for a chance to fight back."

Kai held hard to her natural superiority as a woman. "You can try. You won't win, and some of you will die. Maybe all of you." She turned around, the skin on her back crawling at the thought of armed men behind her, and started up the hill. She'd liked Bally once.

****

"Seventy-one years and they're still itching for payback," Kai reported. "They mean to fight."

"How many are there?" Alanna asked.

"Dozens. Maybe hundreds."

****

"She says they came over here to rescue a little kid. They must of had some kind of trouble in Rightside, and somebody pushed a female kid through a Transfer Door. Anybody know about that?"

All around Bally, men shook their heads. Mike spoke up. "In Bozeman, must of been. Nothing like that happened in Cody."

"Is Willie here?" Bally looked around.

"Nope. Said he was too old."

"Too old, or too scared?" someone asked. There was general laughter.

"Two more things," Bally said. "They don't want to fight, say they'll leave as soon as they can. And there's more women coming up the road behind us. They must of got through Willie's Door, overwhelmed him."

"So what if they did?" Frank sneered. "All this talk ain't getting the job done. Let's spread out, surround the bitch. We'll take Sleeping Woman for ourselves, then we'll be the ones with the high ground when the rest of them get here."

****

Kirannenn's radio was crackling. "That's our backup," she said with relief. Kirannen spoke, then turned to report.

"They've brought four Guard squads, an emergency response team, and our water cannon."

"Your *what?*" Kai gasped.

"I've been briefed on it," Alanna said. "What does it do, exactly?"

"It's a deterrent, a good way to control a crowd without guns. It shoots a high-power stream of water exactly like a fire hose. I thought this would be a good time to test it."

The women had forgotten about Bud, who stood aside, shock evident on his face *What the hell?* He broke in.

"You're gonna shoot them with *water*? What the hell for?"

Kirannen shrugged. "Most importantly, to knock the guns out of their hands. If it works as well as I think it will, we can avoid gunfire. We haven't forgotten the past either, Bud. Men almost killed everyone in the colony with their guns. Ever since we took control, women have made it a priority to come up with ways to keep ourselves safe. This is just another tool."

"We won't use it unless we have to," Alanna promised. "And if there's time, we can shoot it into the hill first as a demonstration."

"Thanks for nothing," Bud muttered. What was he doing up here? He should be down with the men, protecting Wrongside and their way of life. Women had no business here.

The answer to his question wasn't hard to figure out, though. The women did have business here. From where he stood, he could just see the front bumper of the truck where Laran and Hud were tucked away for safety. If the men made the top of the hill, they'd shoot up the place and not even worry about who they hurt.

"When will the cannon be ready?" Alanna asked.

Kirannen consulted her radio again. "They're moving into position now, just behind that outcropping." She pointed to a curve in the road beyond the crowd of men. "They'll advance within ten minutes. Any activity below?"

Jo lowered her scope and turned from the edge of the hill. "The men have spread out," she reported, "circling us. But they seem pretty disorganized."

"Good."

"Will they attack?" Alanna fretted. "Rush the hill and start shooting?"

"They're probably trying to nerve themselves to that," Kai answered. "Bud, what do you think?"

He grunted and walked away.

****

Alanna wondered whether she should follow him, ask what was wrong. Was he having second thoughts? Then she saw him heading toward the truck. She'd checked on Laran herself a few minutes ago, but it would probably do both her and Bud good if he checked on her, too. It was an odd feeling to think someone else was also responsible for her daughter, but maybe, a good feeling, too.

"Upward movement!" Weezy warned.

It was Frank, with the big guy Alanna knew as

Rollie right beside him. They were eeling through the rocks that littered the track, slowly working their way higher. Two dozen men were behind them. All the way around the base of the hill there was similar cautious upward movement.

Louise, who was closest, raised her rifle and aimed it. "Halt!"

Frank's head jerked up. "Why should I?" he barked at her. "This here's our land, not yours. This is Wrongside!"

"And we're trying to get back to Rightside." Louise's tone was calm and reasonable. She hoped they wouldn't realize she was just stalling for time. Squads and water cannon aside, none of the women wanted this situation to escalate. "The only reason we're not back in Rightside already is because you're blocking our way."

"Damn right, we're blocking you. We're gonna blow you off the hilltop, so's all you women know better than to try this again. How many of you's up there?"

"Enough," Louise replied. "Turn around and go back to Cody, and we'll leave quietly."

The men resumed climbing. Louise fired a shot at one side of the leaders.

"The shot that was heard around the world," Kai commented as she raised her own rifle.

Inside the truck, Laran cried out. Hud jerked, then resettled himself and put a thumb in his mouth.

"Stay right there!" Bud ordered. He ran for the edge of the hill.

On the north side, Davy and Tom started at the sound of the single shot. They hadn't committed to firing on their own kind, but they weren't going to let any of them up here, either. They had Hud and the women to think about.

Below them, the men who had been spreading out and up stopped short. Some dove for cover, expecting a fusillade. Others lifted their guns, searching for a target.

Louise's bullet had sparked off a rock just inches from Frank's bandaged hand. He cried out and stumbled backward.

"That's twice!" he shouted, "twice a damn woman's tried to kill me!"

"Wasn't no woman who shot you the first time, Frank. It was me!" Bud shouted down. "Remember?"

"Sheriff, what the Yong hell you doing up there with them women? What have you done with my boy? Where's Chad?"

"He'll make it," Bud answered. "No thanks to you, since you left him laying in the dirt like a stray dog."

Frank was tired of talking. "Get the hell down here with your own kind. We're coming up. Boys!" he shouted downhill. "This is it. Let's get them!"

The fight was on. Their anger boiled up the slope ahead of them. That women should invade their land! They couldn't accept it. Shouting, egging each other on, they climbed.

Chapter 35

"Fire at will!" Louise bellowed. She, Weezy, Jo, and Kirannen, the most experienced, got down to business from behind their trucks. Louise blew Frank backward with her first shot. He landed ten feet down the track in a litter of gravel and didn't move again. Rollie took two bullets before he threw himself sideways, behind a scrub tree, howling in pain. Men surged past them in a frenzy, screaming curses. Rollie lifted his blood-smeared shotgun, propped it on a boulder, and peppered the hilltop. Others paused to aim and fire.

"Take cover!" Kirannen ordered. Alanna skidded to her knees behind a truck bumper. A sudden image of Chad's limp body flashed into her mind. "Can't do it again," she gasped. "Can't shoot anyone, can't, can't, *can't*." The first man topped the hill, a wild-eyed stranger. She aimed for his legs, missed. Her shot caught his attention, and he surged toward her, brandishing an axe. Screaming in fear, Alanna aimed dead center and fired. He dropped.

****

Behind their truck, Jessie and Tenosha crouched, terror-stricken. "I never got good scores in target practice," Tenosha muttered. "Never once."

"I did." Jessie's voice wavered, but her aim was sure. She dropped the closest man with a careful shot to his leg. Her second shot spun another man sideways, clutching his shoulder. She settled into a rhythm with one thought uppermost in her mind. *Protect Baby Boy.* Take out one. Take out another. Check both sides. Guard your position. Don't let anyone past you. *Protect Baby Boy.*

Tenosha finally raised her rifle. "This is for Hud," she declared with a steady squeeze of the trigger. She watched in horrified fascination as a man staggered backward, clutching at his side. "For Hud," she repeated, nodding. She took aim again.

As more men gained the breast of the hill, the shooting intensified. Bullets and shotgun pellets spanged off the trucks, thudded into the ground. A few buried themselves in flesh. Kai was the first casualty among the women, screaming as a shot shattered her elbow. She scrabbled backward, one-handed, from her position. Louise dropped her rifle and ran to Kai, stripping off her shirt. With quick, efficient motions, she wrapped it around the arm.

"I've got it!" Kai gasped, clamping a hand against the makeshift bandage. "Go, go!"

Louise didn't hesitate but spun around to face the battle again, eyes wild, shoulders heaving, wearing only a support tank, baggy pants, and boots. Men were pouring onto the hilltop by the dozens now. She saw two of them head for the young girls, Jessie and the other one, who were facing the opposite direction.

Yanking a knife from her leg sheath, she rushed the men and slammed her blade to the hilt in the nearest man's back. Pivoting, she crashed her fist into the other's ear, knocking him down. Jessie rose from her crouch, stomped a booted heel on the man's hand, and kicked his hatchet away. The man rolled, holding his wounded hand and screeching defiance. Jessie kicked him in the face, and he fell silent.

Louise called out to Kirannen. "It's time to fall back!"

Kirannen rose to a crouch, radio in one hand. "Back!" she shouted. "To the rocks, now!"

Weezy stood immediately from behind her truck. She'd abandoned the scoped rifle for a machine gun, Louise saw. The Guardswoman retreated purposefully, spraying bullets in wide sweeps back and forth across the converging groups of men. She mowed them down, slowing the assault so the women could gather behind the rocks.

Bud ran for Alanna, who didn't seem to be aware of the long graze across her forehead. Blood had sheeted down the side of her face, smeared where she kept wiping it away. He dragged her backward. Jessie jerked Tenosha to her feet, and they backed up, too, still firing.

Louise helped Kai to the rocks. Jo, on Kirannen's order, ran for Tom and Davy on the north side of the hill. "This way!" she ordered. "Close up!"

Kai grunted as she watched the attackers take cover on the far side of the trucks. "Maybe it was a mistake to leave the trucks behind," she muttered.

Kirannen clipped the radio back onto her belt. "Maybe. Can't be helped. They're bringing the cannon up the track. The colonel says they're ready to shoot on your order, Ma'am." She deferred to the president. Bud snorted.

****

Alanna hesitated for a beat. She and her women

had intruded into Wrongside, where they weren't welcome. They had promised to leave if let alone. If they shot the cannon now, would it be seen as a declaration of all-out war? Or would it make the men think twice?

Well. She heaved a deep breath. She'd signed on for this. "Now, Lieutenant."

Kirannen barked the order. A heavy whine signaled a buildup of power. The men turned to look down the path. A half-track growled up the hill, cannon mounted on its back. Ranks of soldiers marched behind it. Some of the men shot at the artillery crew, who were well-protected with bulletproof clothing and helmets.

A stream of water, surprisingly narrow, jetted from the nozzle of the cannon, shooting into the tightest knot of men. It struck with a boom, like a storm surge. A geyser of water, earth, rock, guns, and men exploded up and out.

Bally, who had been close enough to feel needles of overspray on his face, watched bodies fly. When the burst of water stopped, he saw men struggle like beached fish, mud and grit stopping their breath. One of them was Mikey. He was on his knees, sides heaving, breath whooping, trying to spit out mud.

****

Kai nodded to Alanna. "You're up." Alanna lifted a megaphone.

"Men of Wrongside!" All around the hill, heads jerked up to see her standing, spread-legged, atop the inner ring of rock defenses. "We don't want to be in Wrongside any more than you want us here. But there's no need to fight like this. People have died, and more are dying. If you stand down, we'll return to Cody peacefully and go out through the transfer door. You won't see us here again."

****

Bally stood frozen. Mike was down. Frank and Rollie were probably dead by now. Bud was gone. The women had them surrounded, and the men had no leader. He couldn't take it. He wouldn't take it. There was a rage building in his chest, pushing up and out. It was a red, blooming rage that went all the way back to Yong, and it wouldn't be contained. He threw out an arm to the men on his left.

"You!" he roared. "After them women at the rocks. There ain't but a few of 'em, *go!*" He spun around. "The rest of you, with me! Down the hill to that cannon! For Yong, men, for *Yong!*"

His rage convulsed the men. "Yong!" they screamed. "For Yong!"

****

Alanna jumped down from the rocks. "Here they come," she said unnecessarily.

Louise's gaze swept her meager force. Kai held a pistol in her good hand. Alanna was using a wadded-up jacket to wipe blood from her face. Kirannen, Jo, and Weezy were unhurt, ready to go. Weezy had reloaded the machine gun. The two girls, Jessie and what's-her-name, looked sick and uncertain, speckled with blood that she hoped wasn't theirs. The three men just looked grim.

"Form a tight circle," she ordered, "around the shelter and Bud's truck. Don't let anyone get through."

The men came at a dead run, maybe two dozen of them. They were leaderless since Bally was charging down the hill with the rest of the attackers, but they

344

were fired up, filled with what historians would later call Yong Rage. One of them, whose ancestor had fought at Manassas, voiced an eerie, ululating cry that rose as the attackers ran.

"Now!" Louise screamed into her radio. Dimly, she heard the boom of the water cannon as gunfire crashed once again across Sleeping Woman. She shot blindly into the charging mass of men.

Davy, shoulder to shoulder with Jessie, fired his shotgun low.

Men dropped, some howling in pain, some silent. Their battle cries faded as they reached the rocks, replaced by the grunts and snarls of hand-to-hand fighting. Louise went down under the sudden rush of a man with an axe, rolling desperately out of his reach.

Bud rose over Alanna and head-butted the first man to reach them. *I went to school with him!* he thought wildly, reeling from the butt. Rollie's brother Walt dropped like a stone.

Kirannen, trying to keep her head as she fought, could hear sounds of battle from down the hill, but she could no longer hear the water cannon. Had it been overrun? She slammed her rifle stock into a man's head and kicked him away, wishing she could see down the hill. Where was her radio? Another man lunged at her, aiming a pistol. She slapped it aside as it went off.

Behind the women, there was a sudden sound of glass breaking, then a child's scream. Alanna's and Tom's heads turned at the same instant.

Laran burst out of the truck, clutching the baby. Both of them were covered in blood.

"Mommy!" she shrieked. "Mommy, where are you? Bud, help us, Bud! Help!" She stumbled across the rocky ground, Hud beginning to slip through her bloody arms.

Tenosha leaped to her feet and ran to them. Behind her, a single shot rang out, and she was flung forward like a rag doll, skidding across the dirt to land at Laran's feet. Laran's screams pierced through the sounds of battle. Attackers and defenders froze at the sounds. Men gaped at the sight of the small girl. Alanna and Bud abandoned their positions and ran to the children. Tom, reeling from a vicious slash to his arm, staggered after them.

Kirannen rose, stood tall, and stepped onto the rocks. She looked down at the remaining men. She held a rifle in one hand, its stock cracked and covered with gore. In the other hand, she held a combat knife, dripping blood. Weezy climbed up to join her, machine gun at the ready.

"Men of Wrongside," Kirannen ordered. "Stand down."

None of them could meet her gaze. Some backed up a step. Others stared blindly at the children.

Jo and Louise stepped forward and disarmed the men, gesturing them backward. Weezy covered them while the rest of the defenders turned their attention to Laran and the still figure at her feet.

Alanna was running her hands over Laran, wiping away blood. Tom had taken the sobbing baby and was doing the same. "His leg's cut," he said, relief cracking his voice. "But he ain't hurt bad. Is she?"

"I don't think so." Alanna's voice shook with the same relief. "The glass cut her forehead. That's where all the blood's coming from. Honey, does it hurt anywhere else?"

"My leg," Laran whimpered. "When I scooted across the floor of the truck, it hurt my leg."

"Here," Bud said, crouched at her other side. "There's a cut on the back of her leg. I think—yeah, there's some glass in it." He looked at Alanna. "I think she'll need stitches."

"Are they okay?"

The shout had come from one of the men standing at the rock wall. All of them were straining to see what was happening.

"Are them kids okay? They ain't hurt bad, are they?"

"The glass cut them up some," Bud shouted back. "We need Doc Medina. Can someone go get him?"

Kirannen nodded at Weezy, who jerked her head at the man who had shouted. He took off down the hill. Kirannen registered vaguely that the cannon was still silent, and the battle sounds down the hill had lessened.

****

Jessie knelt beside Tenosha. Carefully, she put both hands on her friend's shoulders. "Tennie?" she whispered. "Tennie, can you hear me?" The girl moaned in response. Standing behind them, Jo clapped a hand to her mouth but couldn't suppress a choked sob. Tears started into her eyes. She wasn't much older than Tenosha.

Working carefully, Jessie moved her hands over Tenosha. "I'm a nurse," she said over her shoulder to the Guardswomen. "Bring me your trauma kit."

Jo ran for it and opened it on the ground next to Jessie. Jessie found a sterile pad and pressed it against Tenosha's back, against the bullet hole. "I'm going to turn you over now, honey. It'll hurt."

Kirannen knelt down to help, and they got Tenosha onto her back. The exit wound gaped across her chest, an obscene red hole. Alanna and Bud had already turned Laran away from the sight. Jessie worked quickly, dressing the exit wound, administering a painkiller. She stopped when Tenosha's eyes fluttered open.

She licked her lips and struggled to form a word. "Hud?"

"He's fine," Jessie assured her. "He has a little cut on his leg from the flying glass. That's all."

"Need to see Hud."

Jessie looked around wildly, but Tom was already there, kneeling down with Hud in his arms.

"Here he is, Tenosha. Here's your son." Tom's voice was hoarse.

Tenosha reached out a shaky hand. "Oh, Baby." Hud, with tears still drying on his cheeks, grinned and reached for his mother. He babbled something that might have been "Mama." Tenosha clutched at his tiny hand, closed her eyes, and hitched a deep breath that turned into a cough. A gout of bright red blood spurted from her mouth. Jessie wiped it away.

Tenosha gasped and forced her eyes open again. She searched the knot of faces above her and focused on Davy and Jessie. "Thank you," she whispered. "It's because of you two that I found Hud." Her gaze wavered back to the baby and then to Tom. "And thank you for sharing him with me. You didn't have to."

Tom cleared his throat. "Yeah, I did. He's your son, too, and you love him like I do."

"You'll have to love him twice as much—now." The last word ended on a sigh, and Tenosha's eyes closed again. Her hand slipped away from Hud's.

Chapter 36

Jessie forced her grief into a tight corner of her heart and stood, trauma kit in her hand. "I'll set up inside the shelter. Bring the wounded to me. Tom, you're first. I need to stitch up that arm before you bleed out. Bring Hud and the girl and come with me." She turned away, then stopped, her back still to the defenders. "Put Tenosha in one of the trucks for now."

Kirannen shook herself. "Let me check on the situation down the hill, then we'll re-group. Jo, issue everyone some water, including those men." She waved a hand at the knot of men still standing at the rocks under Weezy's guard. "Find out which need medical treatment." She stomped away, pulling the radio from the clip on her belt.

Louise turned to Kai. "Let me help you inside."

"I can get there on my own," Kai said shakily, still clutching Louise's shirt to her bloody arm. She turned away from the sight of Bud and the young man lifting Tenosha's body, then blanched and sank abruptly to the ground. "Or maybe not." She fixed her gaze in the middle distance, telling herself not to faint. "Oh, shit, look at that."

Louise turned. More men were arriving on the hilltop. It took her overloaded brain a few seconds to realize they were walking backward. The Guard and police units had pushed them all the way to the crest in a pincer movement, as planned. It appeared that the battle for Sleeping Woman was over.

Kirannen turned back. "It's over. I'll take Kai to the nurse and send Alanna out. The colonel's on her way up."

Jo and Weezy, distributing water to their prisoners, were the first to make contact with the arriving Guardswomen. "We have a nurse with us," Jo reported, "in the shelter."

A sergeant nodded and relayed the information through her radio. "Our wounded can be brought up with the med team. Where's the major?"

Louise arrived with the president trailing behind. Alanna had left Bud with Laran, grateful again for his presence. In her exhaustion, her mind wandered. Was this how it had been back on Earth, with mothers and fathers parenting their children together? What a strange idea. She shook herself at the sound of her title.

"Ms. President? We've got one of the men's leaders. Would you talk to him?"

"Of course," Alanna said, forcing her shoulders back and her head high. "Louise, come with me. If I start to fall asleep during the negotiations, you can give me a jab."

"Of course," Louise answered. She turned to Jo and Weezy. "If you need me, call."

The women made their way past knots of bleeding, glowering men. They weren't defeated, Alanna realized with shock. They might be contained for the moment, but they hadn't given up. She needed to remember that.

They led her to Bally, halfway down the hill at a wide spot on the track. One of his arms hung useless, dripping blood. He had an ugly gash across one cheek, a black eye, and looked like he'd been shoved through a rock grinder. He was soaking wet. He limped away from his guards toward the approaching women. He knew Alanna from a Red Cabin encounter or two.

"They tell me you're in charge," he growled. Alanna took his uninjured arm.

"Let's find a place to sit down, Bally," she sighed.

****

Louise had been hanging back, getting reports on her radio. She updated Alanna as they sat at a hastily erected table.

"The fighting has stopped all the way around the hill. The men down there have not surrendered and are not disarmed, but they've agreed to this parley. Apparently, Bally is the one who talked to Kai and later took over when the original leader was shot. He led the downhill charge on our backup units."

At the mention of Kai's name Bally had stirred as though he wanted to speak. He opened his mouth once, closed it, then finally shook his head and asked his question. "She okay? Kai?"

"Injured, but she'll be fine," Alanna said, hoping it was true. "Bally, we need to find a way out of this. Too many women, and men, too, are dead already. What can we do?"

"What's this 'we' shit?" Bally erupted. "It's you women's fault, all of it. You came over here. You shot Frank. Shot his boy, too, according to him. Maybe we owe you some blood."

His words twisted a knife in her heart. If she could take back one single thing in her life, it would be that shot.

She tried to keep her voice steady and reasonable.

"I acted in self-defense, Bally, and Frank knew it. The man with him had already shot Bud. Did you even know that? I'm sorry Chad was hurt. I'd take it back if I could, but I'm not sorry Bud and I defended ourselves from an unprovoked attack. Look around you. The Rightside squads are here to protect us, not to attack you. We'll all leave peacefully if you'll just end this."

Involuntarily, everyone looked to either side, where the Guard forces were still arrayed in battle formation. Alanna knew they didn't outnumber the men, but she hoped the men couldn't see that.

Below, a new cloud of dust disturbed the North Road. More vehicles seemed to be arriving, but she couldn't tell if they held women or men. She turned to Louise, who had binoculars.

"Are those more of ours?"

"I don't think so."

A group of men exited the new vehicles and walked forward.

"I think that's the commander," Bally said. "Seen him once."

Alanna touched Louise's shoulder. "Let me look.

"That's him, all right," she muttered. "What does he think he's going to do?"

"Wait a minute," Bally said. "How the hell do you know the commander?"

"We have teleconferences," she answered without taking her eyes from the binoculars. "Monthly. He doesn't know I'm here."

The commander lifted a bullhorn. "Women of Rightside," he bellowed up the hill. "Can we talk?"

Alanna nodded to a Guardswoman, who produced her own bullhorn. "Come through if the men will let you." She lowered the horn. "That should get him here," she told the president.

They watched him climb with two companions. They stopped briefly to talk to some of the waiting men. The commander shook his head in disgust as he continued his climb.

Alanna, Louise, and Bally walked farther down the rough track to meet him. As soon as he saw Alanna, the Commander stopped short.

"Ma'am?"

Alanna nodded and gestured to Louise. "Major Gallech, and this man is Bally. He's the men's leader. We have a lot to talk about."

"So I hear." He waved at his companions. "My aides, Tim Adkins and Bob Santiago." Nods were exchanged.

"Let's go back to the top and sit down. Our troops are holding. Can you trust the men to hold their fire while we talk?"

"Of course." He muttered an aside. Adkins, a tall man with a competent air, turned and started back down the hill.

The others arranged themselves around the table. No one saw Davy sidle up within hearing distance. He had to know what the president would say. The future of his family was riding on it.

Alanna had sent a Guard to fetch Laran. Bud and Kai, bandaged and looking stronger, had come with them. "Bud is the local sheriff, and Kai Makele is my vice president. This," she continued, putting an arm around her daughter, "is my daughter, Laran. She's the one who was kidnapped. She's the reason why we're here."

Sherman stared in wonder. The kid had a fresh bandage on her forehead, her face was bruised and swollen, and there was blood on her clothing. He shook himself. "As I told you," he began. "I came up to see if I could help but never expected you to be here. The men told me that you personally started this by shooting two men."

"I'll give you the short version, and then we have something more to talk about." She outlined the past few days, including the first shootout with Frank. She didn't tell Sherman that Chad was probably her son.

"So you can see that all we want to do is leave, with no more bloodshed. We're sorry to have invaded Wrongside like this, but it couldn't be helped.

"Before we talk about how to get us out of here, though, let me tell you about another situation we have in common."

"What, more women are invading us?"

"You're not far off," Alanna said wryly. "I didn't know this until an hour ago, but two women came through a Cody Transfer Door yesterday with a separate agenda. One is pregnant and came here to live up on the Plains with the baby's father. You'll remember the situation with Davy Redwolf?"

He nodded. "The boy's dead. We told you that."

"Davy is the baby's father, and he isn't dead. Apparently, the Cody men didn't want to be told what to do, so they quietly let him go, and he came up here to live.

"He and Jessie were smuggling notes through the Fence, and she followed him here. All they want to do is live in peace, away from both women and men, so they can raise their baby together. Davy tells us no one lives up here, that it's mostly wasteland all the way to the ocean. Bud also says there are no actual Wrongside laws to prevent Davy and Jessie from living here together."

"Together? A man and a woman? All the time in the same cabin?"

She nodded. "It's hard for Rightsiders and Wrongsiders to accept, isn't it? That a Rightside woman and a Wrongside man have wanted to be together? You must realize that women and men commonly lived together on old Earth. Milina and Yong were a married couple. That means they'd committed their lives to living together and raising their children together."

He didn't realize that but wasn't about to admit it. She might even be lying, for all he knew, but this wasn't the time to challenge her. She needed a safe way out of here. The men outnumbered them, that was sure. And now she wanted permission to settle women in Wrongside? Hell if he'd do that. Why should he?

"I know what you're thinking," Alanna said. "Why should you go along with any of this? It's all on our side, isn't it? Safe passage, permission for Jessie to settle here.

"And I know," she hastened to add when the commander opened his mouth. "It's a lot to ask, but surely we can work something out. We could talk about concessions, if you're willing."

"Concessions?" Sherman grunted. That put things in a new light. Now she was talking. If he could get enough out of her, it would make the Wrongsiders happy, and he wouldn't even have to admit there would be women living on the Plains because she was right.

No one came here except the occasional hunter. Damn desolate place, it was.

"What do you have in mind?"

"What would you think about a lower rate on import taxes?"

"I think it's a good start," he grunted. "Five percent."

"More like three."

"Perfect," he said, "we'll compromise on four."

"Done."

"What else have you got?"

Alanna was at a loss for a moment, then Kai leaned forward. "We could subsidize their electrical service," she suggested, "now that the new dam is in operation."

"Absolutely." Alanna agreed instantly. "Our new hydroelectric dam is much more efficient."

And they wouldn't even have thought of giving us a break on the rate if they hadn't got into trouble with this kidnapping. Still, he decided, they were good concessions, and he'd take them. Who cared what happened up on the Plains?

"One other thing," he said. "That Red Cabin fiasco caused a lot of hard feelings, and it's probably half the reason the men are so riled up now. I'll need a guarantee from you that we, the two of us and two teams of legal advisors, can get together in the near future to hammer out some more equitable Red Cabin policies."

Alanna pulled back in shock. She shook her head. "You're asking too much, Sherman. Congress will never agree to that."

He half-turned to look toward the waiting, still-armed men. "Do you really want a war on your hands?"

Kai leaned forward again and whispered two words in Alanna's ear. "*Anesthetic gas.*"

"Done," she said again.

"Alanna," he said, daring to use her first name since they were in his own Yong country, "I believe we have a deal."

Alanna put out her hand. She'd never touched a man except in passion. Shaking hands was what women did, to signal an agreement. When he took it, after his own moment of hesitation, she was surprised at the strength of his grip. She hardened hers in response.

"Maybe," she said, "eventually, Rightside women and Wrongside men might learn to get along, almost like they did back on Earth."

"I don't think I'll hold my breath."

They laughed. Alanna had never laughed with a man quite like this, either.

Bud leaned forward to have a word with Sherman, and Alanna went to tell everyone else the crisis was over.

****

Back at the base of the hill, the commander's aide and the threat of the water cannon had kept the men in check. With Bally's and Sherman's return, the aide stepped aside, and the men gathered around.

"We ready to show them women what for?" Rollie asked eagerly.

"We are not." The commander laid down the law. The men weren't happy, but they listened. He'd been in power so long they were used to it.

"We have the upper hand, and they know it, so I've made them pay dear for the privilege of getting back to their own side in one piece. In return for letting them go, their commander and I will meet soon to write new rules for the Red Cabins. We'll get our rights there, finally, because we're letting them leave with their lives."

He raised a hand. "Also, from now on, everything we get from them will be cheaper, including our electricity. Life will be easier for us and for our families, and all we have to do is let them go back to Rightside."

"But what about—?" another man broke in. The commander cut him off with a peremptory chop of his hand.

"Now. I want most of you to go on back home and put your guns up. Bally can form an escort detail, and the women'll be out of here soon's they can. Too many men and women are already dead or wounded, including the boy Chad, who I hear is doing fine at the hospital in Bozeman."

Rollie couldn't just let it go. "Commander, you mean we ain't gonna teach these women nothing?"

"What's the point?" Sherman asked. "They made a bad mistake coming here, but we don't have to shoot anybody else over it. Why start another war? I've forced good concessions out of 'em, and they'll give us a lot more respect, after this."

Rollie hitched at his belt. "But—"

The commander shot up his hand again, and Rollie subsided.

"I figure it's over," Bally said. "Folks are dead. We taught them women a lesson they won't forget, and that's gonna have to be enough." Slowly, the men dispersed to their trucks and began to turn around for the drive back to Cody.

****

Atop the Sleeping Woman, Davy ran to tell Jessie and Tom what he'd heard. "It's okay! She fixed it all, Jess. The president came through for us, just like she said! She understands what we want, and she got the commander to agree to it!"

"The commander?" Tom was skeptical. He'd had a hard enough time accepting the presence of women in Cody. "The commander hisself's here? Arranging things just for you two?"

"Yes!" Holding Jessie to him, Davy could even feel Baby Boy's happiness. He was wide awake and kicking enthusiastically. "That Alanna, she promised him something called tax concessions. And price breaks on electricity, and better terms at the Red Cabins. He even agreed that we could live on the Plains long's we stay hidden and quiet."

"Oh, Davy." Jessie pushed him back at arm's length, almost afraid to believe that what he was saying was true. "Davy, this is—it's everything! We can be together, just like we planned, and no one can stop us?"

He shook his head. "No one."

They melted together again, Baby Boy between them. Tom cleared his throat heavily, then stumped away.

It didn't take long for Bud, Alanna, Laran, and the small team to pack up and say their goodbyes.

"We'll need to set up some sort of regular communication," Alanna told Jessie. "We need to ensure you remain safe here, and I know you'll want to be in touch with your family. For now, keep this radio. The frequency will connect you with the Guard unit in New Washington, and they'll relay any message you need. Oh, and are there any supplies you want?"

"We're pretty well equipped," Jessie said, leaning against Davy. "But thank you. It's good to know Rightside can help if we need it."

"Of course. Good luck to you both." Alanna hesitated, almost said something else, then shook her head and turned away.

"Bye, Hud!" Laran waved a hand to the baby. "I'll come back and play with you again!"

Hud, of course, didn't wave back until the last truck had disappeared over the hill. Tom, holding him, turned to follow the others to their now quiet camp. He already missed Tenosha. He had some good memories of her, at least. Maybe the best, he was able to admit, was the way she'd loved their son. He would be glad when Hud was older, and he was able to tell him what his mother had done to be with him.

****

In the truck with her mom, Laran snuggled close and sniffled. "I'm really sorry, Mommy. This was all because of me, wasn't it? All the guns and the people who died. The men who were so mad and everything? If I hadn't—"

Alanna put her arm around her daughter. "It was the crazy woman's fault. Not yours. And you know what, sweetie? I think it's time we got a puppy."

Laran hugged her mother hard.

Chapter 37

Guard squads overwhelmed the dusty streets of Cody, lining up to move through the Transfer Cabin. Men stood aside, watching resentfully. The commander and his entourage set up camp in front of the courthouse. Tension as thick as a dust storm still filled the air.

Kirannen led her team to the same side street from which they'd originally begun. To keep the isolated entry secure they wouldn't go back to it, instead taking turns at a Door. The colonel had offered Bud, Alanna, and Laran a place at the head of the line, but they had business to finish first.

"Wait till you meet Willie!" Laran was saying. She bounced excitedly on the truck seat, wide awake now. "He's so nice! He made lunch, and he let me hold a male baby, a brand new one, not like Hud."

"We'll have to thank him," Alanna said uneasily, opening her door. "But honey, he didn't tell me you were here. He didn't even try to send you back through the Door. I'm not going to thank him for that."

"But the crazy woman was on the other side, and that mean clerk! I'm glad Willie didn't try to send me back."

As had so often happened in the past few days, Alanna didn't know what to do. It was a strange feeling for her, and she didn't like it.

"Alanna?" Bud held her door, waiting for her to step out. "You look as sleepy as I feel. How long has it been since either of us had any rest?"

"Days, at least." Alanna suddenly wanted nothing more than to melt into Bud's arms. She was tired enough to let herself do just that. "Oh, Bud, it's over. Our daughter's safe."

Bud gathered her in, surprised. They dropped their heads to each other's shoulders, swaying with exhaustion.

Getting out of her own truck, Kai saw them and froze. The sun was starting to drop to the horizon, backlighting the couple, and they looked for all the world like they needed each other. *How could that be?* she wondered with a strange mixture of awe and disgust.

****

Bud eventually found Willie in Bally's nearly empty bar.

"Kicked me out," the old man said morosely into his beer. "Them damn women kicked me outta my own Transfer Cabin. My own home! Good thing I finally got that truck. I'll prob'ly be living in it now."

"Relax, Willie," Bud said, lowering himself with a groan onto a bar stool. "They'll be gone soon." He thumbed the radio Kirannen had given him and told Alanna where to come. Then he jerked his head at Bally, nursing his wounds in a corner. "Beer?"

Bally stood. "Dunno as I feel like serving you, Bud."

Bud sighed. "Can't blame you, I guess. I'll probably be out of a job after this. Never mind, then, I just gotta talk to Willie a minute."

363

Bally limped away, but he came back with a beer. Him and Bud, they went back a long way.

Bud mustered a tired smile. "I met my daughter, Bally. She's the one they pushed over here. Her name's Laran, and she's almost nine. She'll be here in a minute. You can meet her, too."

Understanding lit Bally's ugly face. He nodded once, then twice, and walked away.

"Alanna wants to talk to you," Bud told Willie. "She really is the leader of Rightside. I think she wants to thank you."

"Shit," Willie said hoarsely. "I can't have no woman beholden to me."

"She's probably gonna yell at you, too, if that makes you feel any better."

Kai, having been to the bar before, led Alanna and Laran there. The room was sparsely populated with silent, angry men. As the women entered, Rollie Leon scraped back his chair and stood, half-crouched in a defensive posture. "Here, too? You gotta come in here, too? What right—?"

He stopped in mid-sentence as he caught sight of Laran. She was no bigger'n his own youngest, and she looked hard-used, with bandages, a blacked eye, a swollen nose, and somebody's dirty shirt for clothes. He gaped at her.

Bud stood up. "Rollie, let me introduce you to somebody." He walked over to Laran and put his good arm around her as casually as a man might touch his own son. "This is my daughter, Laran."

Tension bled out of the room, replaced by wonderment. Most of them had never heard the word 'daughter' but they could all see what it meant.

"She's the one, Rollie," Bally said into the silence, "the kid who got put through Willie's Transfer Door. She's the reason the women invaded us."

Rollie collapsed into his seat.

"Come on over here," Bud said to Laran. "Here's an old friend wants to see you."

"Willie!" Laran barreled into Willie in a crashing hug. Nonplussed, he lifted his arms, not sure if he should hug her back.

Bud laughed. "Go ahead, Willie, she won't break."

Willie decided he'd go on ahead. He bent down and wrapped his arms around the little girl. It felt good, he had to admit, and from the murmurs of awe that filled the bar, he knew it made the other men feel something, too.

Alanna joined them, and for the second time in her life, she held out a hand to shake with a man. Willie took it hesitantly. "You got a good kid here," he said hoarsely.

"Thank you," she said. "For everything." The rest of it fell away. She didn't need to upbraid the man for his decisions. He had taken care of her daughter, and that was enough.

****

The door of the bar crashed open, and Mikey limped in. "Pop, I need Bud. Have you seen him? Some of them women found Frank. He's still alive. They wanna know what—" His voice trailed off as he caught sight of Laran and the two women.

"I'm here, Mikey," Bud said. "Come on, let's see about him." He turned to Alanna. "Don't leave before I get back," he pleaded. "I need to say goodbye."

Alanna nodded. "I know."

365

The two rushed out.

Curious, Kai leaned over to Alanna. "Why did that kid call Bally Pop? What does Pop mean, is it a nickname here?"

"It's what boys call their fathers," Alanna replied. "It's like saying 'Mommy,' I guess."

Kai's face drained of color. Her head jerked from Alanna, to the door, to Bally behind the bar. "Oh, no. No. *Hell*, no. This is too much, Alanna. I can't—it's too *much*." She lurched to her feet, retching.

"Kai?" Alanna reached out a hand.

"Leave me alone," Kai gasped. "I have to get out of here."

Alanna stared after her friend as Kai pushed past the men and stumbled out of the door.

"Mommy, what's wrong with Aunt Kai? Is she sick?"

"Sick at heart," Alanna murmured as understanding dawned. She shook herself. "It's been a long day, sweetie. She'll be fine. We'll be home in a little bit, and we can all rest."

"Rest? I'm not even tired. Hey, Willie, did you get any more babies?"

****

It took more than a little bit, it took hours before the last two women were finally ready to leave Wrongside. Bud, Alanna, and Laran stood in the dark in a tight group on Willie's front porch.

Bud squatted down in front of Laran. "I don't want to let you go," he said. "I waited so long to meet you, and now we have to say goodbye already."

Tears trembled in Laran's bruised eyes. "Mommy—" Her voice hitched. "—Mommy said kids call their fathers Pop over here. Can I call you Pop, Bud?"

He caught her up in a crushing hug. "You sure can, honey. I—" His voice broke. "I love you, Laran."

"I love you too, Pop," she wailed. "But when am I gonna see you again?"

"Soon."

They both looked up to Alanna. "Soon," she repeated, taking both their hands. "Bud, we'll come back. You're her parent, too, as much as I am. I can't keep you apart. I'll fix it somehow with Congress. I'll talk to the commander again. Rightside and Wrongside can't stay separated anymore, not after this. I don't think we were meant to live apart forever. There has to be some other way."

"I wonder," Bud said, rising to his feet, "whether Davy and Jessie have a way. They want to live together, raise their baby together. Does that seem like the way it could be?"

Alanna shrugged. "Maybe? Who knows? I'm so tired I can't even think, but—maybe?" She stepped closer, and lifted a hand to Bud's face. "I'll miss you too, you know. Let's meet at the Cabins in a few days once all the dust settles, and we'll talk."

"I'll come," he said, smiling.

A word about the author...

Cathy Hester Seckman has been a published writer since the 1980s, mostly in non-fiction. Her writing credits include thousands of pieces in newspapers and magazines, plus two books. She is also a professional indexer, having indexed topics that range from terrorism to fashion design to ultrasound technology. She and her husband live just outside a map dot called Calcutta, Ohio, and love traveling, hiking, camping, and motorcycling. cathyseckman.com

Thank you for purchasing
this publication of The Wild Rose Press, Inc.

For questions or more information
contact us at
info@thewildrosepress.com.

The Wild Rose Press, Inc.
www.thewildrosepress.com